The Danburg Diary

by

T. A. Powell

This book is a work of fiction. Though the story, The Danburg Diary is based in part on an actual historical event, (the massacre at Moores Ford Bridge in 1946) many of the characters and other events have been created to carry the storyline. Places and names used in regards to the Moores Ford Bridge case history are a matter of public record and already pre-exist within the public domain.

Preface

Danburg, Georgia 1946

The front jib windows stood ajar as the night breeze settled on the porch steps and refused to enter. When the lights had finally gone out in the parlor, he crept into the downstairs hall and tread only the boards that kept their silence. The desk drawer creaked slightly as he pulled it forward, retrieving pencil and pad before making his way to the ironing shed out back.

Dearest M,

My head tells me I need to confess all here and now so that details are not forgotten, yet my heart tells me I have no right to force this upon you.

I was trapped among the briars, a captive audience. They begged for mercy. I tried to call out, but the first round of fire eclipsed my cry. The coloreds twisted and reeled in the ropes that bound them, faces and chests obliterated by ceaseless gunfire. Their writhing bodies jerked with seizures in the reddened dirt as I vomited into the underbrush not more than forty feet from them. Terrified, I choked as fleshless jaws dangled at eerie angles before me, unhinged by shrapnel that flew from every corner of the wood. And the sounds—dear God, the hideous sounds as air whistled through shredded wind pipes and punctured lungs as they slumped into the hemp that bound them.

Too long these men have hunted humans as animals. I must record their horrors and place the evidence into hands that can do justice. There were twenty or more men on the bridge and riverbanks. Most of them farmers, but there were a few whose dress implied positions of power. They were the few who spoke about taking the law into their own hands.

Some faces I recognized from the steps of the courthouse that afternoon, others I can identify because they shouted their names in perverse defiance. Not all carried weapons nor fired, but they dragged the victims and they tied the ropes. I have recorded what I can remember and have placed my ledger safely in our sacred spot.

I cannot bear our continued separation, but this is my only chance for a life of peace. Even now they plot, but there is a more treacherous threat closer to home. She claims to be with child and wishes to brand me the father to prevent our departure. I was foolish enough to flirt casually to keep the family peace... but what she proposes now goes beyond flirtation. Like her ancestors before her, she must be called to account for her deceptions.

I will return for you. Be ready.

H

The smoke from the small hurricane lantern wafted towards the opposite wall as the warped door of the ironing shed swung inward on rusted hinges. The new groom heard her call his name softly, stuffed the diary inside his muddied shirt and his letter of confession beside the glass as his cousin's foot cleared the threshold. Her eyes met his and then seized on the blazing lantern. She reached for the soiled parchment and he batted her hand away. Thinking it a game, she tried again and this time she out maneuvered him. She read with eager eye, while he stammered his regrets. At first she did not understand his unkempt appearance, but reading further it began to make sense. In jest, she offered it back. When he removed his hand from the inside of his shirt to receive, the gold band on his dirty finger flashed in the flame's light and he saw the rage flicker in her eyes.

"How dare you humiliate me like this, and with her of all people? You will not leave this place alive without me. You know I can never allow that now. Think of the family, of what this will

mean to us. The shame you have brought upon this house—"
She spat and pulled the sash slowly from her waist.

"You have left me no other option but to offer up what has always been yours for the taking. There is no other way for either of us to survive if you deny me further. Lay with me...and we'll make a truth out of a lie."

She sent the note drifting to the dirt floor before him, then dropped the gauzy film that framed her slender silhouette. He reached for the paper as her hair fell forward across her face blinding her for a moment. The lantern's flame devoured the last inch of parchment inside the glass and convulsed with flying embers as she bent low to blow it out. Smoke curled into the moonlight, and he knew then he would have to find another way to get a message to his bride.

Seventy two hours later the men from the bridge, having been guaranteed pardon in advance for their sins, strung him upside down at the hog station. When he refused to give the location of his list of names without confirmation that his bride was safe, they tightened the chains ripped from the weights of the hall clock around his legs and hoisted him higher. With one final obscenity, a large man with the black rimmed hat swung a rusted thrasher blade and sliced through half of his throat. His blood blended with the red clay of the earth below. Eleven days later his body was found floating in the swamps not more than two miles from the Danburg and neither his bride, nor an innocent nation ever knew what really happened until sixty two years later.

Chapter One

Danburg, Georgia 2008

Having already listened patiently for over an hour about the Danburg and its shadowy past, the fiery red head across the table from me threw out this further warning. "It's never enough just to tell part of the truth, Caroline. You have to tell it all and be committed to proving it if need be, so that others can recognize it when they come face to face with it. You of all people should have learned that by now."

"I know, I know." I sighed into my empty cup. "That's easier said than done, though. Nobody around here wants to hear about those murders anymore. Especially not from someone with an over active conscience, sixty two years too late to be of any help" I added.

Cecilia fiddled with the chipped handle on her coffee mug while carefully considering my response. "I agree about the level of difficulty in reintroducing this case to the public, but Caroline..."

"Please, don't 'but Caroline' me. To go public with what I've found would not be reintroducing this case—it would only be dragging it out and they have suffered enough. Most of the people in this town won't even talk to me anymore."

She pishawed my objections and gave me one of her looks. I rolled my eyes and in doing so, caught a glimpse of myself in the window. "Cecelia, take a good, hard look at me." My reflection glared back at me in equal disgust. "Trust me. I'm not the best candidate for this job."

Tired and frustrated with an endless stream of obfuscated answers, she began to show the first signs of real irritation since I had dragged her out of bed to meet me for coffee at five in the morning. "Well then, what the hell are you?" she demanded as she wiped a water stain from her spoon.

I looked again at the window and saw myself more clearly than I had in years. "What I am... is a very white, non-native, middle aged, historical preservationist with a slight drinking problem who obviously needs a new haircut and a better dye job."

While I toyed with a wiry gray hair just above the widows' peak of my forehead she cocked an eyebrow, then blanched at the marginalization of my most recent overindulgence and smirked. "A slight drinking problem, Caroline? You crawled into the bottle at five yesterday afternoon and didn't crawl out till two this morning. Then you proceeded to call me six times throughout the next three hours, blubbering about this ghost girl of yours. That my dear, is not a slight anything!" she added.

"Ok, perhaps not so slight of late, but still... I'm not the right person for this mission of yours." I brushed another wayward strand of graying hair from my cheek and wished for a drink. "If I couldn't salvage the truth from the wreckage of my own family, why the hell would anyone think I could do any better for theirs?" She held her tongue in check, but not her expression so I went for the sympathy ploy.

"Even Matt never acknowledged the truth about us until it was too late." I added.

She considered my earlier revelation, and then spoke softly. "Caroline, that's because you never bothered to tell Matt the truth... until it *was* too late."

"Semantics..." I echoed into my empty cup and then shot an annoying glance towards our waitress who was working on her second cigarette break since we arrived.

"Ok, then. Let's approach this in another way." she suggested. "You already know half the population of Danburg's not talking to you. The other half's not telling you the truth, so don't keep going back to them for answers. You'll only frustrate yourself further. Find other sources for corroboration. Use your gut and the evidence you have so far. Go outside the inner circle on this one, my dear. Somebody else either remembers something or knows someone who does! I'd bank my reputation on that!" she boasted. "You just have to figure out whom that somebody might be and then... figure out a way to make them talk."

"With, or without coercion?" I replied sarcastically and fingered the serrated knife at the edge of my plate. "I could always use the good ole boy system of interrogation."

I ran the knife just under the crease of my jowls and smiled wildly. "What do you think? It proved pretty effective once before!" I added sardonically and batted my eyes. "I could do it Miss Scarlet. I could cut them with this knife...'ceptin... I don't know nothing bout no 'chinery." I mocked.

"Don't be so maudlin" she replied, remembering the coroner's report I had shown her. "Besides... you don't have actual corroboration it was foul play yet, only hearsay. And hearsay my dear, is not admissible in a court of law. You need an eye witness, so you'll have to get one of those two sisters to crack. I'll bet there's a boatload they're not telling you and they're the only ones who lived in the house with both of them at the time it happened."

I agreed with the validity of her last statement, touched that she appeared to have taken in most of what I had been telling her. Truth was I already had a pretty good idea which sister needed to be cracked. I just needed to figure out how to get her alone.

Cecelia tried to signal the waitress with a polite wave of her manicured hand. When that produced nothing, she interjected demurely. "Excuse me, miss... could you?" and then raised her empty mug to her lips several times in mock desperation. The waitress seemed to be ignoring us both. "All I would like is one little refill" she pouted. "If that isn't too much to ask."

"Of course it's not." I offered. "It's our right! It says so... right here on their menu under the huge picture of pancakes. 'Free refills with your breakfast order'." Satisfied I had the right to complain, I did so.

"It's fine Caroline. I'll just wait till she notices we're out" she said and lowered her mug to the table.

"Nonsense! We could be old and gray by then." I replied and then caught our reflection. "Ok... older and grayer" I corrected.

"Don't be obnoxious. Just see if you can catch her eye" she said.

"I'll be the epitome of etiquette." I cooed and daintily waved my empty cup in the air.

Cecelia suspicious of my sarcasm warned further. "Caroline... behave."

"Me, misbehave? Surely you jest." I mused and winked, knowing I was still riding on a slight buzz from the residual Jack Daniels in me.

"Caroline...please don't!" she pleaded.

"There you go again, expecting me to make a scene." I volleyed and then made one more pass with the mug. This time with my pinky flagging the way like any good debutante in distress. The waitress saw my reflection in the mirrored backsplash behind the counter, but pretended not to notice. So being the tactful and dignified creature that I am, I decided a more direct approach might produce better results.

When I saw her look our way, I took a small chunk of biscuit and placed it inside the corner of my mouth. Having nothing in my coffee cup to wash it down with I began to cough dramatically, pretending to choke. When that didn't work I faked a small seizure, artistically flinging silverware to the floor about three feet in front of her. At the sound of gagging and bouncing cutlery, the waitress finally jumped from her seat. The long ash that had perilously dangled above her snow white cleavage seconds before suddenly broke free and slalomed down her chest like a tiny gray avalanche. Screeching at the sting of live embers, she hopped frantically in a seizure of her own!

"Mission accomplished" I muttered to Cecelia under my breath and tried not to grin too widely.

When the waitress finally turned to glare at me, I offered a few token coughs then spat out small globules of sodden biscuit onto the table and announced myself miraculously cured.

"Caroline! That was just down right rude." Cecelia chided.

"Noooo, Cecelia. What that was, was down right effective—don't you think?" I chirped back and delighted as the waitress continued to hop up and down and then finally tossed ice water down her front to squelch the pain.

"We'll take some ice water too. You can bring it with the coffee you forgot. Thanks!" I gloated. Cecelia scowled at me over the rim of her glasses.

"What?" I asked innocently. "You wanted her attention. I got her attention."

Cecelia simply shook her head. "You don't do anything in a small way, do you?"

"Nope... in for a penny, in for a pound I always say!" and spat out the last tiny morsel of crust for effect.

The waitress snarled in my direction as she poured two waters, taking her time at making a fresh pot. It took her twenty seven seconds to separate the filters and then another twelve to scoop the coffee. At this rate our next cup would be for lunch, so I coughed again as forewarning. She turned, just as I began to line up the remaining silverware on the table like fighter jets waiting for further flight instructions from the tower. Cecelia glowered at me over her empty mug.

"It was merely an accident." I defended. "I choked... then coughed too hard and it set up an involuntary muscle spasm in my back which triggered my arm to jerk with amazing accuracy in her direction." I watched her face for a reaction. She never even blinked.

"It was unfortunate of course, as I had just picked up all that silverware not seconds before trying to help clear the dishes for her." I added as full of bull as the leftover bits of fried Spam beside my biscuit.

Cecelia tried hard to keep the corners of her mouth tight, but I knew she was secretly enjoying the comic repartee so I un-abashedly continued, incorporating flamboyant hand gestures as well.

"It happens all the time. Things just spontaneously fly out of my hands when I cough too hard, or get angry, or frustrated..." At this point I raised my voice an octave or two in the direction of the counter. "... or have to wait too long for coffee" I sneered and stared at the waitress for good measure and then turned back to my guest who was trying to stifle a giggle with her napkin. Other patrons began to focus on us. Audience in tact, I continued.

"It's an inherited disease called, Nervosous-Projectous." I confessed, keeping my volume high enough for the whole restaurant to hear.

"My grandmother had it. My mother had it, so... it only stands to reason I would have it. If I *could* have kids...which now everyone in this half of the hemisphere knows I cannot... they'd have had it too most likely! I swear on my great Aunt Matilda's grave... even she had it!" I sheepishly cajoled and winked at Cecelia for good measure.

"All right, pipe down silly girl" she insisted. "You'll wake the dead."

"Isn't that what this is all about anyway?" I teased.

"Caroline...I'm warning you! Besides, you don't have a great Aunt Matilda. You were adopted so how could you possibly know what your mother or your grandmother had or had not?" she responded.

"Again with the semantics! You're such a stickler for details." I mused. "Anyway...you were saying?"

"Oh, hell. I believe I've forgotten now what it was I *was* saying" she whimpered. "You always distract me with such silliness."

"You were saying...'Oh Caroline...you're so good at what you do. Really good. I wish I could be just like you!'" I baited.

"Well... ok. I'm sure it was something like that... minus the wish I could be like you!" she teased and then went on. "Now about this diary girl of yours. I'm pleased you never gave up on her...or the research and investigating. It's remarkable what you've been able to unearth, thus far. When you show the authorities everything you've found they will simply have to listen."

"This is the South Cecelia. Nobody ever simply has to do anything. And they generally do not. It's the Margaret Mitchell law of the land!" "Hey... did you know she used to stay in the area?" I decoyed. "There's another plantation just down the road from the Danburg about thirty minutes from here. It's called Callawold or the Calla-something. I remember, because I was out riding one day and saw these huge chimneys in the distance and thought..."

"Don't try to detour me again, young lady. Let's stick with your diary maiden. They will listen, the evidence is over-whelming" she restated.

"It wasn't enough evidence for them back then" I sighed and walked my fingers towards a butter knife.

"Hindsight is always twenty-twenty, Caroline. They didn't have the luxury of that or the diary. You do. They'll listen to you now, kiddo. You can do this. You'll find a way to make them." She moved the remaining potential projectiles out of the way to pat my hand. "Nervosous-Projectous indeed" she smiled. "You have a good heart, my dear. I should have told you that more often. I'm sorry." Compliments from her had always been few and far between and I had never been very good at accepting them.

"Please don't..." I sighed coyly hoping she would lavish more praise, but she misread my intentions.

"OK... I won't. But, Caroline. They'll have to listen this time. Your diary maiden's entries will lead the way and they'll come to the same conclusions as you. You have a gift for finding the truth." she said with absolute declaration. I smiled soaking in the sentiment and noticed the waitress across the way sarcastically smiled too, knowing my mother in law had moved another steak knife several inches beyond my reach.

"Professionally, you've kept things in perspective and been very careful about documenting and vetting your sources. Just because you're not certain you can tie it all together in one neat, clean little package for the state at this point...don't let that keep you from moving forward with this. And as for your personal life being used against you... Well, it shouldn't come into play. It's really nobody's business but yours and Matt's."

"But they'll make it everybody's business if I can't definitively prove everything I suspect. I can just see the headlines. 'Poor Barren Preservationist Obsesses over Mysterious Diary Maiden!' My reputation will be eviscerated in the papers. Not good for the old resume, I might add" and flashed another death stare at the waitress who had forgotten twice now to return with our free refills.

"Well, that's just a risk you'll have to take" she replied.

"Let some one else take the hit this time. I've been beaten up enough this year." I whined.

"Mostly by yourself, my dear" she reminded and then smiled at the waitress who now took pity on her. I shoved my empty coffee cup towards the edge till it teetered to drive home my impatience and watched the waitress make a beeline for the filling pot.

Frowning, Cecelia pulled the cup back from the edge and continued her campaign. "If not you and not now? Then who, Caroline? And when?" she asked flatly. "You may be the only real hope this thing has of ever getting solved."

"Cecilia, please. If I screw up this, I may not even be able to go back to teaching. What university is going to want to hire me if this blows up in my face? I'm too old to start over and too young to retire!"

Her eyes squinted behind the wing tipped frames. "Don't be so melodramatic." I saw the waitress circling, waiting for the safety of a cleared landing so I removed my hands from the table.

"Cecilia, the point is I would be all alone in this. I'm divorced...no children. I play Barbie's Dream House with the government's money and I drink occasionally because Ken had the audacity after fifteen years to walk out on me for Skipper down the street."

Editing my response with a glare, Cecelia lowered her glasses and cocked an eyebrow till I recanted.

"Ok...so Ken didn't walk out until *after*, I shoved him out. Happy?" I tossed in for good measure.

She frowned and squinted again. "And...?" she baited, holding her gaze.

"Ok, ok, fine. And the drinking occasions have bunched together lately into one continuous cocktail hour." I blurted. "But that's just because I don't know what to do with all this information! I'm scared people will think I've gone crazy. You said so yourself, it's almost unbelievable. What if I'm wrong?"

"But what if you're right? Sixty two years, Caroline! Sixty two years these folks have waited for the truth!" she volleyed back.

I raced the net with another more obvious objection. "Ok, how 'bout... I'm not even the right color to approach them about this. What do you want me to do? Charge the hill screaming don't shoot till you see the whites of my eyes... oh and the rest of me too?"

"Drop the theatrics." She remanded.

"Ok, but how do you think folks around here would feel about me going public with all of this without their blessing? And I can't get their blessing, because half of them won't even speak to me about it."

"Which half?" she asked.

"Both halves! White and black! But even if we all were chartreuse it wouldn't matter. I'm not a native, I'm not a man, and I'm not anything to these people but a big fat drunken intrusion into their world." I replied.

"Then you must make them see you as something other than a threat" she said.

"I'm not the real dog in this fight, Cecelia. It's them. Them, and their children and their grandchildren. They talk and every family member white or black, born or unborn will bear the mark of a rat. And you know what happens to rats— and I patted the diary in my purse. They get slugged in the head and kicked to the curb as a warning to other rats to keep their yaps shut!"

Chapter Two

Twenty minutes later the waitress yawned into her own cup of coffee as the streetlamps outside began to flicker. Graveyard shift at the local diner was slowly coming to an end and so was my mother in laws patience. She listened intently for a few more objections, but I could see she was already formulating her defense.

"Besides, that's the least of it." I implored. "Think about the FBI. Do you have any idea the field day they would have with me if I go to them with all this now? I'm sure they'll be more than receptive when I say, 'Excuse me sirs, but you seem to have overlooked about a million clues over the last half a century. But that's ok, because I and my trusty diary here have all the answers for ya!' I'm sure to win an award for that performance!" I spat and popped up like a Jack-in-the-box, waved and took a bow.

"And now, I'd like to thank all the little people who had to die to make this very special moment for me possible!" The waitress, who had finally begun a courageous but cautious attempt to deliver more coffee to our table, suddenly balked and scurried in the opposite direction. "Yeah... that'll make me real popular around here, don't you think?" I stated and slowly took my seat. The quivering body bulging inside the orange and white ruffled uniform behind the counter was now talking to the manger and making odd gestures.

Cecelia pushed my half eaten biscuit towards me. "Caroline, calm down and eat something to absorb the alcohol. You're embarrassing yourself."

My voice squeaked back at her, pitched with emotion. "I'm perfectly sober. I haven't had a drink in..." I looked at the tacky cat clock on the wall, "... what? Six, seven hours now?" I guesstimated. "Besides, you don't know anyone in this town and technically neither do I... except for her." I glanced at the waitress and waved. "She's my new best friend and she doesn't even know it" I quipped sarcastically. The waitress's hand shook as she lit another cigarette and my mother in law threatened to get her coat.

"Ok. I'll calm down. But Cecelia, what if I go through everything. Tell them about the girl, the diary and the bridge and end up with nothing for my troubles but a huge lawsuit? What then? Who's gonna protect me on this?" I demanded. "Whose gonna cover my ass? The state? Locals like them?" and I signaled towards the waitress who now was beginning to get that deer in the headlights look whenever I glanced her way.

"Caroline, you're over reacting again" she said.

The waitress sensing I was about to go postal, rushed over in between diatribes. Hot amber liquid drooled from the pot into our cups as she kept her eyes on the butter knife to my left. Mission accomplished, she slid the check onto the table to encourage our speedy departure.

Cecelia thanked her graciously and then turned her attention back to me. "Forget the hysterics. Get to the point."

"Don't you see?" I implored, thinking about Matt. "I need to learn how to bury my own ghosts first. Not go digging up somebody else's." I brought the fresh cup to my mouth and the steam fogged my glasses long enough to soften my resolve.

"Caroline, honey" she whispered. "What happened to you as a child wasn't anymore your fault, than it was the little diary maiden, as you call her. Not sharing it when it happened, for the both of you was the mistake after the fact."

"I know that academically." I bit back. "So why do I continue to sit here blubbering about a child I don't know; who suffered God knows what, by God knows who... and for God knows how long?"

While she hesitated to find direction, my mind raced over words from the diary that had first thrown me spiraling back into my own childhood. "You tell me why!" I blathered. My eyes glazed with tears and I choked on my words.

"So... so..."

"So, you could make yourself feel better about what happened to you as a kid?" she innocently ushered in trying to help.

"No!" I growled and cut her off. "So, I don't have to relive it alone night after night, while your son— my ex sleeps blissfully next to his new wife, Skipper! The mother of a child that was supposed to be mine!"

Her eyes widened with hurt.

"He got what he wanted. You and Dan got what you wanted—a grandchild! But what about me? What did I get out of it besides an old leather book, a dilapidated manor and a huge headache?" She remained silent while I continued to vent. "And what about the diary maiden? What did she get for her troubles?" I screamed, demanding answers for us both. "He's dead. Hell, she's probably dead for all I know! They're all dead! So what's the point?" I blasted.

Cecelia held her tongue, confounded by my depth of emotion. I burst into tears and waited for the rebuttal, but there was none. She completely by-passed my personal jabs and unfair accusations, placed her hand on mine and signaled the waitress for more napkins and coolly changed the subject.

"Did I ever tell you about a story I once wrote in college?" she calmed, dabbing a napkin in her water glass for my face. She talked softly while I attempted to clean up my mascara.

"It finally got published a few years ago, but a professor at one of the workshops I attended out on the west coast had a ball with me over it before I got it right."

"No...you never told me." I swallowed gratefully and sniffled my way back to composure.

"The story was about your typical southern legacy stuff. You know. Class warfare, racial intolerance. The kind of stuff your Danburg ghosts survived". She finally bit into the edge of her biscuit and washed it down with a mouthful of coffee.

"They are not my ghosts, Cecilia! I never said they were mine." I snapped and then retreated. "I have enough of my own, thank you. What I said, was…"

"Whatever," she bristled, signaling she was finished listening and was determined to be heard. "The point is…that while my story had no tie to a real crime like yours it was still believable. Believable from the stand point that such insanity as wanting to hang a black man for purportedly stealing a pie from the window sill of a white kitchen happened quite frequently in those days. What really irritated this professor was not the ludicrousness of the crime; it was that I had dared to write it from a man's point of view!"

I failed to see her segue, but held my tongue out of respect.

"You see, I wrote it in first person. I became the lead character—this fella I named Willie Oreo. Get it? Oreo…like the cookie? You know. It was a common figure of speech back then. Black on the outside, educated and cultured like a white man on the inside… an Oreo?"

"Oh, my God! What year was this?" I stammered at the gross political incorrectness of her moniker.

"The sixties…" she winked and I grimaced. "It wasn't like that back then. It was an innocent equivalence. Not an intentional slight" she insisted, tossing her bottled red hair away from an ample bosom. "Clever name, huh?" and her cleavage shifted as she readjusted her shoulders.

"No wonder your professor had a little trouble getting behind your… male point of view." I flattered and nodded towards her matronly chest.

She grinned. "Very funny, Caroline. Now, as I was saying" she continued in between bites. "When I explained to my professor that Willie Oreo was a black man, it damn near killed him. And it should have, he laughed so hard at me!"

I watched her eyes beam as she brushed crumbs from her cleavage with amusement, recalling her mentor's annotations. "Anyway…he wanted to know how I, the queen of Norwegian estrogen could possibly know what a man… any man, white or black, would feel or think in any situation."

"Well, Minnesota in the sixties wasn't exactly a haven for..." I began, but neglected to finish suddenly mesmerized by several crumbs that had gathered in the corners of her pink lipstick and danced when she spoke.

"Yes, well... anyways. Isn't that the whole point of creative writing, I asked? Isn't it supposed to take you somewhere different than your reality?"

I marveled at her abuse of the literary poetic license and played dumb. "Yes, but..."

She cut me off. "Soooo... that's what I did. I went somewhere I'd never been before—inside a black man and outside in Tennessee!"

I blanched at the innocent sexual innuendo and saved her dignity by going for the lesser intrigue. "Tennessee?" I smiled. "When were you ever in Tennessee?"

"That's where I met your father in law."

"Ex- father in law, thanks to your son" I corrected and stabbed at the biscuit on the plate, pretending it was Matt's heart.

"That's not the point." She said and pulled the knife from my hand like I was a toddler. "The point I am trying to make is, that just because what I found when I got there didn't resemble anything in that professor's Californian tie-dyed, beach blanket bingo'd mentality didn't make it wrong. It just made it..." and she paused for dramatic effect, "...grossly unfamiliar."

"I'll say." I conceded weakly and inched my fingers back towards the knife. She made a low growling sound from her throat. "What?" I mused. "I need it to spread my butter." She pulled it from my grip and then told me more. She paused occasionally to nibble on her biscuit while I tried picturing her saying things like, 'down in the holler' or singing like Sissy Spacek in the movie, *Coal Miner's Daughter*.

"The storyline was fictional" she said. "But the rest of it was true. I had really known a few guys up north like Willie Oreo. That's why I wrote it!" She highlighted the moment by pulling out her compact, checking her face for signs of breakfast and aging.

"Did you tell the professor that?" I asked.

"Yes... and do you know what he said?"

I began to venture a response, but suddenly a vision of her in a blue gingham dress singing at the Grand Ole Opry popped into my head, making it difficult to concentrate.

"I'll tell you what he said!" she snapped sensing my ambiguity. "'I don't find the motivations of your lead character believable!' Can you believe that?" she said and swiped at her mouth with a fresh napkin, her lips now presenting as raw as her emotions. She took my silence as invitation to continue and sarcastically prompted on my behalf. "Why, you might ask?"

I hadn't, but at this stage of the conversation any objection I might have entertained would have been tantamount to throwing a mill worm in front of a run away locomotive to stop it. I raised an eyebrow signaling my curiosity and tried to erase the Opryland scene from my head by carving my initials in the butter pads. The waitress began to get nervous again.

"I'll tell you why if you'll pay attention long enough" she sneered. I set the knife down and focused on the waitress who smiled at me. I did not return the expression, causing her to fumble with another cigarette and realized Cecelia had moved on without me.

"Because those outside the south, think we make this shit up. They cannot fathom that such vicious and primitive caricatures outside literature like, *To Kill a Mockingbird* still exist, or ever really existed. We are a by-gone misrepresentation of token roy-alty for the nation." A few rounded vowels of her Minnesotan accent occasionally bled through her recently acquired and labo-rious southern drawl. She pretended not to notice my grin and barreled through.

"We are the geographical cartoon that has long since lost its humorous appeal. They would rather pigeon hole and condemn us to narratives like Margaret Mitchell's sacrosanct creations. Forever doomed to flounce around in frilly skirts and oversized sun bonnets planning cotillions and barbeques. Saying tacky things like, 'Ya'll come back now, ya hear'? Plying our guests with sweet tea and mint juleps. Dripping sacrine from our lips with monikers like, 'sugar-pea', 'honey-lamb' and 'darlin'. We are called upon by those outside the borders of the almighty Mason Dixon and the notorious gnat line to spread them thick as peach marmalade throughout our conversations. All the while, charged with the responsibility of keeping the convenient and collective southern portrait alive."

I stopped carving the butter pad long enough to contemplate the exact latitude and longitude of the infamous gnat line, while she took a few seconds to catch her breath and blot her freshly painted lips. She sallied forth across the metaphorical lawns of Tara with her best imitation of Scarlet O'Hara and finished her performance by picking up the check and fanning herself.

"They didn't want to believe the worlds of Faulkner or Tennessee Williams either. The infamous 'they' have whitewashed our southern history so often to make it more palatable to future generations, that when 'we' finally try to tell the truth... they laugh at us and tell us we shouldn't believe our own tall tales! So with that in mind..." and she leaned across the table, batting her eyes and fanning herself one last time for effect or to ease a sudden hot flash.

"I will now ask the question my former prodigious professor from la- la land and half a million others would not think twice about asking you at the drop of a hat, Miss Prissy."

I leaned in to close the distance. "And what question might that be, Miss Scarlet, since I don't know nothing 'bout birthin no babies?" I mocked with the only other famous quote I recalled the little colored servant of the O'Hara household muttered. The irony in the statement was bittersweet and I damn near choked on the aftertaste. She scrunched her blue eyes beneath her black rimmed spectacles and sneered back at me.

"What makes you think you, of all people...a white, non-native woman, playing house with government money has the right to tell their story?"

Sucker punch delivered, she piqued her tailored eye brows simultaneously, reached for a clean napkin and settled back into her haunches awaiting my retreat.

Chapter Three

You could hear the cat clock humming on the wall in the absolute silence that followed.

"Wow, you're good." I said, hiding behind professional etiquette and unabashed admiration. "Well..." I stalled. "I'm not telling *their* story... specifically. I merely have an obligation to ferret out historical information pertinent to the property and the completion of my project. It's just part of my job to unearth what happened there, so I can properly identify artifacts, buildings, furnishings. It's never been my job to rewrite history. Only document and preserve it. There!"

"Ahhh....I see. But it is your job to correct it, isn't it? If what was recorded in the first place was wrong... right?"

I reeled at the implied responsibility. "Cecelia, it's not my..."

She cut me off once again. "According to what you say you've found...you can prove that! Right? So what's the problem?"

"The state didn't hire me to challenge prior historical narrations. Only reconstruct buildings, an era... to preserve a segment of the local history."

"But only part of it, right?" she threw back at me.

"Noooo." I bit back. "Of course not."

"Then how do you intend to do it justice by leaving half of it out?" she remanded.

"It's not up to me to provide justice…just facts." I stammered. "What I present in my work is an overview. A time capsule meant only to represent a composite history of the South."

"Whose South, Caroline? That's all I'm asking. Whose South? Yours? Mine? Willie Oreo's?"

"Don't start parsing." I spat. "You said yourself Willie was only a character."

"No. I said he was a composite character. Pieces of many compiled to present as one truth. Just like your so called facts Caroline!"

I grimaced.

"Okay, okay. No more parsing" she said and immediately changed the subject to ease the tension. "Remember the movie, *'You've Got Mail'* with Tom Hanks and Meg Ryan?"

"Whoa…. talk about a 360!" I said, dumfounded by her conversational dexterity. I was briefly blindsided, but held on for the ride.

"Remember?" she pushed.

Somehow, I managed to regroup. "What? You're reviewing movies now?"

"Yes… apparently I am" she responded. "Let's get a fresh perspective, shall we?" she declared without segue.

Suddenly I wished we were at a bar and not a diner. "Okay…if I were drinking something other than coffee right now, I'm certain this would make more sense."

"Well you promised me you'd quit" she slammed and moved on.

"Remember the part where his character brings her character daisies? And she's all ratty looking 'cause she's been sick with a bad cold and she puts on that ridiculous raincoat to answer the door while shoving hordes of snotty Kleenex's into the pockets?"

The visual was distracting, but I hung in there. "Yes. Is there a point to this movie review, Mrs. Ebert? I have to be home by five to wash my hair so I can watch Elvis on the Ed Sullivan Show." I mocked.

"Yessss…" she hissed. "There is a point, so keep up!"

I blanched, but let her continue.

"Well..." she resumed. "Remember how he—his character Joe Fox started talking about how sorry he was he ran her little book shop out of business?"

"Yes I do. He, I mean his character was a real jerk. Not unlike another member of your family." I added surreptitiously under my breath.

"Okay maybe, but he countered his remorse by saying how it was just good business. It wasn't personal—just business. Remember?"

"Yes...go on." I said rolling my eyes and reaching for the knife again to play with the jelly. Cecelia stalled my hand and the waitress watched the scene unfolding, getting all twitchy again.

"Remember how she— Meg Ryan, aka Kathleen Kelley got all pissy and said how it drove her crazy that people always said that kind of thing right before they did something they wouldn't want to happen to them?"

"Yes..." I patronized and toyed with the wooden handle on the butter knife just for fun.

She ignored my behavior and continued, "... and that because if anything should be anything at all, it should at least start out by being personal?' Remember that conversation?"

"Yes, yes, yes!" I blurted. "Get to your point already!"

"That *is* the point, Caroline. History *is* personal! Yours... mine... theirs!"

"Willie Oreo's?" I smiled and took the butter knife in my hand and faked stabbed myself. The waitress damn near had a stroke and ran to get her pimply faced manager.

"Don't be a shit, Caroline. I'm trying to help you." She sneered.

"This is about the Danburg again, isn't it?" I said and dropped the knife to the table irritated that she wouldn't let things die.

"Yes! But not just the Danburg or even your two ghosts. Although in and of themselves, they have a honey of a history folks would die to hear about."

I lowered my eye brows in disapproval.

"Sorry...no pun intended. But what about everyone else connected with them? What about those people at the bridge that day? Who will record their history?"

"That is not my concern. I have no authority. Not to mention the fact my dear ex-mother in law, this is an on-going FBI case. I can't just throw this stuff out without letting the authority's do due diligence first. People's lives would be changed forever."

She cut me off. "Caroline... people's lives *were* changed forever dammit! The world ignored them back then— they have a right to be heard now!" she blistered. "The Feds may have the facts, but they don't have the truth. You do!"

"Maybe, I have the truth Cecelia...maybe. And that's a mighty big 'maybe' because I'm still missing some of the evidence."

"But you have enough" she reminded.

I balked at the implied obligation. "Even still... it's not my job, Cecelia. I'm not FBI. I'm just a Historical Preservationist, remember? I have a laptop. They have guns!"

The manager and the waitress now made nice and smiled from the doorway of his office. I couldn't tell if that was a pocket calculator in his hand or a tazer, so I smiled and let go of the butter knife.

"Fine!" she hurled back. "But it is your duty."

Shocked by her bluntness I listened tolerantly to more of her observations and then offered a few of my own, including the biggest one of all.

"Southerner's do not take kindly to outsider's butting their noses into private affairs and they have a rather violent history to prove it! Case in point — current dilemma!" and I motioned towards the door of the office where Clark Kent and Lois Lane now waited patiently, poised to dial 911 should I reach for a knife again.

"Your favorite excuse is Moores Ford Bridge still being an open case with the FBI, but that's rather small potatoes in the larger scheme of things. Don't you think?"

"That may be small potatoes for you Miss Scarlet. You can afford to stand there defiant on the steps of your Tara claiming 'as God is your witness, you will never go hungry again!' But you my dear woman have tenure at the University, a fat 401K and a husband to cover your ass! Me? I'm all alone out there in the cotton fields with just a basket of fluff and my knickers in a wad! I wouldn't do well in prison, Cecelia. I'm all for cable TV and three squares a day, but I prefer bathing alone at this stage in my life!"

She smiled sarcastically. "I agree... scooping the FBI on a federal case is a bit of a toughie to get around." She muttered, knowing we had only touched the very tip of the iceberg of reasons why I should keep my mouth shut on this thing.

"Jesus Christ...a bit of a toughie to get around? Cecelia! If I'm right and this diary describes what I think it does, I may have inadvertently tampered with evidence in both a state and federal case! If I'm wrong, I could hang! Or, at the very least...be sued for a laundry list of offenses I can't even begin to count. And.... by not telling the FBI about it to begin with, prosecuted and sent to the big house for at the very least, obstruction of justice! And when I say 'the big house', I'm not talking about the Danburg manor! Any way you look at it...I'm screwed. Royally!"

She finished the last of her coffee in silence, waved a twenty and the check in the air as a white flag and then pricked my conscience one more time.

"But Caroline, darling" she baited, "Forgiving everything else...what *does* give you the right to tell their story?"

"Cecelia..." I whined. "Drop it. I can't afford to be on the 11:00 news tonight. I don't even stay up that late to watch it!" The manager swooped by, grabbing the cash and check while the wide eyed waitress cleared the dishes— especially my silverware! The table now cleared of sharp objects, they disappeared behind the register.

"Hah ha! I knew it. That was no tazer! It was just a pocket calculator! How dare you come to a battle unprepared to fight!" I cackled as the two scurried away.

"Caroline!" She cut through my evasion, no longer amused by my nervous humor. "Caroline...think dammit! What's the one reason nobody, not even you can ever argue with?"

We both knew even if there had been a hundred more reasons just as sound as the myriad before why I shouldn't tell this, there would always be the one incredibly obvious reason why I should.

"Because..." she started, slowly pleading with her eyes for me to finish.

"Have I told you today how much I hate you, Cecelia?"

"I can't think about that today. Maybe tomorrah..." she said in her best Vivian Leigh. "Now go on Caroline. What's the one reason nobody, not even you can ever argue with?"

I paused under the weight of the epiphany and then continued for us both. "Because Miss Scarlet... they are no longer alive to tell it for themselves."

"That's my girl!" she said getting up from her chair. "You better get going, Caroline. I have an appointment with my colorist and you my dear have an appointment with justice!" She touched at the graying roots of her head and smiled. "...and we're both already more than half a century late!"

She touched my hand as I got up, signaling it was time for both of us to move on. I kissed her on the cheek and left knowing I would most likely never talk to her again. It was the first of many goodbyes.

Chapter Four

The Danburg Manor and surrounding acreage had achieved acclaim as a state historical site, and I had been consumed by its restoration for the past eighteen months. On the surface most of the manor's history was rather mundane, but my digging in the Georgia red clay revealed events that invited notoriety. Ironically, it wasn't the reconstruction of the Danburg Manor as a *house* that presented a problem. It was what I unearthed during the reconstruction of the Danburg as a *home* that brought me to my knees.

Built before the Civil War, the Danburg Plantation had been wonderfully appointed, with over twenty-one original outbuildings. Like many other plantations in the path of Sherman's March to the Sea, the Danburg suffered radical damage. Sherman's strategy was to send Union troops in several directions to deceive the Confederates. The Union troops' multiple swathes of destruction left the Confederates confused as to whether Sherman would march on Macon, Augusta or Savannah. Howard's wing marched south along the railroad to Lovejoy's Station. Slocum's wing together with Sherman advanced east toward Augusta destroying railways—the lifeline for southern troops.

After decimating the bridge across the Oconee River, the troops then turned south. This was apparently where the first manor house met with disaster. Reports spread that Confederate soldiers were starving since Union troops had destroyed the railroads, rendering it impossible to send supplies to the front. Hell-bent on bringing Georgia to its knees, Sherman was not content to lift what food and supplies he needed, but boasted that he would make Georgia howl, and indeed he did. Since the march began several months after the harvest, opportunities for greed were abundant. Soldiers that advanced before the columns did their best to ferret out the local rich. These "bummers," as they were called, found the larger plantations ripe for the taking. Their barns were bursting with grain, the outhouses full of cotton and the yards crowded with hogs, chickens and turkeys. Sherman's men took everything of value that could be moved. Many homes were burned.

In wrenching personal letters and recorded accounts, southern plantation owners wrote of gratuitous abuse and thievery. There were whispers of similar documentation hidden within the Danburg manor, but documents giving credence to the rumored defiling of both manor and mistress eluded discovery.

After the war, the family reconstructed its plantation and reputation. Cotton was king in the south and the Danburgs prospered again. But in the new century, family fortunes ran dry and debt mounted. The land was gradually sold off in parcels. In 1946, a mysterious second fire claimed the Danburg Manor. By the time I was tapped for the restoration project in 2007, the fourteen-hundred-acre plantation had dwindled to a paltry sixty acres. On my first visit to the once-majestic plantation, its isolation held promise for personal mending. Desperately in need of personal reconstruction, I resolved to restore my soul through the renovation of the manor.

For me the restoration process had always been about more than just the transformation of old buildings. It was about the opportunity to salvage dignity of place and purpose. For the Danburg, the process had promised a chance to reclaim a rich history. Now, no longer an illegible icon, it rose two stories above an emerald lawn. I stood confidently at its threshold, ready to return it to the world. If one human could be indentured to mere mortar and brick... it was I.

I closed my eyes as sunlight fingered its way through the pines and the warmth of the first rays settled upon my lids. I would have stayed, but like me, the structure had been granted a new lease on life and was anxious to begin it.

For over half a century the Danburg had sheltered its ghosts. With a keen sense of the bittersweet, I locked the front doors. The iron hardware that bolted behind me felt as heavy as my heart. I needed to remember the house, its ghosts, and their haunting secrets while they were still mine alone. Needed to memorize the way sunlight broke across the manor's face, the manor's smells and sounds. Wanted to imprint upon my soul the sacrifices made here so that I could share them with the community of moral souls who would never fail to remember.

The skeleton key to the front door burned in my hand. In a few short hours a new docent would be here to take my place and though I was not yet ready to go, the Danburg had given me the strength to walk away. As a tear slid down my face, I held tight to the key with one hand and the tattered book inside my pocket with the other and told myself I could keep the promises I'd made here.

The sun now blazed with jeweled brilliance through the stained glass transoms of the front parlor. I tested the bolts on the jib windows below and then turned toward the steps. So much of who I was and who I had become were connected to that house. I wondered how it would feel to finally walk away.

I rolled the key over in my palm several times to commit its feel to memory. It had been his, it had been hers, then finally it had been mine. We had each used it to open secret doors in our lives that had revealed both joy and pain. I thought about my ex-husband Matt and squeezed my fists. Now on my right hand, the center diamond of my engagement ring gouged the little finger next to it, leaving a mark. I rubbed the spot and twisted my ring back into place more out of habit than affection. Matt and I had been constantly at odds at the beginning of the project and it hadn't been just about the baby—or rather, the fact that one didn't exist.

After trying unsuccessfully to have one of our own, Matt had desperately pressed for adoption. Uneasy with his solution, I ignored his pleas and found it easier to bear the silent halls of our home if I was less exposed to them. I buried myself in work. In the end it proved to be a huge mistake. Comforting myself with my career made it easier for someone else to comfort him. Eventually, I figured that out when someone other than I was pregnant and we were soon at opposite sides of a lawyer's conference table. The Danburg then became the only place that I could call home.

I looked at my left hand. It was as empty as my heart and the band of pale skin on my tanned ring finger bore testament to failure. Perhaps it was time to call things what they really were. Over! I moved cautiously down the freshly painted front steps of the porch. Stepping inside the stone edges of the carriage walk, I paused to look back for one more moment. The stately elegance of the fresh façade was framed by a magnolia and manicured boxwoods. Without compromise, the manor was the most beautiful home I had ever seen. Yet its real magnificence came from the truth about two of its most cherished residents.

Satisfied that everything was now in its proper place, there was just one thing left to do. Slowly I walked across the dewed lawn to the partially buried foundation of the original ironing shed, bent my head in prayer and placed two long-stemmed, sterling roses atop the identifying marker.

The street lamps signed off and the sun, dressed in the same shade that had been her signature, blazed a trail to where I stood. I brushed away another tear and bent to touch her rose. The petals were cool and soft. I remembered the feel of her cheek against mine in a former moment of goodbye. I still needed her. Needed to feel her guiding hand in mine again, needed to watch the rush of joy upon her face when she knew we had found him at last, but it was not meant to be. Having unlocked the mystery of the diary, she had been anxious to be back in his arms. Determined to fulfill my promise, I made my way down to the edge of the drive where the wrought iron gates waited.

Had I known what I would find the first time I walked that path, I might not have taken the first step. But if I had not, I would never have met her, and that would have been an even greater tragedy. The Danburg Manor deserved to have its story told, Moores Ford Bridge to have its ghosts exorcised, and the world to know their secrets.

I entered the code on the security pad and watched as the two wrought iron panels slowly closed. With closure both metaphorically and physically they came to rest, framing the Danburg with perfect symmetry between the past and the present. I whispered my goodbyes.

It was now time to tell the story about the house, the secret afterlife of the Danburg Diary—and how it came to be mine.

Chapter Five

My heart broke when I first saw the Danburg. The main structure was severely damaged. The challenge was to discover what was blackened from rot and what was charred from fire—and to discover why it happened. How a property fell from grace did not interest most people, but to me the reasons created its mystery and charm. Historic preservation wasn't merely about saving walls; it was about saving the history trapped within them. Typically, the explanation for each structure's deterioration pointed to someone or something to blame. I imagined the Danburg's dossier, once completed, would reveal much the same.

The Danburg had become a victim of flagrant disregard after its darkest episode since the Civil War, the great fire of 1946. My research found that a brick-and-mortar replacement constructed in 1868, after the Danburg's first fire, had weathered several smaller fires until the calamitous blaze of 1946. Generational bouts of mismanagement continued into the new millennium until a generous stranger decided the benefits from its salvage by the state far outweighed its certain demise on the auction block.

When I took the assignment I thought it would provide good therapy. After I started, the assignment became the sole reason to seek therapy! At first, nothing in my research nor the demolition phase of the Danburg suggested intrigue. But there was a consistent undercurrent that propelled me to listen more closely to the locals' speculations about its sinister reputation.

Winter came and left the Danburg. The house continued to dismiss me as an itinerant intruder unworthy of its complete disclosure. I continued to woo its affections. By the time the outer buildings had been rebuilt, spring had bloomed and summer was inspiring the dream of reconstruction. After the plaster was repaired and the dry wall hung on the lower floor, I was finally ready to start designing the interior layouts.

The great effort for acquisition began. I combed the local markets and contacted preservation-minded citizens to find as many original pieces of furniture to the home as possible. After several months of searching, I had procured only three pieces that had survived both fire and family exigencies. I was now forced to populate the rooms with period furniture not original to the home.

Rumors circulated that a fourth piece symbolic of the Danburg still remained in the area. In my search for substitutes, I still hoped for that one signature piece — a stately grandfather clock with a hand-painted face that local legend claimed held clues to all the family secrets, making it a real find if it still existed.

An antique dealer from town told me the clock had made several trips in and out of his front doors as customers would buy it for looks and then trade it for functioning pieces. It seemed no one had time for a clock that remained as dysfunctional as the family who'd owned it and fewer still for a clock that held the collective sins of an entire region! This is how I first came to know of the diary, the girl, and the murders.

Chapter Six

The kitchen has always been my favorite spot in the whole house. It's been the setting for hearty breakfasts, noonday dinners, social gatherings and Saturday night baths. Some of the most important moments of my life have happened there and I need to record every detail so I won't forget if tomorrow finds us in new adventures far from here...or just far from one another...

The diary to this point had been rather pedestrian in nature and although it was enjoyable to examine in a sentimental kind of vein, it had not piqued my professional curiosity enough to warrant much more than a passing fascination. But seeing as I had no other plans for the evening, I decided to pour myself a cup of coffee, settle into my leather chair and allow it to keep me company for the duration of the evening.

Unlike the rest of this house, the kitchen walls are a collection of mismatched, peeling wallpaper, shelves and hooks. The flooring much the same: a hodgepodge of grayed heart of pine and linoleum with colorful, ragged edges in unique starburst patterns, just like a huge jigsaw puzzle. It's always felt like a great game board to me. When I first came and the older girls would ignore me, I would play hopscotch on its blotchy surface or float pint-sized pea-pod sail boats I'd made in the pocked porcelain sink. Six steps beyond the expansive drain board, with dishes forever drying, waited another favorite hideaway for me—the pantry.

The pantry is a huge shelf-lined cavern whose home-canned vegetables and fruits shout vivid colors according to the season's harvest and tease as make-shift kaleidoscopes when I hold them up to the summer sun. When life became hectic and I was shushed out of the way and told to entertain myself, I would hide within its knotted pine walls pretending I was about to embark on a very long and dangerous journey. Pulling a wicker basket from the laundry, I would pack for my adventure everything precious to me in the world. A tiny locket on a golden chain, my lace-topped anklets, my diary... fresh tiger lily blooms or peonies from the yard—picture books, a loaf of homemade bread and sometimes jars of fig preserves or apple butter.

Funny... only now do I recognize how I never packed anything for practical use, only for pleasure. I never packed things that other folks thought were important, things like shoes, toothbrushes, combs, personal toiletries and underwear. Only the things I thought beautiful and fragile. Had I only known life would turn out the way it has, I might have learned to pack more wisely...

"Amen to that, sister. Wouldn't we all? Wouldn't we all..." I sighed as I looked into my empty coffee cup. Closing the cover carefully, I placed the diary back into its container and made my way to the kitchen. What would I have taken on such an imaginary journey had the diary been mine? I poured myself another steaming cup of coffee and then reached above my head, opening the cupboard to my right. There were two cans of baby peas, three packages of Ramen Noodles, a half eaten granola bar, a canister of Crystal Light Pink Lemonade and an empty box of Sweet and Low.

"Pathetic!" I said, closing that cupboard to open the next. I moved a cereal box and found four packages of Sugar Free Jello Instant Pudding—all chocolate—some peanut butter cookies, a small jar of generic instant coffee, a box of oatmeal and a half a bottle of Jack Daniels and a can of cat food called Tuna Delight.

"At least I can travel light..." I mused. I opened the third cupboard and it was empty.

"I have all the necessities for a woman well over forty-fi... Well, I have what I need until menopause!" I barked into the empty kitchen. I took inventory again of cabinet number two, hoping to find something to put in my coffee, playing a child-hood game with myself. "My name is Caroline and I'm going on a long trip...and with me I will take...hmmm..." I canvassed my supplies again, convinced there must have been a second box of Sweet and Low hiding somewhere behind the oatmeal.

"Let's see...I have...chocolate—check! Liquor—check! Caffeine—double check! And last but not least...food for a trusted furry companion who could keep me company on cold winter nights! Aha! Take that little miss dear diary." I blurted back laughing. "I too could embark on a great adventure as long as it led me straight to another grocery store and my therapist!" Not wishing to drink my coffee neat, I reached for the box of Sweet and Low and then remembered it was empty. "Shit!" I muttered, closing the cupboard door and then reopening it slowly, eyeing the can of cat food. When had I purchased that?

I didn't have a cat. I had never had a cat. I had always wanted a cat, but my ex-husband Matt was allergic to animal dander, so the question still remained. How had I ended up with a can of cat food in my rather meager pantry and not a necessary condiment for my coffee? When and why had I bothered to pick up such a charming little accessory and yet not a staple such as Sweet and Low?

It couldn't have come in with someone else... there was no one else! And I hadn't started staying on site until I had officially moved out of our marital home and then wore out my welcome at my friend Connie's. The whiskered face on the label smiled mockingly. I grinned back, but for the life of me I could not imagine why I would have bought such a thing. There was not even a stray on the property.

The green, beady eyes continued to stare at me as I rolled the can over in my hand a few times. Embarrassed that my life now allowed for so much time to be spent on contemplating the sheer existence of cat food in my larder, I returned it to the shelf confused, but not for long. I reached for the bottle to the right of the whiskered face and decided to make my beverage a cocktail.

That's when it hit me. Valentine's Day—the first alone since my divorce.

It all came flooding back. Had I not still been sober at this point, I could have sworn the little vixen on the label winked at me. Irritated, I turned the can completely around to put the petite feline's face in time-out.

"Ah yes... last Valentine's Day. No card, no gift... no sex... no husband... no sympathy and no alimony to make it all more palatable! Yes... now I remember! I was all alone... except for the one man who has always stood by my side —Jack Daniels. Compassionate fellow that he is, he and I spent the night together! And apparently, if you ingest enough of him on an empty stomach, cat food called Tuna Delight and actual tuna at a convenience store at 2:00 in the morning can look an awful lot alike!"

I poured a shot of the amber anesthetic into my cup. Celebrating my excellent memory and the fact that I had been too exhausted to cook that night, I ceremoniously thanked my ex-husband for the cat food and made a mental note to take him and his lovely new bride a delicious Tuna Delight casserole the next time I went into town.

Placing the bottle back in its place, I applauded myself further at having made remarkable strides in dealing with my anger issues. Satisfied with myself I adjusted the can, winked back at the cat on the label for good measure.

"It really is true what they say...Hell hath no fury like a woman scorned!" I blathered, as I shut the cupboard door with a bit too much enthusiasm and tried to recall if the recipe required one tin or two!

"Yes sirree" I toasted, "...an apology casserole is just the thing to let my ex-husband know how I sorry I am that I cannot share in his joy at being a new father... especially since it's with my ex-neighbor!" I downed that shot and reached to pour another.

Medicinally comforted, I crawled back into my chair and prepared to read the next entry. I opened the leather cover, found my place and began to read once again about my diary maiden's simple life...

"You, my precious darling, are so lucky to have lived such a boring life! I hope you knew how fortunate you were to have nothing more calamitous happen in your day than the deciding between which pair of lace anklets to wear to Sunday school and which flowers to pick from your garden to match your hat." I raised my cup in toast to her.

...What has always entertained me most is meal preparation and consumption. It starts early in the morning with dogs quietly weaving between legs, waiting for table scraps to drop. The cacophony of pots and pans shifting atop the range and the wood-burning stove belching soot between the pipe fittings before they begin to swell in the rising heat and seal.

Breakfasts are elaborate around here, with homemade biscuits and preserves, country ham and redeye gravy and fried eggs...

"Damn..." I whispered. "She's making me hungry." I thought about the cupboards and realized there was nothing in them that immediately appealed to me.

Dinners are always at noon and fuel hard labor in fields and barns until the sun sets. When I was younger, it appeared that meal preparation and dish washing extended from daylight to dusk and seldom was I without dishtowel on my arm.

Seasons change here, but rituals never do. Right on time every day, folks sit around the big, circular, oil-clothed table passing mounds of food after the blessing. Conversations focus on crops, livestock and family matters. Family and community scandals are never aired in front of me, and even the frictions of the inner circle are masked, but never enough. There is always too much emotion between these walls, so much so that even the house itself groans at night from the extra weight.

The kitchen is for more than just eating. Often it becomes the stage for Saturday night bathing as well. Growing up, the first labor of this ceremony was to banish all menfolk. In the beginning I knew it was to protect my adolescent modesty and allow the tea kettle's repeated adjustments to the hot water supply. Later I realized this time was my only escape. The few minutes I could be alone without the watchful eyes of my cousins or the glares of my uncle.

As I gazed away from the raw light of suspended bulbs, my blurred vision always lulled me into fantasizing I was a desirable siren, unlike my older cousins. I would climb out of the bath into a waiting, oversized bath towel, pretending I was climbing into his arms. Rubbing the soft towel across my damp, chilled skin, my senses would heighten and I would wait... knowing he would eventually show.

I remember the first time I saw him out of the corner of my eye. I knew I should have said something, or at least made a motion to cover myself, but somehow it didn't feel wrong to let him see. And so I shifted my stance, but did not shy away from the intensity of his stare... the same way I do not now...

The flimsy book fell from my hands onto the floor. "What the..." was all I could muster under my breath. I had not been prepared for what was taking place on the page in front of me. The more I read, the more my head started to pound. This was going to take considerably more than just a few shots of whiskey to get through. What the hell was going on in that house... this house... or wherever that child was?

I bent to pick up the diary and gagged on my own saliva. I could not bring myself to read any farther, as my own childhood memories began to flood my vision...a basement shower... cold streaming water... a window well and peering eyes. The smell of dirty linens. Groping hands and a white Formica table with little metal wheels that grated on the concrete floor as it jerked back and forth in rhythm with his thrusts. The taste of urine and salty tears as they mixed with semen drooling from the corners of my trembling lips...I threw the diary into my chair.

Bile started building in the pit of my stomach and I knew the roller coaster ride was just around the corner. First, sweat would start to bead on my upper lip. My heart would start to race next and then either the hyperventilating or the vomiting would begin in earnest. My teeth began to clench...

I tried to take a few deep breaths to calm myself, but the build had already begun by the time I ran down the hall towards the bathroom and my medication. Forty minutes later I returned. I had not had an episode like that since my early teens. I picked the diary up again and began to cautiously read the remainder of the entry as I paced the borders of the room to keep myself from crawling out of my skin.

My romanticism about him continues to edge toward eroticism. It is those dark and brooding eyes of his that make me feel there is so much more than the history of exotic words from his books between us. I am hesitant as to what to say about our attraction yet and as my cousins have set their eyes upon him as well, it is a secret better kept to myself.

Tomorrow he has promised a late afternoon picnic. It will be my last chance alone with him as Mother and Daddy will arrive to fetch me and then three days later, the long and dismal drive north. Whatever happens between us must last a lifetime as time here may become little more than memory if the job prospect for Daddy in Chicago presents more appealing prospects than familial ties. Until tomorrow then, Dear Diary...

There was another reference to a water hole, a trip to the attic to find suitable reading materials and what picnic items could be comfortably carried and then, abruptly in a dissimilar hand... another entry.

I believe it is a fair assumption that they have discovered our collective escape by now. I am grateful that they will be stalled, having no idea where to begin their search, but I fear it will not be for long. My family name comes with a very clear roadmap that leads to the front door of this house, and that is why I must get to you before them. They know I could name as many as ten, and I shall remain eternally indebted to my silent companion for acting as the courier of truth. I hated leaving him there, but there was no other recourse.

Looking out from the belly of a decapitated silo, I saw the scattered wreckage of broken chimneys, felt the brutal rush of foul air beneath the wings of turkey vultures that circled above me, and counted myself lucky that I was still alive. Liquid continued to drain from his body throughout the night, congealing in small pools at the rim of his silhouette. In the moonlight, his blood looked like silver paint. I began to shovel madly with bruised hands, but animal droppings marinated in urine had now mixed with the taint of my sweat and the first hints of rotting flesh, and my movements shifted the mound of defecation beneath us. Dust clouded my vision and I began to choke on the stench. I wiped at the blood from my own nostrils in an attempt to breathe more freely, but the reek was debilitating. I looked to the sky and prayed for deliverance. The moonlight was all but obliterated by kudzu and briar; coughing into the soft layer of flooring only sent a second round of refuse spiraling into the stilled air. I should have feared for my own demise, and yet my only thought was to get to you.

The cursive was masculine and blunt. The author appeared to press his weight into the pen as the ink moved across the paper. I caught my breath and wondered what other vile secrets remained buried that I had yet to detect.

I knew they would return and I needed to find the strength to travel. Inching my way through the tall grasses along the rutted back roads, I tried to conjure the purity of your smile, but my recollections were skewed by bottled habit and fear.

I thought about the crumpled bodies I'd left behind at the river. Their faces shattered, their limbs broken and shredded by endless rounds of buckshot. Their lives had ended so abruptly and in a sick sense I envied them. No chance for regrets. Most folks die by inches, my darling... a little every day at the murderous hand of an unkind rebuke, a biting criticism or a cold and distant stare. So gradual is the grating upon one's constitution that the sting of insult becomes a faded impression, so that we are emotionally dead before the sigh of final resignation escapes our lungs. I see now it has always been that way for me here and I perceive that same path stretching out before you.

I needed to find you in the darkness and tell you before it were too late. The others never mattered. Not to me. They judged and juried me into tightfisted corners of despair. Like irritating refuse at the edge of their brooms, they swept my inefficiencies from room to room.

The more I read, the more I wanted to wrench the author's heart out and pound it flat with the heart-shaped pastry iron displayed in the Danburg's warming kitchen below me. How could he have left such vile descriptions in the pages of a child's diary? How could he dispense such information to a mind so ill prepared to custodian such weighty burdens? I divorced myself from the grotesque content long enough to delve into the context of what was being transferred. Why would a person describe such horrors in detail and what kind of evil delights in the display of such graphics? Already I was forming an opinion of the author and it was none too favorable. Aside from my repulsion for his subject matter I tried forgetting a past that always seemed to stain my perception. It was clear to me from the very beginning what his intentions were. I had felt the implication of those words crawl down my spine as rough fingers had once crawled up my thighs. I read again: "...*my only thought was to get to you.*" Someone else in a distant past had used those very words trying to convince me I was special. I returned to the diary. It was unbearable for me to be sympathetic to its author's plight.

I am neither as kind as you will want to believe, nor as vile as they will eventually try to convince you I am. Judge my actions in days to come, but not my heart. I am merely a man caught between coincidence and consequence. My only hope is to tell someone the truth. With no one to trust, I must leave this with you.

They have always been suspect. But you, angelic you, always with soft curls and tiny voice, you never condemned, only consoled. You were my only oasis—you and the shed. Even now you lie before me. A woman-child tangled in rumpled sheets...evening slip adrift upon a sea of sun-kissed legs, beckoning. I dare not even startle you with kiss. I must leave as I have come, disheveled and distracted. I grieve knowing that I cannot express my sincere apologies if you should wake and find me not returned as I had promised.

I look out the window above the rise of the roof and see the moon clinging to the bottom of the sky. Hovering above your bed, I beg forgiveness for any unkind act I may have ever perpetrated in your presence, for now you are my only courier and I cannot risk losing your allegiance for want of a moment's bliss.

A breeze sifts slightly through the eaves and you shiver. I want you to know it takes monumental discipline to bend only to softly graze your forehead with fevered lips and not crawl in beside you.

I hear the yelping hounds—somewhere near the old pump station. Keep this and remember me.

The man's signature was lost at the edge of the singed page. Someone knew the truth about the entry in that diary. Sixty-some-odd years was a mighty long stretch for any confession to bridge, but I was willing to try.

Careful not to further compromise the damaged manuscript, I placed the diary back inside its hermetically sealed plastic coffin. His words rolled over and over inside my mouth and brought forth a small surge of bile from the pit of my stomach.

I thought of the child being ogled half naked in the moonlight and wanted to scream for justice for a crime I couldn't prove had actually taken place. Slowly I returned the sealed diary to my desk, closing the drawer on my resignation and disgust.

Chapter Seven

Separated from my husband earlier that summer, I was in no hurry to move on with my life or anyone else's. Perhaps I simply had no room for misery other than my own and that was the real reason I hadn't the energy for due diligence on the diary's origins. Somehow it was just too melancholy to absorb all at one time. Truth was deep down inside, I wanted to howl at the moon at the violation of us both but there was no one left in the Danburg home to care.

I closed the drawer and meant to turn the key in the lock hoping to secure the silence of the voice in the diary for another night, but I could not tear her words out of my mind. It was obvious on some level she sensed and tried to match the lust of her intruder, but I did not feel she truly understood the intensity of its consequence. Her mind and body raced far ahead of her experience, oblivious to peril.

I instinctively hated the man for actions I feared he might have taken, but not recorded. Where were the responsible parties for this child? Why was someone not watching out for her?

Was his entry fiction in any part? What sort of cruel beast breaches the inner sanctum of an adolescent female's memoirs? If not fiction, then what kind of animal would leave such a description of depravity in the hands of an innocent? How could he not know the damage he would inflict with so careless an act? I had no idea who this girl was or if she was still alive. While the gradual elevation of her maturity was evident, there were great lapses of time in between entries. Random references to personal attributes spoke of both physical and emotional evolutions that seemed to span years rather than seasons. The words and the content flowed and then for no apparent reason, shifted without explanation.

What remained constant was this mystery location and the soulful eyes of the dark dark-haired object of her affections. This was the man in the moonlight who spoke of ephemeral encounters and then later of lingering alone with her in her bedroom. From diary notes, I estimated her age to be between the eleven and seventeen. I could not even venture what might be her present age. I felt her pain as an echo from my past, and a peculiar intimacy began to form between us.

There were only a few months left before the Danburg project would be officially turned over to the state and to another curator to run and I would be out. As far as I was concerned, this project had claimed enough emotional victims and leaving this house and its diary behind became my top priority.

I confessed to myself that it made no sense that I had become so consumed with the equilibrium of a child I had never met. Yet I could not help myself. Perhaps it was because she presented herself as less of a victim than I and I needed her to teach me how to do that for myself. She didn't whine with adolescent illogic, she merely accepted how she felt. In some ways she offered more womanly wisdom in her youth, than I at middle age. Without apology, she had claimed ownership of deeply seated desires before, I feared, her maidenhood had been stolen from her by force.

Chapter Eight

I looked closely at the slides in the catalog file of the Danburg family and their manor. While unable to match timetables between diary and slides, I knew not one soul in them could have been her. Yet I flipped through each set over and over, searching their eyes as though they might lend some clue as to who she was and what had happened to her.

Several of the smaller and grainier photos of the manor's inhabitants caught my attention. There was one slide with a singular subject who stood to the side of the front porch that gave me pause. Her face was drawn and her waist thick with child, but there was no glow upon her cheek, no joy in her eyes and I wondered if all the Danburg ghosts were just as sad and worn as her expression.

It was obvious the focus had been on the human subjects in each frame, but the partial backgrounds provided some visual information. I tried to use that as orientation when applying parallels to the specific entries in the diary that made direct reference to interiors.

In the bedroom, structural reminders of age are visible in the once patinaed now grey, bare wooden floor; plaster walls streaked with water damage; and ill-fitting window treatments. In that room raw emotions explode. I hear them even now, fighting over their unhappy station. Blaming one another for their inefficiencies and trading obscenities they think I cannot hear. Spewing emotions that have been contained at the intergenerational round table in the kitchen; emotions that are fed by anger from missed chances; emotions that have been corked in the carafe of desire…this is my education in longing… my birthright to despair… I cover my ears and try to drown them out, repeating a childhood tale about how a cow jumped over the moon… Dear Diary how I wish I too could run away with the dish and the spoon.

I pulled a slide from the earlier dated plates, amazed that it was the Danburg. With so much of the restoration now mere memory, it seemed pagan to look with adoration at the crippled silhouettes of what few remaining outbuildings remained.

There were two rough outlines that stood off to the south side of the large brick manor house. I was certain by configuration one was the well house, but the other was eclipsed by clumps of overgrown shrubbery. It suggested a small chimney and at least one window. The tin roof was slightly tilted and I could not see any other defining features for the several elongated shafts of shade cast by the bank of back porch columns.

I made a mental note to check historical diagrams and locate the possible foundation of either a weaving or ironing shed of the kind so common to the era. Generally those structures for supporting activities were located closer to the main dwelling. I mounted the stairs. Crossing the second-story hall to take in the full views from the upstairs bedrooms, I tried to decipher which room had been hers, if indeed she had been in the Danburg house at all. Most antebellum homes shared the same bone structure, so it was a fifty-fifty chance the descriptions would match. Not convinced she had been there, I returned to my office and placed the slide under my enlarger to study the structures more intimately.

Why was it structural benchmarks of decay never translated as gracefully to humans? Flaws in inanimate edifices are considered character caused by great and significant trials, but not in those who suffer right along through them. I pulled another photo slide of a Danburg matron and traced the lines at the edge of her mouth. In people we see the aging caricature as imperfection and impediment, not as testimony to a life.

Closing the catalog I glimpsed my reflection in the mirror behind my desk. I too had become unloved and compromised, unattractive in my defensiveness. My nostrils pinched from the foul stench of my earlier deposit in the basin below.

I shut off the light, gazed out the window and thought about the woman-child who had bathed in the kitchen and dared the appraisal of a foreign eye. What would she have been like at my age? Would she have worn such a scowl as I? Or would she have found another way to rise above her own destruction? It was foolish to make an oracle of her, but I needed to find a definitive tie to the house and the reason I had become so obsessive in seeking her release.

Chapter Nine

Validating the diary was a major problem from the beginning. The diary itself had not been found on the premises, but rather in a piece of furniture that had once graced the lower hall of the Danburg before it spent its crippled afterlife as heirloom junk.

As with most re-gentrifications, period pieces had been secured either by donation from family members or purchased through grants to flesh out the reconstructed rooms. There were only four articles of furniture that could be verified as original to the Danburg. The first was a tall, spindle-backed, uncomfortable "in-law chair." This was traditionally placed just inside the door of the downstairs front parlor to receive callers. The second, a leather-cushioned corner chair, commonly referred to as a "soldier's seat," which enabled one of military distinction to sit comfortably while still brandishing sidearm or saber. I wondered if any of the Union soldiers ever sat in it before they set the house on fire.

The third, and one of my personal favorites, was an Andrew Bruhle side table. It was an enormously heavy and intricately carved piece that graced the gentlemen's smoking parlor and sat at the back wall adjacent to the fireplace. Seductive to the touch, its delicately laced copper overlay floated above a burnt sienna tortoise shell foundation. The side table glowed with refracted light from the mirror that hung directly opposite it.

But the fourth and final was my most cherished piece. Damaged by fire, its burled oak facade whispered of better days and its hand-painted dial looked with equanimity into the future. The Danburg grandfather clock no longer held court at the foot of the stairs as it once had. It merely witnessed the emotional clock of its owners standing stationary in time, just like me.

Ironically, for all its secrets, it was the only Danburg original that brought a feeling of possible joy to the walls that surrounded it. When I looked into its worn and faded face, it hinted of phantom children who once raced the expansive halls with sheer delight. The painted celestial orbs with cherub cheeks and milk-painted complexions smiled graciously into the mirrored front of the replicated petticoat table. The reflection doubled my pleasure each morning as I crossed the threshold. I felt the grandfather clock was my best chance of tying the girl of the diary to the manor.

I remembered the day the diary arrived in the mail and the first time I had found her words.

I remembered the first time I saw him. Our family rode out to the countryside and for me inside I never returned to the city. The bouncing motion of my perch on a sturdy suitcase intensified my excitement as tall chimneys standing apart from the houses they once warmed signaled the proximity of our approach. These relics identified the antebellum mansions not rebuilt after the Civil War. Turkey buzzards perched on the chimney tops, their defecation icing the broken bricks beneath them.

At the mile marker from the manor, the general store still stands humbly at the crossroads, tin roof bent in salutation. The store was a familiar gathering space for both whites and blacks, whites inside and blacks out back. Sitting around the potbellied stove was encouraged and fresh boiled peanuts were favored. Worn out stories and peanut shells identified the circle of regulars and drew more ants than paying patrons.

Turning minutes later, I push past the front seat and eagerly place my shoes on the sandy backyard. My first thought is always to search for his footprints from the shed. Before my hostess can shove through the tangle of dogs, I am greeted by their swinging tails and slobbering kisses, their paw prints obliterating any chance to confirm his presence till supper. With commands to "hush," she embraces me warmly, explaining that work will be interrupted as soon as the hired man can carry the news of our arrival. Another elegant woman waves gracefully from the kitchen door. Except for grand occasions, the front door takes second place to the side door's sagging screen and ill fitting hinges...but this is not the door I focus on. That door is to the left of the bordered walk, just beyond the peonies, just beyond my reach. This is where I first saw him. He was dark haired, wild eyed... like an animal trapped in a cage too small for his temperament."

It was hard to associate the entries with the same house. Initially, she spoke of childish anecdotes and typical family anthologies. But as the entries and penmanship matured, the banal routine of everyday happenings gave way to those things oft unspoken. It was only after reading the diary several times that I suspected the undercurrent of betrayal. The youthful entries started to blossom with emotional evidence of physical transformation.

A few reminders of elegance from the bedroom suite include a dressing table long admired by me for its accoutrements. The table speaks of the lady of the house's prominent past with its ornamented perfume bottles and red leather jewel box. Inside the drawers baubles lie ready to adorn her. Her chiffonier and armoire are crammed with dreamy lingerie and sensual attire ill suited to her rural life and aged silhouette.

I've never really seen her wear anything frilly. Occasionally I glimpse the edge of tattered chiffon dancing just beneath the bulky chenille of her housecoat, but I cannot not lay claim to witnessing her parade as seductively as the siren Lorelei. The attire for her has become only cloth, and not a source of allure. Comparing the pert youth in my mirror, I imagine the flimsy frocks hanging without purpose on her stilted frame, but fulfilling their purpose upon mine. Tracing the smooth curves of my womanhood, I cannot imagine the desperation of not seeing one's body in the same fashion as in one's mind. Her pain is foreign to me. I shall steal a nightgown to see what it feels like to lounge in gossamer and float on desire. When my hostess is engaged in social pursuits and he is banished from the main house to the shed below, I shall brave the evening air without a night coat. As smoke from the shed chimney curls and licks at the bottom of my window, without shame I will walk the halls and dance in the moonlight for his pleasure.

Often I dream of him watching me as I prance in the upstairs hall. The once grand corridor extends the length of the house and opens to a balcony supported by iron rods that allows the structure to swing gently. Standing before the ten-foot-tall mirror with its elegant Louis XV gold leaf frame, I shall mimic the image of the nymph in the painting on the adjoining wall. The figure, with her gauzy drape and voluptuous frame, resembles an early Rubens and her pose suggests female liberation. In my vivid dreams, I dance dangerously near to the stair with its low balustrade and missing vertical rails. The sense of suspension strangely does not ignite my usual fear of heights, but dreams enable rather than inhibit. My fantasy ends with him joining me on the suspended balcony where we lean forward to touch the branches of the century-old magnolia tree and then... the pounding on the shed door below wakens me. My dreams shatter and I am introduced to his night by the brutal accusations of the lord of the house. I hear his whimpers for help and am caught. Trapped between the moon, my youth and the secret of desire. Some day I will brave the night and the slander of wagging tongues and come to his rescue. No one understands the pain of longing... not for him and not for me. Only the moon hangs as often as we between the dusk and dawn of our emotions..."

I sensed contrived memories, as though they had been masterfully manipulated to hide the decayed morals of a household that did little to protect her. I knew the formula... the coded words... the hyphenated emotions: "...Mister so-and-so spent time with me today. Told me how grown up I had become, how beautiful... how special... and that he wanted to share a secret with me..." I had written the words a thousand times hoping to convince even myself of their innocence. In the end, they defeated me. My defense had been to hide through my own cryptic expressions, and I sentenced myself to the hell of eternal silence. I never told anyone I had been sexually abused.

The warmth from assembled company leads me to see the rooms in their once splendid state. Here I can fantasize that he has reformed his alcoholic wanderings to accomplish a studious, celibate life.

Bedtime requires the challenging trip to my bedroom upstairs. Entering the large center hall, the absence of heat in winter immediately chills my bare feet and reminds me that my nightgown demands an overcoat. The hall is cavernous, poorly lit and leads to the formal parlor, bedroom and a vast back space where a large dining table and chairs sit gloomily for the few formal dining occasions. This is where he always waits. Breath tainted with soured grapes and a thick head of charcoal hair, he baits me from the shadows with winsome looks that melt my heart and put a pause in my step.

Unable to let go of the haunting imagery, I pulled the diary closer and rubbed at the worn and freckled binding. Its edges were like brushed velvet to the touch and I knew somehow the young woman had worried them between her hands, pacing in disjointed contemplation of her sexual emancipation. Each entry appeared to be the summation of calculated encounters.

What else had been her curse, her habit? What did she like and dislike about her own reflection at the end of her days? If the Danburg had been her destination, which was her favorite room and what view did she cherish most, other than the face she admired, ill advised, from afar?

I rinsed the sink and doused it with a bit of lavender toilet water. I tried to focus my mind on something else.

A car hummed past the end of the drive and claimed my attention. Odd as it sounded, my favorite view before finding the diary had been from the front porch through the jib windows of the first floor into the home, and not out. For me the Danburg's open front parlor had meant security. It provided an accessorized peace in direct opposition to my life and I found that comforting.

Chapter Ten

On the south side of the house, wisteria's twisted strands of fragrance fought ivy for sunlight. From the upstairs hall, tubers of brilliant lavender blocked every view, making the second story claustrophobic. Even after the vines had been thinned, the south side of the house suggested something unsettling. With daylight flooding the hall, there was still something dark. Yet on the north side of the house, the upstairs scenes were magnificent, overlooking a high meadow with tree lined horizons that rippled one after the other.

The closet at the end of the hall under the rising stairwell of the attic housed two coffins as required by early rural southern tradition. One large and cumbersome pine box for an adult and one smaller for a child. I knew from familial accounts these had been replaced several times, as the first ladies of Danburg had buried their men and children before them in the cemetery to the south of the main structure. No less than three Civil War markers and several smaller stones now sunk with the weight of their history into the soft red clay.

Just beyond the newly seeded lawn, I suspected the remains of a cremation site. Of course, I continued to chide myself for such a morbid obsession. Nothing I had found thus far could have substantiated such juxtaposition, but just the same I treated the area with caution. The stone foundation in a horseshoe layout matched the height of the main house, plus an additional three

bricks. I had hoped it was an arbitrary addition in the mid-twen-
tieth-century remuddling of the property. The brickwork and
chinking appeared congruent with the site, as the earlier
Danburgs had manufactured and kiln-dried bricks on the property. But credible sources concurred that the site had been used
for something less jocular than picnicking and it didn't take much
for my imagine to run wild.

Naturally, here in the South, the outdoor structure for most
folks would be associated with great barbeques. But there was
something unsettling in the earthen irregularities. Embroidered
by conspicuous layers of moss-covered anomalies, the alleged sac-
rificial altar nestled itself inside the surrounding volunteer pines.
History had the area once part of the hundred-acre wood that
had been cleared by slave labor for the cotton fields. That would
have placed the original clapboard homestead even further from
the brick fire pit for safety reasons, but ever so much closer to
the potters' field and the slaves' quarters than the family cemetery.
Fire seemed to be a prevailing curse for the inhabitants of the
Danburg. Perhaps using it to keep warm on winter nights was
the least offensive of all its uses since just before the winter of
1864, the original structure burned to the ground. Thus, the
brick main house was constructed several hundred feet to the
north.

I had visited the site a few times for the preliminary mapping
of the grounds and several times since then for other reasons, but
not once for what I feared now. A wayward limb had fallen
nearby and so I broke a healthy switch from it and poked at the
contents closest to ground level. Grayed fragments of bone jutted
from beneath the leafy decay and I screamed.

Wishing I had watched more episodes of C S I, I had no idea
what I had really seen. It could have been last Fourth of July's
celebration for all I knew, but my imagination swarmed with un-
natural horrors.

The auxiliary author—he joked in one of his entries about
hiding one's secrets out in the open. I paced the distance off to
place the site within the historical layout of the plantation, and
then turned to search for the girl's favorite room under the eaves.

The south side attic window had the most perfect view. I thought of the Roman coliseum and a shudder of fear chased me down the drive and through the back porch doors.

Chapter Eleven

I understood living with the unspeakable. It was a strange analogy to compare oneself to a house, but it seemed the only one that truly fit. Returning indoors I peered outside the window of my office again at the site. A maple leaf drifted softly away from a branch that stretched its bony fingers just beyond the furthest pile. If summer's luxurious canopy of denial had provided both the Danburg house and me ample shelter from our little secrets, it followed suit that by early winter its absence would provide us none.

I suspected there had been a rape from one portion of the manuscript and from another, a murderous cover up either for the rape or for some other crime I was yet unaware of. There was both great tragedy and mystery in the Danburg Diary's past and I felt duty bound to uncover them both. Since there was no one left of the Danburgs but the Chenille sisters, I figured the truth couldn't do much damage. The fact that my suspicions remained unsubstantiated kept alive my hopes for the Danburg girl's virginity. If I had been so alert for myself, I might have seen the truck before it hit me, but that is the curse and blessing of youth. We trust, we honor, we cherish and then we pay dearly for our innocence! How could I have let it happen to me?

The Danburg diary didn't invent my turmoil; it merely brought it back with a vengeance. For months after my initial submersion in its pages, I had lashed out at everyone and everything that brought back the shame of my personal betrayal. Decades of therapy had never appealed to me, so Matt was the only other soul who knew of my childhood tragedy. I had trusted him with something I thought was sacred information.

After several years of marriage, he announced his desire to start a family. We tried for months, but were unsuccessful. He even presented adoption as an alternative, should something be wrong. I refused to consider such desperate measures insisting I was certain he was just fine. I chalked it up to stress and poor timing, what with the traveling for my job. That was until I received the test results from my doctor. Matt was so anxious to have a son. I didn't have the heart to tell him it was me. The thought of adoption at that point was painfully insulting and not option to me. Hoping that a few months of privacy with information would allow me to gracefully digest the thought of raising some one else's child, instead of my own I stalled.

The more I thought about what I had survived as a child and now what I was being asked to survive as a woman, left me bitter and depressed. With each day that passed I began to withdraw a little bit more and he took that as a sign of disinterest. I knew I should have told him the truth, but he became so fixated on getting me pregnant that I began to resent him. The more he pressured me, the more I played down my interest until one night after too much wine he made the mistake of using his wants as a weapon. That's when the shit hit the fan.

He accused me of using my "problem" as a way to get out of performing certain marital rights. "After all..." he hurled, "...if I wasn't interested in giving him a child, the least I could do was give him something else he wanted!" He felt I was holding out on him sexually.

I knew I should have told him the real reason for my distance right then and there, but I could barely say it aloud to myself, yet alone to him. Hurt that he could have thought such things about me, I went off to bed alone to lick my wounds. He joined me later with wine on his breath and playfully tried to force the issue again. Pulling my head to his crotch, he tried to illicit attention from me and I lost it. Every emotion I had pent up for over thirty years exploded beneath the sheets. I tore at his skin like a caged animal and screamed I would not let any man do this to me again. Dumbfounded, he stumbled half dressed out of the bedroom in shock at my response. I ran down the hall and locked myself in the bathroom hysterically crying and rinsing my mouth until my tongue went numb.

An hour later he tried to coax me out, saying that he forgave me. I screamed back I didn't need his forgiveness, what I needed was his understanding. In his defense he suggested that my response was a delayed reaction to my past—that he was my husband and that that sort of irrational response should have been confined to the man who had abused me.

He didn't understand that my response would naturally translate subconsciously to all men who displayed that pattern of behavior. That it wasn't simply a matter of sexual preference. I didn't want him that way— I didn't want any man in that way... ever! That in the deepest reaches of my soul I prayed to God never to have a son, afraid he could one day grow into a man who could do such things to some other little girl. I knew it was wrong, but I was drunk with anger and hurt. He asked if that was the reason I was refusing to have children. Because I was afraid it might turn out to be a boy.

It was then I decided the time was finally right to tell the truth. I thrust open the door and tearfully told him I could never have his children... boy or girl. The silence hung in the air with my hopes for his understanding, but it never came. He only heard what was said as insult and pay back for his bad behavior earlier in the evening. The more I tried to explain, the harder I cried and the more incoherent my speech. Frustrated he packed a bag and left me sobbing in the hall.

Hours went by without his return. I realized the entire thing had been my fault. By not telling him the truth right away, I had created a war where none existed. Repentant I cleaned myself up, grabbed my keys and headed out to find him to apologize. Sadly, I didn't have to go far. His car was parked a couple of houses over at our recently divorced neighbors. Since I didn't know which one of the couple had retained the house, I decided not to make a bigger scene and wait till the following morning to show him the report and discuss what to do next.

Three days later he came home. I found out which spouse had kept the mortgage and keys when he announced he needed someone who could live with him in the present and not in the past; a woman who could love him and be happy. He wanted a family...an heir he could pass his precious autographed baseball collection on to.

It was in that moment I decided I needed something too. Someone who would listen first and react second— someone who understood 'through sickness and in health... till death do us part'. Someone who could love me and not punish me for the things that had happened to me in the past.

I shoved the manila folder in front of him and told him what was written would explain everything. He never opened it, never even asked what was inside. He simply got up from the kitchen table to collect the rest of his clothes. I knew in that instant, his leaving had nothing to do with starting a family or my past. He just needed an excuse and my infertility had been little more to him than perfect timing.

I got up from the kitchen table and followed him into the bedroom. While he silently unloaded his closet, I unloaded his dressers. And when he asked if I would help him pack the last of his belongings... I did. I took his prized autographed baseballs to the kitchen where I ceremoniously packed them into the blender and ground them into large rubberized junks of history! After all, he was right. Neither of us should cling to the past. I should not be made to feel like less of a woman because I could not appreciate his specific kind of foreplay and he should not be made to feel like less of a man because he no longer had any balls! We left it there.

There was no murder in what had happened to me, No bodies left to decompose beneath the bloodied beaks of vultures out on a lark. No graphic display of slaughter or cryptic innuendos. There was however, the quiet death of innocence and trust and apparently... no time limitations on the mourning period.

After losing Matt I realized that some people went to bed at night and cried for love, any kind of love. And others went to bed and dreamed of greater loves than they already possessed. And then there were others like me out in the world who tried not to go to bed at all. We were the ones so frightened of love that its very mention sent us cringing into dark corners, because for us love meant something else all together. We were the confused, the children of the night who survived the groping hands of fate. Those who believed love brought nothing but pain and unfounded shame. We were the cursed who awakened one day to find someone had come and switched our dictionaries at night, twisting our understanding so that we had no idea what love really meant anymore.

While I could forgive Matt his ignorance, I was still unable to trust my own understanding of love. I thought of the child lying just as innocently in her bed mistaking lust for romance and cried myself to sleep at night. During the day I worked hard and occupied myself with other people's lives. I found it best to keep to myself, laying both my heart and the diary aside, trying to forget our collective fates.

Chapter Twelve

In late August my almost-ex-husband had called and begged me to come back. By mid-September I knew it was a mistake and I called his current mistress and begged her to take him back! It no longer mattered who breached the trust. A sacred bond had been broken mentally as well as physically and I saw little point in carrying out the charade a second time.

In the end it was a fair trade, I thought. I got his remember-when's and what antique furniture I had collected over the years, and she got his dirty socks and his not-so-happily-ever-after's. Not wanting him to walk away completely empty handed, I gave him my pent up anger and the $4000.00 in Savings Bonds. It may not have been equitable, but I finally got the chance to cleanse myself of obligatory, passionless devotion to people and places. And for me, that became important. The only one who truly "made out like a bandit" in the entire ordeal, the only one not asked to suffer the ignorance of us both, was the child. The one I never got to have.

And maybe that was the key to my obsession with the girl in the diary.

***

While the attempted rehabilitation of my marriage had proven to be a dismal failure, the Danburg had proven to be a decided success. Five weeks ahead of schedule, I closed the doors for the holidays. The success of the project's first phase afforded me the luxury of securing other housing in the interim and that was a good thing.

Since our marital home had sold already, I was frantic for another address before the holidays. Luckily a professor friend of mine owned a comfortable estate on the west end of town and had recently lost his cabana boy to his ex-wife. Retired and ready to travel, he invited me to stay in the caretaker's cottage until I was finished with the museum's reconstruction.

It was a gorgeous southern dinosaur and I drooled over its hedge-lined drive and charm, though not its mortgage. Frank was an intelligent, wealthy and handsome man, and his young female consort had no intension of sharing. Grateful, I felt no obligation "in making nice" and let her function under the illusion that I was a lesbian.

"So... I imagine the cottage will be large enough for one" she sidled. "Unless I have misunderstood and you will be entertaining a roommate?" she queried with a raised eyebrow.

"I have enough room for my books and my baggage. Let's not get over anxious about my social life just yet." And I reached for the satchel that was now crushing their perfectly manicured lawn.

"Men trouble?" she piqued.

"Woman trouble, as a matter of fact... a neighbor." I said and threw the bag over my shoulder and paused to reach for the handle of my Samsonite waiting patiently at my hip.

"Ahhh" she muttered. "I thought so. You didn't strike me as the gay divorcee type" she giggled with that irritating high pitched coquette laugh that you hear in college bars. I turned to meet her head on and accidentally dropped the bag from my shoulder onto my top of my foot and swore under my breath.

She raised her over-plucked eyebrow one more time and motioned to my attire. "I guess Frank doesn't mind flying both flags over the pool this summer..."

"Both flags?" I asked

"You know... his Confederate and your...rainbow?" and she winked.

"Rainbow?" I flinched. Other than the cute colorful swirls painted on my nieces My Little Pony toy figures, the rainbow had little personal meaning for me.

"Care to enlighten?" I suggested as my mind was still entertaining the My Little Ponies series.

"Well... never let it be said that I ever made fun of people's personal tastes... or persuasions."

"Ooooh! That flag." I smirked.

Since I had refused to let Matt back into the house and it had sold before the papers were signed, I had been forced to bring whatever was left of his I hadn't burned. Unfortunately for me this included his torn college sweats, his ball cap, a dingy white wife beater shirt and his motorcycle boots... all of which I was wearing! I had decided that morning that once I had finished moving in, I would strip naked, dance in the moonlight and burn them to celebrate my independence. It was part of my process in letting go.

"Yes... well, I hadn't planned on coming out so publicly just yet, but when I do... You'll be the first I call." I said and then winked.

"I beg your pardon? Are you trying to... suggest something?" and she began to fidget with her hair as she stalled to decipher just what the wink was inviting her too.

"Just in case things with Frank don't work out. You know what they say about converts?" I giggled back and winked again just for grins. She squirmed in her thong as I reached for my shoulder bag and cleared my throat in my best alto voice. "My first name's Caroline, but you can call me Carl. It suits me better."

There's no Salt-Peter like divorce, I always say and men were quickly becoming an undesirable taste on my palate. In her youth, Frank's latest took my disinterest in men; especially Frank as both compliment and surrender. In my fledgling antiquity, I took our lack of rivalry as freedom. With a flip of her auburn bob, I had been relegated to the status of tenant, not contender, and the demotion suited my temperament just fine! I watched her supple ass hitch to and fro like a porch swing as she vacated the yard. As part salute for a job well done, I flipped her off with a slightly arthritic middle finger and smiled to myself as I entered the cottage with my emotional baggage trailing behind.

Chapter Thirteen

It wasn't the mechanics of running the Danburg that had me balled up. After all, I had people who cleaned and people who clipped and mowed. I never dusted it, but I never dirtied it either. What tore me up were its unending obstacles to the truth. On top of that, nine weeks after I moved into "the cottage," Frank and the Queen of Sheba eloped.

I thought about the differences between the southern debutante four hundred feet away from me and who I had been at her age. Other than the fact that her "porch swing" was a bit smaller, we had been pretty similar in our expectations. Where had it all gone wrong? I knew—I just wasn't ready to face it yet.

The view from the cottage into the back of my landlord's home promised winter would eventually leave every landscape but my heart. With regret and envy I caught glimpses of the successful companioning that secured the tailored brick and made his house a home and mine a mere memory. Weeks later, I tried to comfort myself with the knowledge that while she had a beautiful face, Frank and an expansive front yard...I had a sixty-hour work week and the Danburg. I had devoted myself to my job because I thought it would be easier to mend living inside someone else's lithograph of life. Framed, flat and dulled, I realized now how I had trapped myself behind the Danburg's insulatory glass. Like the Danburg women in the portraits, I was the perfect picture of independence stuffed inside a monstrous frame with mirrors that glared, yet never reflected who I was inside. The debutante had Frank, I had the Danburgs.

By the time the holiday season began in earnest, the insult of their happiness was more than I could bear. I took a sabbatical from their heaven, licked my wounds along with the top right corner of my address book and let my fingers do the walking across my heartache. I moved in with my friend Connie and her husband for a few weeks, waiting for the thaw.

Chapter Fourteen

With as much nervous energy as White Zinfandel coursing through my veins that Christmas, I invaded their household and took up residence like a belligerent stray. Every nook and cranny afforded me in their tiny bungalow became piled with baggage bursting at the seams with pigeon-holed regret and misguided anger. Amazingly manic, Connie delighted at the intrusion of my chaos.

Constance McCann was an even soul who never seemed to want for anything and quoted often that "the true art in living is in wanting what you have...not having what you want." Of course the rest of the world knows this is bullshit! But having neither her sense of balance nor her gift for delusion, I chewed on bitter root and wished my ex a very merry holiday in hell by plotting to send him a gift.

I thought this was a very big step for me at such a fragile stage in my healing process. Inspired one evening after receiving a baby shower announcement from his new 'dearly beloved', I hot glued the stringy chunks of leathered rubber that had once been his pride and joy together and entitled it; "A Baseball Diamond is Forever... Unlike Your Vows!"

I even signed it, 'Happy Holidays...With Love, Caroline!'

Though I saw the sarcasm of its title as wickedly funny, Connie saw it as creatively therapeutic and let me slide. I had always wondered what to do with those chunks the blender refused to digest that day. Burning them on the hood of his car would have made a terrible stench and didn't seem right, so I kept them hoping for a better solution. When I got the baby shower announcement... nothing ever seemed so right before. It was brilliant! Knowing what an avid fan of modern art she was and sports he was, I created a very contemporary piece I thought the two of them might enjoy. They could even put it on the mantle or pass it down as a family heirloom! My behavior was petty of course, but necessary for my emotional survival through the holidays!

When I showed it to Connie, she wagged a finger and told me, "Now Caroline... be a good sport. It takes two to make or break a marriage."

"Yes... but it only takes one to screw it up!" I said as I licked the forty three stamps it was going to take to get it across town by Christmas!

"You just have to choose the right one the first time... that's all." Then she looked at Tim with those big cornflower blue eyes and I wanted to puke. Happy people were not what I needed at that particular moment. What I needed was someone with as much pent up anger, gasoline, tall sticks wrapped with rags as I to go out with and torch a small village!

I offered the job to Connie, but she replied in true holiday humor, "I'd love to, but I'm much too busy making paper mache poinsettias for the local church craft show to go out and pillage and plunder on such a 'Silent Night' as tonight!" She laughed. Then he laughed and again... I wanted to puke!

"It's not easy being the only small-minded, vindictive vigilante in the McCann house during the holidays. Everyone just sucks the fun out of my depression.... it's so unfair!" I whined. She winced and then shrugged her shoulders.

"Well then..." I muttered. "I shall just have to call Scrooge and the Grinch and see if they're up for delivering evil fan-mail and imbibing all night down at the local drinking establishment!"

"Suite yourself" She sighed. "Tim and I can finish these alone." And she raised her hand full of pasty paper strips to wave goodbye as Tim hid behind his newspaper avoiding the invitation.

"Come on, Connie... I haven't sent him any threatening e mails or letter bombs in over three weeks. It's the holidays and you saw that announcement! How can you deprive me of such sweet bitterness this way? It is so selfish of you not to share in my revenge! It being the holidays and all... how uncharitable of you!"

She smiled. "Well... I won't deny you. It was a pretty crappy thing to do sending you an invitation. But maybe he's trying to build a bridge." she said.

"And I have just the bomb to blow it up!" I mused.

"Caroline, he never did anything bad to me. I can't hurt some-body just because they made a huge mistake. Remember, you agreed part of it was your fault for not telling him about the report."

"Yeah.... but I didn't go sleep with my Doctor just to get even with him, did I?" I asked.

"Noooo. But just the same ...you said it hadn't been right for a long time before that. Maybe in the end, he did you a favor." she hedged.

"Don't be so compassionate! It grates on my equilibrium. Where's your holiday spirit? Do you want him waking up all happy on Christmas morning and...?" I cut myself off.

"And what?" She baited.

"And nothing..." I said. "I was just wondering if you wanted him to wake up Christmas morning... at all?"

"You don't?" she quipped back as the smile drained from her face.

"Not really!" I chortled and then seeing her eyebrows take a dive I knew I was crossing the Constance McCann fair and equi-table line. "Just kidding...." I added weakly. She made another face.

"Oh... all right. He can live. But only till New Years! That's it. My generous holiday spirit ends January first!" and I stuffed the present inside a large paper bag to carry to post December 31st!

"You go out for awhile and take a walk to burn off some steam! Go have a good time. Mail your package if you want, have a glass of holiday cheer and tell 'Little Cindy Lou Who' I said hello if you see her. I'll just leave the light on and the bed turned down for you".

And that was it. My entire "I'll get even with you, evil-Matt-ex-husband-having-a-baby-with-another- woman-evening" went right out the window. I slid the bag into the front hall closet and closed the door on my evil plan, but not on my anger. When I returned to the kitchen she never said a word, but the smirk on her face said it all.

Annoyed, I grabbed a clump of shredded paper and shoved my hand into the bottom of the bowl of pasty mush. Smug in her success, she whispered a small thank you and went to gather more materials. I watched her with calm reserve at the kitchen sink and wondered what gene she had that I obviously did not. Seconds later she returned with more flour and water. I raised my hands while she added it to the bowl.

"Mix it up, okay? I'm going to go cut more newspaper."

"Sure." I said. I rammed my fists back into the bowl and secretly pretended I was squishing Matt's tiny testicles through my fingers. The sucking noise it made caught us both off guard and we laughed out loud.

"I hate you... Constance McCann." I giggled.

"I hate you too..." she giggled back. "Now...quit flinging that stuff all over the table!" she mused and the spell was broken. I had hated Matt for betraying me, but I couldn't continue to hate him forever. Connie knew eventually my emotional baggage would become too much to carry and like a true friend, thought she could help by removing the weight one bag at a time. Starting with the one stuffed in the closet at the end of the hall!

She held the bag and peered inside. "You know... years from now this little pile of artwork might be worth something. You don't want him to have a chance to profit off your work now... do you?"

"You're right." I said as she handed it back to me. "You can still see part of where Babe Ruth signed his name. Course now it reads '...abe uth' because of where the blades had cut through, but still... it could bring some money." I wryly mused. She pulled a tin from the counter and brought forth a handful of sugar cookies as peace offering.

"Want one?" She smiled and raised her eyebrows. "They've got chocolate sprinkles!" she baited grinning from ear to ear.

"You really know how to kill a good bitter buzz don't you?" I said continuing to squish the pasty mush between my fingers.

Connie was a freaking saint. I tried not to resent her contentment, but the more I watched her the more I marveled. Everything arrived for her in the same perceptual package. Whatever life brought, gift or garbage, she unwrapped with the same generous spirit of acceptance and never complained. We had known each other from fourth grade. She was an eclectic mix of practicality, mayhem and ego, and I adored her quick wit and rounded accent. Above all, she was a great sport. Since fellow Midwesterners were a rather scarce breed in the rural South, I relished her friendship as I would the blooming of wisteria in the artic circle.

Apart from the sterile grist mill of her husband's world of academia, Connie lived 'real' in a marvelous place just outside of town. Surrounded by bee hives and chickens, her house lazed amidst a meadow just above the river. Just beyond the double ponds in the back, the burled whispers of the shoals rose into the air and beyond that, an ancient dress shop she owned with her friend Charlene.

Together they reminded me of an old vaudeville act, reigning as costume queen and make-up artist supreme for several local theatre houses. From time to time I solicited their help in repairing period clothing and painting museum mannequins for displays.

Charlene was born and bred in the land of collard greens, but she had gone to college in Ohio and the length of her drawl had been eclipsed by her education. Her home was across the street from Connie's and though their places were forty minutes further from the Danburg than the cottage I had been renting, their company suited me better. Both shop and residence were but a stone's throw from the high shoals and I found at the end of my day, I was more in need of their frantic beauty than of freedom from my gas tank.

Chapter Fifteen

While Charlene was accommodating, Connie was a darling about my melancholy and I did my best to stay out of their way. Hedging against the probability my depression had overstayed its welcome, I obligated myself to assist them with a summer stock program later that year. As part apology and affirmation of my gratitude for their grace under my fire, I easily surrendered to their whims.

The summer theatre raised its curtains one county away, but the ride was beautiful and I enjoyed the regular contact with people who saw me less foreign than the red tinted soil beneath our collective feet. Sober I thought I had made it fairly clear that getting the Danburg and its museum opened and then a short respite from humanity was my first priority.

But when they told me the local theater had lost its director to embezzlement charges and its back up assistant to the musical *Gypsy* two towns over... I folded like a Japanese lantern. It was no surprise. After all, I saved demolition fodder for a living and besides, I owed them both.

In my best inebriated guestimations, I had calculated during the cocktail hour I could open the museum by late spring. By the time the Cornish hens made their dancing debut on the tabletop in lemon rind tutus, I'd promised to take two weeks off in between to study the script and design the set. Just before the crème brûlée and another glass of wine, regret arrived on the sideboard, but by then it was too late. Somewhere in between mulled wine over an open fire, a game of charades and a second helping of chestnut dressing, I had sacrificed common sense for nostalgia and left myself no out. I'd have committed myself if I hadn't already committed to directing Connie's revival performance from *Wait Until Dark,* a dramatic murder mystery by Fredrick Knott. Talk about being blind sided by a refrigerator twice in the same evening!

It was not until I had left them and the county three weeks later with my artificially induced good cheer and handful of ibuprofen that I realized what I had done. It had all sounded so very doable and exciting in contrast to the cold and barren landscape of my drunken December. Now sober, I wanted to shoot myself.

Intellectually dry-docked back in Danburg, I had not even looked at the script, let alone considered the construction of the set, when Connie called me. Stalling, I allowed her to ramble as I scavenged my desk for the prop list.

She started by telling me she had lined up several folks to audition for the peripheral parts and that she had pulled costumes and props and set them aside. Most of the missing things she thought she could secure from the shop, but a few articles would have to be bought. I agreed to purchase them, happy to have skirted the issue of my profound ignorance. By the time she finished making her grocery list of delinquent props; I had captured and perused the sheet. It all appeared rather stock for theatre folk, so I dismissed its level of difficulty until she asked about the refrigerator.

"The what?" I blurted. There was nothing about a major kitchen appliance! I flipped the page and found it there on the back, next to the stove and kitchen sink. "Who the hell doesn't put a thing like this at the top of a prop list?" I admonished.

The phone went silent for a second and then she asked again, "Do you have one that will fit the set?"

A refrigerator? I didn't even have a set! Where the hell was I gonna find a refrigerator, a stove and a sink already detached from somebody's house in an afternoon? She grunted at my silence. I hadn't seen the play since high school and had completely forgotten about the ending of the damn thing.

* * *

"Couldn't the guy just die by light from a microwave instead?" I asked. "After all... this is the millennium!"

"No, silly. It's gotta be a refrigerator!" Suddenly her calm and grace under my fire irritated the shit out of me. I had a museum opening in two days. How the hell was I gonna find a couple of major kitchen appliances and get them to the theatre between now and then? "Charlene and I were talking and...."

I lost her somewhere after "Charlene and I were talking..." because she and Charlene were always talking! I let her chatter and pondered my predicament. It wasn't that I regretted my original offer, even though I felt she had obtained it under dubious circumstances. She purposely bought my favorite wine to seduce my commitment! I wasn't going to renege... it was just that the interruption of her obligation meant I couldn't afford the luxury of getting caught up in the emotional cobwebs of the Danburg's tainted history till later. It would be weeks before I would be able to get back to it, as auditions and rehearsals would consume every available spare moment for the next two months. By then, my influence in the area would have faded and folks would be less available for independent investigations on the diary.

I looked at the clock. It was amazing what a slave I had become to time. Either suffering from the lack of it or the burden of too much of it, I began to resent time! It continued to alter everything but my pessimism. A year ago I had been married and happily at home. Okay, relatively happy and relatively at home. I couldn't help it. Traveling was part of my job and this project had been the closest one to home in a long time. Unfortunately for me, it was so close it had been easier to go home on the weekends... just in time to introduce my husband and my next door neighbor! Enough said.

Connie was still bubbling along about something she and Charlene had discovered, so I mentally checked out again as I eyed the empty spot in case thirteen. But then I heard her voice break cadence and looked at the prop list again. The list mentioned silverware and a small kitchen knife. She balked and asked if I had been paying attention. While I looked at my wrists and contemplated the virtues of serrated or straight, Connie plowed on. I remembered she had said something about my suitcases, the light at the end of the hall and something about the condition of her shop and the lack of space.

I answered "Right…" to everything. She grunted. I told her I had a brief window of opportunity in the morning to get the remaining props. She said she would help pull together her pile and whatever her partner Charlene could gather and we could borrow her husband's pickup and take them all to the theatre, dump them and then grab a quick bite. When she asked if I had a dolly, I double-checked the list. There it was: (1) Toy doll stuffed with heroin.

Trying to impress her, I mentioned there was a doll at the museum, but it was too valuable to be used as a prop. She laughed and corrected my interpretation.

"Not a dolly, as in plaything—I mean a furniture dolly. You know, for the refrigerator!"

There she went again with the refrigerator. I had to fess up. "Connie… I never found one. Hell… I never even looked for one, to tell you the truth. However if you find one, right now I'd like to climb in it. The AC has yet to be turned on here and the windows are still painted shut!" And then I waited for the heavy sigh.

Instead she laughed. "I just told you. There's no more room in the shop. I threw out your old suitcases and I have an old beat up fridge in the back that came with the shop when we bought it. Other than cooling a few Cokes, we don't use it. We'll take that and it will give me back an entire corner for Charlene's new things."

I returned my imaginary gun to its holster. "Then the heroin dolly… was just a furniture dolly… right?!"

"You really need to take some time off, kiddo. Go home. Take a cool shower and hop into bed! Meet me at the shop by 10:00 AM and we'll head out from there. I need to show you something anyway! See you then." And she rang off.

Ten o'clock in the morning was going to roll around sooner than I hoped, so I got back to my inventory lists for the museum and concentrated on the final walk through.

Chapter Sixteen

I agreed to help Connie move the fridge and clear the shop of my marital fallout. In an effort to make her world less disorderly, I packed that night and decided to move my things into the site trailer. In the process of transferring, I also contemplated applying for a grant to finish my research on the diary.

I thought about the true significance of the Danburg diary as I unboxed several of my own journals. It was one thing to base an extension on a real find, but that wasn't my true motivation for delaying the conclusion. I had heard rumblings of a collection of papers dated from the Civil War era by one of the earliest matrons, from when the Danburg had been in Sherman's path, but this journal was far too new to present that kind of historical interest. I was still searching for concrete ties between the journal and the Danburg to validate the monetary investment. Emotionally though, I knew it would never matter. I could not calculate either cost or return value for me as it was becoming far too private to measure.

There was just as much hedging in the Danburg entries as in mine. It was a typical stalling tactic. You told just enough around the edges so if someone tried really hard, they could figure the rest of it out from the clues. Problem was you had to know they were clues to begin with and not merely random thoughts. All that the puzzle provided was a false wall of safety, and it was about time that I broke it down.

Desperate to avoid internal confrontations, I had convinced myself that forestalling knowledge of the Danburg authors' destinies provided shelter from my own. But I could not change what had happened to me or what had happened to either of them. And unless I took off the emotional blinders and dug in with both fists, I would never know their fates.

The real trouble was whether I could deal with what was found when I pulled both fists out of the muck. Already I was confounded by local legend disputing Union soldier activities in the immediate area of the Danburg in the fall of 1864. That legend contradicted the assumed origins of the first great fire. On top of that, a birth was recorded in the family Bible that went well past the feasible gestational period if in fact the death certificate for the master of the house on file was correct. Jeremiah C. Danburg was killed in the War Between the States three and a half months before the child could have even been conceived. Mrs. Jeremiah C. had some "splaining to do"! Coupling that with rumored documents revealing improper relations between slaves and masters, and the Danburg was showing promising signs of a Civil War soap opera that could rival the Young and the Restless.

One era of dysfunction was bad enough to deal with, so I decided to concentrate on the more contemporary of the two. The auxiliary diary entry in blunt penmanship had mentioned a silo entombing a body. I comforted myself with the fact that there was no silo on the Danburg property now, nor in any of its recently recorded history. But that did not speak to the thirty or so silos that had graced my travels from my former marital home in Athens to Danburg.

I only knew that in order to deal with what had happened to me, I had to know what had happened to her. Somehow the girl of the diary had become the passport to my subconscious. The silos were a different story. I decided they would simply have to wait until I had built enough reserves to deal with whatever reality they might bring.

Drunk, but not delusional— I was aware of the lunacy of my rationalizations, yet remained emotionally devoted to them. The diary was like my life; echoing with moments of intuitive clarity, but mostly shying away from the truth. The question that continued to riddle remained. Was it an honest reflection of the maiden's girl's life? And further still... who had this disarming changeling been? This person who lived so much on the inside of her eyelids and the edge of her pen? This woman child who dreamed of a world kinder and safer than the one she lived in, who danced the halls of a home that sheltered but did not protect?

And who was this mysterious entrant? There was a reference to an older alcoholic male in another section of the diary. Could this have been the man who perched above her bed in the moonlight and confessed his desires? If I could only corroborate the foreign pages as having been tied to the Danburgs in real time and place, I would have a chance of making that leap to the mysterious masculine as well. But it was all so fragmented. There were no dates, no recognizable family names... nothing that could point to its spatial relationship to the Danburg exclusively.

By bringing in the restoration project early and under budget I knew that I could press the Historical Society for more time and funds for document research. I just wasn't certain the Society would see the diary as having the same level of historical value without empirical proof that it belonged to one of the inhabitants of the house, especially since the 1864 papers they had hoped would turn up had yet to materialize. Though we had found letters and various personal documents in the attic volumes alluding to their existence, I had found nothing thus far dating back to the Danburg's colonial origins. I needed more time until I could authenticate my suspicions and this play of Connie's was going to squash all hopes of that.

It was after 11:00 p.m. by the time I had showered, poked at a salad and tossed the script aside to crawl into bed. My little mystery girl and her co-author would simply have to wait, but the words on those last few pages scrolled across my mind like a ticker tape and refused to depart even in slumber. Tomorrow was finally the last day before the private, family viewing. Though I was getting closer to solving some of the Danburg's mysteries and should have been thrilled, there was a lump of undigested suspicion in my stomach that refused to settle.

I needed to know if the girl had been violated that night or if the arrogant intruder had shown compassion and left as he had intimated. And what of the bodies he referenced? Who were these people he spoke of so callously? Were there records of any deaths that involved silo burial sites? Or had they been part ploy in his sexual game? How the hell was I going to be able to track anything when I could not even assign authorship to either one of them?

So many questions I wanted to ask of them both and yet not one more word had ever been written by either of them. I had no way of knowing if she had been spared my fate. No way to know if she had lived a life riddled with doubt and guilt for provoking a crime committed upon her by someone else. The remainder of the diary was charred and other than an unintelligible two line scrawl on the bottom of the following page…empty.

And that's when I realized I had just recognized the first clue. Singed pages meant but one thing… fire!

Chapter Seventeen

After several hours I awakened in a cold sweat, nauseous. I had a full day ahead of me and could ill afford the loss of REMs, but the images from those words continued to frustrate any attempt to fall back asleep. In two weeks we would open to the public and my obligation to this place would be fulfilled and I could walk away. I should have been happy, but there was something missing.

The structure had begged me for help and I had delivered it from demolition, but not from its original downfall. No matter how much excavation had taken place, there were memories here that refused to be exposed. They clung to the rooms like faded wallpaper unwilling to respond to the temptation of steam. I had failed the Danburg emotionally as much as myself and in the end we were both left standing structurally, but not whole.

The night unfolded uneasily and I dreamed about the diary intermittently until just before the dawn. In the suspended haze of waking I sensed some sort of latent message in a fading dream. Closing my eyes tightly I lay in bed, trying to recapture what it was.

My first impression was that there had been an endless supply of people crowding into the front parlors waiting to take the tour. I tried to join in the conversations of those nearest me, but they averted their faces, whispering behind my back. The parlors continued to fill. Everyone was becoming fidgety and it was making me nervous. Suddenly the assembly hushed as a young child appeared alone in the hall.

I maneuvered my way to where she stood. I inquired if she'd seen the docent. She nodded. I checked my watch. Whoever she was, she deserved a sharp reprimand for being so late, but I decided to curb my tongue. Five more minutes passed in silence and the guide was now extremely late. When no one appeared, I asked her again if she had seen the tour guide.

She pointed to the face of the clock. Confused, I searched the crowd for explanations. Where the hell was the docent? When no one came forward to volunteer information, I pressed her again. She smiled politely, addressing the man in the moon on the clock face with a question. I made the assumption it was a child's game. Aggravated I went to make apologies to a group nearby who were now demanding a refund for their tickets. Since no one stepped forward to lead, I decided to give the tour myself, moving the velvet rope aside. When I did, the child told me not to bother. She was very sorry, but the man in the moon had instructed her that the tour would not go on as planned that day or any other day. When I asked why, she said he had told her that he could not return. I asked her what that meant. She merely pointed to the face inside the wooden cabinet as if it should be evident to everyone why.

Curious, I moved closer to inspect the clock. There was nothing there but my reflection superimposed over the hand painted dial. Nothing was different from the moment before, with the exception that the weights had been relocated to the floor and the clock had stopped ticking. I reached for the weights and noticed that one had been dented in the fall. By the force of habit, I reached for the key in my pocket to open the cabinet and search for the chains, but the chains were missing too. She touched my sleeve, unfolded my fist and placed a piece of coiled paper inside.

She whispered that the man in the moon had showed her that the secret key was rolled up in the paper. I looked at the face of the clock again. The caricatured orb had swept three-quarters of the way across the face of the milk-painted sky, chased by the sun, and stopped. He was her man in the moon. Cherub-like, with plumped cheeks and cheery expression, the moon slumped in its orbit. I had to tilt my head to look him squarely in his vacant eyes.

She explained the man in the moon had died the minute the weights had fallen and the clock stopped ticking. That was why he had not returned to her. I froze. I tried to remember the positions of everything inside the case, but the sun began to rise outside my window and the display inside my lids began to fade.

I forced myself to the desk and poured over the diary, studying the entries again. From the damaged pages I knew there had been a fire. The dilemma was there had been more than one fire. According to several interviews, the Danburgs boasted Sherman's torches had set the first fire, and there had been several in between then again in1946. A more careful inquest might ask had the diary been in a fire in that house or somewhere else? So far the first clue was it had been in a fire, period. The second clue came from the dream.

There was no mention of a clock on any of the previous pages of the diary, yet there was a real grandfather clock that originally stood in the lower hall of the Danburg and for some reason seemed to symbolize the Danburg past to everyone I had interviewed. Had I missed something? I searched again. Page after page revealed the same parade of adolescent monologues until the disclosure of her situation, followed by his entries. While it was highly common for structures of that age to have survived a great many small disasters, this fire was a turning point for the Danburgs and it showed in the collective memory of the community. My next chore would be to chart the dates of recorded fires and try to find when the clock had first appeared in familial inventories or photos. That might provide a common timeline to what details I could glean from the entries.

I continued to reread the diary to see if the clock had been mentioned even peripherally, and suddenly the third clue presented itself in the midst of childish drivel about a picnic: a waterhole. There was no waterhole on the current property that I recalled, but then the diary never said where it was located. Then again, if the entry had been recorded before the turn of the century, prior to the sale of the outlying parcels... there might have been a waterhole in those acres. So was the diary from before or after the Civil War fire? Pinning down the diary's dateline was becoming as impossible as nailing Jello to a wall!

The girl's diction lent more weight to the theory that her journal had been composed after the turn of the century, so I decided to begin my research with the lesser tract of acres. If the waterhole had been for a private rendezvous, the pond would have been out of the way. If the Danburg maiden girl was inching her way toward sexual surrender, she would have made certain of its sanctity. If it had been the perpetrator's forcing of submission, he would have made certain of its seclusion. There was a small pond for livestock located in the northwest corner of the property recorded in the plats of 1912, but it didn't fit the description of the diary and by 1937 those acres had been sold off. Either way, the waterhole of the entry would have been somewhere others would not have had the casual opportunity to watch nor the inclination to follow. I would look into that later. For now it was back to the clock.

There was no mention of an actual timepiece in the account, not in the physical sense. It only referenced a point in time: a man looking over a roof top at the moon from an upstairs window. I looked at the entry again. His view was from a window that gave him access to a visual. What portion of the roofline? What portion of the sky? What time of year? Where in the lunar revolution did he see the moon? What other clues were imbedded that I had glossed over in my anger? These could have been greater clues that required more than just my intuition and guesswork. I logged my questions as quickly as they appeared in my mind.

His hiding his writing in a child's diary was the most obvious clue. He had not been trying to violate the sanctity of her diary; he had been counting on it! My heart began to pound inside my chest and my pulse quickened. I gathered the pages to my chest and took a deep breath. The last time I had overreacted and prematurely condemned or applauded the intentions of another, it had cost me a marriage. It would take a clear head to do the intention of this man's entry justice so I laid the diary down on the table and then paced a few minutes to work off the excess energy to calm myself.

On closer inspection, his writing style spoke of something altogether different than first suspected. I chastised myself for my previous ignorance. I had to learn to read not just what had been entered, but how and when. It was necessary to note the words that were used and those that were not. In that vein, the manuscript seemed completely different and I became more forgiving of them both.

From this new perspective, it soon became his overwhelming lack of self-protection that caught me off guard. How had I missed it before? The author wasn't trying to boast belligerently or hide anything; he was trying to divulge information in the fashion he knew best. This man was educated. A poet of sorts, he could not bring himself to write such vile things without the gloss of intellect. He used vivid and elevated words that allowed him the grace to write without reducing himself to the same primitive level as what it was he was describing. Gradually, I saw his handwriting as the result of hurried penmanship, not overbearing masculinity. He was being as gentle with his dissemination of horrific bulletins as could be, bent in a gentle arc above her as lover. I suddenly realized that his concern for this woman-child was real and not the product of false bravado. The potential deflowering was about *his* loss of innocence, not *hers*.

I had been so wrong. My life had been so tainted by my own bitterness that I saw everything as threat and innuendo. In my ignorance I had missed the whole point of the entry. No wonder I saw her as such a victim. That was how I saw myself! I wiped a hard won tear from my cheek and returned to the diary to see what other mistakes I had made in my premature condemnation of their world.

Chapter Eighteen

Forgive the breach if I do not return. It is not the insult of rejection, but the compliment of protection. Some day you will understand. Keep this close. Remember those things best kept from discovery are those things kept in plain sight...

If indeed he lived there or visited on a regular basis, why would he not return and why would she need protection? Why would you hide such a message inside a young girl's diary? You wouldn't. Unless he was certain that if she found it, she would know what to do with it. Who was this young woman and what made her the perfect keeper of his secret?

I had no answers to offer. I was back to square one. He referenced secrets hidden in plain view. What other than her diary would have been in plain view from that room where it was written? There was a bedroom at the back right of the upstairs hall that looked out over a warming kitchen. The view opened toward the pasture and the old school house from the lee of the old hay road. From the left back bedroom the view swept out towards the barn and the tool shed. And if you looked out over the wisteria...dear God...the cremation pit! I thought again of its location south of the house and the hog killing station to the back and right of the kitchen. In our tour monologue for the docents, only the empty family coffins in the upstairs storage closet and the stone-walled family cemetery were publicly mentioned. No one ever mentioned the burial rights and practices for the slaves who had worked on the Danburg's land since its time as a plantation.

The clues were starting to pile up and began to resemble every moss-covered burm in the area. My stomach rolled as I contemplated beings other than hogs being lowered by tethered feet into boiling water pots at the killing station. Suddenly the sickening smell of burning flesh crept into my nostrils. I gagged at the thought.

Local lore and family histories confirmed there had been several fires on the Danburg property, both small and large. How could I ever decipher which flames had singed the diary? The house was endowed with fireplaces in every room, not to mention the warming kitchen and all the outside buildings. I thought I was getting warmer and the warmer I got, the sicker I felt inside. Had something more horrible than an inappropriate tryst happened to my Danburg maiden? Was this why she was not mentioned in the family annals? Was she more than just a possible sexual abuse victim?

The tears began to well in the lower lashes of my eyes and the page before me became awash in a sea of salty fear. If the secret was hidden in plain sight, then perhaps...so was the answer to what had befallen her.

I saw them. God help me, I saw them, but I was not one of them. I swear this to you. I was not one of the men in the sunlight. You must never forget me, but do not remember me as the foul beast they will tell you I have become. You know me. Remember my eyes. Did you not say to me once how kind they were? Remember them if you remember anything of me at all when people speak unkindly of me. Remember me as the smiling man in the moonlight who brought you his heart, and not one among the frightening men of the sunlight who left naught but tragedy in their wake!

What was this man's obsession with the time of day? Why was it so important for this girl to be able to distinguish between sunlight and moonlight? I feared this might be another reference to those things hidden in plain view that I had yet to decipher, just like the importance of the clock at the end of the hall.

Chapter Nineteen

The Westminster Abbey chime had always been my favorite and I smiled as the clockwork moon teased me with its secrets. The grandfather clock was a beautiful piece that had required quite a bit of work after being donated by the Chenille sisters last spring. Meeting them both had been such an adventure; the antique clock at the time had presented merely a perk!

Orphaned young in life, they had grown up with their aunt and uncle in the Danburg and their input was invaluable to the reconstruction. Miss Celine, whose friends referred to her occasionally as Linny, wore white evening gloves and smelled dreadfully of toilet water. The two reminded me of characters from *Arsenic and Old Lace*. It was hard for me to take them seriously, but they were my only sources for much of the familial history, so I smiled a lot and disciplined myself to listen. At our first meeting, Miss Cattalieu Chenille had argued forcefully with her sibling over the history of the time piece. Catty, as her sister called her, stated it had always graced the front alcove at the foot of the stairs. Celine insisted that the clock had stood in the furthest alcove just outside the library until the great fire and its subsequent banishment to the cellar and then beyond to an auction block. At least I could confirm the piece had once been in the lower hall...somewhere!

I enjoyed watching the theatrics as they carried on, pointing in different directions to indicate where other objects had been in reference to the clock's installment.

Cattalieu squealed with excitement when she entered the front parlor. "Oh Linny, remember the teas we used to have with the tiny little cups and saucers from our aunt before she died? And the little cornmeal cakes we used to bake out back in the warming shed? Remember? You used to stamp them with that heart shaped thing and it made them look so pretty! Oh Miss Horton, it was such a delightful time in this house until..."

Celine cut her off without batting an eye. "Nonsense, Catty. We rarely had such frivolities and our aunt was a stingy old bat who never shared her precious porcelain with another soul... alive or dead!"

"But you remember the heart cakes, don't you dear?" Catty whimpered. "I always loved when you made them. Don't you re- member we used to steal the doilies from the parlor tables, lay them on top and then sprinkle sugar over the doilies to make pretty patterns? We used to get into trouble for using them that way, but it made the little cakes so glorious ... remember Linny?" And she turned from her sister's gaze and smiled at the table that now held an array of photographs and a vase of colorful flowers atop similar lacy mats.

"So very, very pretty they were. Reminded me of the Queen Anne's lace that grew right outside that window there... such in- tricate patterns." And she turned to address me.

"Hated that they were called weeds... Lucy's little sister and I used to gather them and make bouquets. We used to spend hours in this room during the happier times. We'd play and dance... bakes those tea cakes and then you'd leave two or three of the leftover ones out behind the porch for..."

Linny bit into her. "If said I don't remember, then I don't! You must be mistaken Cattalieu. We were never allowed to play in this room. Uncle wouldn't have allowed it."

"No, I distinctly remember it was in this room and the kitchen out back is where we used to help make the batter and then... beyond the walkway, past the peonies we used to spy on..." and Catty pointed towards the rear hall.

Celine pulled her hand down and patted it patronizingly. "Perhaps it was at another house with another set of young girls. Lucy and her younger siblings' maybe. You used to play with them. Lucy was always a fool for such youthful fancies. Or maybe it's just one of the hundred silly little things you've dreamt up in your foggy little brain! I never spied on a single soul... no reason to." she spit back, and then holding her breath she turned to face me.

"You must forgive my little sister. She suffers from early stages of Alzheimer's and cannot be held accountable for her babblings."

Catty gasped and Celine shot her younger sibling a death ray stare.

Embarrassed, the younger sibling clung tightly to the velvet ropes that kept her from her past. Celine continued to explain her sister would unfortunately not be of much help, since her mind tended to wander and distort even the simplest of details. She proceeded to educate that her interviews then would most likely provide little more than entertainment and should not be taken to task as they could not possibly be substantiated. Catty stared out the window across the parlor and bit at her lower lip in concentration.

"I do remember some things quite clearly, Linny. There are some moments in life one can never forget." She grimaced and then turned quickly to face me. "Don't you agree, Miss Horton?" Her gaze was so direct and her implication that we shared some sort of common goal so strong that if she had the onset of dementia... she certainly had it selectively.

I tugged at my sleeve and rubbed at one of my wrists and smiled weakly. "Yes...some memories are printed indelibly upon our minds. Even those we would like to forget."

She took my smile as invitation to continue. "I quite agree. Especially those we would like to forget. Like for instance..." her fingers began to loosen on the velvet rope.

"Cattalieu! Enough of these games! Miss Horton here has serious business to attend to and listening to the fanciful flights of your idyllic youth is not one of them. Besides, if I don't remember these little tid-bits of nostalgia... then how could you possibly?" Celine barked, but the younger sibling continued despite the glowering presence of her agitated keeper.

"For instance..." Catty cleared her throat as challenge and began again. "The in-law chair you have placed here, sat in the opposite corner. I know, because it used to be my favorite view from the room. I used to sit in it and watch the smoke curl from the burn pit through that window. It was where I was sitting the day I saw you put..."

"I said that's enough, Cattalieu. And the chair was never at that window."

Catty shot back a glare at Celine. "But I'm certain that is where I saw you..." and the words died on her lips.

"No. Not that window. Never that window. I am older... I think I would know better than you where a chair was or wasn't placed and what view would have been best. There's nothing out there but an old pile of bricks and overgrown scrub. Now, be a good little lamb and wait for me in the front hall."

Cattalieu continued to mumble under her breath about the placement of the chair while her sister critiqued the placement of other furniture pieces in the room.

They argued one more time about the clock and then eventually realized the futility of their argument, since the clock was in no condition to stand at either end of the hall. Celine toyed with frustration at the upper edges of her gloves, trying to make her final point and it struck a cord with me. It seemed odd for her to wear such a formal accessory that early in the day, but perhaps she was trying to keep the charcoal smudges from the wooden clock from tarnishing a manicure. Commanding Cattalieu to return to her side, she asked for the small package that had accompanied them inside the door.

Gushing with gratitude, I blushed when they pressed the blackened key crank into my hand. Twelve seconds later, dry rotted, it crumbled in my palm. Reminding myself that beggars should not be choosey, I smiled and thanked them. I set the pieces aside carefully. I was informed the remaining guts and weights were in a box on the front porch beside the charred cabinet. Their driver had placed them there as they were too heavy for either of the sisters to carry. Celine warned that the clock had never worked properly to begin with. The weights and the chiming were always off!

This time it was Cattalieu that blushed and then laid the cloth-wrapped pendulum on my desk, begging forgiveness for its tarnished condition. Celine chided under her breath, but Cattalieu continued. She explained that the damp cellar had wrought its revenge because the heirloom had been removed from its place of honor prematurely. Much to her sister's surprise, Cattalieu added that a similar occurrence had happened to an heirloom family member as well. Celine pishawed her sister and bit at her lower lip. Readdressing me, Celine focused on the scorch marks upon the wood cabinet, saying they were nothing more than "tragic wounds of consequence."

I had the uneasy feeling we had stopped talking about the grandfather clock. The look in Cattalieu's eyes confirmed this, but I had neither the courage nor the inclination to question further.

Sensing my hesitation, Cattalieu elaborated on the original craftsmanship of the clock and the intricately painted face, rushing briefly over the condition of the charred spots on the wood. Celine allowed the marks were "blemishes on the surface of second grade timber made by second class citizens". I assumed she was alluding to the first fire of the Danburg set by Yankee soldiers on their march to the sea.

The disparity between their personalities was fascinating. Both had been as generous as their accents with family anecdotes and sisterly accusations, but there was something thicker than peach marmalade that separated the two of them and I surmised it to be the truth after so many contradictions. As an only child, I enjoyed the comic relief of their sideways glances and glares. But when I pushed Cattalieu to explain further the origins of the great fire, Celine threw her sister a daggered stare that cut her to the quick and the blood drained from Catty's face. Shortly after, the younger sibling retired to the family car and Celine finished the interview alone.

A history of something less sweet than Madison Jasmine clung to the edges of their smiles under the veneer of civility as they waved goodbye. Something reeked just beneath their eau de toilette and I sensed a greater mystery between them than the origins of the great fire. I watched with fueled interest as they pulled away, smirking as they rounded the curve of the carriage walk.

It made no sense that Cattalieu made me promise to be so careful with the clock after so much neglect. She had been the one to push for the donation, yet Celine had seemed so completely exasperated with her sister's sentiment. I decided to take their conflict and the clock's condition in stride.

***

Two weeks later, I was shocked when the clocksmith called to explain why the clock had never worked. Aside from the fact that one of the weights was missing, the others were grossly disproportionate in their calibrations. When he opened the capped ends to remove the lead cylinders and re-calibrate, he was confused at what he saw. Inside the cap was a thin layer of candle wax and behind that what appeared to be silver, not lead. Not wanting to disturb the artifact's value, he suggested I send the weights to a jeweler. Beyond that, the mechanicals ranged from poor to fair condition and one of the chains was missing as well. As to why the remaining weights refused to descend, it was because they were blocked.

Inside the back corner of the cabinet he had found a thin leather book had been jammed into the mechanicals, preventing the movement of the remaining chains that raised and lowered the weights.

***

Everyone who had been interviewed denied knowledge of the diary's existence, expressing their disappointment that the more important Civil War documents apparently had been lost to the fire of 1946. I assured them I would continue my search amongst the papers housed in the attic library.

In the case of the Chenille sisters, their refutation was understandable. They had spent a lifetime busily keeping score of their own battle wounds and tallying each other's offenses. From the sheer number that had passed between them in my office, I doubted they had time to do anything else. Still, there was something behind the older sibling's eyes that suggested she had known more. When I told her others mentioned they thought she might know the location of those records kept by the first matrons of the Danburg, she smiled and referred to "small minded people seeking their fifteen minutes of fame". When I had questioned Cattalieu about the Civil War documents, she shrugged her shoulders, stating her sister Linny was the family archivist and that only she would know about such things. But when I asked about the current diary, Cattalieu's eyes danced with panic. Celine dismissed her edgy sister immediately to the front parlor and then answered for them both.

Without confirming or denying its existence, Celine reasoned that if a diary had been found in a clock that had been bartered around the countryside for over half a century, anyone could have placed it there. There was no way to prove it had anything to do with them. She almost dared me to find a connection.

It was the way Celine had said the word "prove" that caught my attention. Celine was haughty and arrogant, but not stupid. Her younger sister seemed less entrenched in the southern aristocratic charade of class warfare. Cattalieu had a tender heart. If I needed to find a hole in the Danburg dike, it would be through her.

As Celine pontificated about the statistical probability of the diary's ownership, I watched Catty toy with fringe on a table lamp down the hall and tried to imagine her as a child within these walls. Her nimble fingers delighted at the tactile pleasures of the parlor room while she kept a keen watch out for her sister's wrath. In an odd way she reminded me of the child from the dream standing there, uncertain of where to keep her hands. Perhaps if I dreamed again, the child would return and tell me about the clock, the key, and the man in the moonlight.

Chapter Twenty

Remembering how the diary was discovered, I reached for the new mechanicals behind the clock's frame and wondered how long before I heard from the jeweler on the originals. The clocksmith had done a marvelous job restoring the cabinet. The worn patina was now mostly freed of obvious blemishes. Sanded and rubbed with linseed oil, one could scarcely distinguish the burn marks from the burled strands in the tiger oak. I noted the error in time, adjusted the strike and set the new pendulum in motion. The freshly oiled veneer surrounding the corbelled key hole slicked the edge of the key as I removed it. Looking akin to thinned molasses, the oil clung to my fingertips.

Adjustments made to the pocket door enabling me to enter the original dining room, I turned before closing them and surveyed the opposing parlor. The Danburg home was a typical four on four with a large center hall and two alcoved areas in the rear perfect for housing the glassed lawyers cabinets and buffed surfaces of the matching marble library tables. Everything was perfect, but for one thing. There was a vacant spot in case thirteen at the top of the stairs yet to be filled. I was counting on the diary to fill it.

I pulled the heavy pocket door along its track and paused. The sudden silence of the usually garrulous mockingbirds in the freshly planted azaleas caught my attention. I looked up. I hadn't expected anyone till later that next afternoon for the public ribbon cutting ceremonies. A behemoth Lincoln perched itself in the left hand turning lane at the edge of the driveway. Polished and pedigreed, it idled longer than necessary and missed the light. I was curious about its driver's debate as the winking blinker flirted with my concentration. I reminded myself I had only intended to stop briefly at the Danburg on my way to Connie's.

Any intrusions at this point would put me behind in my schedule and rob me of the few minutes I had to identify the author of the uncaptioned artifact that was waiting to lie in state in case thirteen. I checked my appointment book. No one was scheduled until 6:00 p.m. the following day, when the local paper would arrive to do the meet-and-greet photos, and then there was the cocktail hour beginning at 6:30 for city officials to preview the house before the family viewing the next afternoon.

The long black sedan pulled forward onto the driveway's crushed gravel. I watched as the car dallied at the front gate, wondering who would breach southern etiquette and appear so many hours before an invitation's appointed time. My truck was in the back and if I hurried, I could pull away before whoever it was hit the front porch. I thought about the long drive to High Shoals and the possibility of a long wait if Connie wasn't finished with her scavenger hunt for props. I decided to take the diary along with me.

I considered a quick dash back to the hall, but there was something mesmerizing about the way the shadows danced across the grill of the approaching front end that held me fast. I had been visited by every crone within three counties, but the tags on this one didn't register. I bent forward to get a better view. The sun bounced wildly off the windshield as the car snaked its way into the curve of the carriage walk and stalled for a second, blinding me. Annoyed at the interruption, I determined to let the groundskeeper ferret out the mystery visitors' needs, resolved I had far more pressing matters to attend to. But the determination on the driver's face made me think twice. Had I scheduled an inspection by the Historical Society and not recorded it? I thought about the diary and my inability at this point to divine its authenticity. I had explained to the Society I'd been holding that particular dossier apart until authorship could be verified, but I held it apart because I had become so attached to my mystery girl that I refused to place her under the unforgiving microscope of the insensitive public.

Given the time constraint imposed by my obligation in High Shoals, it was unlikely that I would get the diary identified and placed into the exhibit for the private showing. But if she visited me in my slumber again and gave more clues…perhaps I could substantiate its ownership and importance before the public viewing and then file for further grants to delay my departure. With few clues to lead me, it would be a long shot, but it was the only one I had worth pursuing.

I heard a car door open and saw the driver unfold himself from behind the steering column. Adjusting his posture, he tapped on the tinted glass to make inquiries of the passenger in the rear seat. The window scrolled slowly down. The bowed rim of a red meshed bonnet fluttered with punctuation as the bearer spoke, like the long sweeping eyelashes on an elephant. The driver shook his head in response and motioned to the side yard, then back towards the house. The window edged its way upward and stopped half-opened to the summer air.

Today was not the day to waste time being cordial to another of the papier-mâché matrons of Danburg and so I reminded myself to remain focused. The driver returned to his station. Relieved that they were leaving, I returned to mine. Four Armoralled tires ground the crushed gravel underneath the columbined overhang as the clock in the foyer chimed the quarter hour. I dismissed the intruder, assuming all interest had been satisfied. But the sedan stopped again fifteen feet from where it had parked the first time. The clock to my left at the bottom of the stairs had ended its cadence. I shuffled through my key ring, checking the clock. Either the grandfather was thirteen minutes fast, or I had been thirteen minutes distracted. I signaled the groundskeeper outside I still had several hours before I was obligated to open the doors for anyone and suggested he wave them on.

He did so and went back to laying pine straw. I closed the facade of the grandfather clock, listening to the crush of uneven gravel as the weights rewound themselves, chugging behind their painted face. I watched the calculated climb and made the connection with the dream and the diary remnant that mentioned how people die by inches. I pondered its relevance to the Danburgs as I watched the chain click along its ascension, inch by inch.

Shaken from my distraction by the rumbling of the engine, I heard the raised voice of the landscaping engineer. The driver had emerged from the car again. I saw him motion toward the far side of the house. Following his gaze, I noticed that one of the doilies atop the drop leaf table was off center from the lamp, so I moved behind the velvet ropes to reposition it. The Danburg family in the framed photo on the table approved with frozen smiles, and so with careful hand, I wiped at a line of lint just inside the matting. It refused to budge.

Bending closer, I realized it wasn't lint at all. It was the slight figure of a young female in a pinafored frock. How had I missed that before? She was a tiny thing with a bow drawn up through her curls, slivered next to the daunting, darkly clad figures of matrons. Joined by their male counterparts, the Danburg matrons poised themselves sternly beneath descending wisteria vines that overshadowed the tiny waif.

Having not discovered her silhouette in any other photo plates, I dismissed her immediately as either a neighbor or a distant relation. Had she been of any familial importance, I felt certain that surviving family members would have pointed her out and provided extensive education as to her inheritance. Each one of them had been interviewed and each one had been quite clear about his or her standing within the family hierarchy. There was no mistake... this child could not have been a Danburg or I would have known about her months ago. Replacing the frame, I checked the glass for smudges and returned to the office upstairs.

Chapter Twenty-one

The private family viewing was scheduled for 3:00 PM that next afternoon. The general public would be allowed entrance at the end of the month in two weeks. The local paper had been posting updates for months and while the public opening would prove to be a logistically larger headache, the family logistics proved to be a larger headache.

I watched as the driver followed the groundskeeper the length of the Lincoln. As they passed out of view beyond the front wraparound porch, I wondered where they were headed. There was no window in the back hall and so I scuttled back down the stairs to decipher their destination. The massive magnolias that chaperoned the front lawn curtsied to the breeze and threw dappled sunlight across the figure in the rear seat. Sporadic splotches of light across her skin echoed the printed pattern of her gauzy scarf and she suddenly became more intriguing than the errand she had sent her driver on. Her nails were glossed with clear polish and bulky rings circled her fingers. Unaware that she was being watched, she checked her lipstick in a compact, sending a shot of sunlight through the etched glass of the front door directly into my eyes. Blinded, I slipped on the runner and bumped into a milk glass lamp, swearing under my breath.

Clearly, whoever she was, she was in no hurry to vacate the leathered comfort of her chariot and I had not the patience for dispensing drive-by public service announcements should she try to engage me. However, my anticipated abrasiveness went untested, as she had not even noticed me. Quite absorbed in her presentation, she tossed back her head to rewrap the scarf in the mirror. No doubt she was another local aristocrat come to appraise the setting before the next evening's gala. I decided to continue my pursuits and leave the curious onlooker to her continue her own, and resumed my preparations to leave via the back porch. As I paced I took note of my efficiency. Every artifact had been catalogued and tucked neatly inside its velvet bedding behind shiny stainless steel butterfly catches. Every artifact now but two! The first, the diary that had caused nothing but headache since its discovery and now the lithograph in the front parlor that housed a lovely little maiden who appeared nowhere else in the Danburg file.

I was furious with myself for having committed so much time to Connie. Had it not been for the promise to her, I could have been knee deep in photos slides trying to identify the little orphan in the parlor. I had never noticed her in the photograph before that moment. In some warped fashion, I was grateful to the intruders for diverting my attentions long enough to make such a discovery possible. Now thirty minutes later in leaving than I had planned the rear door of the sedan opened. She emerged, and I saw her face. Something in her smile reminded me of the girl in the photo on the parlor drop leaf table. If she was a Danburg, she was a Danburg no one ever talked about, and suddenly that made her more interesting than a hundred other leaves on their family tree.

I knew I had to leave, but I was unable to drag myself away from the screens at the back porch. I watched as this woman stepped slowly from foot to foot and cleared the distance to the backyard with even tempo. If I walked out there now, I would never make it to High Shoals on time. I tried to get the groundskeeper's attention, but he was busy chatting with the chauffeur, gesturing with large sweeping motions across the lawn and then back towards the fenced in area.

I tried to follow her from screen to screen across the back porch, but it was obvious she had no intention of talking to anyone. She was on a mission and her dedication reminded me I needed to be on mine. I watched as she stopped approximately twenty-five feet in front of the barn and brushed the blades of grass beneath her with her silver-tipped cane.

I had never seen anyone study the area with such concentration. Her pause was definite. There was nothing there. Perhaps she had merely run out of breath. I gathered up my things, grabbed the plastic box with the diary inside, and waited by the back door for the woman to relocate herself. Two minutes passed, and just as I thought I should check for a medical issue in the making, she turned and pulled a handkerchief away from her eyes. She crooked her head towards the second story as if getting her bearings.

What was it about that site that brought her grief? I made a mental note to recheck the original drawings of the outbuildings just in case there was some relevance to the spot that I had not registered. She wiped at her cheek, dipped toward the ground and then began the trip back to the car in the drive.

I waited at the back door until I could see her no more and then dashed out to where she had stood. Beneath my feet there was a sterling rose resting gently upon the wave of green blades under it. At first blush, there was nothing different than any other patch of ground that surrounded the Danburg except for the rose.

Tapping with my foot where I thought her cane had touched, I felt the quality of unyielding ground. There was a thin layer of several of the flat-edged stones that were used as foundations for chimneys. I didn't remember seeing anything like this on the schematics. What could be there that generated such reverence? A grave? I turned to look at what had caught her attention before her departure and there it was. The small window in the south side of the attic eave glinted in the morning sunlight. I thought about the book *Green Mansions* and smiled. It had been the favorite of the Danburg Diary maiden.

The attic? I should have thought to check the attic for clues. After all, it was the least tampered with space within the Danburg prior to the state taking it over. I could have kicked myself for not turning it inside out before. I looked at my watch. I was now more than forty-five minutes late leaving for High Shoals. I dug my keys out of my pocket and headed for my vehicle. Whoever she was, she left as unexpectedly as she had arrived. I heard the persistent crunch of gravel and then nothing as the Lincoln pulled onto the paved road and headed in the direction of town.

Chapter Twenty-two

I spent the better part of my drive into High Shoals trying to divine the significance of her intense expression as she stared at the attic. What was her connection? She didn't favor any of the Danburgs. Cattalieu and Celine had distinctly substantial silhouettes. They sported the broad shoulders and elongated features that dominated the Danburg genetic landscape, but not this woman.

This woman was slight in the shoulders and her waist was trim and confined. Thinning hair cut just at the jaw line curled slightly at the ends. She was tailored in every fashion but her expression. She had not stayed long, but I felt certain that this was not the last time I would be seeing her.

The road stretched out before me, the tires humming in tandem with the radio. Insulated from distraction by the white noise, my mind was free to wander. Before I knew it I had crossed over into Oconee County and was just fifteen minutes from Connie's shop. I was desperate to get back to the Danburg and look at the attic with fresh eyes. I had spent so much time looking for Civil War documents; I might have overlooked more pertinent information to this diary.

The attic had been nothing short of a bonfire waiting to happen when the state had finally taken over the Danburg. Inches deep with pigeon guano and shredded family mementoes, it was a wonder that this portion of the house had not burned first.

Both eaves had been piled to the rafters with every conceivable form of literature—encyclopedias, law books, novellas and period works. I had been through more than three-quarters of the attic library without finding anything of real historical value, and I wondered if the older documents had been lost in the first transference.

There were so many books that the Washington-area library became the depository until the library itself ran out of shelf space. Still even with a generous portion of the contents removed, the southern eaves of the attic remained full.

It was unlikely that either county workers or volunteers had documented each book taken from the Danburg. If such documentation did exist however, I would check the files for Civil War correspondence, and then to see if the book *Green Mansions* appeared anywhere in its inventory. Because the book by Hudson was not home-grown enough for rural readers, I was surprised by its introduction in the diary. My darling Danburg maiden girl had drawn innumerable parallels between her dark-haired mentor and the character Abel, so naturally I was intrigued.

I crossed over the bridge at High Shoals and pulled into the parking lot of the dress shop. Connie shoved her nose into the pane of the storefront bay window and signaled she would be a minute as she chatted into her rotary phone. There was no such thing as one minute with her. I bargained for fifteen and pulled the plastic case from the passenger seat and searched for the entry about the book.

Released from the boundaries of formal schooling, he left home early and began his borderless existence. Empty pockets required jobs ranging from grocery delivery boy to garage hand. His good looks attracted young matrons eager for escape from their constricted lives. He soon discovered that trading on his body rather than his mind produced higher returns and required far less effort. Lacing his hours with alcohol, he tumbled through women and money mindlessly. When he reached the certain abyss of his excesses, he dried out and made his way back to the manor... back to me.

His rehabilitations and my family's residency seldom matched those first few years, but I remembered his occasional morning visits to my bedroom. While I was making the bed, he would stand across from me talking about books as though I lived through them as much as he. I recalled his favorite, Green Mansions, *and felt the small tremors below when he recommended that I try to align the characters to individuals in my life. He explained that by this exercise I could absorb not only the book's content but could call upon the characters when reality required escape. Of course, it was obvious he meant himself to portray Abel and I was hopeful that he saw Rima when he looked at me. I wasn't the exotic, raven-haired girl of the pages he fondled when reading, but I burned for him with as much primitive desire as I thought she might have had for Abel. Our encounter across the bed swept me into the fantasy of intimacy. During the next twenty-eight days, I struggled with the terror that such intense feelings would open my body to him.*

Late at night I could smell his cigarette smoke and hear him humming from the walkway beneath my bedroom window. Half covered in the moonlight, I would imagine myself as the wild, brown-skinned sprite whose home was the woodland, and he, the man of great heart. I even took on extra outside chores to insure a more tanned appearance. It of course backfired as I was too fair to achieve more than sun burnt shoulders and freckled brow.

I thought about the Danburg maiden waiting with innocent desire in the quiet of her second story sanctuary and wondered if it had been her favorite book only because of him. The book was of little help to me other than as a barometer of time. Published in 1904, the issue date presented only as the alpha for a time line and the attic as a plausible place to begin my search.

The content of the attic shelves was more sophisticated than I would have envisioned. There was more depth and intellect exhibited than in most bucolic settings. The collection contained little of what I had expected and according to the diary; the girl had much the same reaction.

Once my eyes adjusted, I could feast on the rows of makeshift shelves. The subject focus surprised me. I had expected religious tomes, southern histories and discourses on honorable living, but instead discovered rows of law books and digests with peeling leather covers. The laws of contracts and property led me to discover the Danburgs' family concerns about perfecting the homestead title and lands granted their lineage in the early 1800s.

The family's pre–Civil War land wealth had been eroded by the thievery of Yankee soldiers and the need to sell off parcels to make up for the severe deficit in cotton crop returns as a result of the fires they set. Instead of selling parcels to related families in hopes they would sell them back when times got better, they sold parcels first come, first served. Those that had diversified their crops into tobacco, corn and seasonal produce were the first to snatch them up. Twice-removed relations had also purchased the Danburg general store, whose customers paid their charges annually, providing significant cash windfalls for land purchases.

I knew of his mother's family and their wealth, but I also knew the pantry cupboards always looked thin except for what goods were raised on the premises. He seemed sensitive about both money and station and so I kept observations to myself and poked at another shelf.

Knowing that my guide would resist any "digging up the past," I moved on to a small section of books considered classics. Their shredding covers led to cautious reading of titles, and when I found Charles Dickens' Tale of Two Cities, I asked my mentor if I might call it my own. The restraint evident in his answer told me more about him than I ever expected to know. My companion said that he would have to ask his stepfather, since none of the books was his to give. Pragmatically I responded that this was not a first edition, the spine was barely in place, and the cover could not protect the contents. When he yielded, I saw his shoulders hunch in defeat. He had traded his freedom before to too many other dominant women in his life: his mother, his grandmother and the two female cousins who shared the family quarters seasonally and dogged him constantly. His only male role model, his stepfather, despised his very existence.

Chapter Twenty-three

You must never confess that I saw them, that I heard the muffled screams of horror and watched the last dark figure crumple into the bloodied mass below as their phantom white hoods pulsed with frantic rhythm. Echoes of pain bounced back and forth between the wooded banks as the wind picked up its heels and then slowly died along with the victims. For a moment Mooresford lay silent, riddled with guilt and buckshot. I gagged and ran deeper into the woods...

Who the devil was this mysterious author or the man named Mooresford? No document offered evidence of such a familial name. On top of that, neither of Celine nor Cattalieu admitted to keeping a diary. Cattalieu declined comment with their eyes. She simply shriveled at its mention and left the room. The diary had either been brought to this place or had been here all along. Although the cast of characters and settings remained relatively constant, the memoir had been written in sporadic bursts, providing an uncertain timeline. The secondary author was another anomaly. The first entry of consequence suggested his residence, since she had searched for his footprints in the sandy soil the day of her arrival. Scribblings later, she referred to his occasional banishment from the main house during alcoholic bouts, presenting him as a relatively constant but stigmatized fixture. As a sometime resident, he would have had access to her room to inscribe the diary upon his desperate departure. Other observations placed the bulk of writings during the warmer months, suggesting a summer retreat for one or both. Their identities simply had to be hidden within the pages between the two covers. I flipped back and forth.

None of the references appeared to have anything to do with the Danburg specifically, and then I realized the problem was that the Danburg itself, while gorgeous and massive, was no more special than any other glorious antebellum beast in the region. Situated on the cusp of Sherman's anger and military agility, the uncharacteristic generosity of Sherman and his geographically selective unlit candles did little more than confuse. For every plantation that had been decimated, another five had been untouched. There were many structures fitting the same representation displayed within the diary and it became impossible to decipher the exact location without name or context to act as guide rail. While we had local reference to the Danburg as fire victim, we were still lacking personal accounts of the Danburg's destruction in 1864. If the diary was tied to that century, I was at a complete loss. If it were this century, there was still hope.

Obsessed with the identity of the diary's author, I was unable to separate myself from its mystery even in my sleep. What had the clock been trying to tell me under the glow of the moon that I had missed in the glare of the sun? Even more importantly, could any part or parcel of the dream hold any truth? I was beginning to sound to myself like a broken record. Clearly the enigmatic diary had been placed inside the clock as a way to hide it from eyes hell-bent on seeking it out, but why would you hide something so well when you needed it to be discovered as evidence? And further, if its value was so great, why had it been left in the custody of a child youthful enough to find fascination with the thought of a man in the moon?

It made no sense. None of it! What sort of beast described such horrors? I wanted to scream at the inconsistencies! Had the author counted on the confusion? Or was I missing the point? The bottom line was that this man had counted on the maiden to pass on the message to someone who would be able to comprehend its shorthand better than I. Obviously the relay had not occurred, and so my only line of attack was to go back to the intended recipient: the girl.

I looked up to find Connie still deep in conversation and the one minute finger stretched its way into five fingers, which meant at least another fifteen. I returned my attention to the diary, grateful for the extra time to make some notes. Having established her role as courier, I could then move forward. When and to whom had the diary been directed beyond her? Assuming she was still a minor when the message was written, her influential contacts in the rural area would have been relatively few. So where would she have directed such contents? Someone within the household or her immediate circle?

With no name mentioned, other than this Mooresford character, who cold not be traced to a branch of the family tree, and the author's inventive signature of the man in the moon, I was left with little to go on.

Once again I was reduced to chasing shadows in the dark.

Chapter Twenty-four

Connie's five minutes appeared to be up for renewal. Slightly annoyed, I hopped out of the truck with the diary inside its plastic case and made my way for the door to rush things a bit. I had a ton of errands to complete and while I had relished the extra time to read, the day was not getting any cooler and I was no closer to solving anything. I decided I would share my maiden with Connie in the hope Connie might see something my eyes had missed.

The door chimed and she smiled while she continued to discuss the pros and con's of a crinoline slip with a bridal client and motioned me towards the kitchenette to have a cup of coffee.

Grabbing one of the mismatched mugs off the counter, my attention returned to the maiden. Who was this little girl who haunted my dreams? Frustrated, I tried to clear my mind. Connie's eyes rolled to the back of her head as she ran an imaginary knife under her throat and I knew I was in for at least another five minutes more of waiting.

I turned her portable television on for diversion and then reached for the generic brand of instant coffee in the cabinet. The local small town grocer carried only two kinds: somewhat fresh and somewhat stale. As I reached for the jar, I decided it was choice that messed with your head, not consequence. The dial was set on TCM. The Turner Classics always made me feel better, so I fired up the volume on the remote. It was comforting…always the same shades of gray. Always the same faces, the same shoes. Real men wore fedoras and the women, flowers, a ribbon and a mischievous smile. You bought your heartache with a ticket and your release with a song and a dance. If only the price were so easily paid for my troubles. I tried to forget about the dream and concentrate on the day's agenda.

An old Shirley Temple movie was playing, so I watched while I waited for the microwave to deliver my steaming sanity in a cup and then suddenly, there she was—this dainty little thing with a ribbon and a smile and a piece of paper in her hand… talking about her knight and her charger! Something about what she was saying was familiar… her knight, her charger and her marker! I thought of the Danburg girl of my dream… In some ways she resembled the curly headed blonde tap dancing her way across the screen. My dream girl had been trying to tell me something about the clock. This child was trying to tell me something too. I listened to the child star speak her lines and became inspired.

Something about '…her knight, her charger and her marker"

"A marker, huh?" I whispered into my cup and the steam curled and rippled at the introduction of my breath. Fascinated I continued to conjecture. "A marker could also mean a headstone, couldn't it?"

There was no one in the room to answer, but the confirmation came back just as loud as if there had been. A marker could be a headstone and Danburg was full of them. I swallowed hard. The coffee was still too hot and I burnt my tongue, but the epiphany was worth it.

There simply had to be more information imbedded in the diary. I kissed the screen and brought the plastic case over to the small kitchen table. Thanks to Ted Turner I decided to take another look at the entries and sift for more clues. Equally frustrated, Connie was now wrapping the cord around her neck in a mock suicide attempt and it made me laugh. Constance McCann would not die of anything but old age and we both knew it! Terminally polite, she would die of nothing shy of good manners! I let her off the hook. I mouthed I would wait patiently and finish my coffee so she could finish her business and sat down to read another page or two.

...The two adjacent bedrooms were furnished with mahogany Victorian high-backed beds, heavy chests of drawers, and marble-topped side chests. The bed in my room displayed a crotch-mahogany mirror image on the head and footboard. Porcelain pitchers with faint Blue Willow design nested in matching washing bowls and soap dishes, shaving cups and glasses adjacent. Embroidered linens were set symmetrically on towel racks to complete the ensemble, but I never dared to use them. The bedrooms had a northern exposure which amplified the chill in winter, and their fireplaces stood vacant each summer. I could dance barefoot easily. A few pictures hung listlessly from the walls, and even in these bedrooms, one felt a keen sense of abandonment as if the whole house shared a loss of enthusiasm for life.

One of the rooms on the south side was clearly forsaken and served as a storeroom. The floor presented a disordered array of oil lamps and assorted discards of the household. That room functioned as a makeshift bedroom during the episodic visits of the object my fascination. Ringed by parts of broken furniture and dusty boxes of books, he fed his rapacious reading habit and yearning for rehabilitation. He visited the main house only when he was sober, since his stepfather demanded such conditions for bed and board.

It was a double-edged sword. Drunk and banished, he would lie beneath my window and coo like a wounded dove and we could talk till morning. Sober, he was allowed to enter the house, but our visits were confined to the attic and limited in length. There we were left dangerously alone, reveling in our collective affinity for literature and art and each other.

The two bedrooms were proximate, but not constant. Often there were references to other portions of the upstairs and her observations seemed to change as often as the seasons. There was an obvious age difference between my maiden girl and the alcoholic object of her obsession. I gauged the spread as a minimum of six years and did not rule out a disparity of up to twenty!

With deep set eyes and dark hair he does resemble Abel from W. H. Hudson's Green Mansions. *Abel's description is far more apt than that of Rima, my stand in. I never see myself in such a light, but when*

I tightly close my eyes and repeat Abel's words, I can soothe the sense of separation from his side—

"...in what real or fictional world will we find a sister to Rima?...a dream, a wish, a nature goddess, a singular elfish hummingbird, a disembodied passion...larger than life, and more real than truth."

Oh... I pray he sees me just the same in his world. Good night then Dear Diary...

Thus far the only concrete clue was their mutual fascination with literature, specifically the novel *Green Mansions* and one of the Greek tragedies by Aeschylus, *The Oresteia*. The Greek tragedies had been in circulation thousands of years ago, and *Green Mansions* had been in circulation since 1904. To have reached the attic library of a rural derelict, I presumed a ten year gap. If he'd had the book from 1914 on, he'd probably be dead. The probability of his demise had never sunk in before that moment. Adjusting to its likelihood set me back. I felt an unexpected pang for the Danburg maiden's girl's loss. A small tear jerked from my lower lash, surprising me. I was flooded by memories of a funeral that had held both sorrow and relief for me. It was the Stockholm Syndrome effect. I had naively loved and simultaneously hated the man that had abused me and the older I got, the lines kept wavering until it was all just a blur.

Suddenly it became important to find all the masculine cemetery markers in the area with a date of death between 1904 and now. I would start there right after the refrigerator run!

I looked up from the diary and saw Connie reach for the sign on the door and flip it over. She motioned and I pulled the truck around to the front door and lifted the dolly out of the bed. Just like clockwork, Smudge the cat leapt from a front porch rocker and headed up the hill to meet Charlene. I waved and then followed Connie back to the corner of the shop where the fridge sat kitty-cornered into the wall. We waited for Charlene, and then together we got the white beast on the dolly, then hoisted to the back ledge of the truck, sliding it as far as the cab window would allow.

While Charlene tied a rope around and through the handles to prevent the doors from opening in the wind, we chatted casually about the Danburg and the imminent opening. I wanted to share my suspicions about the girl's sexual sacrifice with both of them, but thought better, since I had abused their friendships enough through the New Year with my speculations.

We decided to eat at a small diner on the east side of Athens before heading to the theatre. Connie decided to ride with me and then return with Charlene when we were through. Turning left out of Connie's driveway, we headed toward town. At the end of the road I asked if I should turn left or right at the upcoming stop sign.

Silently going over lines, Connie never raised her head from the script. "Go until the road dead ends and turn right onto Moores Ford."

Startled, I tapped the brakes, and the truck jerked, sending the fridge forward into the cab window with a bang. Connie glowered at me over her script. I had never thought of the name in the diary as reference to a place. I had always assumed it to be someone's name. Was Mooresford then perhaps not meant to be one word, but two words? Could the author have merely run them together in ignorance or haste?

"What was the name of the road I turn on again?"

"Moores Ford. If you turn left it will take you over the bridge, but that's the long way around. If you turn right it will take you out past the University's farm research centers and back to the highway...highway 53 I think." I paused in the middle of the road fifty feet from the stop sign. She raised her head and glared at me. "What are you waiting for?"

"Fate, I think..." I said, staring straight ahead. "It's just ... this is the second time that name has come up today and it caught me off guard, that's all." I hesitated to hit the blinker, not wanting to commit to turning yet. I tried to remember what the entry had said about muddy banks... "Is there a stream or something there?"

"The Apalachee River. It's actually quite famous in this area for a lynching that took place there. They have the re-enactment coming up in a couple of weeks." She said matter of factly. I blanched.

"I know… I know" she continued, unaware of my facial expression. "Seems a bit morose to do such a thing every year, doesn't it? But they're like elephants, these Southerners! They have memories longer than an elephant's eyelashes for this kind of shit… why?" she asked and finally brought her head out of her script.

"I… I was just thinking…" I managed weakly.

Thank God Southerners had long memories, as mine was beginning to fail me! Flustered I tried to recall any facts that could corroborate what I was about to see to the diary. If southerner's had such long memories, how come the Danburg folk had proven to have only short and extremely selective ones? I tried to recall whether there had been a name attached to the body of water referenced in the diary, but couldn't remember. The diary talked about a bridge, but a lynching implied ropes, whereas the diary entry mentioned a silo and gunshot holes in the body. I hit the blinker to turn right and sighed.

The clicking of the blinker echoed in my ears like the ticking of the Danburg clock. There was something in the cadence that said not to turn just yet. The truck rolled forward slowly, but I could not bring myself to breach the main intersection. Cataleptically I watched the hood eat up tiny segments of the faded white line on the asphalt beneath us as I waited for divine intercession. If only she would speak to me, I would know what to do. I placed my hand on the box near my side and said a small prayer.

Each blister of tar that covered the cracks and crevices of the heated road hissed as the tires crawled forward. The squeezing and sighing air beneath the tires began to sound like a message. *Hss…tn… hiss… ten… lss…tn… liss…ten…listen…listen!*

Suddenly I sensed it as his voice speaking from beyond the diary, and I picked up speed. The truck hood began to eat up several more inches at a time as the tires spun biting faster into just as many below. The bubbles in the tar began to pop in measure. *Liss…ten… liss…ten…*

He was trying to reach beyond the grave. *Liss… ten… liss… ten… listen…*

"We'll never get there by noon inching our way... I'll die of old age before lunch at this rate! Let's go." Connie said as she flipped another page of the script and closed her eyes to go over them in her head.

It was all I could do not to stop. Hadn't he used similar words?

'Death by inches, my darling...' Wasn't that what he had said? Wasn't that what I was doing? I was inches away from where death had reigned supreme. He had written that to her... trying to warn her. I knew his original intent had been meant to be metaphorical, but I could feel my heart pulsing violently inside the walls of my chest as the truck jerked forward. Had he also been trying to caution her about what he may have seen?

I could barely keep my hands from shaking on the steering wheel. Was this what he meant— this loss of confidence and the erosion of my ability to follow my own lead? The Danburg was more than ninety miles away. There was no way it made sense to tie the house and the bridge together. Which to follow? Gut instinct or rational thought? I looked in the rear view mirror and saw what listening to my head had produced. Perhaps if I had listened to my gut and not my head thirty three years ago, I might have been able to protect myself. It was my head that had betrayed me, telling me I could trust someone because he was family.

What if her Abel of *Green Mansions* had been here that day? It was possible. She had mentioned waiting for him to *return* for their picnic. What if this was where he was that day? Ninety miles away in the middle of a situation he had not bargained for? I had been so close for a moment to reaching her that it was as if we had brushed each other's faces.

I saw a car approaching in the bend and held tight to the stop sign pondering what to do. The word lynching had left me upended. All the speculation was making me dizzy.

"You okay?" Connie inquired.

I tried to answer with a lilt in my voice to distract her from digging further. "Sort of... just thinking about your history lesson for a second, that's all. I'll let this car go by and then we can be on our way. I have so much to do... maybe we can just drop the fridge and then I can head back. The private viewing isn't far from now and I'm not really ready."

"Well...okay. If that's what you need to do. I'll just catch a ride back with Charlene. She won't mind. We can skip the diner but...Sure you don't want to grab a bite at a drive- thru or something on the way then? You look pale."

"I'm alright. I just had a mental picture of your local attraction and I've lost my appetite... that's all. I'll eat later."

The words from the diary ran like wildfire through my mind. If Mooresford had not been a person but a place, an event described by my mysterious author ...God only knew what he had been privy to.

"You know," Connie continued, waiting for me to commit to a destination, "you really should check it out sometime, you being such a history buff. It's pretty compelling. They called it a lynching, but the reality was," she turned the page in her script, "those folks were executed in broad daylight! Usually you would expect that kind of butchery to take place under the cover of nightfall... but not this time. That's what makes it so outrageous. And to top it off, no one ever came forward to tell the truth. At least no one that could be corroborated. I think one fella tried in the 1960s, but nobody could substantiate his story. It's a real tragedy...you should Google it."

My stomach crawled up into my throat. I had never told her about the auxiliary entries, just the girl's narrative. "What year did this happen?" Thinking about *Green Mansions* and the girl's entries, could she have been in her mid to late teens at that entry sequence?

"Sometime in the forties. Wait... it was an election year. 1942? No...1946, I think. Why?"

I tried to do the math in my head. If it had been 1946, my Danburg girl would be in the neighborhood of seventy-some-odd years old and possibly still alive. Random information flooded my head. It happened in daylight...not moonlight...bullets holes in the body at the silo, not rope burns... Mooresford a place not a name...1946... the same year as the Danburg fire! The same year as the heated gubernatorial election that had rocked the state!

Could my secondary author have been participant, witness or both to such a heinous act? My head was swimming with possible scenarios as I changed directions towards the bridge. Connie put down her script, raised an eyebrow at the switch in navigation and asked, "Now where are we going? I thought you said you had to get back to the Danburg," I handed her the plastic coffin with the diary tucked neatly inside.

"I do, and I'll get there. I'm heading back by way of Moores Ford Bridge and if my suspicions are right, we're about to enter it through the gates of Hell!"

I made the left turn into the bend and kept my eyes forward. The luxury of turning back had long since expired. I was on my way and hopefully the dark-haired author was waiting on me.

Chapter Twenty-five

Small houses and dirt yards hugged the edge of the road. Sensing my desperation, Connie remained quiet till I heard the lid of the plastic box burp and then a small sigh escaped both their lips.

"This is it, isn't it...the diary of Danburg? This is your little girl? The one you worry about all the time. She's in here isn't she?" she asked and touched the binding with reverence. With the delicate hands of a seamstress she lifted the treasure and placed it squarely in one hand and looked at me with care I knew to be sincere. Connie had known me so long the shorthand of my eyes gave me away. This could have been her girl... my girl, if I had been healthy enough to have her. I smiled weakly. Watching her fondle the leather binding led me to realize how passionate about the Danburg maiden girl I had become. My inner reaction astounded me. Not jealousy as if someone was playing with a favorite toy, but something altogether different. I feared that someone would rush to judge her words and pass sentence upon her without understanding who she was. From the beginning of her journey, I had made terrible mistakes I now feared others would make. All those ridiculous assumptions and accusations that biased my compassion had been based upon my own shortcomings and trials.

Connie eased open the mangled cover and I watched as a small tear came to her eye. Connie had a little girl, Emily, who was just approaching the age of eleven. In some fashion I had made the Danburg maiden girl as real in my world as her own daughter was in hers. I bit back the urge to prologue and left her to discover the girl on her own, returning my attention to the road.

It was amazing that at such a crucial moment the scenery on either side of me seemed seedy and unimportant. How could ordinary chain link fence be present as margin when I was about to find my link to her through something as horrid as what Connie had described?

Two miles later I slowed to a crawl. Connie pointed out the large concrete barriers that lined the sides of the bridge and motioned to a wide shoulder at the other end. I drove across the bridge as though it might break under the weight of our collective angst and felt a pang of disappointment at its pedestrian appearance. The bridge barriers had been washed in shades of gray and commercial green to cover graffiti. The only symbol of the significance of the site was the bronze marker just beyond the rutted shoulder of the highway. I rolled past the sign and pulled over to the side. Connie nodded and I got out of the truck and walked back the ten or so feet to read the marker, bronze with gold lettering. I tried to piece together the tragedy from its content.

"2.4 MILES EAST, AT MOORES FORD BRIDGE ON THE APALACHEE RIVER, FOUR AFRICAN AMERICANS—GEORGE AND MAY MURAY DORSEY AND ROGER AND DOROTHY MALCOMB (REPORTEDLY SEVEN MONTHS PREGNANT)—WERE BRUTALLY BEATEN AND SHOT BY AN UNMASKED MOB ON THE AFTERNOON OF JULY 25, 1946. THE LYNCHING FOLLOWED AN ARGUMENT BETWEEN ROGER MALCOMB AND A WHITE FARMER. THESE UNSOLVED MURDERS PLAYED A CRUCIAL ROLE IN PRESIDENT TRUMAN'S COMMITMENT TO THE CIVIL RIGHTS MOVEMENT. IN 1998, A BIRACIAL MEMORIAL SERVICE HONORING THE VICTIMS WAS HELD AT MOORES FORD BRIDGE.

ERECTED BY THE GEORGIA HISTORICAL SOCIETY AND THE MOORES FORD MEMORIAL COMMITTEE, INC."

I gasped. Is this what my Danburg diary author had witnessed? Four people had died and for what? I knew the sign was just an abbreviated imprint of the horror that had actually taken place, but for the life of me I could not understand what infraction would require such aggressive and vile acts. I thought of the secondary author and pondered what monumental courage it must have taken to describe what he must have seen. How could I be certain this is what he meant when he said Mooresford lay riddled with guilt and buckshot? Cautiously I eyed the sign.

I looked back at the truck and saw Connie's head crooked in concentration. The girl had made her introduction, and seeing my friend lost in discovery, I decided to continue with my own and walk the edge of the bridge. Shrubbery clogged the river banks with every shade of green imaginable. What sunlight could filter through danced amongst the rocks anchored in the thin water below. In another setting this play of light would have proven poetic, but this was not another setting and the echo of what had happened here reverberated inside my head. The slight current produced eddies among the rocks; I was queasy watching the whirling movement and grabbed at the concrete barrier to keep my equilibrium.

A pregnant woman had died here. Small birds lamented overhead and I bent in empathy with a sorrow of my own. Dear God in heaven, what had my girl's obsession seen and what possible reason could he have had to have been here? To partake in such a ritual slaughter as this was inconceivable. Was this the work of the KKK? I searched the barren patches that led down to the river's edge. Had he traveled this same path? I stepped off the asphalt and felt the instability of the ground beneath me, both physically and metaphorically.

It wasn't enough just to be where it had happened. If he had seen all that had taken place, then I needed to see through his eyes. I went around the back side of the concrete margin carefully and started down the scarp towards the water. The earth crumbled slightly under my steps and I slid a few inches and caught myself on a low hanging vine. The image of a pregnant woman making this same journey under duress was a whiplash I was unprepared to sustain. I let go of the vine and lurched forward awkwardly. Stumbling, I stopped shy of wetting my shoes and caught my breath.

Suddenly I felt him all around me. On the shore... hiding in the briars, crouching in horror. His voice whispered through the trees, telling me he had not wished to be party to such a crime and yet had not been able to extract himself for fear of suffering the same fate. And I was there too, not wanting to hear the screams that must have ricocheted inside the hollows just beyond the edge of the wood. I slipped on a stone. The tip of my shoe thrust a clod of red clay into the swirling water. I tried to catch my balance, slipped again and the clay began to collapse and liquefy. Bright tendrils of red elongated away from my footprint and streaked into the oncoming current. I watched as the river itself seemed to bleed anew with the memory of what had happened upon its shores.

Just then Connie honked the horn and I screamed. Moores Ford would have to wait—I had a refrigerator to deliver.

Chapter Twenty-six

During the entire drive back to the Danburg I could feel goose bumps as they mated, multiplied and gave birth to several million goslings which continued to the parade up and down my spine each time I thought about the bridge. I had been so anxious to verify the girl's Abel as one of the Moores Ford witnesses that I damn near ripped the plastic box containing her diary out of Connie's hand. I explained I needed to finish some research on it before the showing. I think she knew deep down Moores Ford had affected me in a way even I could not explain, and so she let the slight go without reprimand.

When I returned the groundskeeper had finished his work and the place looked magnificent. The freshly painted front porch glistened in the sun and a breeze set leaves sailing from the magnolia. Shaped like gilded plates, they slid across the threshold in artistic patterns as if by ethereal effect. I climbed the steps, and the worn spots whispered of other shoes and their moonlit search for entry. Inserting my key into the door, the clock chimed in salutation as the tumblers clicked into place. Another golden leaf bumped into the window to my right and I reached down to pick it up. I noticed one of the hinges had been partially un-pegged during the painting process and made a mental note to re-peg it. The jib windows that graced the facade were one of the Danburg's finest attributes. Opened from floor to ceiling, they allowed ventilation when summer stalled in her retreat from the gracious lawns. The maiden had spoken often of how they were frequently left open to circulate the night air on the lower level, and the windows in the widows walk opened to circulate on the upstairs level.

As I entered, the door creaked loudly even on its recently oiled hinges and the clock continued its revelry. I rounded the corner into the front parlor and thought about the night the diary had seen its last entry. I suspended the peg above the slotted hinge and felt certain this was my mystery man's entry point. The rear of the house would have presented too much distance and too many obstacles. I entered the hall and thought about a man desperate to behold something normal in the throes of his terror, training his eyes on a small lamp steps from where her diary rested upon a bedside stand.

To breach the main entrance while intoxicated with booze and fear would have been brash. Her Abel would have opted for a less obvious entry point to reach her side. I looked up the stairway and suddenly felt the need to trace his steps. He would have known which boards would keep their silence. I worked my way up, noting that numbers three, four, seven, and seventeen held soft spots in the centers, but their outside edges held firm and kept my passage private.

When I reached the first landing I stood at the foot of a mirror that could reflect an entire family history at a glance and imagined the woman child as she danced for herself half naked in the moonlight. Oh how I envied her daring and self love, wishing in my heart that I could find her still there at the end of the hall waiting to teach me how to breathe again. Stripped of guilt and shame, could I have pranced so nimbly through my youthful devastation? I wiped a tear from my cheek.

The house was empty but for me and the echo of her wisdom. I brushed a stray piece of graying hair from my brow and smiled at the woman reflected before me, struggling to find her inner smile. If I could just forget for one moment what had been and float on gossamer wings as she had shown me, I could survive my own destruction. I held my breath, closed my eyes and did a small pirouette in front of the mirror. Slowly and laboriously at first I moved across the floor and then bravely committed to a second revolution... a third... and then another and another until

I no longer counted. I spun away years of doubt and self-efface-
ment. Forty nine… thirty six… twenty three… seventeen… thirteen… and then and finally forgave myself for not being able to
protect the child I had been.

With calm stride I mounted the remaining stairs and came
face to face with the attic door. I remembered the woman with
the red hat, her steady gait across the yard and the intensity of her
gaze in the direction of the attic eave that lay just beyond that
door…

*Finished with my chores, I have flopped on my bed to rest. The days
are growing longer and so the night shorter and I miss the company of
his sighs beneath my window at night. I have not heard from him the
last two evenings and cannot think of what has removed him from
pacing the path below my sill. No doubt he has suffered further punishment for some unforeseen crime and now I am without both consolation and entertainment. How much longer shall I be forced to
continue my charade of innocence? I should return to fetch the linens
from the line and yet I know that once I do, I shall be thrust back into
the sameness of the day and the hours will drag.*

*…Everyone had gone to town to greet the new Preacher, his wife
and family. I feigned a headache. My heart was suddenly lifted when
familiar footsteps thundered up the stairs. He tapped on the bedroom
door and that familiar ripple pulsed down below. He whispered that
today we might undertake the long promised visit to the third floor
again.*

*The entrance to the stairs held such intrigue that I was able to pass
the nearby coffin closet without the usual sense of suspended terror. I
watched as he disengaged the wooden latch of the attic door and led the
way upstairs, forcing his shadow forward.*

*The pine stairs and bordering walls were smooth to the touch and
invited calm. Seldom used, the passageway preserved the fresh pine smell
of the wood. At the top of the stairs, he turned and smiled…here was
his real home— his refuge from those who sat in constant judgment of
him…*

When I lifted the latch the smell of pine wafted toward me. I saw the space with a newfound affection. This had been her sanctuary with him and I felt her arms wrap around me as I launched my fragile sense of security up the stairs. They were on equal footing here. Inebriated, he was denied access, both to the house and to her. Here, sober and unchaperoned, they could display their affections for one another and share the written word without fear of reprisal. This was their domain and I entered with respect.

No longer frightened of the shadows in either of our pasts, I went from step to step with confidence and breathed in the pungent smell of molded, leather-bound books and weathered wood. The rail was well worn and I rubbed it with affection knowing that where my fingers touched, she too had touched. We were separate and yet we were as one in our ascension. When I reached the top step I bent forward to exercise the single bulb that hummed and glowed before it took full light.

To the left rows and rows of shelves bowed under volumes of law books. Between stacks of worn journals and periodicals, novels of various genres were shelved alphabetically. The central rafters bit into the sky, but dipped at the gables where this shelf stood and so I bent in submission. I ran a finger down the spine of each book and whispered its title in anticipation until I came upon a breach in the order between ..."Grea" and "H"...

The opening caught me off guard. *Green Mansions* was missing and it didn't take long before many of its most cherished verses began to swim in my head! I understood my maiden's affinity for Hudson's writing. His verbiage flowed with such exquisite emotion as was as cerebrally seductive as the Bronte sisters. That was one of the passions we shared; a love of the written language. Yet it wasn't just enough for them to engage emotionally— they were cemented by more than just superficial attraction. They had the overwhelming desire to consume one another mind, body and soul. Theirs was another realm where souls meshed on every level. They saw the beauty of who they were both separate and together. They were boundless in their appreciation of each other's potential and it made me cry that I lacked such a connection to another human being within my own life.

I dug in my memory. There had been one entry much longer than the rest that encapsulated such a struggle. Its raw emotion scraped at my heart.

"...with months between our meetings, I deliberately began to explore the spiritual dimension to our relationship. Religious traditions since early childhood coached me in practice on the mechanics of life— such teachings that we are born into this world with sin upon our souls. That we must do good in order to die with forgiveness and a clean heart—but no longer is that enough to get me to the other side of my longing.

My Uncle belittles and berates you. He calls you vile words I cannot repeat and I grow sick of his hypocrisy. How would you find such supplies so abundant if left to your own devices? You have so little money independent of his hand outs. Your mother has nothing beyond the pitiful parceled out pennies he awards her... Your mind is much too vast to be content with mundane chores and you have nary spent a week in consistent employment to garner such a bankroll as would be necessary to sustain such a costly vice. Besides, his secret is not sacred. I know where he hides his precious hooch. I have watched from the windows of the upper floor at dusk as he sways from stall to stall within his own alcoholic haze.

While my cousins sleep and dream of family inheritances I am forced to listen to the guttural offenses he slathers his frightened wife with each night before the bed coils screech with her violation. I cover my ears and pray for her release. Their room is beneath my own and there are times I wish I could reach through the cracks and cradle my weeping aunt as she wastes herself in such inebriated afterglow... but she is lost to her own regrets and I cannot save her from herself. I hate what liquor has done to them.

Look into their mirror and see something different for yourself. I beg of you!

You my darling even in your exile, remain still a poisoned prize. Each time you are banished to the shed I pray for your release from what holds you there. I hear my older cousin quote bible verse after bible verse outside its tiny door and it makes me laugh.

'Do not cast pearls before swine' she reminds herself under her breath even as she throws her virginity at your muddied feet and begs

the intrusion with her eyes each time you return from the fields. I am at great loss as to the equilibrium of her rationalizations and yet when I myself look into your eyes... I understand the absolute conviction of her need. You should however not toy with such dangerous affections, even for appearances sake. I fear she is less than stable and may do you great harm if she finds you less than sincere. She has compromised her religious moorings for you and there will be no safe harbor for you if she decides to set sail to her anger.

I know you do not always support the same pillars of faith as she, but you do acknowledge a greater path than the one you are currently on and that gives me hope for your salvation. Like you I often flounder between the rights and the wrongs of my heart. My faith tells me how to come and go in life, but not what to do about all the in between times. The times filled with the needing and the wanting of things. How to govern myself when the necessity to be held is stronger than the strength to deny?

I look at the people in this house and how they cower from life and wallow in bitterness and regret. Is this the only reward for such stringent stewardship? Is this what piety and self denial crown you with at the end of your days? I look at my aunt and know she is dead inside... there is no woman left within her frame, only the duty bound plow horse meant to suffer the gee and haws of her marital harness. I pray I am meant for more... and plead that you see you are too.

We are so different you and I ...and yet we are the same.

Not a member of this house, or my schooling ever taught me how to be who I am...or how to love someone better than my own heart may guide. To my diary I now declare that without walls or window I have built my house inside your eyes and I am forever at home in your arms.

The reflection by Abel as he struggles with the death of Rima leaves me without guardrail and tearfully I struggle to memorize the passage hoping to one day tell you as artfully how I feel —

'You are you and I am I – why is it?' – the question asked when our souls were near together, like two raindrops side by side, drawing irresistibly nearer, even nearer: for now they had touched and were not two, but one inseparable drop, crystallized beyond change, not to be disintegrated by time, nor shattered by death's blow, nor resolved by any alchemy.'

I can withstand anything, but your distance. Where are you? I should die from loneliness... should you be gone forever."

I traced a heart in the dust between two neighboring manuscripts and the intrusion sent rebel specks to flight in the sunlight. This was her safe harbor, her vantage point...she had been right here. I moved around the furthest end of the shelf and stood in front of the window. At this height she could survey the better part of the south lawn all the way out to...

The cremation pit lay in the distance and I averted my eyes, thinking of a line from Green Mansions she had quoted in the diary:

Now it was accomplished; the sacred ashes brought so far, with such infinite labor, through so many and such great perils, were safe and would mix with mine at last.

Had she been trying to tell me something? There below to the right was the small patch of grass that surrounded the single rose the visitor had left behind. From my elevated view, I could see the angular outline of what had been a foundation for a small building... the shed!

According to the lithograph the small building to the south side was what was commonly referred to as the ironing and weaving shed. It was a small ten by twelve foot structure that boasted a single chimney within a single room. I had seen one at another plantation during my research and its primitive interior had no window, merely a humble hearth with scissor-shaped andirons and a scrubbed floor. This was the shed of the diary—his oasis and the destination of her secret desires.

Moores Ford had changed everything for me. If in fact my Danburg maiden had been victim even collaterally to such a tragic event, I needed to know. The night had ended and so had the entries. If I was ever going to find the answers, I would have to go back to Moores Ford Bridge and trace the events that brought him to her bedside and provoked his entry. How had he arrived at Moores Ford Bridge and what circumstance held him there until he could come safely to her side? Even with the new insights about Moores Ford Bridge, I did not know how much more I would glean from the entries made by our mysterious Abel. If I could just find his name...

My senses replenished, I climbed back into the book, discovering that our real life bond had progressed far beyond that of the early stages of Abel's and Rima's relationship. I could indeed walk beside, sit beside, and converse with my companion. My fears of his fierce passion have now subsided. I am "... the fiery-hearted little humming bird that flashes into sight, remains suspended motionless for a few seconds before your face, then, quick as lightning, vanishes again."

Re-reading the novel, I find his comparisons of Rima to me exaggerated. In reality my pear shape differs from the exquisite, my halting motions diverge from the graceful, and my plain visage deviates from the divine. Yet I think he sees me better than any vision I afford myself. He transforms the image I see in the mirror to a more confident creature, a companion who can unlock even the most sacred of all doors to his heart. I begin to take pleasure in what gives him pleasure, to see what he sees and exploit what it is he waits patiently on the other side of passion to explore.

In Rima's forest I am released from the confined space of my second floor bedroom. In Rima's form I am liberated from my mediocre existence with its mediocre standards. And with Rima I am freed from my restlessness. Repeating Rima's name becomes my mantra and helps me escape daily banalities. I celebrate the name as I recall the author Hudson's explanation of tribal tradition that "...in these latitudes a person is rarely, perhaps never, called by his or her real name, which is a secret jealously preserved, even from near relations." By rehearsing the name Rima I can emerge into her character and release myself temporarily through the great good gift of imagination. As myself I must remain confined, but as Rima I can be his."

Who was this tender little hummingbird who would willingly forsake her own identity for fictional renown?

I thought about calling the Chenille sisters and grilling them for all they were worth, but they were worthless as sources of information. Whatever the truth was, I would not be retrieving it from them. So I challenged myself to find another avenue of information. The private showing was fast approaching and I had little time to pull together this mystery. It was late in the afternoon and if I hurried I could make it to the cemetery and research headstones before it closed.

* * *

Since it was a small graveyard, I exhausted its resources within an hour. I was heartbroken. There was no marker which fit into the Danburg's scenario. Frustrated, I had started down the hill to my car when a woman pulled up beside me and got out. I mindlessly watched her, thinking she would ascend the hill. Instead she closed the door and made her way across the street to a church parking lot.

Embarrassed but desperate for information, I caught up with her as she started to climb the front step of the church with an armful of linens. I introduced myself. Her smile was genuine and she was quick to provide information. No, the Danburg cemetery was not the only cemetery in town. Two other church yards housed eternal inhabitants as well. Duly educated, I was rounding the corner of the building when she called out to ask if I could use any background information. I gratefully accepted her help, and she walked me from row to row of markers, searching for the dark haired rascal of the Danburg. I mentioned the family and the alcoholic trait of my query and she led me straight to him.

The graveyard sloped away from the church and ended in a barricade of woods. Each family section was dotted with stones of variation and size. Glanced at with squinted eye it resembled the aerial view of a large farm with odd parcels cordoned off to denote separation of different purpose. I smiled at its bucolic simplicity and structure as we navigated its checkerboard layout.

She began my education as though giving a tour, bending every now and then to pluck a wayward weed or wild flower.

"He was the son of a socialite from Atlanta who had married into the Danburg clan."

"Atlanta?" I repeated surprised his roots began so far from his eternal doorstep.

"Yes. Delia had been a Madison of the Atlanta Madison renown and fortune." She said with slight contempt. I clicked through my mental catalog for a connecting reference and came up short.

"Renown for what?" I asked. "I'm afraid I don't recognize the name... should I?"

We passed another plot and I followed as she turned to navigate down another small pathway. "Not from this part of the state. The Madisons were somewhat concentrated to the central portion of the state. They owned a successful dairy company in Atlanta back then. Just on the outskirts of the city...in Decatur, I believe."

"So she was from old money, then." I commented.

"Yes, but that was not her real claim to fame. Her real claim to fame had been that she had publicly disgraced her family! She walked out on an arranged marriage, abandoning another aristocrat for a fling with the garage help's oldest son!"

"Ooooo... I'm betting not a good headliner for the social columns come Monday morning, eh?" and she laughed.

"No... Not a good headline at all. Her parents did their best to keep it under wraps. But it did throw a mighty big kink into their plans. Alignments between the wealthy and influential were still quite common then."

Astounded I replied. "You were serious then about it being an arranged marriage?" The woman nodded and bent to pick up two spikes of Queen Anne's lace that had volunteered themselves amongst the rod iron fencing.

"Arranged marriages in the twentieth century? What year was that?" I asked.

"A later one than you would think plausible" she replied and placed the wayward weeds at the edge of the stone edging for the sexton to gather later.

I bent to help her and plucked another of the lacey weeds, marveling that anyone would find its intricate beauty unwelcome.

"There was many an alliance made for profit and not for passion in those days, I fear" she added. I stared at the flower contemplating her quip. I found its erratically displayed personality more appealing than the perfect symmetry of a rose and noted that the world was full of such irony.

"So who got thrown over for the help?"

"Oh, I was certain you would ask that and darned if I can recall his name just now. I do remember he was a young politician. Had a very promising future in the Democratic Party too... What was his name?" she pondered.

Not wanting her to loose her train of thought I told her she could tell me later and begged her to continue. "Tell me more about Delia."

"Well, like I said... her behavior was a disgrace! The family publicly humiliated. After a few months when she found her new companion could not afford to support her in the manner to which she had become accustomed, she came running back home to mamma and daddy... pregnant!

"With the young man whose grave you're going to show me now?" I baited.

"Yes... our dear little black sheep. He's just a bit further down... away from the family plot."

I looked across the sea of granite and tried to ferret out which stone would be his.

She side stepped another budding fire ant hill and continued.

"After she moved back into her parents' home things settled for a bit. They allowed her sanctuary until a gentleman more suitable to her station could be found. There was no argument this time! Her parents orchestrated the quiet elopement, and offered a small stipend to encourage dedication, but the results remained the same."

"She ran home again?

"Well she tried. The bags never made it off the running board of the truck. Her father patted her head, wished her luck and sent her right back to Danburg and told her to put herself right with her husband and her God. They were tired of the drama. So, trapped in a loveless marriage, she withered, and her son became part of the ransom for her loss of dignity."

"How old was she?"

"She wasn't more than twenty by then I guess, but she aged quickly after that."

"Wow... burnt out on life at twenty. At twenty I was still in school... still hopeful." I muttered.

"Well... things don't always work out the way we plan" she mused and we changed our direction at the end of the row.

"Sorry... one more down. Yes, there it is. Over there..." she pointed. She waltzed me down a third row and over two head-stones stopping in front of a simple but handsome marker that lie partially hidden amongst the knee high grasses. I began to pull the thinned stalks away from the marred granite so I could read. After three more handfuls the face of the pitted stone became visible.

Haydon Edison Fitzgerald
March 13, 1918
August 9, 1946
Beloved son of Delia Evelyn Madison Danburg and Joseph Washington Danburg

Haydon had never taken his stepfather's name or his fanatical approach to religion. It became the cross they both would bear until his early and unheralded demise.

Curious I asked, "Why haven't I ever heard of him before? Eighteen months of working on this reconstruction and their family background and his name was ever mentioned!"

"Doesn't surprise me a bit... he's lucky they consented to give him a decent burial marker at all. They blamed him for the fire of 1946. 'Haydon's Revenge' they called it, you know."

I raised my eyebrows. "No. I certainly did not know. How could I? No one ever brought him up." I chalked it up to another selective memory I would have to research.

"They did their best to erase him after the scandal. It was a terrible turn of events. His mother was broken hearted of course and was unable to identify the body. I believe her husband did so for her. It wasn't a pleasant task. He'd apparently been in the water for quite some time. They found him lying face down in the swamps just outside of town."

"He drown in a swamp?" I gasped. The thought of my maiden's Abel, bloated and unrecognizable, drifting among a sea of grasses made me ill. I took note of the fact she did not confirm a drowning and slowly the rest of her words made contact.

"Haydon's revenge? That's what they called it?"

She nodded as she pulled another set of stray weeds from the side of his marker. "They refused to pay for perpetual care. I try to keep it nice out of respect for Haydon if the weeds have gotten out of hand, but I've been out of town. Despite his rather unruly lifestyle… he'd always been good to Lucy and me." She tugged at the few remaining wisps of grass that embroidered the base and set them to the side.

This was now the second time I had heard the name Lucy, but as the clock was ticking that was not uppermost on my mind. Though many small fires had been mentioned by the family, and the evidence was clear that this was the fire that brought the house down around their ears both literally and financially, I was shocked they had not elaborated on its origin. Since none of the Danburgs attributed the fire to Haydon previously in their conversations with me, I suddenly felt a call on Miss Cattalieu was demanded. She of all of them would crack if I could get her apart from Celine long enough to interrogate her. It started to sprinkle and the tiny woman in skirt and blouse motioned that we should start back up the hill under the threatening skies, but I was glued to Haydon's marker and did not want to rush her reminisces.

"Why would they have called it revenge?" I ran a finger across the pitted brow of granite. A distant rumble of thunder rolled around inside the mouth of a cloudbank like a jawbreaker and the sky finally bit and broke it in two. Lightening flashed and I felt a charge of emotion as I pulled my hand away from the marker. She shot a glance toward the horizon anticipating the next volley of thunder, but allowed me to stall a moment and absorb the current that flowed about us.

"He was quite a character, Haydon. More mischievous than malicious, I think. He was just a reflection of his mother's unhappiness. You see, they never meshed with the rural folk. She never set herself above them mind you…" She bent and pulled another weed growing too close to the stone. "Never above, just apart. As though it would have been pointless to try. That was a sad house, and Haydon, poor child, did his best to fit in, but there was no place for him to fit. There he was with not a friend in the world… his mother that could not forget where she had come from and his stepfather…I'm not sure he had the capability to express any emotion other than anger. Lucy and I did our best, but there was only so much we could do. The child only came twice a year to visit."

"They were members then?" I asked as she started to pull away under the threat of a downpour. I followed as she motioned to head for the steps, twisting the weed stem in her hands.

"Yes, his stepfather was very active. An elder. Very devout, and that drove a wedge between them once Haydon had acquired a nasty habit of drinking when they weren't there to supervise him. Lucille and I found him more than once out behind the pump station with the local rabble. Mostly blacks and whites that never seemed to know what the line was, let alone toes it, if you know what I mean. He liked to run with them for the thrill and the moonshine. It wasn't healthy, but we never thought it would get him killed."

"Killed?" The thought crossed my mind then that her not confirming a drowning perhaps had been intentional.

The thunder cracked overhead and we picked up our pace. I thought about my maiden's entry at the beginning when she wrote about the general store and the distinction between the front and back door clientele. It was there that she referenced the strict religious upbringing of the locals and her cousin's rejection of such.

Remembering how he had enjoyed my curiosity the day before, I pushed toward him the once elegant wooden wheelchair with cane seat and back. Relishing the contact, he imitated his stepfather sipping sweet tea on the front porch, reprimanding him for sipping something other.

Following his playful lead I edged my way around the eaves of the attic to the tattered fainting couch and slunk into its lumpy landscape, striking a seductive pose I had once seen in one of his art books. Taken aback, he sputtered with embarrassment about memories of his paternal grandmother, whose staunch Baptist upbringing did not permit admiration of the human anatomy. She had always said, "Vanity kills."

What little I knew about the tradition surrounding the fainting couch could be capsuled in a few words – none of which ended with a kiss, but hopeful I kept my pose. He paused just for an instant and I saw something run behind his eyes that took the smile from his lips before he pulled me quickly from the chaise and reminded me not to court danger. I could hear the cousins below discussing the upcoming church social and knew he would not raise his voice for fear of attracting their attention.

I stiffened in his arms. The feel of his touch was not the velvet I had anticipated in such a setting, yet it eased as I brushed against his side. As we turned to leave, a cracked hip tub caught the light and for a second blinded me. He caught me just as I was about to fall and our eyes met again. There was no velvet in his touch a second time either, only need, and as his hands reached out a second time with clear destination— I finally understood the sacred necessity of the fainting couch.

A flash of lightening raced across the sky, breaking my reverie, and we made a dash for it. I would ask about the maiden as soon as my guide had finished with Haydon's history. For now I needed to get as much information as possible about him before the storm abated and my docent would be gone. The sky cracked open like a ripe melon as we started to make our way from the back row of the cemetery. We ran awkwardly through the outer edges to the front steps and into the church with the summer tempest on our heels. In my eagerness to arrive I tripped on the mat just outside the door. I swore as I crossed the threshold, and not meaning to be irreverent I bit at my tongue. Introducing herself by way of soggy hand as Cheryl, she smiled politely, inviting me to wait out the storm inside the church with her. Having no intention to do otherwise, I watched as she scurried to the side wall and promptly excused herself to get some towels.

Alone, I turned to assess my surroundings. As a Catholic, I had never been inside a Baptist Church before and was struck by its aged beauty and simple structure. The building had been built and dedicated in 1785 and its doors were huge and swollen with the seasons of many years. Wide woodwork and plastered walls supported the interior roof which climbed to a vaulted peak as high as the trees that lined the outside. I heard her footsteps travel between two rooms. A phone rang deep in the cavern of one of them and the door closed and the conversation became muted. I walked the center aisle and took in the red velvet padded benches that aligned themselves one after another, then followed the same bright hue upward as lightening bounced off the inside of the windows that banked each wall. Tall and narrow, filled with stained glass, they amplified the effect of flashing light in stark contrast to the dark outside.

* * *

While I waited for Cheryl to return, I moved forward to read the very large document framed upon the wall just behind three glorious chairs that resembled thrones. Completely out of sync with the rest of the furniture in the room, they sat on a platform that ran the length of the front walls. Obviously this is where the highest in the hierarchy of the congregation would have sat.

Curious about the proclamation under the title "Church Covenant," I began to read and was amazed at the simple approach to living church members endeavored to apply to their daily lives:

"… We also engage to maintain family and secret devotions; to religiously educate our children; to seek the salvation of our kindred and acquaintances; to walk circumspectly in the world; to be just in our dealings; faithful in our engagements and exemplary in our deportment; to avoid all tattling, backbiting and excessive anger…"

And then the statement that had obviously caused the conflict in the Danburg home on a nightly basis:

"… To abstain from the sale and use of intoxicating drinks as beverages; to be zealous in our efforts to advance the kingdom of our savior…"

Poor Haydon. It was clear from what both Cheryl and the diary had said that the only advancement of the savior's kingdom for Haydon would have had to come with a cover charge! How he must have suffered under such a keen eye and tight rein.

I was getting irritated at the amount of time I had been left to drip in the aisle. Had the information not been so important, I would have braved the rain and lit out for my car on the opposite side of the road to return to the Danburg. Portraits lined the halls and there was one with the name Lucille underneath. I made the connection to my new acquaintance with the phone glued to her ear. Just as I was about to read the portrait dedication, scuffling noises came from behind a door, followed by a large clatter as an older phone dropped and rocked inside its cradle. Agitation showed on Cheryl's face as she entered and I ascribed it to church business and my interruption.

"She says I'm not to talk to you anymore about this." And she handed me a towel with a terse smile.

Brought up short, I took the towel with trepidation, dabbed at my face and then drew it across my bare arms, stalling for an explanation. "Who?" I asked casually.

"She saw you across the street. It's a small town. What did you think?" A smile broke over her face. "She's so touchy about all this. Silly as that is. Everyone knows…"

"Everyone knows what?" I asked in complete confusion.

"They tried to cover it up… said he'd been out on a drunken binge and got tossed in some rural pokey to sleep it off. Came home late that night and accidentally fell asleep with a lighted cigarette. But that didn't explain why he ended up in the swamp, or why the FBI was interested in where he'd been before he ended up there. He had ties… well not him exactly, but through his mother's family. Big money in Atlanta… very influential and even though they disowned her for being so free with herself in her younger years they remained very protective of the family name and their grandson." And she took the towel from me and carried it down the hall, wringing it in her hands.

"The FBI?" I shouted and staggered down the hall after her. "Shit!" She stopped dead in her tracks and cocked an ear. I couldn't believe I had just cursed in a church. "Oh damn! I just said shit, didn't I?" I blurted and wished I cold have just stuffed the towel in my mouth.

She turned on her toes to face me squarely. Silence would probably have been the more prudent thing at this point, but prudence had never been my long suit. Without thinking it through I advertised my own suspicions. "Excuse my... vulgarity. It's just that I was so... so shocked by my epiphany. They thought he had been at Moores Ford Bridge that day... didn't they? That's what the FBI was after. Evidence that he had been there... right?"

The look on her face told me cursing again would have been a much better choice.

Like Connie said... if Southerners' memories were as long as elephant's eyelashes... she had just batted me with forty footers!

* * *

The oak doors clashed behind me. I wasn't certain what had pissed her off more—my cursing in a holy place or my accusation that Haydon had been at Moores Ford Bridge and brought that shame back with him. Either way, I had just screwed myself out of further information about my Danburg maiden. Information that was now more important to me than ever. The bigger question now loomed...who was she to the Danburg family?

The rain had stopped and so too the magic of the storm. I was alone again with just a handful of clues and a fistful of chaos. Whoever the "she" was, she had been influential enough to pre-empt my investigation and I felt like a pawn on a life sized Monopoly Board... 'Do not pass Go. Head back to Jail or pay $200.00.' I pulled out my keys, started to cross the street and then decided to return to the churchyard to look at the marker again; hoping Haydon had something more he wanted to tell me.

The afternoon had flooded my head with information and the dates burned behind my eyes, but I was left with no impression that I could put on paper with confidence. I studied the letters and tried to gauge the depth of the affections that had placed them there. Haydon, beloved of no one in the world save his mother and a small girl who grew to womanhood in his shadow, hoping to be devoured by his passions lay just below the soggy red clay. A woman-child who borrowed a treasured book and kept vigil over his compromised conditions from a second story window of a home that was not her own... my maiden.

I walked the cemetery knowing the minutes were ticking away till the night. Again I would be alone with her, yet no further along in my search for her identity, other than knowing she had traded her heart for the affections of a troubled soul. Maybe that was enough. Maybe that was all I was ever supposed to know about her. And maybe she had only been the vehicle to discovering the truth about Haydon's entries and my past.

I brushed a leaf from his grave, angry at his silence. What the hell was I supposed to do with this information now? I stomped my shoe on the top of the dirt and asked Haydon why, if it was all so God-blessed important to get it recorded... why the hell had he stuffed the damn thing in the stupid clock and then died! What kind of an idiot hides something he needs to be discovered and then dies without telling anyone where he hid it?

Haydon was talking to me and I continued to listen...

I must try. I cannot erase memory of the lips that begged for mercy before me if I cannot replace them with your own. Go from this place as soon as you can and mention not our trysts...

But whom would she have told? One of her earlier entries referenced her parents returning to retrieve her, so the threat of disclosure would not have been immediate with them. It made no sense to go to all that trouble of documenting everything and then not document everything. I looked one row up and saw the multiple stones declaring Danburg territory. Haydon had not even made it into the family lineup, not even in death.

And then it dawned on me—neither had he in life! Separately and combined they had all let him sit the sidelines. Celine...she had made the comments about the clock and the wood being second grade, like second-class citizens. Family heirlooms and family members being buried prematurely! That entire dog and pony show about Cattalieu's mental incapacity was for my benefit. A detour meant to divert me from picking her diatribes apart. Catty knew things... things she had unearthed as a child and Celine was doing everything in her power to rebury them!

The more I thought about things, the more I came to realize it was quite possible Celine had not even known the diary was there when the clock was donated! Catty had counted on Celine's ego superseding her caution. After some of the things Cheryl had told me today I would have banked my paycheck on it. Celine may have not known about the child's diary, but Cattalieu certainly had! She had tried to hint at so much, but I had been numb to the prompting. It was all finally beginning to make some sense.

They didn't mention Haydon because they hadn't needed to, in the same way they had not had to mention her...it wasn't a lie. They had not had to breach their staunch religious upbringing. They had merely had to wait out my ignorance. The maiden was not a Danburg; a relation perhaps, but not a scion of the Danburg family. All along I had been barking up the wrong family tree! He was a Madison, not a Danburg. Celine knew that! Knew I would have been blinded to looking outside the Danburg lineage, because I wouldn't have known I had to.

My maiden must have been related to the non-Madison side of Haydon's family tree, the Fitzgeralds. I now knew I had to discover more about Haydon's biological parents. The Danburgs had drowned this guy's name and reputation in the swamps to service their own and left both him and it for dead. Haydon had been a bad Baptist...a drunk... a letch. His associations questionable and of the wrong color! Haydon had burned down the house with his less than Christian habits. Haydon had had an uncommonly intimate relationship full of sexual innuendos with an underaged female in a house where she lived only part time. The insult of his behavior must have been infuriating to those who tried to convert and control him.

And if my Danburg maiden had spent her evening hours at a darkened windowsill watching and waiting for him to crawl out from beneath the fog of liquor to exchange a loving looks...who else might have been watching and waiting with the same unrealized desires from another darkened windowsill one floor below? Someone who equaled his age and station...someone who spent her time trying to control his darker side as opposed to reveling in it. Someone who watched with envy as a freer, younger soul danced, displaying her naked silhouette in the moonlight for his pleasure. Someone who let the insult of his disregard gnaw away at her interior enough that she would hold even his life in the balance to exact her revenge! The same someone whose bedroom overlooked the other side of the shed where the dark-haired devil lay heavy with drink and drank water from a cup held by another's small hands.

There were only two other young females in the house, both of whom had no blood relation with him them to quell such an attraction. Hell hath no fury like a woman scorned and apparently neither did the Danburg! I wouldn't get Celine to expose more about the Danburg than what she had, but now that I thought about it… she had already said a mouthful!

Chapter Twenty-seven

I returned to the Danburg late that evening. My head was swimming with as many facts and speculations as the twisted Danburg family's DNA. Haydon had spoken from the grave and now it was up to me to put it all together and find the young woman who meant everything to him.

I pulled out the research forms and began to sift through the interviews to decipher if she had been mentioned either by name or by coincidence in the oral histories I had taken. I grabbed a salad and a Diet Coke and sat down to read. Four hours later, I had three pieces of paper that I thought might help me build a bridge to her. There was a woman named Maria who had been a close friend of Celine's in their younger days. Maria admitted that she and Celine she both had had a terrible crush on Haydon. But mostly that his little cousin from Atlanta had been a royal pain in the ass. Several years younger than they, she had the habit of following Haydon doggedly about and questioning him about his books. They laughed at her and joked at the thought that they could have had anything in common. She volunteered that Haydon had always gone out of his way to be kind to her. When it went on far longer than they thought it should have, Celine told her Uncle she thought there was something unfit about the relationship. She suggested the little cousin be kept at bay, which resulted in limiting visits to when Haydon could be stabled at his biological father's hotel to earn a small stipend during the summers.

I was now able to discern that the child had come from Atlanta, and that explained the seasonal occurrence of the entries. Now, the big challenge was to find out what the name of this hotel was and where it might have been. I went to my laptop, brought up the internet and Googled "Fitzgerald + hotel + 1946" and got nothing for my troubles. I tried again. "Fitzgerald + hotel." Only thirty-seven listings popped up, but that was thirty-seven more than I had had ten minutes earlier. After going through nine, I hit pay dirt!

"The Fitzgerald Hotel is located in lovely downtown Washington, Georgia, between Athens and Augusta. The hotel is also convenient to historic Madison. This historic hotel allows guests to experience luxurious accommodations reminiscent of another era, while providing all the modern amenities our guests have come to expect. The Fitzgerald Hotel features ..."

The rest was just marketing, but the location made perfect sense. Washington was a progressive small town on the highway between Athens and Danburg. That go-between location would have allowed Haydon to be close enough to his mother, but far away enough for his stepfather to tolerate. It also would explain how he could survive away from home without earning enough for bed and board of his own.

I read the rest about the hotel and its current owners, but there was nothing relevant to my search. What I needed was history about the owners and whatever relatives might have been involved in the ownership of the Fitzgerald. I traced a finger around the rim of the turreted corner room displayed on my screen and wondered how many women had stood at those windows and watched the shuffle of life below. Had my maiden been there and done so? It was more than possible if Haydon's family had been among the owners of the place.

I visited the rest of the Fitzgeralds' home page. The photo boasted a marvelous turn of the century building painted in my favorite shade of green with copper trim and a turret that graced the south end of the structure. In my appreciation of its architecture and ambience, I almost forget why it was I needed to go there. It was no more than thirty minutes from the Danburg. I pulled up the e-mail form, fired off a reservation request for the following night, and asked for the name of a local historian who might have the background history of the hotel. I could do the private showing, weather the steel magnolias and get to the Fitzgerald before sunset. I clicked away at my laptop, receiving a scripted "Thank you" message for my reservation, along with a reminder to check in before 6:00 PM and an invitation from the concierge, who was delighted to expound on the Fitzgerald's colorful history to me. Happy to be finally on the right track, I decided to move my attentions back to a Google search for Moores Ford to discover what else had gone wrong that day in 1946.

The phone rang, interrupting my mission. Seeing Connie's number, I wanted to shove it in the drawer. I was not up to idle talk, but considering how rude I had been to her earlier in the day, I felt guilty and answered with a weak hello. Connie asked if I'd seen the local paper. Having not read a local paper in weeks, I confessed to having been covered up with work. I continued to search online. She advised me to get out for a walk, breathe some fresh air, and buy a copy of the *Athens Banner-Herald*. I decided to get her off the phone by lying. I said ok. I'd just grab a cup of coffee, since I surmised it was going to be a long night at the laptop. Certain that my clipped statements would put the chatter to rest and she would let me get back to the web; I waited for her to sign off.

As the Moores Ford site popped up, she recommended that I drink my coffee with a shot of whiskey! Distracted, I asked why, and she told me I should sit down if I wasn't already. "There is a huge article in the paper today about Moores Ford Bridge. They think the 1946 race for governor between Eugene Talmage and Joe Carmichael may have been somehow involved in what happened there. You gotta see this, kiddo. It'll blow your mind!"

"1946? Politics? This was about a political election?" I held the phone at bay and tried to remember a line from the diary—"...politics made for strange bedfellows and desperation made them even stranger..."—and decided to forego the coffee and go straight for the whisky. I hung up the phone, grabbed my purse and headed out the door. Surely Washington was forward enough to have a package store!

At this point I really needed to unearth information about the hotel and the girl. A field trip was now definitely in order for the following day. I understood immediately why it had been a good thing I could not put it all together before the private showing. This was big. Somewhere deep inside I had held suspicions this thing that hung over the Danburg was huge... I hadn't realized just how huge till Connie called.

I found the whiskey and the article. The Associated Press had plastered it everywhere. The papers, the internet... all airing the filthy laundry of the rural south. I devoured each word. The very thought that the impetus for the killings could be this degraded, made me sick. I read every article I could. The shadows this event cast were longer than one could imagine!

FBI Investigated Ga. Gov. in Old Lynching
By Greg Bluestein
6/15/07
MOORES FORD, Ga. (AP) Newly released files from the lynching of two black couples more than 60 years ago contain a disturbing revelation: The FBI investigated suspicions that a three-term governor of Georgia sanctioned the murders to sway rural white voters during a tough election campaign.

The 3,725 pages obtained by The Associated Press under the Freedom of Information Act do not draw conclusions about the still-unsolved killings at Moores Ford Bridge. But they raise the possibility that Eugene Talmadge's politics may have been a factor when a white mob dragged the four from a car, tied them to a tree and opened fire......The investigation of Talmadge began in the months before his death in December 1946 and it appears he was never interviewed. The allegation of his possible involvement was not included in the FBI's official report, but was sent to Hoover in a letter "as it may be of some possible future interest."

The lynchings of Roger and Dorothy Malcom, and George and Mae Murray Dorsey on July 25, 1946, came eight days after the election and followed weeks of simmering tensions. There were rumors that George Dorsey, an Army veteran, had secretly been dating a white woman—a taboo in the segregated South....

...White farmers were described by the FBI as "extremely clannish, not well educated and highly sensitive to 'outside' criticism." Harrison, for one, told police he couldn't identify any of the participants. Black families, who often sharecropped on white farms, were "frightened and even terrified" when approached by FBI agents. One farmer fled into a cotton field and had to be chased down, eventually telling an investigator he had been warned not to talk...

...Eventually, the FBI identified 55 possible suspects, including George Hester, but no one was ever arrested. After a federal grand jury in December 1946 could not identify any members of the mob, the FBI retreated from the case..."

Amazed at the amount of press this event had received over the years, I pooled information from every article I could find.

Wall of silence surrounded Moores Ford lynchings
By Wayne Ford
Oconee Editor
The crime at Moores Ford Bridge has been called a "civil rights milestone," and it has not been forgotten by the people of Walton and Oconee counties. Richard Rusk of Oconee County, a founder of the Moores Ford Committee, said the crime was probably the last mass lynching in Georgia after World War II. "I think Americans were outraged that lynchings were still going on," he said. The crime added to President Truman's efforts to address racial injustice. He pushed for the country's first anti-lynching legislation and desegregation of the military, Rusk said. Truman also ordered the FBI into Walton County to investigate the slayings. Yet despite the FBI's efforts, the investigation failed.

No one was ever prosecuted for the slayings of Roger Malcom, 24; Dorothy Malcom, 20; George Dorsey, 28; and Mae Murray Dorsey, 23. George Dorsey was a World War II veteran. What happened on that late afternoon of July 25, 1946, and why it happened is still open to conjecture...

Then in another article, I saw folks who were doing their best to heal. It seemed that was all I could do too. I rifled through a handful more articles and began to lose hope of finding a tie to my maiden's obsession. Sixty-some-odd years later, the case was cold as the bodies that were still waiting for justice. I spent another hour searching the web, but no new names or evidence significant enough appeared on the written horizon since Clinton Adams had hit the scene with his statements. I rummaged through and found another, more current article, but still it gave me no more insight as to why Haydon should have been among the killers that day.

"Justice can't just forget" long-ago racial killings
By Bob Kemper
The Atlanta Journal-Constitution
9/13/06
The letter landed on Chip Burrus' desk about 18 months ago. Two black couples, George and Mae Dorsey and Roger and Dorothy Malcom, had been brutally killed by a white mob in Georgia, it said. And the details astonished the FBI's assistant director, even 60 years after the crime was committed. "I'd never heard of this [case] before, and I kind of fancy myself a student of the South," said Burrus, who had just taken over as assistant director of the FBI's criminal investigative division when the letter arrived. "You sort of start asking yourself, 'How many more of these are out there?'

After ordering all of the FBI's field offices to comb their files and revisit people and groups who may have information about unsolved slayings from the civil rights era, Burrus had his answer: There are at least 35 to 50 such cases across the country, predominantly in the South. But can these cold cases from 40, 50 or 60 years ago be solved? "We won't have the ability to bring closure to a lot of them, probably," Burrus said. But "you just can't forget. Justice can't just forget. Even though they're 50 years old, it still doesn't mean we shouldn't take a look at them and use whatever laws we can to try to address them."

The only Georgia case on the FBI's list is what is known as the Moores Ford Bridge lynching — the slayings described in the letter that landed on Burrus' desk...

Scattered hearsay and personal speculations filled in the gaping holes left in the investigation from there. Someone mentioned hearing about a cop from Walton County who claimed a relative of his had confessed he'd been a party to the crime and given him a gun that had been used that day at the bridge. Someone else had suspicions of an elderly neighbor from Barrow County, rumoring he had seen him mount the steps of the local courthouse wearing the sheets of the KKK as recently as 1996. Lots of folks whispered, but no one declared anything one could reconcile with hard evidence. It was as if we were all reading off the same lead sheets, but no one had a clear way to find out if any of the rumblings were true. My eyes were tired, but I thought if I just keep looking, something somewhere might trigger a clue as to why Haydon would have been involved in such a travesty. Weary, I pulled another one from the internet and read...

Moores Ford Lynching: The Long Route Home

On July 25, 1946, two young black couples—Roger and Dorothy Malcom, George and Mae Murray Dorsey—were killed by a lynch mob at the Moores Ford Bridge over the Apalachee River connecting Walton and Oconee Counties. The four victims were tied up and shot hundreds of times in broad daylight by a mob of unmasked men; murder weapons included rifles, shotguns, pistols, and a machine gun. "Shooting a black person was like shooting a deer," George Dorsey's nephew, George Washington Dorsey, said. It has been over fifty years and this case is still unsolved by police investigators. It is known that there were at least a dozen men involved in these killings...

... The motive appeared to be hatred and the crime hurt the image of the state, leaving the town in an outrage due to the injustice that left the victims in unmarked graves...They were so savagely beaten and overwhelmed with bullets that their bodies were ripped to shreds. "The only way to tell the bodies apart was by their lips..."

...No one was ever prosecuted for the slayings of the African Americans and why it happened is left too much conjecture. The six month investigation following the incident that came to be known as the Moores Ford lynching garnered sensational headlines that horrified the nation, but yielded nothing. FBI agents eventually left the county unable to break the code of silence that protected the killers...

The approaching anniversary date of the lynching always brought the worms of discontent crawling to the surface of every conversation around Monroe. White folks played the tragedy down as if it was nothing more than ancient history. African Americans however felt its sting as perennial as the grass. For them it was never over.

In fact as recently as that afternoon, Connie told me she had spoken with an elderly black woman about the affects of Moores Ford Bridge. The woman had shied away, refused to give her name, and begged Connie to stay away and drop it. Said white folks weren't ready for that kind of resurrection and there was no telling what kind of damage would be done if folks were to re-open that can of worms. She warned Connie to keep to herself and let sleeping dogs lie. She said, "They's dead... leave them and their families alone... Only God gonna ever know the truth about that day and it's up to the good Lord Hisself to exact punishments as He sees fit."

And with that story, Connie cautioned me to play it safe. But I couldn't. Not for her or even for me.

***

I couldn't play anything safe until I had the answers, and they weren't just for the four that had been slain, but for Haydon. His only crime as far as I could surmise was the same as the others': they had simply been in the wrong place at the wrong time. Even Roger Malcom had not deserved to die the way he did. He had stabbed a white man, been placed in jail, and would have stood trial for his crime had he lasted long enough. The other three had merely gone along for the ride. That had been the sum total of their crime. Could that also have been the sum total of Haydon's? Or could there have been something more to his crime that I was yet to discover?

There were so many questions now that ran through my head. Had Haydon's family shared subversive political ties with the Carmichael campaign agenda? Had Haydon himself been some sort of activist? His mother's family in Atlanta had financial and political prowess...but had they been part of something more subliminal? Perhaps a right-winged political machine hell-bent on trying to move the mindset away from the traditional roles played by most "coloreds" in the rural South? Or was it perhaps something as simple as Haydon's associations with the local "coloreds" that had infuriated those in his immediate surroundings?

When random citizens were asked what was they thought the motivations for the murders might have been, folks rationalized with a laundry list of suspicions. Some said it was over the stabbing, others that bootlegging money was owed, and others still speculated that someone was exacting revenge for alleged interracial relationships. What did any of these conjectures have to do with Haydon, whose home and life were over ninety miles away?

Unless one of those suspected issues been Haydon's as well? Could he have been involved with the illegal distribution of moonshine? Or had he been caught in a compromising relationship with a woman of color? If Haydon had been there that day, then surely somebody else had to have known why. And if they knew why and were still alive...whoever that someone was, they obviously still believed that keeping the reason for Haydon's presence at the bridge a secret was more important than helping solve the mystery of why four lives were sacrificed sixty years earlier.

I closed my laptop and ran my fingers through my hair, tired and frustrated beyond belief. Where would one look to find the truth? I stared out the window and heard the chiming of the clock below. The clock had told me things before...why now could it only chime? Fatigued, I shoved myself away from my desk and listened to the last of the clock's chiming. The rest of the house was silent as the last hushed tones mounted the stairs and then faded into the night. I thought again how much I loved that particular sequence. We had a clock that played that same series of musical notes when I was growing up and it always comforted me. I distracted myself with trivia. What was it called? Ah yes...the Westminster Abbey chime.

With a final gong, the echo left me simmering in my past and still no further ahead in my investigations. I stared at the lighted screen with another fifty Moores Ford Bridge sites all over it and then at the huge pile of papers in front of me and sighed. How would I ever find the one clue that could lead me to him in all of that? I doodled on my writing pad to try and settle my thoughts. I thought perhaps the comforting memory of the chime might help me, so I wrote the words Westminster Abbey... and then began to draw swirls and circles trying to recreate the face of the clock. Again I thought of the little girl and the dream. She said the answers were there. I just wasn't looking hard enough. I stared at the drawing and then began to hum the chime, thinking. And then it hit me!

The Westminster Abbey... an abbey! An abbey was like a church...

That's when I began to smile. The clock had spoken indeed. Where would one look to find the truth? In an abbey or a church of course! The man in the moon had pointed me in the right direction again. I'd start at the church from this afternoon and work backwards from there!

Chapter Twenty-eight

I studied the timelines carefully. Gone on a holiday either voluntary or enforced, our mysterious Abel must have left the Danburg shortly before the 25th of July that 1946 and traveled who knows how far initially. Perhaps to Decatur to visit the branch of the family whose extensive dairy operations and affluence earned them influence with political figures across the state, or perhaps to one of the many political rallies supporting his father's favorite candidate.

I pulled out the vast stack of personal interviews that had littered my desk before Connie's call and tried to filter them through my newfound enlightenment, but there were still too many fragments missing. I recalled the name of the woman from the church cemetery and though the hour was late I called information and said a prayer.

She sounded irritated at first, so I told her I was trying to identify an artifact for the showing the following afternoon and was desperate for information. Sensing this would place her on the inside track, she got up to excuse herself from the bedroom where I could hear her husband snoring like a freight train. Once I heard her close her door, I pressed for more information about Haydon. She cleared her throat and reminded me of the phone call she had received earlier from Celine. When I assured her that I was asking for purposes of historical reference, and that our conversation wouldn't fall under the heading of behaviors admonished by the covenants on the church wall, she told me with zeal.

She and Lucy had taught Sunday school and though Haydon had not attended often, he occasionally came when his cousin was visiting. His relations on either side carried a great deal of influence politically and though the weight never translated to his mother, Haydon still exploited the roots of his family tree whenever it seemed most advantageous to do so. On his mother's side, the Madisons were staunch supporters of the Carmichael campaign and saw both economic and social growth in the young man's vision. The Fitzgeralds on his father's side had done their best to climb the economic ladder rung by rung. They had no intentions of dispersing their wealth to those not willing to earn it. Following the mantra of the Republican Party they employed according to abilities and not color.

While his maternal grandparents were less than happy with his womanizing and drinking, Haydon's intellectual prowess served them well on his visits to the city. They took pleasure in his company for short spans of time. With passing years his visits to Atlanta lengthened. Frantic for affection and acceptance from his grandparents, he became chameleon-like in an effort to make everyone happy. Each trip he tried harder and harder, hoping they would see that the rural constrictions of Danburg were unfair to such a cultured soul as he. He read to his grandmother from the great books and played golf with his grandfather. With his uncle, the lawyer, Haydon would present himself as perfect guardian and chaperone of his charge, a much younger cousin who would periodically visit the countryside.

Haydon's grandparents lived the "Old South" traditions and regarded leisure as a right. Supporting the exercise of that right was a staff of "coloreds" for kitchen and home management. They received payment for their services, but their contribution was seen no differently than those who had served before for bread and butter. Haydon's father, on the other hand, like his candidate of choice, saw the blacks in a more liberated light. Employing them as more than just menials in his hotel, they were paid according to job not color, treated with respect thus preserving their dignity.

Color was no barrier for Haydon. He and they both had been set aside as outcasts. The bottle had forged a communal tie between Haydon and some of the lesser fortunate, first out of mutual need and then addiction. These associations led him into troubled waters and occasionally resulted in small fines and house arrests commissioned by stepfather's anger. On rare occasions his Uncle was called in: a lawyer from Atlanta who admonished him and encouraged him to seek other, more noble outlets for his energies... such as politics.

I interrupted her to ask if the lawyer was the same relative whose child was left in Haydon's care at times. She answered yes and started to continue, but I stopped her again.

"What was his name?" I asked. I threw in, "For the record?" for good measure.

"I told you...Haydon Edison Fitzgerald. Who did you think I was talking about? Now really... it's terribly late and I'm exhausted." she asked, exasperated at the hour and my apparent ignorance.

"I'm sorry... I meant the name of Haydon's cousin. What was his name? You know... for the record?" I sounded like an idiot even to myself.

"For the record, he was a she! And the she was the daughter of his Uncle Floyd and her name was Magnolia. It's really late now... Is there anything else or can you call back in the morning so we can discuss this at a more reasonable hour?"

"I...I...think that would be fine. Goodnight and thanks... by the way... do you know her full name?"

"For the record?" I thought about the church covenant and then the Ten Commandments. Especially the one that says, "Thou shall not lie or tell falsehoods."

"No..." I said and took one for the team. "This one is for me... no record, on or off... I just wish to know who she was. And I waited with a lump in my throat. The name Magnolia was so clichéd, so unlike the character in her diary.

"Yes ...Magnolia was her first name, just like her grandmother's. But since she was so small for such a big name, we all called her Maggie for short. Magnolia June Fitzgerald. Adorable little thing when we first met her. No bigger than a minute… curls drawn up in a bow… I can see her now. Precious child… spent her time in the attic amongst all those dusty books like Cinderella. She and Haydon! Like two peas in a pod! Countless hours together in the attic with their noses crammed in between book covers…they went everywhere. She saved him, you know? Well…she saved him up until the end and had she known….perhaps things might have ended differently for them both.

She was the one that figured out as long as he had a book in his hands and something to occupy his mind, he wouldn't carry a bottle! So she carried a book in one hand and his in the other every time she could arrange it. She adopted his favorite book as her own, you know. Very heady stuff…It was a bit boring and difficult for me to plow through, but she was such a smart and haughty little thing. Hmmm… what was the name? It was the book that they made into a movie… Audrey Hepburn starred in it. What was it again…?"

The attic shelf with the missing book in the G column flashed in my mind, and I realized there was limited need for the helpful church lady to continue to guide me. I could find my way to them from here as soon as I was brave enough to dispel the sanctuary of my own illusions about them. While I was lost in thought, the church woman rambled underneath my mental segues. I focused on her voice just long enough to interject an appropriate response and insert a quick goodbye before I went to look for their faces amongst the many Danburg files. Cheryl continued to mumble about the opening and I glanced at the clock and was astounded at the hour. I had so little private time left to be alone with them.

"I'm sorry it's so late. I'll let you get back to sleep. Thank you." There were the sounds of shuffling feet and a door creak. "You've been very generous to share this information with me and…" The squeaking of rusty coils signaled her return to the bed and I was anxious to get off the phone, but something she delayed played back in my head. "Did you just say something about the opening tomorrow?"

The coiled squeaked once more and she replied. "I imagine she will be there for it. I'll have to prepare for the wrath of Celine for telling you this, but…" She sighed heavily into the phone.

"But it will be worth it after all these years to watch them square off!" She chuckled. "Celine's always been such a witch to everyone! Hah! It'll serve her right for being such a..." She trailed off, then whispered, "...a bitchy prude!"

Feeling much better about the untangled tongue I'd had in the church confines earlier that day, I snickered.

"Like I said..." She cleared her throat for effect. "I can't imagine she would not be present. It's sort of her shrine to Haydon, really. I would have thought you of all people would have known who she was from the very start. After all, she's the one who donated the house to the county to save the wretched thing in the first place. The name Magnolia J. Fitzgerald doesn't ring a bell?" I recalled an M.J. Fitzgerald from the initial hearing almost two years prior when the house was deeded over to the county, but had always assumed it was a man. "She was bequeathed the house after her father died in 1997. He was Floyd Haydon Fitzgerald and was the last soul to own title to it after he bailed the Danburgs out of bankruptcy in the late forties."

I made a mental note to Google the name when I hung up and listened further. No longer anxious to shut her up, I asked, "So... how did her father end up with the Danburg home?" trying to figure out how it all fit together.

"You see, the fire damaged the house terribly. The outer buildings, including the shed where Haydon slept most of the time, along with the surrounding cotton fields, appeared to have been set ablaze earlier, which ... never really made sense to me. Unless... the flames from the shed caught the main house on fire...I never knew. But there again, the shed was separated a good bit from the house and the house is brick for the most part. Plus, the fields are, what, 150 yards away from the shed and the house? I didn't think it through at the time. Everyone was so distraught. I do recall thinking at the time there was only a slight breeze that night, but the Sheriff never questioned any of it, so...I never made the connection. But Celine swore it must have been Haydon who knocked over the oil lamp in the hall. She said he rushed out of Maggie's bedroom and down the back stairs that night. He was drunk, and then he fell asleep in the shed with a lit cigarette...

"But how can that be? You told me Celine had said the young woman was yelling out the second story window to him as he headed for the woods through the pasture, not seconds after he was discovered by her in the house? You said yourself... neighbors saw the smoke from the front of the house first." And I heard her rummage through the facts in her mind like a card file.

"You're right. They kept the oil lamp on the hall table in the upstairs hallway...not below...and he wouldn't have even had time to get into the shed to have smoked if things happened at the break-neck speed Celine described." She hesitated. "Not only that...the jib windows were left open that night and they would never have been left ajar unless it was a still night."

We both heard the ramifications speaking louder and louder with each fact remembered.

"Had anyone else suspected a sexual relationship between the two?" I asked with absolute candor and much to my surprise, she responded in kind.

"It always comes down to sex in the end... doesn't it?" she mused. "Of course Cattalieu was oblivious to most of the goings on, but Celine was obsessed with clearing the family name and grew intensely bitter. She blamed Haydon for ruining their lives with his drink and uncomely behavior. She had a crush on him, you know?"

"Haydon?" I supplied.

"Oh yes...from the very first day he arrived. He was handsome. Dark eyes, substantial build, captivating smile. We all drooled into our hankies, to tell you the truth. He had danger written all over his face and there's nothing more seductive than that to young girls forced to live such confined lives." I could hear the roar of the freight train she slept next to as she reminisced. "Anyway, we all did our best to hide our feelings about him, but Celine never hid hers from anyone. She wanted everyone to know she had marked him as hers. She even told me one time she thought she might be pregnant and was going to force him into marriage. But we knew she was a virgin." And she giggled like a school girl.

"Everyone knew she was too chicken to go through with it! I knew what she was after, but the more he rejected her advances, the more rigid she became. After a while she claimed it was her duty as a good Baptist to save him from himself—ha! She just wanted to have an excuse to follow him everywhere he went. Didn't matter. She'd trail him when he was with Maggie and if he struck out on his own… she'd even follow him to the store or out behind it just to have the chance to speak with him. He'd ignore her or wave her off and it stuck in her craw that he preferred spending his time with the 'coloreds' more than her. Chapped her fanny something fierce!" And she let go another laugh that sent her husband's snoring off the charts. "She told everyone she'd been with him, but we never really believed her. Hell, if just once he really had invited her out to that little shed of his after dark, she'd be a different woman today! Hah!"

I thought of those matronly lips pursed in the throes of passion and laughed out loud. We both laughed and she continued in a softer voice. "It was painful to watch, really. She was desperate for his affections. When Maggie began to blossom into something more than a freckled little girl, Celine became livid with envy! Each summer Haydon spent days in preparations for her visits stockpiling library books. And as much as Celine tried to interject herself intellectually into their conversations, the more she tried to impress him… the more he perceived her as a snobbish know-it-all.

"Haydon wasn't unkind, now that I think about it. He just never saw her on his radar, that's all. Maggie was his… his delight. Soul mates, I think. I know it sounds crazy—there were so many years between them… But they were so well matched and he adored her company so. We all thought it was a harmless infatuation that would run its course, but…

"Celine must have been furious," I guessed. "Can you imagine wanting someone so much and having to watch as somebody you thought beneath you stole away with your prize?" I thought of my ex-husband's Skipper and snarled under my breath.

"Uh-hum. I imagine it ate at her something fierce" she added.

I thought about Matt and his new bride. Even though I had long since let go of any real affection for my ex-husband, I had to confess I felt less than Christian toward the woman who had given him the one thing he truly cherished in the end... a family. Cheryl shifted the phone and continued.

"Oh yes. Even in her absence, Maggie held greater allure than all the lowered necklines and come hither stares Celine offered on a nightly basis across the dinner table."

For an instant the image of how I had come to create my modern art piece ran through my mind. Angry enough to physically damage inanimate objects, wishing it was him in the blender was just the bottom rung of what I really wanted to do to Matt those first few weeks and I considered myself relatively well adjusted...relatively.

"Was that why she claimed Haydon started the fire, do you think?"

"Oh, it's more than that. The last summer before Haydon died, Lucy and I visited often. Cattalieu and I were best of friends. There wasn't that much to do in Danburg so we were left to our own devices for entertainment. We had splendid tea parties in the front parlor! It was a wonderful time—little girl games and the such."

"Did her sister join you?" I asked.

"Not often. Lucy and Celine were so much older and of course humored us, but it was clear Celine had graduated well beyond tea parties and pig tails. She and Lucy used to keep secrets from Catty and I. They hid behind doors and whispered a lot about the cousin who spent too many nights sleeping it off in the shed. Lucy shocked me some summers after it all happened."

"How so?"

Lucy told me Celine had broken down in tears one night. She claimed she'd been with Haydon—in the biblical sense. That's why she lost her temper the night it happened. Celine said she'd become violently jealous when she caught him in a compromising position with the young Maggie, who was already in bed and half undressed.

"Lucy told me Celine had claimed she'd heard the girl crying and so ran into the room. She confronted Haydon yelling and screaming, banishing him from the house. They quarreled in front of Maggie, who kept blubbering something about her diary. Convinced it was some sort of a perverse love letter; Celine tore the book from her hands and locked her in her room so she could confront Haydon further in the hallway.

"There was a struggle over the little leather book between her and Haydon and she held it over the oil lamp on the hall library hutch, threatening to burn it if he didn't leave the house at once. Haydon pleaded, but she said she could not let him have the evidence of their incestuous relationship. It was for the church elders to decide his fate! That he, the diary and his flirtatious little cousin would both burn in hell for what they'd done."

"Did she know what was written in the diary?'" I asked, wondering why she had not asked about the final entry that night.

"I doubt it…but it wouldn't have mattered if it had been full of nursery rhymes or baking recipes. Celine was hell bent on finding dirt or supplying it if necessary to get Maggie out of the way once and for all!

"The way she told it, Haydon dove to the hutch to retrieve it and at that point, the whole house erupted into the fray. His stepfather took the front stairway two steps at a time, brandishing a shotgun. The pages started to singe, Haydon charged Celine—she was hysterical—and her sleeve caught on fire. He smothered the flame with his body, reached for the book, and then ran with it down the front stairs. When the stepfather fired a round of buckshot over his head, Haydon dropped the book and it slid under the petticoat table and he could not retrieve it. He bolted for the back hall and out through the warming kitchen.

Frantic with the smell of smoke filling the upstairs middle hall, the young Maggie pleaded through the window to him below not to leave, but by then it was too late. As he was halfway to the pasture gate, Celine yelled from the opposite second story room window to her father that Haydon had flown into a rage when she told him of her condition, and that he'd set the house on fire.

I can't imagine what was going through the child's mind hearing all the accusations, not to mention the rifle shots and smoke billowing from portals other than chimneys. Panicked for Haydon's safety, she made a desperate attempt to climb through the window and down the lattice. She made it as far as the shed before Celine caught up with her, throwing her to the ground.

Lucy heard from another friend that had heard it from one of the field hands that Celine had pinned her down, calling her a whore and a harlot… screaming that Haydon was no longer fair game, that he was to be wed to her! They said the child bolted from her side into the night. Celine went in search for her and dropped her lantern in the shed when she heard the child run screaming back into the house trying to collect her precious diary. But neither the diary nor Haydon were anywhere to be found.

Folks said it was a miracle Maggie got out of the fire alive. She was dragged from the house kicking and screaming about her diary and how she couldn't leave without it. It was a horrible scene. The house blazed and the child slumped into the front yard sobbing hysterically, waiting for Haydon to return. Her parents made the trip to Danburg and took her back to Atlanta. We never saw her again.

"What did they tell the police?"

"The Sheriff's report was basically Celine's story. Celine stated that in a drunk and belligerent state over the news of her unexpected condition, Haydon and she had argued terribly. When she refused to handle the situation by means other than marriage, he flew into a rage. She locked him out in the hall, yelling for her Uncle. When Haydon could not break through her door he tried getting into Maggie's to make her jealous, knocking over an oil lamp in the hall in his haste. The hall caught on fire and when Celine's uncle hit the scene with a rifle, Haydon ran away like a coward and hid out in the shed. When it too caught fire, he fled the manor into the woods. In his shame, he spent the night away. When he came home the following afternoon to make amends, she rebuked him. And well, you know the rest. Guess he went out and tied one on and the next thing we knew… they found him face down in the swamp."

"Celine… pregnant?" I stammered. I was reeling.

Cheryl claimed that even the mighty could make mistakes and Celine was so desperately in love anything was possible. Celine said one night in the ironing shed, after a particularly bad bout with his stepfather, Haydon was so in need of comforting that she lost her head. He was drunk…one thing led to another and…she said he promised to marry her."

"There's no mention of a pregnancy, not in any of my research. Not even a marriage. How do you explain that?" I asked, somewhat impatient with the detour.

"Well, because no child was ever born and no one ever asked to marry her after that. She claimed the trauma of the event caused her to miscarry. Course the family was so hush-hush about so many things...we just never knew for certain. Bottom line, true or not, she never gave birth then or ever. She was apparently barren, poor thing."

I wanted to be sympathetic, but could not muster enough compassion to do so. Something didn't feel right. "Did *you* believe her?" I asked pointedly.

"Her uncle was a pretty rough character and pretty rough on her. I can't say for certain. She'd never lied before about anything as far I knew, and she was so in love with Haydon... but I can tell you this. You didn't mess with Haydon's stepfather. He had connections, if you know what I mean. If you said you were pregnant, you better have been pregnant, and if you said you'd lost the baby, he'd have demanded proof on a silver platter! The house of Danburg would not suffer the insult of shame without retribution."

It was all too much to take in at once. Celine had intimated she had seen Haydon through some of his more demonic phases with the alcohol and that Maggie had not been the only one to catch his eye...but this? This was a goddam soap opera! Too many, "Celine said..." and not enough corroboration by what anyone else ever saw or heard. Once again it seemed to be the gospel according to Celine. I tried to replay it all back in my head and piece it together chronologically with what else I knew about the nights events. Most things didn't quite add up, but there was one thing that bothered me even more. Celine had never once said Haydon had ever returned after the fire.... never!

"Who said he came back home? Neither of the Chenille sisters ever confessed that to me."

"No doubt... why would they?" Cheryl added. "He could have come back 10,000 times and it wouldn't have made a difference. He was never gonna love Celine. He'd already given his heart away to Maggie."

I began to feel the first throbs of a migraine coming on. Everyone in Danburg was sending me on a wild goose chase. It was time I demanded accurate answers. While a few had talked openly about the feasibility of a family scandal, no one ever spoke about the day after the fire or Haydon's imminent return. Not until now at least, and I found that amazing in a little town this size.

Since I started the project, everything anybody did was fodder for gossip and even I as an outsider knew more about half the folks in town than I cared to! If somebody heard a cat had shit purple in the alley behind the Quikmart, they'd have filmed it by 9:00, written about in the paper, posted a bill board announcing it to the world and had it on the 11:00 news that night! Everybody would have talked about nothing but purple cat shit for decades!

"No one but Celine ever could have said that with any confidence...after all, she was the only one there that next day when..." she added as an after thought.

The receiver seemed to pulse with the revelation. Haydon had basically been accused of rape and arson by Celine, but had no way of knowing it at the time since he had left the manor in a desperate sprint for the woods at the first round of buckshot. If he'd come back at all in those first few hours after, it would have been for another reason altogether and not to explain to Maggie that Celine had lied.

I let Cheryl ramble for a few more lines before I received what I needed to hear. All of the family had conveniently been relocated to neighboring houses by the time he returned... everyone that was except Celine. She had left the neighboring estate telling her Aunt she wished to be alone to collect what few family mementos could be salvaged from the smoldering ruins of the Danburg and her heart. The phone receiver dangled from the cord along with my patience.

"Hello? Are you there? Hello?" Thinking I had ended the call, Cheryl hung up while I searched the cabinet and pulled out another file.

***

I had never heard of Haydon before, let alone that he had come back, until Cheryl's eye opening conversations.

Celine had lied through her teeth about everything all along. Lied about her so-called condition, the true nature of the argument, the real reason Haydon had been in Maggie's room that night... And her sniveling little sister Catty had backed her up with her silence! I was furious with the entire community. It was amazing how everybody talked, but nobody ever said anything! For a fire that had been put out over 60 years earlier, it was unfathomable to me how much smoke still got blown up my ass every time I asked a simple question about it! I pulled the files and started going through every interview that had anything to say about the fire and the night Haydon went missing. Somebody simply had to have said something I missed the first go round!

If Haydon had truly set the fire and not cared about Maggie or the rest of them, why the hell would he have returned to the scene of the crime a day later and faced certain confrontation with his stepfather and possible arrest for arson and rape by the local law? And why the hell would the FBI give a rat's ass about some backwoods love triangle or a farmhouse fire? Fires happened all the time to older structures and rape was something gentlemen didn't do and ladies didn't suffer and nobody ever talked about so... why would he have returned?

Why? I'll tell you why! Because it didn't have a damn thing to do with love or Celine's misplaced honor. Neither arson nor rape... ever occurred! Oh sure there had been a fire. But just like the original flame set by the supposed Yankees...I had a gut feeling this one too had been set by more feminine hands. Perhaps someone in the family who had more to loose than trinkets and family treasures if discovered.

It was clear to me that Haydon had not set the house on fire anymore than he had supposedly raped a woman that night, or any other night. Either it had been an accident or someone else had set the fire as decoy. It wasn't so much of a stretch. I thought about the gloves Celine had been wearing the day we first met. Formal wear was only necessary during cotillions and high teas, and then only if you were 450 years old and lived in a time warp! The only other plausible reason was one I was all too familiar with. If you had something to hide... I looked at my wrists. I wore four bracelets on my right and a wide banded watch on my left to hide my scars. Another person could do the same.

Hiding something like burn scars might be such a reason. But Cheryl had made it clear; Haydon had gotten the flame out before Celine had gotten burned. Only the diary had suffered damage from the lamp. So what was she hiding under those gloves?

Perhaps that was why she didn't want me to speak with Cheryl at the cemetery. Celine was afraid a less native set of eyes would notice details that stood out as incongruent. She feared someone who was free to question inconsistencies, someone who would be able to reconstruct what Cheryl had tried so hard not to say...

* * *

My research continued to point to anomalies in the Danburg story. Haydon had been set up for crimes he did not commit, but why? And there was still an obstacle from the very beginning that needed to be cleared. He wrote he had been with one of the bodies in a silo!

I believe it is a fair assumption that they have discovered our collective escape by now... They know I could name as many as ten...Looking out from the belly of a decapitated silo, I saw the scattered wreckage of broken chimneys, felt the brutal rush of foul air beneath the wings of turkey vultures that circled above me, and counted myself lucky that I was still alive. Liquid continued to drain from his body throughout the night...

How was this possible? Haydon clearly stated his position as being within a silo and his companion was obviously none other than one of the four victims. And yet, I had seen the photos of the gurneys, with all four of the bodies atop them. They had all been accounted for at the Dan Young Funeral Home. Their families had buried them all. Services rendered, lilies faded, dried and left in the wind to take flight. How could it be that Haydon described himself lying next to one of them at least forty eight hours later in the bottom of an overgrown corn crib?

Unless I was dealing with a similar lynching that fit all the factual evidence but this one major detail, something was not right. There was a hole in someone's story and apparently that's where the truth had fallen out!

* * *

The more I looked over documents, the more it bothered me. There were inconsistencies everywhere that could not be denied, some directly within the descriptions of the burials and gravesites themselves.

There was an excerpt from the book *Fire in a Canebrake* by Laura Wexler that had stuck in my mind.

"'There was hate amongst those two people' says Mattie Louise." "'I see the hate in both of them.'" (two people = Weldon Hester, the Malcom farm overseer; Roger Malcom) "She'd thought of that hate when she saw Roger's body in Dan Young's funeral home. 'I seen folks kill hogs. Four or five hogs, hang'em up, and let the blood drain. I'm a strong woman,' she says." "'I looked at that, and I fainted...'"

I thought about the Moores Ford web site and the mentioned loss of one of the gravesites. Then I thought about the reference to the hog killing segment in Wexler's book. Intimidated by the aforementioned description, I had to force myself to look at the hog killing station beyond the warming kitchen and cringed. Something the woman from the church had said... about Haydon's body having been so unrecognizable and revolting that the mother had fainted at the sight of the hideous glob that had once been both the apple of her eye and the bane of her existence. The stepfather had been the one to make the final verification of identity and I heard told he never batted an eye. He just nodded his head, turned away and walked out of the mortuary room. These southerners not only had memories as long an elephant eye lashes, they had cast iron stomachs as well... almost as though they had known what the body would look like before the viewing. I consulted the web for information on typical practices of bloodletting. I was appalled.

I read further from Wexler's book. There was no funeral for the one family, as they had been stalled by citizens too frightened to assist them with transportation that day and they had not made it to the graveside on time. The two coffins were lowered into the ground and covered with dirt and that was that. Across town, the others were laid to rest and the night closed on them all, shutting out any ray of hope on that unforgiving day referred to later as "Black Sunday."

I rethought the parallel to the Mattie Louise's statements about the body of one of the four and the slaughtered pigs she had seen. Could there have been even more atrocious acts committed beyond the soggy ending Haydon suffered in the swamp? There was an obvious disparity between what shell game facts the family applied to Haydon's death and what was ground out by the rumor mill. The coroner's report simply stated he had drowned and that there were other marks upon the body. But I was looking for more specifics...something along the lines of what I had seen on the internet about bloodletting or what was described in Laura Wexler's book. Right now it seemed to hold the most palatable account, yet even that made me want to vomit.

The descriptions were almost too vivid to read.

"...bodies riddled with bullets, bones shattered. Plaster used to fill in and reconstruct the gaping wounds left by close range firing... faces obliterated; tissue shredded by buckshot... identifications hampered and done by lips alone..."

All this carnage committed in the name of southern justice... why? It made my skin crawl with contempt for those capable of committing such atrocities. Just like Haydon, I felt it was more than anyone should have been asked to view, yet alone suffer. I closed my eyes on a single tear. My heart ached for them all, especially Haydon. I thought of his words. No man with that kind of poetry inside his soul could have been a willing party to such a thing.

I heard the echo of my own thoughts. Even my own prejudice showed. Black or white, none of those people, poets or not, deserved to suffer such a fate. No wives, no lovers deserved to be forced to stand by silent as their mates were slaughtered and left like animals to jerk in the final throes of surrender like dying catfish strewn upon a riverbank, gasping for air and suffocating in their own bloodied mud.

I thought about the families and tried to put myself in their shoes. I looked again at the photos from the mortuary. The plain white sheets pulled tight above the hairlines of the victims in the photos. It was time to take off the gloves and get dirty in what had really happened that day. Good or bad, I needed to know how Haydon had been involved and what that had meant for my maiden. I wiped my face with a fresh towel and got down to business.

I pulled the file that held interviews and peripheral items of interest concerning Moores Ford.

According to chronicles in the local archives, tensions began to ease a couple days later. Folks began to trade again in the shops lining the square and commerce picked up in the peripheral shops that lined the side streets. Everywhere things were returning to normal, but for the "colored" sections of town. For them, time stood still. Local law made their presence known, but many started to imagine there was more to come when GBI and suspected FBI agents began questioning the help at the Fitzgerald. Pointed questions concerning the whereabouts of the owner's son and how much they knew about the "coloreds" that had been taken care of at Moores Ford Bridge. Naturally they pleaded ignorance of both the crime and the location of the prodigal son of the owner.

According to the whispers of those brave enough to remember, Haydon had been gone for quite a few days when the "necessary event" took place. Shortly after the "coloreds'" funerals, Washington began to swarm with "concerned citizens" that imagined the same things might migrate from Monroe and happen there. The rural blacks had pretty much kept their silence and their distance, fearing reprisals. Entering from the rear doors of their respective working establishments, they kept their eyes down, avoiding all contact with the local white folk... save for one who needed a favor.

No one ever confirmed the rumor that Haydon had shown his ashen face at the rear door of the hotel four mornings after the slaughter at Moores Ford Bridge. No one ever asked if it was true he had begged the concierge to get into the safe for his monthly stipend five days earlier. No one ever suggested he hitched a ride with a colored who worked in his father's garage. In fact, not one person said they saw that same green sedan headed in the direction of the smoldering frame of the Danburg that first day after the fire at ninety miles an hour.

No one in charge ever asked, because they already knew.

Chapter Twenty-nine

If what I suspected was true, Haydon's familial political standings and affiliations made him a double threat. His mother's family had money...big money. His step-uncle the attorney from Atlanta carried clout legally, so both money and influence coursed through the familial veins. Their standings on both fronts wielded power that turned heads at the state Capital's steps towards whatever cause they deemed worthy. Civil Rights was one such cause and it was Haydon's lack of border recognition that placed him in double jeopardy. Others less privileged than he still sought to draw the racial lines at every turn and his disregard for their southern tradition appalled them.

There was another issue at hand about the burial sites that unsettled me. There were too many questions about the locations of the four graves. The black church whose congregation buried the victims had been built on outskirt acres of a family plantation in the area late in the eighteen hundreds. As squatters, the church members had no legal claim to the grounds when the last white inheritors of the land decided to sell and move on a century later.

Though many of the church's elders tried to argue their case, no one cheered in their corner so the congregation's graves remained with the land. Unmarked and unheralded, the eternal inhabitants were as devoid of dignity in death as they had been in life. No chain link fence installed to surround them, no buffer to honor the sanctity of their eternal resting place. I wanted to know more, but it felt cruel to reopen their wounds and so I tried to focus on less invasive research methods than asking church members about the graves.

According to various accounts, the mortician had been rushed because of the growing tensions that surrounded the murders. Funerals were brief and those that attended kept their memories to themselves. In hindsight I wondered why local law hadn't protected the graves. So many folks had tampered with the crime scene by collecting souvenirs, one would have thought grave robbing not beneath them either.

I chastised myself for being such an idiot and paced the floor to try and clear my head. Why did I continue to attribute nobility and compassion to members of local law enforcement who had supported the killings? I picked up a photograph of the bodies lying on the mortician's slab and held it under my desk light. I reached for my drink and watched as the shadow I cast on the wall behind me took on an eerie, familiar silhouette. Like a carnie-barker outside the Big Top I waved my arm up and down, fascinated at my own outline as it twisted and turned in the bent light.

I was as naïve as I was blind!

Nobody saw stealing bits and pieces of body parts and shredded skin as sanctimonious! Nobody saw their guttural curiosity as vile and contemptible! Nobody saw their poking and prodding as tampering with evidence... because everybody had known there would be no trial! God it was infuriating! It hadn't been a crime against humanity; it had been a fucking carnival. A freaky sideshow! I fingered through some of the more ridiculous personal interviews. The words practically screamed contempt for the "coloreds" and it wasn't hard to imagine the festive celebrations that night in households who held no sympathy for these four people. I grabbed my whiskey, waved the photos of their mangled bodies in the air and hollered into the night. "Step lively now...Come see the dead niggers! Hurry! Hurry! Step right up folks and get a tooth or a bone before they're all gone! Come see the wild and primitive great black apes as they contort in a pool of their own blood. Careful not to touch, young man! No telling what kind of disease or taint you might get! Come on now...Step right up and get yourself the traditional southern hickory switch!

One poke for a dime! Two pokes at the bodies for twenty-five cents!"

I heard myself mock and couldn't believe what was coming from my mouth. Even tipsy and in jest it was vile. There was simply no way to sit on the fence about this thing. You were either dedicated to the disclosure and prevention of another Moores Ford or you weren't. It was then I realized the power and the weight of what I was trying to do. This wasn't just about doing my job or placing an artifact within its proper domain. I was about to make history. Not by rewriting it, but by exposing it!

Was I prepared for the kind of demons that would be released from this Pandora's Box? Every day I was surrounded by evidence painted on pick up trucks or yard ornaments that touted the stamina of the southern legacy. I looked at the photo again. Was I even capable of understanding what reactions my research would trigger? What repercussions might occur in the aftermath of any further discoveries? I had an ex-husband whom I wasn't overly fond of...but he had a new wife and a child. Could my disclosure bring harm to them if the names could be associated?

How safe was I in the twentieth century from the hangman's noose for bringing this into the spotlight again? This was still an open case for the FBI and I was about to pick a very large scab off a wound that had never really healed. Was I stupid enough to think the KKK didn't still exist in the seedy garages and moldy basements of the rural south? Not only that, but why would the black community want to trust me? Who the hell was I kidding?

I really needed to put down the whisky and walk away until my head was cleared, but there was so much gray area still left to plow through. My desk was littered with notes on my speculations and I was exhausted. Emotionally spent, I pulled together the wayward stacks and another article, with all four bodies displayed under tarps, fell to the floor. I bent to pick it up and read, "...only 3 of the 4 gravesites had been located when the memorial ceremony took place in 1997."

Suddenly everything became very real. The people in that photo had loved ones: mothers, brothers, sisters, people who cared about them. People who had waited at the edges of their porches on them to return that night. Folks whose worlds depended on them for bread and butter, love and compassion. Real people whose hearts broke at the news, whose stomachs rolled at what little was left of the flesh and bone of the beloveds they were asked to identify.

My fingers shook so badly I decided to leave the article there and went to the sink to rinse out my cup and calm my nerves. For whatever reason, the diary had been bequeathed to me. Unless I turned it over to the authorities, I was now the only one who had access to its mysteries and it was up to me how far I was willing to go to find the truth.

The water ran as lukewarm as my resolve and I watched mesmerized as it filled and flowed over the edges of the cup and slurred down the drain. After a few seconds of absolute waste, I shut the faucet off. I could bury it. I could burn it in the cremation pit I suspected it had visited before and walk away. I didn't owe anyone. This was a job... just a job, not a cause I had signed on for.

I wanted to throw something, but everything in the room was a valuable piece of the Danburg's history.

"Damn it. I need to talk to someone to about this!" I shouted as I picked up the phone. Wanting the comfort of a mothering voice I began to dial Cecelia's number, before remembering we had mutually severed ties just days before. I hung up and then dialed the only other person I knew I could depend on—Constance McCann. She answered sleepily. "Connie... I ... I just can't. It's asking too much of me and I just don't have anything else to give..." I sobbed.

"It's late...are you okay?" she muffled into the phone. "Jesus... it's three in the morning."

"Shit... I'm sorry. I had no idea of the hour. I'm just... just..." I began to sniffle.

"You're just, what. What's wrong? Has something happened? Did Matt call?" she demanded.

"Matt?" I had had a whiskey moment and forgotten Matt had ever belonged to me before the blonde bimbo. "No... I never hear from him. I may as well be dead for all he cares... for all I care.

Cecelia made it very clear when I saw her the other day that we all need to move on." I sighed.

"Is that what this is about?" she cooed into the phone with compassion. "Losing a rotten husband to somebody just as rotten? Caroline... don't be so..." and I cut her off.

"Nooo..." I slurred. "This is about injustice. I am this close, Connie... this close to walking away from this job and getting on with my life and this stupid diary won't leave me alone. It calls to me every time I shut my eyes. Every time I see that stupid fucking clock I hear her voice in my head."

"Oh Jesus, Caroline—this is about that girl? Honey, get a grip. You can't possibly still be dragging that around with you, are you? She's old. Probably even dead and there's nothing you can do to change what happened to her. It's over. Get some sleep and call me in the morning. Okay?"

She didn't get it. It wasn't over. Not for her or any of them. There was a grave missing out there that hadn't been found yet. A soul who had not been laid to rest and the clues were here in the diary and I was just too stupid to figure them out.

"I can't do my job, Connie!" I vomited and then heard her object with a round of compliments for my dedication and attention to detail.

"I preserve what I *wished* happened to them and not what really happened to them because it's nicer! It fits with all the pretty furniture and the tailored lawns. But this isn't the real history here, Connie. Not what I've shown. It's a fucking post card from Neverland compared to what they went through! They were both too good for what happened here..." I sniffled into my sleeve.

"You didn't do this to them, Caroline. You couldn't have saved them anymore than apparently they were able to save themselves. It's history, honey. It's over." She whispered trying to ease my conscience.

Thinking about the condescending way I had treated Cecelia and her southern fried morals over her hokey caricature of Willie Oreo, I openly confessed, "I am a real piece of shit, Connie! I made fun of Cecelia and her story because it was so stereo typical... but at least she tried to make a difference."

"Caroline, honey..."

"No, really... Think about it Connie. At least Cecelia wrote what she thought was the truth. I don't even bother to try. I just steal from other people's lives and leave out the crap I don't understand because if I get it wrong... it's bad for my career. But by leaving it out, I will never ever get it right... and those people... Those poor people will be... left burning in hell for all eternity because I didn't have the balls to put my self out there. Some mortician scarred shitless of being slaughtered himself 61 years ago tried to put their faces back together with plaster of Paris... just so they would look human again! And I put the lie about what really happened to them back together with Duct tape and pretty paint. That man put his life on the line for their dignity and I just put down my credit card. Don't you get it?" I blasted.

She remained silent as I continued to sound off.

"Who am I to do that? Who am I to rewrite history? What kind of fucked up historical preservationist am I?" I screamed into the receiver and heard Tim grunt at the intrusion to his sleep.

I heard the mattress springs creak as she tried to get out of bed to spare Tim the noise.

"Calm down.... calm down. Let me go into the kitchen. Have you taken your medication lately?"

I had not taken my Zoloft in months, functioning under the misguided impression that I had cured myself of depression.

"I... I'm fine... sort of." I minced.

"Pull yourself together then. Are you drinking?"

"Connie! Mixing anti-depressants with whiskey would have been completely irresponsible." I said, trying to applaud my noble instincts and set the bottle down sniffling my way around incrimination, but she didn't buy it.

"Stop this! Stop this stupid drinking of yours right now, dammit. I thought you promised Cecelia the other day you were going to quit?" she asked.

"Yeah well... her son promised me I'd get my 'happily-ever-after'...and he didn't follow through on his promise either, so I figure we're even!" I shouted back like an idiot trying to defend my deficiency.

"Get a grip, Caroline. She didn't cheat on you... Matt did." Her voice came back solemn and stern. "Besides...liquor never solved a thing. This isn't your real problem, kiddo. Your problem is *your* past. Not Matt's, not Cecelia's and certainly *not* theirs. Deal with that. Get the Danburg and its museum opened, turn this thing over to the FBI or whoever the hell wants it and let them deal with it. They're trained for this. You're not. You're just an antique freak who got to play house in somebody else's world for a while!"

I had never heard her so pissed off before.

"Do your job, Caroline and be done with it. Fix that old place, make nice with the family, put the spit shine on the collection and get the hell out of there. It's changed you, Caroline...You've become obsessed with this diary girl and it's not healthy for you. Let it go. Let her go... move on. Find some one else to love and go adopt a few girls of your own. Protect and love them. Don't let this mystery child be the only kid you ever have. Stop thinking every little girl gets ra..." she let the unarticulated word "raped" dangle over our heads for far too long.

"Finally, you didn't invite it, Caroline. It happened to you... not because of you" she eased.

I remained silent, sucking in air and holding my breath alternately, trying not to hyperventilate.

"Caroline? Caroline, honey...are you ok?" she whispered softly. "Do you want me to call Cecelia? She's still in town I think. We could come over if you want?"

"No...no. She was right. I have to learn how to move past this." I said. Maybe there was a difference between the diary girl and me. My maiden seemed to have had a handle on who she was and what she wanted. Maybe she was even mature enough to have wanted the intimacy when it found her. But me? I was barely eleven. I was just a kid, still wearing my stupid little plaid skirt and writing Jesus, Mary and Joseph in the upper right hand corner of my papers. I never saw it coming. Never knew such a brutal world existed until...I began to sob uncontrollably.

"Get some sleep. I'll call you in the morning and maybe we'll go out for breakfast... okay? Let *her* go, Caroline. Let *them* go. You can't save any of them now, honey. They're already dead, but you're not. Save yourself, Caroline...save yourself." And I cried until she finally gave up and closed the connection.

I sobbed for another fifteen minutes before chasing the remaining whiskey to the bottom of my cup. Everyone in my life who was real...wasn't here. I had my diary girl, but she wasn't real. She was just the distant echo of somebody else's life I had latched onto because the present in mine seemed so unbearable. So whose death was I really mourning? Haydon's...the victims of Moores Ford Bridge or that of my own childhood?

I saw the bottle sitting to my right and wanted to drown inside it. How was I supposed to handle something the magnitude of this when I had been such a complete failure at less global crises like my marriage? Even more to the point, how could I find justice for these folks when I had never solicited justice for the crime committed against myself? Before sharing it with Cecelia, I had only told one other person than Connie about being sexually abused as a child—my ex-husband. And we all know how that turned out!

Looking in the mirror, I took stock of myself and was uncertain I liked what I saw. The whiskey had left my vision slightly skewed, but the confused look on my face would probably have been the same sober. No wonder the waitress from the diner had been so terrorized. My reflection looked like the crazy woman I had become. All my life I had been a victim, but in truth...the greatest abuse suffered was by my own hand. I had kept silent. I had hid inside myself and worst of all; I had not let myself heal.

Who the hell was I now to stand as beacon and educate an entire nation about their history when I had been so ineffectual at successfully navigating the truths of my own? No one had listened to the facts in 1946. Why the hell would they listen now? Hadn't I said these very same objections to my mother in law earlier in the day? I looked again at the paper on the floor and then again at the woman in the mirror above the sink. I heard the words of my ex-mother in law turn over and over inside my conscience.

"'If not now...when? If not you... then who?'"

Where the hell was Cecelia and her Willie Oreo character now when I really needed them? I added coffee to my emptied whiskey glass and returned to my desk trying to get away from the emotional aspect and refocus on the facts. "Come on Willie Oreo... don't fail me now." I whispered into my cup.

Clearly information had been poorly recorded if a gravesite had been lost in the span of only fifty years. Somewhere in between 1946 and 1997, the fourth grave had been destroyed or lost, but why? Surely someone should have been able to recall where the dearly-departeds were buried. How did such a renowned gravesite disappear?

"Pretty much the same way four people got slaughtered in broad daylight by a crowd of unmasked people!" I reminded myself as I pranced around the edges of the floor not covered by articles. An 8x10 glossy of the four bodies stared back at me and the truth of the statement settled hard in my stomach like too much late night pizza. Unable to digest the implication, I asked myself again.

How *do* you commit such crimes and loose a body without anyone knowing a single goddam thing? And why the hell wouldn't the local law or the white communities have aided those people in collecting their dead, when the cemeteries were eventually compromised for progress? Wasn't that possibly the better question of the day? What possible injury could have been inflicted by doing so?

Why was there such a lack of funds to assist and such a rush to develop the land? And why was a single inch of asphalt allowed to cover known burial sites when clearly the law stipulates such sites to be sanctioned as sacrosanct and handled otherwise? Why not give credence to the sanctity of a cemetery and protect it from destruction or inaccessibility with the traditional chain link fence and 50 foot buffer zone? I got up from my chair and began to pace. I thought about the plight of Willie Oreo. A character who was hung for a pie that in the end, proved not to be stolen by him at all.

There simply had to be more rational, plausible reasons for an entire community's behavior, but the only ones I could come up with, like those in Cecelia's story made me sick.

"And the reason ..."

I took a drink of my coffee to stall the shock of the epiphany.

"The reason was...because someone already knew one of the graves would be empty."

"There!" I had finally said the reason I suspected out loud. It didn't make it any more offensive than having said it inside my head, but somewhere in the back of my mind I knew Willie Oreo applauded my efforts for bringing it out in the open. I understood it all now.

"Allowing the victims' families the chance to reclaim their dead, would have meant the discovery of an absent body authorities were not prepared to explain or advertise. Why? Because everyone in positions of authority already had the answers and so the questions were really a moot point! Oh my God...Willie. That's it! That's the reason why they never found the fourth body!" I shouted, but by then Willie had faded into nothingness.

I really could have used another shot, but I was still trying to work off my earlier buzz and limit my self destruction. The hundreds of small family plots and memorials I had seen dotting the Georgian highways and hillsides swam inside my head. Those folks had won their rights for sanctity, why not these?

Was it because unearthing the victims from the lynching at Moores Ford Bridge would unearth another crime? If their deaths had been such a pivotal point in the history of the community, the state and the federal government, pivotal enough to realign responses to Civil Rights efforts...why had their loss not been sanctified by either blacks or the "righteous" whites in the area? For a minute the plausibility of grave robbing flashed across my mental screen.

"Whoa Willie...grave robbing?" I muttered under my breath. "Jesus, I'm beginning to feel like Nancy Drew strung out on crack" I said and turned to the woman in the mirror. She had nothing to add, nut no other feasible option presented itself either. Moores Ford Bridge began to play over and over in my head like a bad B-rated film with no intermission. Vivid scenery from the bridge that day with Connie colored the background behind flashbacks of descriptions of the mob from Laura Wexler's book. Images collided with the autopsy conclusions after the slaughter, the recorded accounts of the burials and then...then what? The finale produced by the overactive imagination of an inebriated preservationist running amuck with half truths and hypothetical theories as to the disappearance of one body? Was that what I was willing to go to the police with? My amateur theories on the sacrilegious excavation of a body in the moonlight by a man who existed only in my dreams, without one shred of quantifiable evidence that he had actually been there?

I remanded myself to stick to the facts. But that was the problem. There weren't enough of them to make a real dent in this thing. The phone rang and I stared at it, but refused to answer. It was probably Connie calling back just to check on me and I could not bring myself to talk trivia with such psychotic possibilities racing through the air. The buzzing ceased after six rings and I was glad as my head was beginning to hurt.

I drank in the coffee and noted its ratio to alcohol in my system. I thought of Cecelia and my half hearted promise to quit. Sobriety might have been a better choice at this point, but I was still weak of constitution for this kind of work and needed whatever bolster presented itself. Willie would understand I thought, so I added a shot of Jack Daniels and thanked both Jack and Willie for their contribution to humanity. This kind of researching was way beyond the scope of my job! We weren't talking about fissures in foundations of buildings or glorified Civil War ghosts that refused to stay buried. We were talking about the fissures in the foundations of human nature where people exercised their demons on innocent souls without conscience.

I inhaled the remaining tepid liquid and felt the burn of alcohol inside my throat. After so long a time at the nipple of intoxication, would Haydon have still felt the graze of alcohol as abuse to flesh or comfort to the soul?

My Instant Messenger flashed with an e-mail address I did not recognize. I ignored it and explored the idea of grave robbing further. My Inbox flashed again with urgency. Too distracted by my theory, I ignored it a second time. The insanity of grave robbing on top of everything else that could have happened that day to Haydon rolled around in my head like that same weighted marble without a level plane to stop on. It was crazy to think he could have... that he would have...but if he had been desperate enough, might he have?

My laptop told me I had mail, but what I really had was a migraine the size of Texas. Two more e-mails from the same address popped onto the screen, but my mind kept returning to the photos. Hadn't the entire event been just as insane as what I was proposing? Witnessing the lynching of four people over the color of their skin, booze, money or even over something as ridiculous as interracial sex was bad enough. But now I was tossing in blasphemous behavior by an innocent on top of it! Had my maiden's poor Abel been as innocent as I presumed, or had he actually been crazy enough to remove a body from its grave?

My AIM flashed again. Whoever it was, was beginning to piss me off. I tried to round out my thoughts. If Haydon had robbed a grave, what reason could there have been for such a sacrilege? Or if it had been somebody else who robbed a grave...why would Haydon have ended up with the body? A body whose description sounded remarkably the same as one of the Moores Ford Bridge victims?

I reached for the diary and revisited the entry again, more to talk myself out of my own madness than to confirm it, but there it was.

"They know I could name as many as ten, and I shall remain eternally indebted to my silent companion for acting as the courier of truth. I hated leaving him there, but there was no other recourse..."

Jesus! It was staring me right in the eye. A courier was a diplomat, a soldier—someone with the responsibility of carrying and delivering official documents. Or...someone who carries and delivers something secretly—illegal drugs, smuggled goods, information gained through espionage. A secret bearer of information... a vehicle for delivery of a package or document—a courier!

Suddenly it all became clear. Haydon had moved one of the bodies after the burial to protect himself from incrimination that he had been either participant or spectator willingly. One of the four had served in the war—could he be the courier? He had been the one chastised for his uppity and haughty attitude toward the rural immigrants. Even to the point of flirting with white women of the community as he had in Europe.

Was it possible Haydon had planted the names of the men he could identify in the murderous mob with the body as insurance? In a silo somewhere between Moores Ford Bridge and Danburg? If so, the entry in the diary had been meant only as backup information in case something happened to him and he was unable to return and show someone where the fourth body was hidden! Oh dear God…my stomach lurched into my throat as the brutality of the possible truth stretched out before me. The diary would have then been his only backup policy should they get to him first, and that backup of the truth had been trapped in the belly of a scorched grandfather clock for sixty-one years, his only chance for survival lost!

The scenario was speculative, but it made more sense than anything else I had read. It was now 3:53 in the morning and I had a full day ahead. I was too tired to drive home, so I decided to spend the night at the Danburg. I glanced again at my screen. The address of the sender still did not register, so I simply applied my away message and let it go for the night. My head still pounding, I finished my whiskey, turned the light off and climbed the stairs to the first landing. Executing a small pirouette in the mirror somewhat ungracefully, I mounted the stairs to the upper hall and headed for her room, smiling to myself, and whispered to her we were both almost home.

Chapter Thirty

Exhausted, I lay half naked in the antique bed, distracted by the luminescent glow from a full moon that broke even outside the window of its original host. Through the lacy sheers, the moonlight projected a kaleidoscope of shadows. Even though my eyelids were heavy with anticipation, they refused to close. I rose to shut the damask draperies and then stalled as the view over the treetops took my breath away. His words came to my lips...

I look out the window above the rise of the roof and see the moon clinging with the same compromised desires as I to the bottom of the sky. Alone and desperate I hover just above your bed, begging your forgiveness for any unkind act I may have ever perpetrated in your presence as now you are my only courier and I cannot risk losing such an allegiance for want of a moment's bliss...

I placed my palm on the curve of my cheek and felt the warmth. Was there still hope another's hand might one day follow the path that now guided my fingertips down my breast, that I might feel that hand without shame? As I held my eyes shut, his impressions continued to stroke my mind.

A breeze sifts slightly through the eaves and you shiver with delight. I want you to know it takes monumental discipline to bend only selfishly to kiss your forehead, whisper my goodbyes and not crawl in beside you ...

If he had been in the room, the seduction of his language alone would have made the tremble in my throat descend to where my ardent desires resided. The moon dipped behind a cloud and a slight breeze teased through the eaves. For a moment I felt the rush of scented jasmine climb up from the columns beneath, rising to the occasion with my desires. I held my breath in an effort to capture the magic, inhaling the musk of leather-bound books. Is this what she felt standing here draped in gossamer, waiting for him to speak from beneath and heavily sigh his affections into her dreams? The perfumed air and the power of his words were intoxicating. I finally understood the addiction they shared. Had he walked into the room then I would have surrendered myself without thought of consequence.

Even now clinging to the hope of an involuntary invitation...

Tremor after tremor began to swell and involuntary invitations ran up and down my body for a man whose charm echoed within the walls, but whose touch would forever evade me.

Suddenly I needed to hear other words. Words that had nothing to do with death and injustice, crime or punishment, Maggie or the past. I wanted pretty words that told me I was wanted, needed, desired, here and now. That someone could devour my soul and return it with a smile. That I could dance naked in the silhouette of moonlight and bring a man to his knees in thanks that his words had wrought such liberation.

I ran down the hall, flipped the latch, threw open the door to the attic and slammed the light switch on. My heart was pounding and my ragged breath raced the sprites of unsettled dust to the top of the stairs. Reaching the landing, I canvassed the attic with frantic need. There simply had to be another book, another entry in another diary, a letter or note. I no longer cared about what was real and unreal for her, only for me. There was only insatiable need at this point that begged not to be denied. I wanted him in any manner left to the sane.

Even in my delirium, I realized how crazy it all was. I had fallen in love with a ghost. How dare he touch such private realms of my very being and leave me so raw and painfully aware of my own inability to engage with him physically. My heart continued to hammer away inside my chest begging, for the intimacy I knew would never come. Perched at the edge of madness I ran to the last shelf and fanned through every book, desperate to find anything. Bent in anguish, I recalled the final entry's soliloquy…

Should you wake, no matter how you might beg and I should want to surrender, I still must take my leave. I have borrowed no kiss that cannot be publicly repaid, but have without remorse stolen your precious book, hoping that one day you might read and know that there was one in this house who put you above all others, who never saw your youth as handicap or flaw.

Keep this and remember me. My hours are numbered, but yours… Alone, yours will stretch out mercilessly before you and all that you will remember of me is that I once held your hand, kissed your sweet cheek and broke a promise…

My heart broke in two at the tenderness that this man expressed for her. He had stood at this window that night and watched her… had written to her of his hearts desires and his deepest fears for them both, living a lifetime in between her shallow breaths. Committing to her heart and soul for all eternity, to touch without greed… to surrender without regret or rancor for the loss… to borrow but a kiss and leave his heart as ransom until she could return it. Oh, to be so loved! In a fit of jealous frustration I banged at the window sash and cried for want of such passion and heard nothing in return but the rustle of leaves.

The wind stirred the trees just beyond the roof of the warming kitchen and the moon danced between the patches that raked their way across the lawn below. I tried to imagine looking upon another person so lovingly, sacrificing your very soul to make certain they might understand the desperation in your every word as you fled their side, uncertain as to whether you would ever be allowed to return.

I had wasted eighteen months of my life on mending someone else's heartache instead of my own. Maggie had become me, and I her. Despondent, I slumped to the floor and sobbed for the terrible waste in our lives. Minutes passed as despair racked my soul. In between sobs I heard the faint chime of the five o'clock bells from the grandfather clock on the first floor below. A quote floated up through the passages of a book on the floor beside me:

"...Who casts not up his eye to the sun when it rises? But who takes off his eye from a comet when that breaks out? Who bends not his ear to any beel which upon any occasion rings? But who can remove it from that bell which is passing a piece of himself out of this world? No man is an island entire of itself; every man is a piece of the continent, a part of the main. If a clod be washed away by the sea, Europe is the less, as well as if a promontory were, as well as if a manor of thy friend's or of thine own were. Any man's death diminishes me, because I am involved in mankind, and therefore never send to know for whom the bell tolls; it tolls for thee..."*

The last chime struck and the vibration gonged through the floorboards and rattled the window. I took it as an omen. It was time to bury the past—everyone's. And when I lifted up my head to dry my tears and stare once more at the moon descending in the early morning sky, I saw the corner of a parchment wink in between the casement and the shadows cast by a towering pine and smiled.

Haydon had heard my prayers again.

Chapter Thirty-one

From the amount of soot and decay that fell from the brittle parchment, I thought I had finally found one of the Civil War documents, but quickly realized that was not the case. It was a letter from Haydon to Maggie. I knew it wasn't mine— that it should have remained sacred, but I no longer cared. If what Cheryl had said was true, just for the few hours I had left alone... I needed to pretend it was mine.

Darling Maggie,

If I were to tell you exactly what lies within my heart there would not be parchment enough to do justice to depth, nor border enough to attempt to measure. When I wrote once that the gift you grant is expression, I had no idea how much of me it would take to accomplish such a feat. I have ransomed my very soul as down payment for the slightest taste of you.

You seemed to have so little comprehension of the great gift of passion I wanted to give you. I felt I was standing upon a mountainside alone, overlooking the great precipice I had climbed without guide to show me the way back down. Had you not confessed your own passion, I would have left you yet unpoisoned by my emotional fatigue, and I would not have returned. Perhaps never again will there be such a chance to tell you that my heart is full, my mind ablaze with everything that pours from your lips, and that there is such electricity in your touch that the current carries itself through me with endless charge, so be certain not to tease.

Lost in the sea of my affections for you, I no longer care to find the shoreline of our collective insanity. Its margin is now so foreign to me that its purpose is lost. I am mad with joy, and if this is all I ever receive, it will have been worth the admission price of my heart. Whatever depth of affection is granted by God for such a humble being as I, whatever can be contained in so marginal a vessel... I want you to know I have been filled by you to the extent that I can barely maintain any conscious equilibrium, be it day or night.

I miss the feel of your tender hand in mine, the crush of morning kisses that brushed my fevered brow at the cusp of dawn and the way I opened my heavy eyes to find your gaze upon me with such appreciation and quiet longing. I write now only for you... of you... to you... about you... it is all the same in inspiration and I am dizzy with the onslaught whenever I put pen to pad. You are now my only dictionary... the thesaurus of my life... the punctuation in my days.

I can add nothing to, nor subtract anything from the moments that you graced my side at the Fitzgerald, but my gratitude for your touch and your impression upon my soul. May I live worthily enough to validate any pain brought to you by loving me.

My undying affections and admirations,

H

The dawn arrived without my permission and the sun began to kiss everything in its path except me. In the days before his death, she had been at the hotel with him, and I realized there was so much more to this story than even I had ever imagined.

I touched the margins of the page with a reverence and a humility I had never felt before. The words were beautiful, intelligently seductive, but most of all...private. As I folded it back up, the parchment bowed with salty tears that had no right to breach its sanctity, and I knew what I had to do...

Deliver the letter in person to a damaged woman who had waited sixty-one years for its arrival.

Chapter Thirty-two

I quietly spent the better part of the day inside. Emotionally exhausted, I tread more softly through the house than usual. The ghosts of the Danburg had earned their rest as well after such a fitful night. In an effort to regain some equilibrium, I drank a hot cup of coffee at the window of the attic and looked down upon a new day. The cremation pit looked less threatening than it had before, and suddenly it dawned on me.

If you had a fire, where would the evidence of it be most likely overlooked? Someplace out in the open. Someplace you would already expect to find ashes. On a whim, I sent instructions to the landscaper to dig as far as could be managed into the interior of the pit, and then set my suspicions aside to get back to the more pressing elements of my day.

The sterling rose had paled but had not yet dried. No doubt the morning dew had kept it alive and supple. It too was doing its best to survive and it made me realize, no one is guaranteed anything in life. We receive only what we are meant to receive and give back whatever we find ourselves brave enough to accommodate. I placed the letter to Maggie inside in the shelf space left open by the missing book and hoped that if she came that day, she would travel to where she had last held his affections. No one else would have known to look there and she deserved to find her shining knight apart and private from my prying eyes. I felt I had already disturbed enough of the Danburg ghosts without permission and it was the least I could do after they had shared so much of themselves with me.

The ghost of Haydon had shared with me a rare gift; the gift of true love. Not his for me of course, but of his for her and though it pained me, I knew it was not my place to receive Maggie's letter any more than it would have been my place to try and intercept his love. So, just as the fourth body of the Moores Ford massacre still lay somewhere waiting to act as courier, I replaced the envelope and waited too. The sun danced across the tops of the tin roofs as it mounted the horizon and I sipped another mouthful of warm brown liquid. The steam condensed on my eyeglasses and toyed with the reflected light as it crept between the yawning pines that lined the outer edges of the lawn. Each flower that lined the bed woke and spread its petals, giving back to the air the fragrance they had been gifted. I recognized that all of life was give and take and that I had lived long enough through other people's lives and resolved that I needed to get back to the management of my own. Frustrated, I decided a visit with Cattalieu was the quickest way to discovery.

I thought of Maggie and wondered if the Danburg could ever feel like the same haven or nightmare for her as it had been in her youth. I had tried so hard to stay close to the original personality of the house and maybe that was my mistake. Because who is to say what a house feels or does not feel about the lives that grow within it? How could I as an outsider, judge what was or was not meaningful to the hidden voices trapped within the halls? I left the letter and closed the attic door silently behind me.

Back downstairs I stood at the back alcove with my dust mitt and decided it was time to let the dust settle where the house decided, not where my white gloves willed. After carefully surveying the manicured grounds from the front porch, I turned and ran inside the front parlor and pulled the pegs that held the jibs fast. Let the magnolia leaves enter where they dared! They had more right to be here than I. The trees, along with the shed, woods and stone walls of the cemetery had seen it all from beginning to end, so who was I then to bar their entrance?

Happy to release and be released I refocused on details for the afternoon's event. The grandfather clock's original weights finally sat nestled in their velvet cocoons. Polished and glistening beside them, the silver-cast cylinders that had resided inside them with an explanation of how they had come to be.

Everything was ready two hours ahead. The caterers were in the back of the warming kitchen preparing trays as the first of the county officials began to arrive and posture, offering their contrived statements of admiration for and dedication to a harmonious preservation. I finished filing some papers and then went about clearing my emails and my slate for the remainder of the day. The AIM flashed again and I saw the same email address as the one from the night before pulse in the lower right hand corner of my screen. Annoyed, I went to click my away message on and then decided to read it, since whoever it was persistent and seemed hell-bent on getting my attention...

Ms. Horton,

I am delighted to be in touch with you. I had no idea your questions were directed more towards the Moores Ford murders than the trials of the Danburgs. If you will answer a few questions concerning your Moores Ford work, I shall be very grateful.

What is the aim of your Moores Ford work? In other words, what do wish it to accomplish with your investigation?

What was my aim? Investigation? Who the hell was this? The address didn't ring a bell. Caught off guard by the frankness of my mysterious mailer, I reread the message and responded.

Who is this? I appreciate your concern, but will reserve responding until I understand what it is you want to know from me and why. Have we met?

The emailer replied:

Ms. Horton,

I have a very long interest in the Moores Ford case and wish to know more about your work. What Moores Ford literature (books, newspapers, magazines, etc.) did you consult? For example, did you use Ms. Wexler's account or others? And did you read any of the original FBI interviews? In other words, where exactly are you getting your "facts" from concerning the Moores Ford murders?

I stared at the screen for a minute. Who the hell knew I was researching Moores Ford, other than Connie? I read the message again with caution. Who was this person and why was I being interrogated as to what my intentions were regarding Moores Ford Bridge? The screen blinked at me.

Are you there?

My first instinct was to shut it off. My second was to blast away and demand knowledge of my electronic host's identity and his intentions. His message suggested there was a difference between the information available within the public domain and what was available elsewhere if one were to seek it.

With fingers poised above the keys, I tried to formulate a response in my head. One that would buy me time to check my address book without giving away or pushing away too much information necessary to what it was I was trying to accomplish... namely, knowledge of Haydon's whereabouts that day. If this person had access to information I did not, what would be the cost or the benefit for them to share it now?

I scrolled through my address book and then did a search... nothing! The laptop hummed as pop-ups with dancing figures over lower mortgage rates filled the borders of the screen and kept me company while I formulated a response. Without knowledge of who it was, my posturing was of the utmost importance. If I acted offended too easily, I would lose credibility. If I begged, I would invite further chaos I had no time to entertain. The screen blinked again.

Miss Horton? Are you there?

The caterers were busy in the background setting up in the kitchen and the cacophony of their chatter and clattering dishes bounced inside my head. I couldn't think clearly with all the distractions. I tried to read the message again and reorganize my thoughts, knowing my hesitation was eating away precious seconds and leaving an impression of indecision I did not want to give. I decided I would use honey instead of vinegar. My hand moved to the keyboard to reply and then suddenly the AIM shifted again.

I sense the timing is bad for you, what with the festivities this afternoon. I shall try to re-engage at a later time. Please consider the following in between times...

Does your work respect and honor the Moores Ford victims and their loved ones yet in life? If yes, in what manner does it do so? Please give an example. And does your work thoroughly condemn the Moores Ford killers and the white establishment which supported and protected them? If yes, in what manner does it do so? Please give an example. I see that you have used "incident" when speaking of the murders at Moores Ford; why not use "lynching"? I realize that these questions are difficult ones; however, please answer them as best you can. Do you know of a Mr. Welborn V. Jenkins and his work?

I shall certainly monitor your work with keen interest. With all good wishes, I look forward to hearing from you in the very near future.

I tried to type a response and the screen blinked. My AIM box sent regrets. The sender had signed off.

Nothing could have been more frustrating. The connection had been broken and the sender was gone leaving me with a laundry list of motives to consider. I swore under my breath. Murphy's Law!

The dancing mortgagers were now in a full kick chorus line, scrolling across the tops and bottoms of the screen, and I wanted to reach in and strangle them each as they hoochie-coochied their way into cyber space. I hit the keys with fervor and shut their performance down along with my anger. I should be happy someone was reaching out. If I could just keep myself in check, I could make it through the day and discover what the intentions were of my mystery mailer later that night. Though the message did not specify a time of re-engagement, it did relay the party was knowledgeable of the showing. That and the fact they had reached out several times the night before led me to believe they would know when to reach again. What I needed was patience.

Footsteps coming down the hall reminded me I had other duties to attend to. A uniformed woman stood politely as I closed and locked the door to my office. Turning the key in the tumbler, I pondered the messenger's questions. First of all, how had this person heard I was digging around for information? Secondly and more poignantly...was what I was doing to honor the victims? Was my intent to condemn the killers and those that continued to protect them, or was it something else? And thirdly, who the hell was this person Jenkins and why should it matter if I knew of him or not? I had not recalled seeing that name appear anywhere on any document I had thus far reviewed, and the fact that this was the one name mentioned among the hundreds that could have been intrigued me. I reminded myself to Google him later that evening.

The woman tapped me on the shoulder and I jumped. In my distraction, I had not heard her request, let alone responded to it.

"I'm sorry. I didn't mean to alarm you. I just needed some information for the staff."

Hell, didn't we all, I thought, and shoved my keys in my pocket. I replaced the smirk on my face with a smile and she eased.

"I really didn't mean to interrupt. I just needed...do you know the location of another wall outlet inside the warming kitchen where we could plug in a large urn? For the reception?"

"An urn...?" I repeated, and chided myself. Everything had taken on double meanings for me since the Danburg. She had said "for coffee."

"For coffee... right? The urn... it's for coffee... for the reception?" and I looked back at the door to my office thinking about the question relating to the so called *"facts."*

She looked at me with large eyes. Of course she had meant coffee. Right now her entire world consisted of securing steaming cups of Maxwell House coffee and electrical outlets. For my mysterious messenger, his reality consisted of his concerns over my intentions... and my reality consisted of my concerns over my maiden's consort and what it was he was preparing for almost sixty years ago to the day. I glanced at the date and time on my watch and said a silent prayer that the instant messenger seek me out later that evening and remanded myself to be more focused on the matters at hand. I let the images of the numbers on my watch fade. The anniversary of July 25th was creeping up fast. Oblivious to my hesitation, the woman's eyes narrowed to slits as she was now being paged by her superior.

First task... coffee.

"The outlet, ma'am?" she insisted.

"Follow me. I'll show you where," and I moved past her and walked the steps back down the hall to where the day would take another twist.

* * *

Distant Danburg relations and invited press and project officials spilled over the tailored lawns with their champagne glasses and their arrogance. I watched carefully for the long black car that would bring my maiden girl home. Casually I answered questions about the minor alterations and concessions made in the reconfigurations of the rooms as each member of the private party worked their way through the upper chambers and closets. Comments both kind and catty fell on my ears without consequence. It didn't mattered what they thought... only she mattered, and she had yet to arrive. I stood poised as docent until I could no longer bear the brunt of their insignificant comments. Where was she?

The grandfather clock began to chime six bells and I prayed the Fitzgerald had received notification that I would be arriving later than previously anticipated. She had not yet arrived and I worried that there was but another hour left until the gala would break up into smaller groups that would infiltrate the Morrison Cafés of the world and agnatic points beyond. Respectful, I had pulled the blank tag from case thirteen earlier in the day, leaving a slight indentation as personal tribute to Maggie. Her diary was not an artifact. It was her life, and neither I nor anyone else had a right to display it as if it were no more than reference material or historical fodder. I rushed past the case and went to the small window that jutted out over the back entry of the servants', stairs searching for her slight figure.

Misses Celine and Cattalieu Chenille were holding court with a local commissioner and it took Herculean efforts to stand still and not budge as I watched Celine traverse the lawn to where the rose lay untouched. Cattalieu anticipated the collision and bent in an effort to pick up the rose. Without breaking her stride Celine put her hand out, staying her sisters' hand. Devoid of hesitation she charged forward and ground the rose with the toe of her shoe as she pivoted in place atop it and made way for the rear of the porch, still chatting with the commissioner.

Appalled, I banged at the window pane and grunted my disgust. Holding fast to the arm of her male escort with those long white evening gloves I had seen her wear on the first day we met, she swiveled those big brown eyes upward, smirked and continued her navigation out of my sight. I banged again and bit at my lower lip, swearing under my breath. Cattalieu caught the gist of my rage and scuttled under the columns to avoid my gaze further. Furious, I decided I had had enough of the Danburg selective memory and chased my anger down the back hall to the rear alcove of the center hall. Just as I reached the final set of doors to the patio beyond, I caught the sound of faint and steady footfalls. The cadence sounded familiar and I recognized it as the woman's steady shuffle from the day before. Freezing mid-step, I listened as she stood quietly before the grandfather clock that smiled back at her and announced her arrival as 6:15 p.m. on the dot.

Chapter Thirty-three

My heart skipped several beats and I clutched my chest. The sudden movement attracted her attention and even though I tried not to intrude, I was involuntarily drawn further into the hall by the power of her presence. She turned slowly and I held her gaze. She knew who I was without need of introduction. Knew I had done my best to give her back a small part of who she had once been within these walls and a tear brazed her cheek as she weakly smiled.

I was so overcome with her grace that I held my breath, not wanting her to fade from view. I knew this woman instantly as my maiden. As intimately as I knew myself, I knew her. And though I had seen her in my dreams, she was so different than I had ever pictured her. Younger and older at the same time, I saw who she had been somewhere just below the gather of her skin. Underneath all the trappings of time ran the smooth and un-blemished innocence of the child who danced in my dreams at the top of the stairs. I raised my eyes to the landing before the mirror where two spindled rods still remained vacant and smiled.

She tilted her head upwards and then recognized where I had focused. She then smiled with great enthusiasm at our now col-lective memory. The depth of the blue in her eyes ran as deep as any ocean and there was such pain and forgiveness in them that I was speechless. Timidly, she offered her hand and I crossed the great bridge of our communal heartache and took it without hesitation. It was small and nimble, thinned with age.

As if I had done it a thousand times before, I brought her hand to my lips and kissed it lightly. She covered mine with one of her own and I cowered inside, in awe of such a learned heart that spoke so wisely without ever a word passing from her lips. Forgiveness was an unspoken theme in her eyes that told me it was not only time, but it was right to let go of the hurt and the pain. A tear slipped from my lower lid and she graced my cheek with a kiss that lit upon my skin as soft as any butterfly. I thought of Haydon and his description of her kisses, "...*As soft as a butterfly that tarries only long enough to catch the color of the flower beneath it, leaving in its wake only the impression of having been touched.*"

I graciously returned her hand and she slowly removed a simple band of gold from her left ring finger and bid me take it for the slot in case thirteen that lay empty. Her voice was small and laced with compassionate authority. I took the bauble and turned it over gently in my palm. She nodded with her eyes in patent approval of my tenderness. The evening light that filtered through the etched glass door struck at just the precise angle and I knew her secret.

The man in the moon had never been the cherub in the clock... it had been the man in her heart. The man who spoke to her in the moonlight from the columned walkway beneath her bedroom window sill and begged her to reply in kind was one and the same. The man who had stopped his ritual drink and instead wore it as perfume to ensure the destination of a shed that sat just below her bed where he could gaze and she watched, waiting patiently for his return each night. Theirs had been no sordid tryst... theirs had been a secret engagement and elopement... its public announcement eclipsed by the event of human tragedy.

As she reached forward and touched the cherub like face of a timepiece that smiled back, I read the worn inscription just inside the thinned curve of her wedding band: "Forever and always, Haydon, 7/24/46."

In an instant I knew what had eluded me, why there had been no more entries after that night. I could not contain the tears as I watched her mount the first of twenty two steps.

* * *

I sat at the edge of the stairs fingering her treasured gift as she made her way, one step at a time. With all the audible clatter of the reception yards away, I strained to hear the careful calculation of her footfall as she made her way to the outside corners of stairs 3, 4, 7. Touched by her efforts to commemorate the night's events of her memory, I reverently waited for her to navigate the swollen edges of number 17 and then left her to private reverie. Her hands ran softly atop the wooden banister and made no sound as her bare finger tapped the successive inches away without its golden band to accompany it.

It all made sense now. There would have been no change to her maiden name in any record, since she and Haydon shared the same surname. There would have been no consolation for her grief in the light of the commitment that had been made one day prior to her loss. No family legacy important enough to have buried the truth...except for Celine's!

I made it to the rear alcove of the hall and heard the haughty laugh of the woman who had done her best to burn every bridge and memory of nobility the Danburg had to offer. The landscaper came in through the front and informed me he had found something in the pit. When he described it for me, I sent him into town to the usual place with instructions it be cleaned and restored. If anything of value were found inside, he should call me as soon as possible. I made a mental note to add another slot to case thirteen just in case and moved towards the back door with measured steps.

Pacing off my steps to the patch of grass where the rose lay, I bent and gently gathered it in my hands. As I did, I felt her eyes upon me. Though it was not necessary, I looked up towards the attic. My maiden's palms were wrapped lovingly around the envelope I had left in the breach. With arthritic tenure, her other hand rose slowly to her heart. She made the connection and I nodded that it had been there waiting for her all these years. The tears streamed from her eyes and I averted mine to give her space within her own grief.

With another clue to the Danburg's secrets now safely in the landscaper's bag, I searched the lawn with absolute conviction of purpose and found Cattalieu beyond the back patio standing beside her sister near the warming kitchen. Culling the weaker sister from the herd was easy. She took note of the direction of my gaze and knew the charade had come to an end. I motioned her inside the kitchen, where I shuffled caterers out into the yard in twelve different directions and told them not to return until every champagne bottle was emptied and every tray devoid of decoration. Then I locked the two of us in, set the rose on a silver tray under a glass pastry dome and demanded to know the true history of the Danburg and the second great fire!

* * *

Outside the warming kitchen, Celine paced the length of the columned porch, wringing her evening-length gloves in her bare and battered hands. Seeing Catty take a seat opposite me sent sparks flying from her eyes. When I rose to close the curtains, she began to storm the door but was cut off by a local politician asking for a tour of the grounds. Her lips smiled and her eyes burned as I closed the curtain. Safe inside behind locked doors, her sister Catty emptied three tulip glasses of champagne before she spoke.

Bolstered by years of abuse and booze she began spilling her guts about a truth she'd been holding inside for over sixty years and did not stop for nearly forty-five minutes. Everything seemed to hinge on that one infamous night... the night of the great fire.

"It was July 25th, 1946..." she began and I did my best to remain silent while she emptied herself of everything she could remember.

She told me how the house suffered substantial damage, and three out of four outer building were completely destroyed, along with the first fifteen acres of cotton. That the loss of crops and the cost of what little reconstruction could be managed to make the house inhabitable did more damage to the family finances than they could afford to weather. How she and Celine took on the role of live in help and how they all did their best to recoup, but the family just never bounced back. The fire was the first in a long line of tragedies that summer that followed the discovery days later of Haydon's body floating in the swamp.

"Maggie was beyond consolation at the news. Then her father accepted his position up north immediately after the fiasco, hoping the change in scenery would help her deal better with the trauma, but to no avail. She was distraught with sorrow and tried to commit suicide, claiming they had been married just days before, countering my older sister's claim that Haydon had finally agreed to wed her."

I could not imagine the despair my maiden must have felt. "Go on..." I directed.

Cattalieu looked towards the window. Celine was still on the arm of a local commissioner, but remained obviously agitated. Gripping the stem of the champagne flute with white knuckles, Catty refocused her attentions on the rose and continued.

"Since Maggie had nothing other than the thin band to document the union, the father dismissed the incessant declaration as delusion. After all, the word was out about Haydon and Celine's situation, which made Maggie's claims even more difficult to believe. I tried to tell the truth... but nobody would listen to me" she implored.

"What happened to Maggie then? Did she go north without knowing where he was?" I asked.

Catty told me Celine took her sweet time in informing Maggie and her parents about Haydon's death. Stalling before she sent them word of his demise, she used the time to concoct an alibi that would cover the multitude of sins committed that night on her family's behalf. She told Lucy that she and Haydon had been lovers. That once she discovered she was pregnant, she told Haydon they must be wed and his drinking and wayward days were over. Including the idle flirtations with her younger cousin. She said he flew into a rage, saying he would not be trapped like a caged animal. Demanded she "do something about it," and when she refused, he set the house to flame.

"Celine claimed the trauma of the fire and the discovery of Haydon's body in the swamp led to her depression and the miscarriage weeks later. The day it happened... I was forced to carry the bloody evidence of the loss to our demanding Uncle. I will never forget the muffled screams behind her bedroom door and the bloodied walls of the chamber pot as it slid through the opened doorway. I vomited for hours after out back in the peonies. No one ever said another word about Haydon... or the baby." She downed the rest of golden liquid in the bottom of her glass and closed her eyes.

She continued after several minutes, telling me days after his death and Celine's "confession," the second copy of the marriage certificate mysteriously came to the Danburg house by way of a young man dressed in military garb. Enraged at the truth of Haydon's betrayal and the compromised position her confession had left her in, Celine took the certificate and Maggie's diary to burn in the cremation pit.

"That's what I had seen out the window that day from the front parlor. That was the memory I was trying to tell you when she and I brought the clock back, remember? We fought about the position of the stupid chair by the window. I was trying to tell you then... but she cut me off and told you I was unreliable."

I told her I knew there was something to what she was trying to tell me that day and that I had taken everything Celine had said about her with a grain of salt. Anxious for the information I kept my comments brief and let her continue.

"Curious as to what she was doing, I told Lucy I didn't want to plat tea party anymore, then watched out the window for a few seconds before I followed her into the woods. She screamed obscenity after obscenity into the air, openly confessing that she would suffer the fires of hell and have him beaten and hung again for the pain he had caused her. I didn't understand everything she was yelling, but I knew there was something terribly wrong. She became hysterical when the diary smothered the marriage certificate and it refused to take flame. I had never seen her so out of control before. I couldn't imagine why she would go to so much trouble to burn something that didn't even belong to her?"

"So you knew it was Maggie's diary?" I asked.

"Yes... but we all had one when we were little. They were nothing special. Just nonsense..." she added. "That's why it didn't make sense. She could have burned mine and I wouldn't have cared. It was just gibberish."

I tried to pull her away from the flames but she turned on me like a rabid dog. As I cringed with fright, she thrust the certificate further into the flames and held it there, searing her own flesh. Dumbfounded by my sister's delirium I tried to pull her away from the pit again crying for help, but no one ever answered my pleas. Not even my Uncle who watched from the dining room window as she writhed in pain upon the ground. I will never forget the look of disgust on his face..."

I watched the younger sibling take a long hard pull on the tulip glass to her left, drain it completely and reach for another. "I never even knew it was a marriage certificate till later... I swear. I never knew..." and she sipped silently on the champagne as tears ran down her face. Every word Celine had said about that night and the following day had been a lie. Crushed by her disappointment both in her family, her sister and herself, Cattalieu began to explain what followed in between sobs.

"You don't know what we went through..." she blubbered. "What she did to prove she had lost a child. You can't understand. We were elders in the church, pillars of the community. She was beyond desperate..."

Released from the politicians grasp, Celine rushed the kitchen and clawed like an animal at the back screened door but it was locked. Caught off guard by the noise and the sudden appearance of her face, I jumped. Her eyes seared with hatred through the glass pane and I felt the flesh on my hands and arms begin to blister. We locked eyes for a moment and a shiver went down my spine. Her nostrils flared as she spun on her heels and began to pace again. Suddenly there was a change in her posture. She began heading out towards the side yard and the portico. I couldn't remember if the front parlor door had been left unlocked. Fearful of the outcome if it weren't, I visually canvassed the lock at the end of the hall as Catty renewed her monologue and I renewed my courage.

"Scattered throughout the community's households for shelter after the fire, there was no one near enough to hear either one of us. Drunk with pain, Celine continued to spout bible verses, swearing she had been forced to save the Danburg name from the incestuous stain the document would bring to bear if made public. I finally recognized the document for what it was and did the best I could to save what little was left of the diary; hiding it in the bottom of the clock."

"So that was why it was so important for you to bring it back...the clock I mean?" I whispered.

"Weeks went by. I stayed at my sister's side. At the time I could not have imagined anyone capable of..."

"Capable of what?" I asked, watching for Celine to re-appear any moment.

"Celine's "evidence of a miscarriage" had been produced by painful, barbaric and unsanitary means. Toxic with fever from infections to her burns, she laid in bed with bandaged hands for weeks after. And by the time she was well, the community had moved on to another scandal that rocked the South, some ninety miles away. Whenever anyone asked about her hands, she simply said they had been damaged that night in the fire as she had tried to save Maggie. With Maggie gone and Haydon's mother and stepfather both in an emotional and medicinal fog, Celine was left to fabricate whatever blanket of truth covered multiple lies best.

When news of Haydon's death circulated and folks started asking questions, Celine swore me to silence and we stuck to the story she had told the Sheriff. Months later, guilt overruled my fear and I devised to get the diary back. Unfortunately, the lot of damaged furniture had been sold or given away for work in kind to help with the reconstruction of the manor. The clock, the diary and the truth had been bargained away to the highest bidder and so I could do nothing without it as evidence."

Catty took a deep breath as her story came to a close. "That was until the owner of the Danburg gave the house and its land to the state to restore...the rest you know. Had it not been for you trying to gather some of the original furniture, the diary would still be out there rotting, and no one would have ever known the truth. The clock was only returned after someone saw your advertisement of its description in the local rag." She sighed, wiped a tear and drained the last bit of pale liquid from the bottom of a tulip glass as the last little bit of war paint lipstick rubbed off on its rim.

"The truth would have been buried and forgotten by everyone... just like Haydon."

"Except by you... and Celine... and most of all...Maggie..." I said.

I heard the front door close and I panicked for a second until I saw Celine's head through the corner of the curtain. Thankfully it wasn't Celine who had just entered, but Maggie who had just left. I knew my maiden had been standing just beyond the threshold for quite some time. Her soft shuffle had given her away, but that was okay. She above all deserved to hear the truth and have the time to absorb privately what had been said. I heard the heavy door of the Lincoln slam and the gravel spit from beneath the tires. Lulled into a false sense of security, I did not realize Maggie in her haste had left the door unlocked. Minutes later Celine made quick work of the opportunity. Storming the front hall she demanded my presence, screaming injustice and bad form from the top of her lungs. Catty took her awkward leave by way of a back one.

Chapter Thirty-four

I caught my breath and my heart continued to pound in my chest as she edged her way into the kitchen looking for her sister. I thought about the diary, the church covenant and the section about back-biting and tattling. Had the fire, "Haydon's revenge," been misnamed after all? Or had there been something else implied in the moniker other than fire?

Celine crossed the threshold with deliberation, rounded the table and then began to open the curtains one at a time in an attempt to canvass the landscape and locate her sister. Catty had positioned herself across the lawn safely sheltered amongst other local matrons. Celine unable to interrogate her sibling turned her attentions to me. She crossed the room one heel click at a time and did not sit, but motioned for me to do so. From directing I knew that when one actor sits and one stands... there is a distinction of power perceived by placement. I refused to be seen as submissive and so remained standing, pouring myself a glass of champagne to steady my nerves.

"So... my younger sister finally found her tongue, did she?" she baited. I raised my glass and saluted her smiling to stall my response and gauge her stability. She took note of my shaky hand and calmed her voice.

"I know all about you, Caroline. Your anxiety attacks. Tsk, tsk. You women with weak constitutions... Such a shame not being able to cope with the complexities of life" she patronized. "Have you taken your medicine yet today?"

I was aghast. How could she have possibly known?

"No sense having two hysterical women coming unglued today." She sighed. "I was surprised Catty would have mixed hers with alcohol, but then her judgments have never been very sound."

I lowered my glass to the table. The only one who could have known about my prescription was the pharmacist.

"That's right Caroline. The pharmacist is a very dear old friend of mine. A bit of a chatter box, but then you know all about small town etiquette. Those kinds of friends come in handy when one is in need of information."

I thought about my earlier appraisal of small town behavior.

"Does this friend have a cat? Perhaps one that shits... purple?" I asked and then let go a nervous laugh.

She never broke cadence. "Why don't you sit down, relax and tell me what our dear sweet little Cattalieu was so intent on telling you and then... if you have any questions... I can explain it in more rational terms." And she reached to empty the champagne bottle into a glass for herself.

"I don't usually drink. It being a nasty habit and all, but I will make an exception this one time. After all, it's a special occasion. It isn't everyday the entire population of Danburg comes to pay homage to one of its founding families."

I flinched as she poured some into a glass and then pushed it forward. "Here... why don't you join me, Caroline? I hear you have quite a love affair with the grapevine." I left the glass where it was.

"Why Caroline...not thirsty?" she questioned and then paused in her sarcasm long enough to push the glass a few inches closer to me. "Oh, how rude of me placing such temptation so close to your trembling hand...without even a clue as to how desperately you must want to take it."

I bit my tongue and kept silent, all the while wishing I could suck down the bottle with a straw. Still, spite was now the greater motivator than alcohol. I kept my hands pinned under the table and my lips closed.

She smirked at my tentative resistance. "Oh, I see. Trying to dry out a bit, are we? How admirable of you, Caroline. I suppose it wouldn't do to have public officials knowing too many of your secrets now, would it?" she baited. "Oh... I so hate wasting such a fine libation, but no matter..." she sighed and then dribbled the golden liquid slowly onto the floor of the warming kitchen. "Can't have you going about half sloshed, spouting lies and misgivings about this family and not sharing some of your own. That wouldn't be fair. And we want to be fair to everyone now, don't we?"

I had no idea where she was taking things, so I waited to see which direction her ill wind would blow.

"Oops...almost gone." She said as she tilted the bottle one more time to tease. "Since your services as preservationist are no longer required here, you may mop that up when I'm finished and then take your leave. By the servants exit preferably..." she mocked while I metaphorically bled from the inflicted wound to my pride. "...you remember where it is, correct?"

"Of course I know where it is. I'm the one that put this place back together." I blathered egotistically.

"Yes. And you did a fine job as well. You simply cannot imagine how proud I am that the Danburg has once again been restored to its grandiose beginnings. And that is precisely why I cannot have you or my deranged, little sister out there spreading untruths about our family or its origins. So... what did she have to say?"

I picked up the bottle and inhaled the remaining champagne to calm my nerves, wishing it had been Jack Daniels.

"There...have another." She said as she pulled another bottle from the case on the floor. "It will help ease the pain of your long awaited departure from our lives!" I winced and she continued. "So...did you allow Catty just to ramble... or was there a point to her silly childhood fantasies?" she baited.

I shrugged my shoulders and watched as she pulled the curtain one more time to check on Catty's whereabouts. Not finding her sister amongst the crowd, she readdressed me with an eerie calm. "You know Caroline... you're much too smart to fall for such rubbish. Let's not trifle with the preposterous. Let's try to concentrate on your real interest—Haydon. Now there's a real story to get worked up over."

My hand steadied as my fear began to turn to something else. "Struck a nerve, did I?"

I set the champagne bottle down rather abruptly.

"Ah yes... I believe I have. Well then," she deliberated. "Let's start a little bit lower on the food chain then. Ah yes! Maggie, my annoying cousin! Let's talk a bit about her and how she tried to commit suicide!"

I flinched and she took note of the scars on my wrists and raised an eyebrow. "You are a lot like her in some ways, Caroline. Inquisitive, book smart, not unattractive... damaged goods."

I hit the table with my hand and my bottle toppled to the floor.

"You shouldn't be so sensitive about your shortcomings, my dear." she toyed.

"You have no right to judge the way I..." I hammered, but she cut me off.

"To what?" she demanded. "To judge you the same way you judged me from a few facts and tasteless innuendos?" and she plowed through. "While I did my best to keep the family together, she did her best to draw attention to herself. It was a disgusting narcissistic ploy for sympathy, but that had always been her way! Poor dear little cousin, Maggie. She thought we didn't know about where she really came from—that we were stupid just because we lived in the country."

"What are you talking about?" I asked. The randomness of her statement had taken me completely off guard and I had no idea where she was heading with it.

"No one ever questioned why she didn't look like the rest of us...him too! The family name was at stake. Of course, she was from Haydon's side of the family. But he was dark, as dark in the soul as he was in the eyes. His mother's brother apparently had the same disease. Promiscuous they were... couldn't commit to just one mate for life! He divorced his first wife and married a woman who had already had a child."

I suddenly saw the reason why the alliance between Maggie and Haydon rankled her so. They were related only by marriage and not by blood… same as she and Haydon, but without the same results.

"Bad blood, that's what's was wrong with her. Weak and pasty. Couldn't deal with the harsh realities of the world!" and she slapped her gloves against the table and bit at the air.

I motioned towards her scarred hands. "And what would you call that?" She blanched with anger.

"My cross for the sins I have committed!" she blurted and my heart broke for her as though the wounds were fresh for us both. I rubbed at my wrists and held back a tear. She had self mutilated out of shame for her lustful longings.

"I understand," I said trying to empathize. She recoiled at my compassion and lit into my flesh with words that cut like a fresh hickory switch.

"You know nothing of my pain! Not of the way they mocked me behind my back! She cooed like a dove and he would salivate and follow her every step like a love-sick puppy. He had no concern for the fool he made of himself! She was the daughter of a stained woman and he, even worse, was too consumed by his primitive lust to see it! She flaunted her form in the moonlight like a common whore… stole him from me is what she did!"

I was horrified at the extent to which this event still riled her after sixty-one years.

"I imagine that was how her mother had enticed her victim into marriage as well. We were never privy to all the sordid details, but enough of them to piece together the past. Everything Haydon's mother said was highly suspect—so many exaggerated displays of melancholy! Did you know she went insane with grief? Catty and I were practically sold into slavery, caring for the feeble-minded bitch while our uncle, Haydon's step-daddy, took to drink. Rather ironic, all things considered! Bad blood all around in that household. I couldn't wait to get away from them, but they had a stranglehold on the land as long as Haydon's grandparents paid the bills."

I wanted to interject compassion to try and counter balance the violent mood swings, but she had started to ride that emotional roller coaster and there was no stopping it once it left the guardrails of her equilibrium.

"When they found Haydon's body, the wealthy grandparents cut off the stipend. Blaming the old man for his puritanical short sightedness and for pushing poor Haydon to the limits. Naturally Catty and I suffered greatly under everyone's inability to rise above the family trials. No one more than I, as you can see" she said, shoving her scarred wrists in my face, "but at last we were free of the Danburg curse."

I was astounded at how unrequited love had devastated so many lives, but that was not the first time I had heard about the Danburg curse. Everyone in town seemed convinced of its existence.

"Haydon's revenge... the Danburg curse? What exactly are we talking about here?"

"When my mother, who was a Danburg, married into the Chenilles, she lost her inheritance as the bulk of the wealth stayed with the land and my mother's brother. When he married that whore from Atlanta, she squandered the family wealth on her precious little Haydon, selling off parcels for his education and his poor habits."

"I thought the mortgage fee was already being paid for," I said, implying there was no need for her to lie about the facts with me any longer.

"That was just to meet expenses... not get ahead of them!" she spit back. "I didn't mind so much in the beginning as I saw the chance to make him mine. It was a short term loss that I knew would pay off in the long run after we were wed. My aunt and uncle's health was always questionable and with their eventual deaths... the Danburg and the remaining lands would fall to Haydon. With a marriage, I could reclaim the family wealth and him all at the same time."

I watched her circle the table and kept my eyes trained on the scarred hands that edged closer and closer to the caterer's knife set. Celine was becoming completely unhinged, but I wasn't certain she was capable of physical violence to someone other than herself. None the less, I continued to monitor her movements. Every time her fingers flinched, so did I.

"Everything was fine, till... her. The first time she came, nobody, including Haydon, gave her the time of day. She was a pouty, beastly little thing. But the older she got, the more she filled herself out and draped herself like a carpet at his feet. They talked of books and art, of fine museums. By the time she was seventeen and had filled in all her darts, he was drooling like a St. Bernard.

I saw her bathe naked in the kitchen uncovered for his delight. Twice, that I know of, she stole my Aunt's negligees and pranced like a two dollar whore in front of the window for his pleasure. How was a Christian woman like myself to compete with the likes of such a Delilah?" and she reached for the nearest knife, fondled it for effect and then stabbed it into the table for effect. I was shocked at the display and began to re-evaluate my safety.

"I wanted her dead!" she screeched. "Still think you understand my pain you shallow little piece of shit? You read a few words, frame a few photos, and suddenly you think you know how everything was! What do you know about this family...the Danburg...its ghosts?" It cut me to the quick. What did I really know for certain about any of them?

"You write the history you think you see. You imagine you can piece back together people's worlds with a few strokes of paint and a new door or two. You sit in that office of yours and pass judgment."

I moved as far away from the table as I could. The skin across the top of her knuckles went white as she tightened her grip on the knife.

"You make assumptions about people's lives. You look at their faces, chart their wrinkles and think you know where they have been in life....".'" She grabbed at a photo that lined the wall above a plaque that pictured the house and a few of its inhabitants in the mid 1800's. "What do you see here?" she demanded.

Frightened by her proximity, I edged toward the opposite side of the room from her, but she followed and shoved the print into my face. It was a grouping of matrons on the front lawn of the Danburg just after the reconstruction of the first main house that was purportedly burnt by Sherman in his historic March to the Sea. One of the matrons appeared to be pregnant and wore a sullen expression.

"Well...speak child! What do you see?" she insisted and pressed the print closer.

On closer inspection the face presented a distant echo of the one before me. "I see a bunch of bitter old women who wear the same scowl as you," I spat back with vehemence and soon realized it was a bad move on my part. She threw the frame at my feet and the glass shattered.

"Look closer and learn, you naïve little bitch. Take a good long look at the one in the middle..." she demanded and toyed with the handle of the knife for effect.

"You think that's the look of bitter? That woman was my great, great grandmother, born and bred right here in Danburg. She's buried out there in that cemetery beyond the stone wall with her husband and six of her children. Look again at her crippled fingers, the bend in her shoulders. That is the look of pain, you pathetic girl. She paid for the rights of her southern heritage with her bones and their blood. Tended this house and the fields during the War Between the States and even for months after, when most of the man slaves ran off, thinking only of themselves and the freedom your Yankee president afforded them. Alone without help or money to hire, she spent every penny to build the Danburg back from destruction. Yet you stand on the backs of my ancestors and claim a successful restoration as if it were your own!"

I looked at my watch. The landscaper should have been back from his errand in town thirty minutes ago. She thrust the knife forward to get my attention.

"Unlike you, she didn't run away from her troubles. She stayed and fought for her children, her home and her land. She was raped when the Union soldiers came through. They took everything they could carry off, including her honor, and she was left alone to survive. She lost her husband, her home...you think you know her life, now from one sorry assed little photo Miss Preservationist?"

"Is that what they led you to believe?" I whispered.

Her eyes narrowed to fine slits. "What was that?"

I cringed. She was wrong about me. I had never judged the people represented in the photos of the past. It was none of my business. I merely pieced the historic accounts and put together what evidence could support. I had only been trying to make a point with my comment and obviously had misjudged my opponent's level of knowledge about her own heritage. But since I had yet to garner all the facts, I kept what little I knew close to my vest.

"Is that what they led you to believe?" I repeated. Her eyes darted towards the knife and her face twisted with anger. Perhaps she had she not really known the truth after all. I would have taken it back, but it was too late. She pressed for more information waving her knife and my only defense was to present a good offense by using what little I knew to wound.

"I said... is that what they told you?" My head was spinning.

She stared at the picture on the floor and studied the features on the face. "What are you implying, Ms. Horton? That she wasn't raped or that it wasn't a Union soldier?"

My silence stymied her.

"Who else could it have been? There was no one left. She was all alone in the end. Just like me...alone. Left to clean up everybody else's garbage! All the men had gone off to fight the war and all the cowardly slaves had headed for the hills. Her husband was killed in battle and she was a widow. There is no other plausible explanation!"

Nothing in my personal experience taught me how to read her response. Did she know the truth of what I suspected or not? I watched her face. It didn't matter. Either way, she now knew... we both knew the Civil War documents possibly held a sin far greater than Haydon's birth out of wedlock.

"You don't save history, Miss Horton... in your arrogance and ignorance— you rewrite it! The world according to Ms. Caroline Horton... the pathetic barren little divorcée".

The blow hit me in my solar plexus and stole my breath away. She held my glare and returned it as I tried to catch my breath.

"You're not the only one capable of doing a little research, my dear. Got benched by a bitch half your age, eh? Must have put a real hurt on you, Caroline. How does it feel... my making assumptions about your life based on one little juicy tidbit of gossip?"

I reeled. Where had she gotten her information?

"Your kind of history comes scribbled on bathroom walls, so don't judge my ancestors by your pathetic standards!" she gloated.

"It wasn't an assumption." I said. "She confessed to an affair... in her own hand. I have recorded statements... other documents that support its existence. She penned it and left it somewhere in the clock for someone to find." I figured out the clues Haydon left behind.

"What clues?" she demanded. "You don't know Haydon. Certainly not the way I did... you couldn't possibly understand who he was" she insisted.

I was confused now. Who did she think I was referring to; Maggie or to her great, great grandmother? Aside from the generous bloodletting slight about my failed marriage, and my inability to produce offspring, had she been right? Had my obsession over the Danburg and its ghosts obscured my objectivity about them and the events they appeared to have been involved in? Was it possible I had been too hard on Celine and not hard enough on everyone else in my search for the truth about the Danburg's past? Had I indeed rewritten history according to my interpretations of the facts and not according to actual facts? I looked into her watery eyes and thought about the hole in case thirteen at the top of the stairs. She kicked at the picture frame and brought me back to the moment.

I peered at the torn print on the floor. The lines on the woman's face became huge in the light of revelation. Could I have been wrong about the woman in the print and about the innocence of Maggie or Haydon's role in all this? I looked at the print again. There was pain written in the lines and creases that crisscrossed every face. Endured or self induced? Cautiously I reached forward to pick it up, but she kicked it further across the floor.

"She looks different to you now, doesn't she?" She raised an eyebrow.

I blinked. She was right. I had seen only what I had wanted to see. I mouthed the word yes and held her gaze.

Her shoulders eased for just a second and then she leaned into the table. "Knowledge is life altering, isn't it, Ms. Horton. And without it, you're only guessing...same as everybody else" There was no arguing that point, so I squared off my shoulders and looked her straight in the eye and took my medicine. The pain rimmed the outer edges of her lids with red as tears built in the corners.

"Think you know who Haydon and Maggie really were from a couple of love letters? Think you know who they were from that ridiculous diary? Did it tell you how they snubbed the very people who paid dearly for their pleasure? Did it tell you how they placed an entire family at risk for their adolescent longings? Did it...did it tell you what I was forced to bear for their betrayal?" she demanded.

I had never thought of my maiden as anything other than victim.

"I want to know, Miss High and Mighty, how you were able to divine an entire family history from a bunch of rotted old photos and a dime store novel about misguided lust! I lost an entire life because of them! I damn near died—but that would have been a joy compared to what I was forced to endure!" And she twisted the knife from the tortured grain in the wood and held it out for my review. My reflection bounced in the blade.

"Jealousy and bitterness rot you from the inside out. But you know all about that, don't you my dear? Your husband left you for someone else who could give him something you could not." My teeth began to clench and I held my tongue.

"Oh, that's not to say you wouldn't have... if you could have." She patronized and I felt my blood begin to boil.

"A marriage comes with lots of compromise, but on one point... he just couldn't. And I'm not talking about the sexual acts you find... shall we say...offensive, Caroline. I'm talking about children. Sweet, little golden haired carbon copies of himself. That's what you couldn't give and what he couldn't forgive."

"You really are a heartless bitch, aren't you?" I whimpered.

"I do what I have to, to survive" she snarled. "If I had been the wielding the knife... her attempted suicide wouldn't have been called... attempted!" she boasted and stabbed the knife back into the shredded wood.

"Then it would have been called homicide..." I muttered back and tried to reach for a knife of my own.

"No!" she slammed her knife back into the table three inches from my hand and sneered. "It would have been called... justice!"

She pulled at the knife, but it had wedged itself too deep into the grain. As she struggled, I dashed around her to the outer alcove, where the heart-shaped iron stamp rested on the top of an antique wood burning stove.

Brandishing a weapon of my own, I thought I could reason with her. Panicked, she used both hands to free the knife as I came bolting back into the room. "What was your real objection to their... romance?" I asked, keeping my voice calm.

"The wedding banns wouldn't have read different names...don't you see the horror their association would have meant to the local rabble? People who couldn't ferret out the truth would have claimed incest within the house of Danburg! And which would have been worse? The truth or the lie about the truth?

Dear God, how many more trials should we have been forced to endure based on the silly scribblings of a woman? First Hannah, then Maggie—do you not know the shame their union would have brought upon our house?"

Just then the phone rang and she froze. I knew answering it was out of the question, but I prayed that the machine would kick in and someone's voice would save me long enough to distract her and get my hands around the iron stamp.

"Miss Horton, this is Mr. Barron. I think I've found what you've been looking for. Please call me at your earliest convenience. You have my number. I'll be here for another hour." And the phone clicked and the hum recorded for a second and then the machine shut off. Thank God I thought... that was all I needed to hear.

"Hannah? Who was Hannah?" I asked, now confident I had her on the run.

"Ancient history... no doubt you'll be digging up her skeletons soon as well." And she wheeled around the table. I countered and grabbed at the iron as I went.

"I had no other choice but to have Haydon... removed!"

The woman was now clearly unstable and I needed to stick to current history, praying for the intervention of those who clustered at the edge of the drive. She saw the crowd waved and smiled, placing herself between the window and my opportunity to make a plea for help. Unaware of the nature of the conversation some waved back and glanced at their watches before returning to mingling. I kept the heart-shaped iron behind my back waiting to get a bit closer to strike a blow if necessary.

"Removed?" I asked, hoping that in the spotlight she was egotistical enough to tell finally how brilliantly she had orchestrated such a crime. I watched her toss back her head and laugh at my naiveté. As her shift in stance cleared my view of the window, I saw the landscaper returning with the truck and tried to make eye contact. I circled the table and she stalled to pull at the curtain, and that gave me the chance to signal for help in another fashion.

I brushed up against the wall and bumped the button of the intercom system we had just had installed earlier in the week. It connected the main house with the garage and as the landscaper got out of the truck, I began baiting Celine to tell me the gory details.

"You had Haydon killed because you couldn't stomach the thought he could fuck someone other than you?" I said and watched through the crease of the curtain as the landscaper's head jerked toward me. I never spoke like that in front of staff, but I needed to attract attention. "So what was it that really tore you up… the way he looked at her? The way he held her close and fondled her in the moonlight? Watching and knowing you couldn't even masturbate your way into their heaven?" The word masturbate was all it took to push her over the edge.

She flew into a rage and hurled the knife into the wall above my head. I ducked and accidentally lost my grip on the iron stamp and watched the landscaper whip out his cell phone and dial for help. I had no idea how long it would take for anyone to arrive, but saw the landscaper moving quickly but cautiously towards the side of the house.

"You filthy-minded little tramp. Who are you to speak with any authority on what I did or did not do with Haydon

Fitzgerald? We were to be married!" She picked up the remains of a bladed cradle scythe from the display behind her and threw it across the room.

Suddenly I wanted to shoot the historical society for wanting me to keep things such as those available to the public and not inside a locked glass case! I needed another distraction to keep her off guard.

"So... was that where the rumor came about your pregnancy? That was your feeble attempt to snatch him from Maggie? With a lie?"

She looked shocked and held her tongue.

"I never pushed you about the pregnancy because at the time I thought it irrelevant. There was no entry for a child in your family tree." And she grabbed at another frame upon the wall and threw it at me. The frame splintered against the wall, but her eyes never left mine, so I continued.

"You know, when I first heard about it I thought perhaps I had been mistaken. That I had gotten my facts wrong and that the rumor had been about Maggie, not you—"

She snapped and reached for the nearest missile, throwing the glass dome with the rose inside to the floor. Dancing with rage she ran her heels through the flower and shattered glass, shredding the tender petals into botanical confetti. If she had pummeled me with one of the bulky cooking pots that hung overhead, it would have hurt me less than to see Maggie's rose trampled and abused. The landscaper signaled he would try to enter from the front of the house and I tried to signal in return the jibs were open, but the door to the warming kitchen had been locked. Celine had pulled it tight and hid the key.

It was somewhere on her person, but God only knew where. Right now I was more concerned with where her hands were reaching than where I might have to reach to retrieve it. She lunged towards the remaining shards of glass on the floor and picked up one large enough to wreak havoc with my flesh. She ran it through the dangling curtain for effect. As ridiculous as it was, I seethed at the fact that I would have to replace the glass dome and the curtain before the grand opening in two weeks— but then I realized her eyes were trained on my wrists.

She grabbed my left wrist and ran the sliver of glass along it as I yanked my hand away. Tiny droplets of blood appeared on the surface of the cut. It was shallow, but the significance of the act ran deep and adrenaline flooded every pore of my body.

"You're just like her you know... ill equipped to handle the harsh realities of southern life. A woman needs to be strong enough to support her man, not just bed him. She needs to withstand the brutal work of working the land and keeping the fires going. She needs to be able to take whatever spoils she can receive in bed and not cry after he's finished with her and moves on to someone else...younger... prettier."

I had no idea she was so compromised. This is what she thought life was about? This stagnant version of North and South where Negroes still worked the fields and the white men bedded their kitchen help, while the wives held their frigid tongues and dreamed of something more? She spoke as if the twentieth century had arrived everywhere but the Danburg and she was there alone on the front steps, waving as the soldiers marched to South Carolina to fight for the Confederacy.

She tossed the glass to the floor. She had also cut the inside of her palm. I motioned that she was bleeding, but she laughed as she licked at her hand and came around the table again. This was child's play to someone who held her hands to seer in open flames.

"Do you know what I had to do to save my already tarnished reputation? They could forgive fornication. Women are weak by nature... lustful creatures. Eve was a woman...but a lie? A lie was inexcusable. Haydon knew about lies. That was one of the things we did share... his mother's shame and his step daddy's abhorrence for lying. My uncle was a harsh man, Miss Horton, with a quick temper and a heavy hand. Do you understand? The longer Haydon stayed away after the fire, the more my uncle became suspicious and focused on my belly. The fact it didn't rise festered in his mind and when he could stand no more... he called for a doctor to determine my truth! Do you know what would have happened to me if he'd found out I'd lied?"

I was shocked that self mutilation had been a better option for her than confessing a sin. What kind of house had these poor children grown up in? I suddenly felt compassion for her. How desperate and terrified she must have been.

"I feigned a miscarriage and lay in bed to hide from his accusations. I was caught. What more could I do? I built a small fire and did my best to sterilize the instrument of my destruction, but it was in vain. Do you how many times I had to jab myself with the charred end of a fire poker to get enough bloodied clumps in my chamber pot to fake a miscarriage?"

The mental image of her violation made my stomach revolt.

"I made Catty sit outside the door while I plunged a poker inside myself, biting at the corner of my bed linens to keep my screams from being heard."

Out of compassion I reached for her hand and her eyes flashed like a rabid dog's. She bit at the air and swatted my hand away. I thought about an entire life lost to something as forgivable as a lie spoken in the throes of desperate infatuation and then the epiphany of her sterility finally struck home. There was never a record of children from her, not necessarily because she had never married... but because she could not have them! Whatever physical torture she had rendered herself to protect from her Uncle's discovery had left her barren.

Sensing my compassion, she hurled another frame from the wall above my head in fury. To have crumbled in my presence would have been a sign of weakness and that was one thing Celine could not abide! She would rather be whipped than held and it was then I realized she was capable of anything. Suddenly all bets were off for my safety. I stalled her charge by circling the edge of the table, forcing her to follow.

"I know all about your ploy to keep him from leaving you, the marriage certificate you burned, and the diary you tried to destroy. I know about the way you used to follow him everywhere and the way he used to send you packing because he preferred the attentions of others. Even the Negroes who hung out behind the pump station offered more entertainment than he felt you could afford him. He preferred the local kitchen help to you!"

Incensed, she screamed obscenities that turned the heads of meandering guests who heard them vibrate off the warming kitchen windows. Patrons darted from the scene.

"You fucking whore! How dare you associate my name with those niggers!" and she threw a pot at the window and cracked it clean through.

"He paid for his associations, trust me!" I said, now judging the Mores Ford Bridge association to be more credible than ever, given the level of her fevered response.

"He paid all right! They came you know… looking for him. Every fucking idiot that carried a badge crawled in and out of our lives for days. They all wanted to know what happened. But I never gave him away," she whimpered. Desperate now, I toggled the light switch, trying to signal that I needed immediate assistance.

"Those agents knew he'd been there that day, that he'd seen everyone who had their hand in it and was willing to name names. I knew he'd turn them in just as soon as he'd gotten Maggie back and then they'd be off. I couldn't let that happen. He was going to hand over the diary. It was my only leverage."

I flipped the switch about ten more times to get attention.

"I told him I'd help. That I was sorry I had gotten so jealous over his little affair and then I begged his forgiveness. It makes me sick now, just thinking how I lowered myself."

I began to feel the sweat bead upon my upper lip.

"He told me they'd gotten married—married!" she cackled. "Can you imagine that? And worse yet, that he'd consummated the marriage in his father's hotel while the rest of us slept through the night thinking she was in her own bed! I thought he was playing me for a fool so I played right back. I said I had suspected as much and that I'd called her parents…explained they were in love and that I had sent her to the church to pray for forgiveness for deceiving them. That she was waiting there with Lucy for him to arrive, so that they could explain to her folks together." And she twisted the rose under her foot again and I tried to keep the table in between us. I searched the side yard keeping my eye opened for the landscaper. Why was he not coming to my rescue?

"Of course it was a lie, but I was hurt and by then I was up to my neck in them. I'd read parts of the diary. You're right. At first I thought it was Hannah's, until I saw what he'd written her. When I realized my great, great grandmother's diary was still somewhere in the house, I told him I had to have it. He could keep his wife, but I wanted that fucking Civil War diary! Nobody was ever going to know the truth about what she'd done."

At this point even I was unsure about what exactly Hannah had done, but Celine's reaction was so over the top, I knew the ramifications of it must have loomed catastrophic. Where was the landscaper! I was certain he had understood my need and called for help, so I committed to keeping things from escalating. The fact that the jeweler had found something meant it would just be a matter of time before the entire county knew too. I comforted myself with the knowledge that the purple cat syndrome could actually be of help this time and searched the yard again with my eyes. She caught me.

"Don't bother about your help coming to the rescue. Maggie was foolish enough not to lock the door on her way out, but I never make a mistake! He couldn't get in if he wanted to. Quite an array of hardware and safety devices you've installed here... my complements. Besides, I told my politician friend and the caterers you and I had several important issues to attend to and could not be interrupted."

"You can't hide from the truth forever, Celine. It always unearths itself, just when you least expect it." I submitted.

"Don't be foolish child. It's stayed buried this long. Even the FBI has never been able to unearth it...as you say. And besides... the truth has many facets. None of which I'm game to bet match yours!"

I saw something blue flash out of the corner of my eye. The light on the intercom system was lit, but I could not tell if the speakers were still broadcasting. Hedging my bets, I continued. "So the FBI wouldn't be very interested in your version of the truth?" I queried.

"Perhaps, if I chose to tell them... the fools. Nobody needed a road map for this one Caroline, but they were so uppity with their Yankee accents and their shiny shoes, condescending to us as though we were the hired help—Out of fear or spite, nobody wanted to help them. Least of all me. You see, they had nothing to offer for my troubles.

Certain individuals however, were very happy to receive the information about Haydon's whereabouts that day. I didn't really care what he had seen them do. Things like that happened all the time and nobody else paid any mind...but that was my only leverage. I could not let him go to her."

"It was you? You told them where to find him?" I hissed.

"Don't be an idiot. Anyone with half a brain knew he'd beat a path back to her side. Besides... they didn't need my help. He'd practically left them a goddam map."

"If you loved him, how could you have sacrificed his safety for your..." and my voiced trailed off as I watched this hideous creature before me twist and contort in the consequences of her actions.

"How could I? How couldn't I? You said yourself you had heard rumors about the pregnancy and that was over sixty years ago! Everything dies, but the lies! Everything changes, but the goddam past!" and she stamped her feet into the glass.

"So if it was just a fabrication to trap Haydon into staying, why didn't you just let it go? Tell them the truth and beg for forgiveness?"

"I was desperate to keep him. I tried to reason with him. I had even gone to the ironing shed to bargain with him that night. I even bared myself for him, but no! As soon as I began to unrobe he blew out the light to keep from shaming us both. He gathered my nightgown from the floor and asked me to put it back on. He would not even look at me. He told me he would never tell anyone—that he had merely been trying to be kind—that he had to have his Maggie and nothing I could offer up would ever change that! What was I to do? I had already told my Uncle I was pregnant with his child— that we had been with one another! Don't you see? I had sacrificed my honor and reputation to be his wife..." her eyes began to water. "I only meant to force a wedding... not a funeral!" She sighed, and I believed the weight of her recklessness had finally caught up with her guilt. Her shoulders slumped for a second, and then she shot up rigid again and continued.

"I just assumed he would comply and the rest... the rest would follow naturally after. I didn't count on Maggie's hold over him.

I thought that once people got over the disgrace of what I had done, they would see how much I loved him and we would be wed. And in time that he would come to love me... that children would be a natural part of the progression. I figured if I didn't get pregnant within a reasonable amount of time, I would simply claim I had miscarried and when I finally did have a child, they would all forget and we could be happy.

But then he refused me—for her! What was I supposed to do? I was a pillar of the community. I had never lied before, so they all believed me. When he denied me, I knew I would be seen as just as soiled as his mother! I couldn't bear that kind of shame. I would have become a pariah in my own house, the church and this tiny shit hole of a town. Don't you see? I had nowhere to go!"

I winced at her justification. "You're mad. You lied and you justify his death because you couldn't face your peers?"

"What would you have done in my shoes? Don't think with your flimsy twentieth century morals—think with what I lived under! They would have called me a whore. I thought being called a widow would be better than being called a whore. I tried to steal his ring and claim it as mine, so I could tell folks we'd eloped, but they'd gotten to him before I could get to it and it was gone. He died... and I was branded a sinner without the opportunity to repent..." she began to crumble.

Had she not been so wicked I might have felt compassion, but when I thought about the devastation she had caused so many people, I just couldn't.

"I wanted to die beside him there in the swamps. I hated her and what I had become because of her. So I told them she was a nigger lover too. Said her daddy the lawyer could cause a lot of trouble for them, if Haydon got to him. I thought they'd just go after her and scare her a little. I never thought they'd use him to get to her... or me. I never thought they'd do more than just rough him up a bit. Frighten her off and bring him to his senses and then he'd see the only woman he ever really needed was me..." and her hand rested again near the blade in concentration.

I maneuvered closer to the wall and bumped against the red button. This time it began to flash. I knew then it was working properly and what came next would be over all the grounds.

"The men confronted him when he arrived here trying to find her. Said they couldn't allow him to testify. Said Maggie was being held in a silo and would die there unless he agreed not to testify. Frightened for Maggie's safety he agreed and begged them to take him to her. They beat him and threw him in the back of an old pickup truck. But they lied. There was no Maggie waiting for him; she'd already been carted off by her folks."

Heads began to turn and direct their gaze to the windows. I prayed that the volume had been turned up loud enough.

"They hauled him around to the backside of the Danburg, drug him in through the back hall and threatened to kill him if he didn't produce the diary. I didn't know they would demand that it be turned over to them. I only told them I had seen him with it, not that he still had it... I told the truth, but they didn't believe me. They continued to beat him to make me talk. He didn't know where it was anymore than I. Catty had hidden it somewhere in the clock, but never told me. Desperate for them to stop beating him, I reintroduced the lie that I was pregnant with his child and suggested they allow me to search Maggie's room for the diary... hoping and praying someone would come to the house looking for me. But no one came. I had told them all I wanted to be alone. Klan members had sealed off the area and we were trapped ... just like those folks at Moores Ford.

When I returned from upstairs empty handed, Haydon bargained. He told them he had dug up the grave of one of the Moores Ford Bridge victims and was willing to trade its location and the list of their names for safe passage to Maggie. They didn't believe him. Two of them who still held him tight, said they'd been to the funerals and made certain the bodies were buried. When he tried to explain he'd gone back that night, they tied me to the spindles on the stairwell and threatened to beat me if he was lying.

They asked again where the diary was and he confessed the last time he'd seen it was the night I chased him down the stairs. Said it had fallen somewhere during the pursuit, so they ripped through the downstairs or at least what was left of it searching for the diary. Finding nothing, they began to throw furniture into the center of the hall to set it on fire, determined that if the diary was somewhere within... it would be burnt along with us both. When the heap only smoldered, they threw the clock in on top. The glass face shattered as they tossed it onto the pile, the mechanics rolling out onto the floor. Haydon panicked and swore he would lead them to the gravesite if only they would listen.

Still damp from the fire wagon's water pumps, the clock but never completely took to flame. They ripped one of the chains from its guts, tied his hands behind his back and beat him with one of the fallen weights. Haydon pleaded for them to stop and swore he would lead them to the Negro's grave, but they thought he was just lying out of desperation.

I pulled at my bindings. The fire had damaged some of the wood and I was able to break free of the weakened spindle and run up the cindered stairs to hide. No one came after. I hid inside the largest coffin in the attic closet until I heard them yelling outside beyond the pasture fence. When I was certain there was no-one left in the house, I crept down the hall. There was smoke, but no fire coming from the pile below and the foyer was empty. Panicked by a sudden lull in the noise, I raced to the nearest window.

Apparently when the furniture refused to ignite, they dragged him from the house and strung him upside down at the hog station by the chain and beat him further. With no warning, the large man with the black rimmed hat left the frenzy and then returned from the hollow of the barn. I watched as with massive forearms he swung a thrasher blade and sliced through half of Haydon's throat like he was nothing more than common livestock.

I screamed as Haydon's body jerked back and forth. Frightened they had heard me; I broke through the opposite window with a chair and tried to climb down the lattice work outside to get away. My dress caught on the jagged edges and tore in two. The burnt rungs splintered beneath my feet and half clothed, I plummeted the remaining distance to the brick pathway below. When I came to hours later, I was soaking wet and half naked. The downstairs was clogged with smoke and everything was silent but for the patter of the rain. They were gone...and so was his body."

I could scarcely breathe. It felt like my heart had stopped beating in my chest minutes before and I could not keep from hyperventilating. Where the hell was the local law? Celine dipped her head in emotional exhaustion and I saw the unlit top of a squad car roll behind the garage and two more uniformed men place themselves in strategic positions next to the window behind the traumatized woman to my left. I heard scraping sounds at the front porch and assumed the first flash of blue had been a cop working on releasing the jib locks at the front parlor. Suddenly I was glad I had forgotten to re-peg the one closet to the door.

"I thought perhaps I had dreamt it all... that something evil had crept inside the house while I wasn't watching and taken my reason with it. When I finally made it to the hog station, there were no traces that his body had been there; save for the bloody water that still trickled in the rain across the wooden platform. The missing chain and dented weight were all that were left. I ran back towards the house and buried them; afraid they would return and try to use them on me.

Then I went back inside to look for the diary. I tried to block the front door behind me with the first piece of furniture I could find. The cabinet of the clock was the closest and the only thing large enough. The face read 6:15 p.m. and the man in the moon no longer smiled. I knew then the minute they had taken him to the slaughter station... the last minute Haydon had been in this house."

While she paused to catch her breath, I thought of my dream and the little girl who had told me much the same. The weight and the chain. Four more blue uniforms gathered in a semicircle just beyond the hedge and they motioned they were about to enter. In Celine's disorientation, she no longer even needed me as audience. She continued as blue uniforms quietly herded the confused hordes outside the window, moving them to safety out of my line of vision.

"I knew in my heart he was dead." She let out a high pitched nervous laugh as she pounded the edge of the table and the last champagne flute hit the floor and shattered. "The next day I told Haydon's mother there would be no money coming from the burnt cotton fields and that it was best to accept the fact that everything would have to be sacrificed in order to survive. Most of the furniture was sold locally to neighbors and friends hoping one day to return it, but I refused to sell the clock to anyone. I couldn't stand to see its face staring back at me, knowing what I knew. There was an antique dealer up from Washington who bargained for a good bit of the parlor furniture and so I threw in the clock making him promise to sell it far away."

The front jibs were kicked open down the hall and though there was no mistaking the breach, she continued as though in a fog. They still had the bolted second wooden door that separated the main house from the warming kitchen to contend with, but that would prove to be a minor conquest. Frightened, I silently applauded their efforts not to provoke a more violent solution than necessary and watched as blue fabric began to flood the hall behind us.

"FBI agents came and went. They asked what I knew about Haydon's whereabouts that day, and I lied. No one from the local law ever questioned me. They knew. Fearful for my life, I had pledged my allegiance to the Klan as well. It wasn't hard. I never knew their names, only their faces, and they have haunted me all these years.

Haydon died and along with him, the location of the only other document that could have supposedly identified the twenty or so men who had committed the atrocities at Moores Ford Bridge…I never knew if he had been telling the truth about that. I only knew…" and she raised her head and looked me straight in the eye, "…he had never lied to me about anything else." And with that, she slumped into the chair and sobbed for all she was worth while the local law read her, her rights and began to handcuff her scarred hands behind her back.

Moved by her confession, I touched the officers' hand and asked for permission to replace the woman's gloves before he cuffed her and he shrugged but allowed the indulgence. As soon as the cops had placed Celine inside their car, I called and asked the jeweler what he had found. When he confirmed my suspicions I told him to keep it in a vault till I returned to examine it further. He promised he would. The next call was to the concierge of the Fitzgerald Hotel in Washington, Georgia. When I asked him to take my credit card number to guarantee a room, I was not at all surprised when he said not to worry. It had already been handled!

Chapter Thirty-five

The pieces were finally in place, with the exception of how Haydon had gotten mixed up with the mob from Moores Ford to begin with. After a series of interviews and statements, they allowed me to gather some of my things and make a few phone calls. When all the commotion began to die down and people had been allowed to leave the grounds, I asked if I could be excused for a few minutes while they finished gathering names and contact information from some of the remaining guests. Released, I gratefully retreated to my office to calm myself and pack. Finished, but not cleared to leave I checked my e-mail. Still nothing more from the mysterious intruder, so I tried to Google the name he'd left in his earlier correspondence...a Mister Jenkins. Unable to find any biographical info on the internet under the full name, Welborn V. Jenkins I used only Jenkins and added the words Moores Ford Bridge to search for a possible connection there.

Nothing appeared under that heading. I tried again removing Moores Ford from the equation, but adding racial intolerance to the mix. Suddenly a thousand sites filled the screen. It was uncertain that this was the connection that the instant messenger had intimated, but I read curious to what it had to teach.

The first article I glanced at mentioned the so-called one drop rule, which sounded familiar. An article called "How the Law Decided If You Were Black or White: The Early 1800s" refreshed my memory. After centuries of arguments over the legal status of mixed-race people, in the 1830s the "one drop rule" emerged. It designated a person with even a drop of African blood a "Negro," keeping such a person subject to all the economic and personal injustices that accompanied being black in a prejudiced society. Was this what the mysterious messenger had meant for me to learn? How people had determined color? I read further, knowing the intention had to be greater than what I had digested thus far.

In an article called "Physical Appearance, Blood Fraction, Association," I found an idea that caught my attention: "Until the advent of the one-drop rule of invisible Blackness in the 1830s (discussed elsewhere), courts relied on a combination of three rules to determine whether someone was Black or White. The first was the rule of physical appearance. The second was the rule of blood fraction. The third was the rule of association..." Association? Had that been Haydon's crime... association? Or was my mentor trying to allude to tainted blood in the family line? I read further hoping to discover a reason why this information had been selected for my perusal.

It was too much to take in all at once and my mind was so frayed at the edges, I could not retain an intelligible thought long enough to construct a plausible theory of why Haydon had been involved in the Klan's activities. Or why they had been forced to involve him. What did one thing have to do with the other and why had the messages stopped? I tried to AIM the previous entry and got nothing but an away message for my troubles.

I thought about the accusations that had spewed from Celine's mouth the afternoon before. In my efforts to defend myself, I had missed something important. I closed my eyes and tried to recapture the words she had used: "...No one ever questioned why she didn't look like the rest of us...him too! The family name was at stake. Of course, she was from Haydon's side of the family. But he was dark, as dark in the soul as he was in the eyes..." What had she meant by dark? I thought of the Jenkins case of 1792. What else had she said that I had not seen as metaphor for something else? I recited the bits and snatches of her words that I remembered: "...Bad blood... that's what was wrong with her. Weak and pasty… couldn't deal with the harsh realities of the world!"

I thought of her hands and arms, scarred from flames. I rubbed at my wrists anew and tempered my fear. My first impression had been that she had self mutilated out of shame for her lustful longings outside of marriage… but what if I had been wrong? What if it had been about more than just carnal impulses without sanctity? I looked at my own wrists. I played the scene over and over in my head: "She was the daughter of a stained woman and he, even worse, was too consumed by his primitive lust to see it!"

What had she been implying by the use of the word "primitive"? That my maiden or possibly her lover had been compromised in their southern legacy as well? That somewhere in the family archives somebody had taken a side tour off the long and whitening road? Was this the link my instant messenger was trying to send me… that either Maggie or Haydon had family secrets of a different color in their closet?

This certainly would have filled the coffins in their closets with skeletons no one would have wanted to identify! Celine's irrational behavior could have been further explained by such knowledge. Would having lost Haydon to another woman been the issue? Or rather would having lost him to a woman of questionable bloodline sent her diving off a cliff? Crazier still…what if it had been Haydon? What if Haydon had "Negro" blood running through his veins?

How could one of Danburg's staunchest Baptists have rationalized her behavior then? It was bad enough he was attracted to a younger woman and had a drinking problem. But if you compounded that with being colored… her lust could not have been rationalized and her shame would have been intolerable.

My endless theories multiplied until I thought my head would explode.

Having not heard back from my mysterious messenger and frustrated as to where to venture next for confirmation, there was no one left to tell me now but Haydon's wife. Mrs. Magnolia June Fitzgerald. The present day proprietor in residence at the Fitzgerald Hotel in Washington, Georgia!

Chapter Thirty-six

Hours later and weary I checked myself in, then made my way quietly up to the second floor and wandered the few doors down to room 201. My key stuck sluggishly inside the mahogany door and I was unsure if I'd received the right room assignment. Working the key more deliberately I tried again. The tumbler rolled and finally clicked. The door creaked open and I adjusted my eyes to the dim.

There was a high backed bed with stepping stool on the right side... a table with the room telephone and lamp and small card in an envelope that read "To Caroline Elise Horton". As I fingered the stationary, the phone buzzer rang and the red light ignited, telling me I had a message at the front desk. I debated whether to answer it. I had asked the local police office to allow me a few nights rest before I had to commit to another round of interviews with the GBI. I had already surrendered the files from my office for evidence and made my preliminary statements. The Danburg had been sealed off. Certain there would be more questions to come; I had begged for a breather and made the appeal to stay in the next town over.

I tossed the key on the bedside table and surveyed my quarters. There was private bath and behind a set of pocket doors a parlor that boasted a fireplace, a Victorian couch, two wing backed chairs with a library table dressed with a lovely floral centerpiece atop a table that divided the room in half. Two smaller tables lined opposite walls serving as makeshift wet bar and writing desk. I kicked off my shoes and flopped on top of the waist high bed, drawing my legs up with me. Adrenaline depleted I hit an emotional brick wall, curled up into a ball and cried for several minutes until the phone buzzer went off again and the light blinked berry red with great impatience.

Was there no end to this day?

I ignored the intrusion and set about appointing the room. With my suitcase unpacked, I opened up my laptop and waited hopefully for a message from my mysterious mailer. Seconds later, there it was... another message. This time there was no mistaking what it was this individual wanted me to know.

Dear Ms. Horton,

Here is one of the interviews I'll bet you never read in any of your reference materials. Try reading from the <u>View of Victims</u>...

'...The four victims of the Moores Ford lynching were perfectly innocent. As regards to Roger Malcolm, he had the right to defend himself against his landlord—and master. For doing so he paid with his life. To my mind, Roger Malcolm is a hero, and I have never believed a word said against him by white people. To my knowledge none of the victims had ever been convicted of a crime.

The four victims, Roger and Dorothy Malcolm, and George and Mae Dorsey, were poor, downtrodden, African-American field hands. Their murders were premeditated. The Moores Ford lynching was indeed a Klan action. Loy Harrison, a member of Klan 5 of Athens and Bogart, Georgia, was the Klan's point man. While in Monroe to get Roger Malcolm out of jail, Harrison organized the members of the Klan lynch mob from Walton County. For example, he was seen by Lamar Howard speaking privately with James B. Verner, an undoubted member of the lynch mob, outside the Monroe ice plant. James B. Verner and his brother, Tom, later beat Lamar Howard almost to death. The Klan had obviously decided to kill as many African-Americans as Loy Harrison could deliver to Moores Ford. If this were not so, Loy Harrison could have let George and Mae Dorsey out of his car at their house, which he passed on the way into Moores Ford. The

Moores Ford lynching was a political statement inspired by Eugene Talmadge and his son, Herman. It was in fact an act of terror to keep rural African-Americans from voting. Alas, it worked for many years.

During the afternoon of 25 July 1946 Riden Farmer and his family were at home on the Moores Ford Road. Riden's house was quite near the road. Indeed, the Moores Ford Road was at the very edge of his small front yard; hence, those passing along the road could be seen quite clearly. Riden's house was two-tenths of a mile from the old Moores Ford bridge.

When the death convoy passed in front of Riden's house, he was resting on a cot on the front porch. When he heard the cars approaching, he sat up to see who it might be. Riden's two sons, Emerson and Ralph, were working on a wagon wheel at the end of the front porch. Mrs. Farmer and her three daughters were sweeping the front yard. All saw the death convoy pass before them. According to Emerson Farmer's statement to the FBI, there were five cars in the convoy. The first two cars were filled with men. The third car was Loy Harrison's and the Farmers saw him and the four victims inside. The two cars following Harrison's were also filled with men. Shortly thereafter the Farmers heard many shots coming from the direction of the river. Soon after the shooting stopped, one of the cars filled with men came out of Moores Ford at a high rate of speed; it was being followed quite closely by Loy Harrison.

On the Walton County side of the Moores Ford bridge (on the right) there was a field road, perhaps 12 or 15 feet off the river bank. It was in the middle of this field road that the victims were slain. They were dragged and beaten from Loy Harrison's car; and they were dragged and beaten out the field road while screaming and begging for mercy. Their bones were broken by unmerciful blows from members of the lynch mob as they continually begged for their lives. Finally, they were shot down in the dirt to die like dogs. When Dorothy Malcolm would not stop screaming, a member of the lynch mob shot her in the mouth. The victims' bodies were mutilated by being shot through over 60 times with shotguns, rifles, and pistols.'

So Ms. Horton—had you ever read this account of the killings before? I imagined the Moores Ford killers then returned to their homes and families—to kiss their children and pet their dogs. They no doubt enjoyed a good supper, etc., feeling that they had done important work, and knowing full well that they were supported and protected by those in power. And they have been supported and protected by many until this very day. I hope to send more notes tomorrow.

All the best...'

"J"

"All the best?" I muttered to myself. What the hell kind of send off was that after what he had described? Jesus Christ! What was it with these people? I started to close the lid of my laptop out of frustration. I didn't need any more questions, for God's sake! What I needed was some God blessed answers and nobody was supplying them, including Mister 'You've Got Mail'! He just kept piling on the same old shit and I was becoming emotionally exhausted and immune and that... that was a very bad thing. That was how things stayed buried, when people got so overloaded that they shut down and tuned the horror out.

I read through the essay again. I had to admit there were some names and statements in there I had not seen anywhere else. But still not a word about Haydon, so... here was yet another question to be answered. Where was *this* person getting his facts from? And why not sign a whole name? Did the "J" stand for Jenkins?

I reread the signature. All the best what, *J*? The best answers...the best questions...the best bullshit!? Everyone had an opinion, yet nobody had the facts! Or rather... they all thought they had the facts! Everybody was right, but everybody was wrong because not one of them said a thing about a young man being there with dark hair who had been madly in love with a girl I had spent the last eighteen months trying to save!

Disgusted, I shut off my computer, crawled back onto the bed and rocked back and forth while tears rolled down my face. The diary was asking way too much of me and I was too weak to do battle with both its past and its present, a present who now sat waiting inside the hotel somewhere with even more questions I would most likely be unable to answer.

The blinker on the phone flashed again and I tried to ignore the intrusion by covering my head with a pillow. Suddenly there was a knock at the door as well and I shot up in bed. Jesus! Why couldn't people just leave me alone? Hadn't the chaos of the afternoon been enough?

I held my tongue and waited to see if it was housekeeping. Half a minute went by and just when I had decided it must have been from the next room down… a card slipped under my door and I heard the soft footfall of my maiden as she walked slowly away. I wasn't prepared for her.

Five minutes passed before I unfurled my legs and slid the length of the bed to the floor. My feet hurt and my back was stiff from the rigors of the suspenseful afternoon and so I was not eager to meet the floor with any part of my body. I bent in exaggerated pain and pulled the card from the polished boards and crawled to one of the wing backed chairs to open. The penmanship was drawn a bit, but I recognized it immediately as my maiden's hand.

I shall be awake in my room if you wish to speak. The number is 307, the turret room on the third floor at the end of the hall. I have a bottle of wine and the kitchen at my disposal. Change into something comfortable and join me please. Simply call the desk and have them send me your reply. If I don't hear from you by 10:00 p.m., I shall assume you have retired to bed and wish to engage at another time…or perhaps…not at all.
Sincerely,
Magnolia J. Fitzgerald

I did not know if there was enough left in me to go where I feared this invitation would take me. There had already been far too much honesty dealt with for one day. I read the card again. She deserved more, but any reserves I'd had earlier in the day had been eaten alive by the confrontation with Celine and the mailer from hell. The clock read 8:36 p.m. and the sky was darkening, but still pink around the edges, much like my eyes. I had not slept much the night before and I was shot.

Reluctantly I went to the phone and told the front desk to let room 307 know I would be unbearable company and begged off for the night. My sincerest regrets extended, I prepared to hang up and then heard the slow southern drawl of the man at the other end.

The concierge notified me there was a bottle of chilled wine and some fruit outside my door and that should I require anything else I should just ask and it would be provided. I thanked him and requested that hot coffee and Sweet and Low be sent to my room around 7:00 a.m. the following morning. He assured me he would handle it himself and that his name was Joe. He reiterated that if I needed anything, anything at all, he was on strict orders to provide whatever it was I desired without question or cost.

I thanked him again and told him I only required enough energy to crawl into bed, and that I was fairly certain I could do under my own steam. I rang off and did just what I had promised to do.

Chapter Thirty-seven

At exactly 7:00 a.m. the knock on the door echoed in my sleep and I woke with a start. It took me a minute to get my bearings in the darkened room and then another minute more to get down out of the bed with grace, minus my glasses or the ceiling light. Since I had fallen asleep in my shirt, I threw on a pair of old cut offs I had hastily stuffed into my bag at the last minute the night before, swept my hair to one side and wiped the sleep out of my eyes. The morning had come earlier than my body was prepared to receive it, but grateful for the prompt service, I felt it necessary to make sincere and early apologies to my hostess. Apparently she felt the need for me to do so too as I opened the door to Magnolia J. Fitzgerald, and not a middle aged man named Joe.

"Room service..." she winked and then smiled. I heard a key tumble inside another lock in the sitting parlor and then suddenly a trolley of breakfast items made an entrance through the opposite door along with a steaming carafe of hot coffee accompanied by a man I presumed was Joe. Stunned by her immediate camaraderie, I was helpless to resist smiling in return. I suggested that my room was her room. She smiled and vociferously agreed that they were all her rooms! With that, I made my way to the bath to brush my hair and teeth. She chose a seat in the parlor and motioned for the breakfast to begin. Watching from afar as I spit into the sink, I was amazed how much she still resembled the small girl I had once mistaken for lint. Without fanfare the coffee table was soon set, complete with linens and silverware. Joe poured the coffee and then offered a small pink blossom of Sweet and Low, nestled inside a ring of tiny creamers with various flavors for my selection.

I accepted graciously and then apologized to them both for my ungracious behavior the evening prior, explaining I had been over tired. Without going into detail I intimated that her invitation had been the most pleasant of the day's events. Joe excused himself as she patted the empty side of the couch, stating she already been informed about the scene with Celine.

While I stirred in two packets of sweetener, she poured herself a generous cup and added nothing to it but her lips waiting for me to initiate conversation. When I balked, she accepted my apology and let it go. The less I felt I had to explain, the better. I was still uncertain as to why it was she was so adamant to meet with me again. I couldn't imagine why she would want to know anymore than she already did and so sipped slowly, stalling for an appropriate opening. It was unnecessary. She spoke and came straight to the point.

"I assume you found the diary then…" she asked and then waited while I lowered my cup.

"I did. Of course, I had no idea to whom it belonged until late last night." I said. "You'll forgive me for not knowing who you were the first time we met." I quipped and she looked puzzled.

"When did we meet before yesterday?" she asked and set her cup and saucer on the table.

"The first time was about two years ago when you signed the deed over to the county. I was there in the court room watching from behind a set of railings in the balcony. So technically we never really met, but…"

"I see…go on." She said.

The second was when I found a spec of lint on one of the lithographs that turned out to be a snapshot of you at a very young age. The next time was the day the diary was returned from the clock shop and every day after when I read you between its covers day and night and couldn't get you out of my head." I smiled into my cup as the steam toyed with my vision.

"So technically... we really have never met... in person. Just through images and words, correct?" she added.

I tried to keep from staring at her, but it was such a wonder to see her right in front of me that I felt an uncanny urge to touch her to see if she was truly real.

"Yes... I'm sorry. I'm staring. Yes... just through your words and that print." I managed. "But... I feel as if I know from them both."

Without prompt she reached forward, took my hand and squeezed. "I am not that same little girl anymore..." she mused and I kissed her hand and held it tight. There was a current of affection that flowed between our collective pasts, and such comfort in her touch.

"You are such a part of who I am now...I can't imagine that this will come to an end in a few more days with the public opening and I will be put on task with another project and you.... I suppose there will be little point in your staying around." The very thought of her leaving pierced my heart and produced a tear.

"I'm sorry," I whispered and used a napkin to wipe at my eyes. "I just... have been so consumed by your words and my affinity for the child in the diary—you, that I can't believe I went through all this to finally find you and then... Like a book, just close the cover and... What I'm trying to tell you is... I'm not ready to say goodbye to you yet."

She squeezed my hand again. Sentiment sloshed rapidly through my veins and I started babbling like an idiot.

"... I waited so long to find out who you were and what had happened to you. I cried myself to sleep with worry over you. Read that damn diary so many times trying to find out where you had gone, if you were all right and what had happened to the mysterious Abel in your life and..." I was rambling but she never once gave the impression she thought I had slipped a cog. The adrenaline that had evaded me last evening rushed back and the desperation of my attachment publicized itself from every expression.

"Oh my..." she breathed. "You have quite overwrought yourself on my behalf." And she patted my hand with maternal concern.

"I was so worried about you. The book... your book.... *Green Mansions*? I knew... I knew how it ended and I couldn't bear it. Rima dies in the end and you kept making parallels and I kept thinking... if I could find you. If I could somehow save you from that fate. If I could have saved you the way I was never able to save..."

And the words floated through the air and I watched as they finally settled on us both. I lowered my eyes and stared out at the rain that fell softly from everywhere, including my eyes. "The way I was never able to save..." and she reached for my hands, understanding that it had never been just about her past. It had been about mine as well. Embarrassed at the barrage of emotion, I whispered, "I just couldn't let that happen. And then when Cattalieu told me about what occurred in Chicago... I knew I had failed us both. And when it turned out that Abel..." and the hurt in her eyes sent up flares.

I broke off there. There was no reason to tell this woman what she already knew... that her Abel had died. Or, to tell her what she did not know... that I had fallen in love with the ghost of her childhood sweetheart.

"Abel..." she sighed. "I had forgotten all about that name... and the *Flaming June*." And she smiled very privately to herself and changed the subject.

"The flaming what?" I asked, but she avoided the segue.

"Now... just where is it you would have me go?" she asked. "This hotel is the only consistent home I've known since 1946. I wouldn't know what to do with myself if I were to leave here now." And she picked up her coffee cup and watched my face.

"Here? You mean, you've been here all along?" I blurted. She crinkled her nose and nodded at me as though I were from Mars to have thought otherwise.

"I thought you moved to Chicago with your folks. That's where you tried to...I thought that's where your life now was." I felt I had overstepped my bounds by alluding to the suicide attempt again. There was no use in rehashing the tragic past, hers or mine.

She set down her half empty cup and pulled at the fluffy pink sleeves of her dressing gown and grinned. "See anything out of whack there... other than these damn age spots of mine?"

I bent and surveyed the thin wrists with the blue racing stripes for veins and saw nothing to give evidence that she had ever tried to slit them. I turned them over and then back again. Nothing but age spots!

"I never went to Chicago with my father—oh not that he didn't try to persuade me," she said. "I just refused and vowed that I would not leave without Haydon. I knew Haydon would never have left me behind and so I persuaded my father not to push me. I knew something was wrong and I warned that Celine had a dark side. It was no secret that she fancied him, that she was obsessed. I felt certain she had been the one to set the house on fire."

I remembered my conversation with the church lady. She too had suspected as much.

"Haydon hadn't smoked in weeks before the accident that night. My father of course, always the lawyer, said he would have need of evidence before approaching the Chenilles with such a suspicion. On the heels of subsequent events, everyone became rather tight lipped. My father allowed me my privacy and told them I had traveled with them to Chicago, while really I waited secretly here for Haydon's return home."

"Home...here?" I asked confused.

"Yes... here. Haydon and I had eloped on the 24th of July, 1946. It was very romantic, but very stupid! Neither of us had any money and so the only place we could afford to go was here, because his father owned the hotel. It certainly wasn't very well planned out... but we were so in love, it never mattered to us. It did, however, matter to his father as he did not want my father to wring his neck. You see, my father was a very powerful attorney in Atlanta at the time, my mother a social icon. Haydon's father had no intention of angering such potentially powerful in-laws!" and she took a bite out of a small piece of pound cake and shoved the rest towards me.

"You would have liked him, my father. I always felt protected by him. Quite the self-made man. I thought he would be a marvelous influence on Haydon. Father had dropped out of school at the age of thirteen to support his mother, but he reached marvelous heights in spite of it all. You see, alcoholism did not merely run in Haydon's family, it ran the family—which is why I had to be so hard on him. His father and brother were destroyed by the disease, in turn destroying the family's financial health. So when Haydon came to speak to my father about our potential engagement, my father took him to task about his drinking, just as I had for months prior.

Encouraging Haydon to return to school, my father told him how he had gone back, finished his basic studies and then entered night school at the John Marshall Law School relatively late in life. In his first months of study, the school's effectiveness in integrating blacks and women into the student body fired my father's populist ideals and ignited his interest in serving minorities throughout the state. Surprisingly, given his mild mannered gentility, my father chose criminal law upon graduation. That he chose the plaintiff side of the battle was a tribute to John Marshall's ethos and my father's character. I always felt Haydon could have learned a great deal from him if only..." and she sighed.

I poured us more coffee and because she seemed uncomfortable on the couch, I suggested we move the coffee to the bed. I climbed on top of the covers and fluffed my pillows and settled in. Not to be outdone, she came to the opposite side of the bed, handed me her cup and then used the ladder to seat herself accordingly. I laughed and she giggled in return as she swiveled her legs and housecoat upward in one fluid motion and then solicited for the extra pillows to be placed behind her back for support. She winked. "Thank you..." she sidled and snuggled up to the headboard for additional support and then continued.

"Everyone thought we were related because of our names. But we weren't even of the same bloodline. My mother had been widowed early on in the war. I was so very young when she met my father, or rather stepfather... he adopted me right along with all her other bad habits! He truly became the only family I ever knew."

I thought about the article on the color of blood. Had she just said, "...but we weren't even of the same bloodline"? Had she been talking about the familial tie to Haydon? She continued to speak but my ears were numb. "My mother had been widowed early on in the war..."

I heard Celine throwing stones in the back of my mind. "The war...A convenient alibi for explaining away a missing father, don't you think?"

Once the floodgates opened on that, other words began echoing in my ears. She had said, "...he adopted me along with my mother's other bad habits..." What other bad habits? Smoking, drinking? Sex outside of wedlock? Sex outside of...her race?

I looked closer at her features and then tried to remember the description of Rima from the book, *Green Mansions*. Wild unruly hair, sun kissed pigment...fleshy lips. Suddenly Maggie's face and voice came back into focus and she continued in her train of thought.

"...In changing my name to Fitzgerald, Haydon became related to me by name only. In fact, for a long time that was just about all we did have in common. He was so pig-headed and self absorbed when I first met him. To tell you the truth, I was glad Celine had an eye for him in the beginning. Until one night when I heard his step father beating him in the ironing shed for having gotten in the middle of a fight between his mother and him. Later, he got into some of the moonshine kept out back in the hay barn in an attempt to relieve his pain and I heard him drunk and crying."

I tried to dispel my suspicions and keep to the conversation at hand. "You mean his step father had been abusive to his wife and a closet drinker the entire time?" I recalled her very long entry made one night about such disturbances.

"Oh... there was a great deal of closeted everything going on in those days. That's why everybody was so thin lipped and bitter all the time. Everybody hid from the truth, but like I always say... hoping something's true or not never made it so!"

"So how did you end up here?" I asked and bit into the cake, hoping I was not reading things into her statement about hiding from the truth. The cake stuck to my teeth and I tried to scrape at it with my fingernail while she looked out the window onto the square and softly began...

"I suppose you've heard just about everything by now. A good amount of what Cattalieu told you, I already knew. And over the years I've come to suspect a great deal more. But I'll wager there's a fair bit of what Celine gave up that I don't know and may never wish to know."

I continued to study Maggie's features to find some roadmap to a hidden lineage.

"Caroline...am I right about what Celine had told you?" she asked, raising an eyebrow.

I regrouped tracing her cheek with my eye, assessing the contours and bone structure with a new appreciation.

"In time... and you'll know in your heart when. You tell me what really happened. It won't be easy. But you'll do that for me... won't you?" and she held tight my gaze and then reached for my hand. I knew she had imagined terrors as real as what I now knew happened and her eyes dug deep into my soul. There was the desperate need to place Haydon at rest within both our broken hearts.

"I need to know the truth. In the end...we all do." She said and then blinked away a tear. I agreed internally. "So... for now, you might as well hear this too and then we'll see how all the pieces fit and we can put this thing to rest once and for all."

She turned and looked into my eyes again and I saw another tear swell at the farthest edge. This time I raised my hand to brush it aside and she placed her hand upon mine and I knew we each had been long in waiting for the warmth of another humans' touch. Timidly I pulled away from her and replaced the tear with a kiss. Her mind already gone on ahead of her... a third and fourth tear slalomed down her hollowed cheek. Absent mindedly she swiped at them with an arthritic hand. When she did, I noticed the slight depression on her left ring finger and remembered in the chaos I had forgotten to place the single gold band in case thirteen. Ashamed I had let the nightmare with Celine disrupt my original destination the evening before, I felt compelled to explain my inefficiency and retrieve the sentimental piece for her safekeeping.

I adjusted my weight upon the comforter. She never turned... never noticed as I went to search my clothes for the treasure. Grateful it had not been lost in the warming kitchen struggle, I plucked the ring from its denim cocoon and carried it back to the bed and waited for her attentions to shift, but they never really did. Her eyes searched the square below as people rushed under oversized umbrellas from stores to cars to get out of the pouring rain. Had it been any other day, in any other little town the scene would have made Rockwell blush. But this was Washington, Georgia... this was the Fitzgerald Hotel and somehow in her mind it was 1946 all over again.

I placed the ring into the warm center of her palm. Her fist snapped around it like an alligator turtle's jaw and I knew then she had regretted giving it to me in the first place. I smiled and she slowly refocused on the sound of rain that ran in tiny spirals down a dimpled pane of glass that had watched the same reaction from a less weathered face sixty-one years earlier. I crawled up next to her and tugged at the comforter and covered us both.

"I think I fell in love with him the moment I met him..."

Chapter Thirty-eight

"At age thirteen, I was little to look at... scrawny and uncomely with a keen eye for wayward literature. Really...anything that made the drudgery of being an only child exciting. Haydon seemed to understand that as he too had been sandwiched in between his biological parents' dreams and the reality they eventually settled for. We were like two orphans he and I...

Celine didn't understand. Couldn't understand that what drove us was pain, not possessions. She wanted the things the Danburg money could buy. Haydon wanted what he thought the money could give... importance, purpose... freedom from failure. In the end he found it afforded only a bottle of it at a time."

I tried not to speak, but the pause was brutally long. "Are you all right?" Even as I said it, I knew it was a stupid thing to say, but she was so gracious.

"No..." she whispered softly. "...but part of growing old is learning to understand when not to lie about it." I had to think about what she meant. And it dawned on me that she too had been a hoarder of secrets and the choice to remain silent about significant and painful events in her life had proven to be wrong for her as well.

"Silence is never golden, my dear," she said and swallowed hard as she twisted the ring around her arthritic finger and looked into my eyes. "It's just silence... and what is silence but an endless void that aches to be filled?" The blue ocean in her eyes suddenly darkened.

"I had been naïve about so many things, Caroline. Thought I could deal with my pain... as did you." And she motioned towards my wrists. Suddenly realizing my arms were exposed. I pulled at the sleeves on my shirt. She never wavered in her stare and I became uncomfortable by my inability to hide. I looked down as she traced the thin, white crooked lines that crawled an inch and a half across my wrists on either side. With my watch and bangles too far away for camouflage, I pulled from her touch and tugged again at my sleeves.

She reached again and I bit at my lower lip and raised my head to take my medicine in her stare. "Curiosity didn't kill the cat. It was keeping the secret about what he'd swallowed that did him in...Understand?" she questioned and touched my cheek. "It's not important what it was any longer my darling. It's just important that it's over."

I smiled weakly and held back the urge to hug her. "How did you get to be so wise?" I winked and she winked back.

"Practice, my darling. But even practice does not make perfect... always remember that!"

The rain continued to pour and the world no longer seemed quite as lonely. Joe came and went several times that day answering various requests and concerns of my host. We spent most of it in bed or later back in the parlor with wine and cheese. I had never felt so comfortable with another person.

By late afternoon it was clear the rain had settled in for the night and she ordered room service for two to be set up at eight in the turret room. I offered to pay, but she refused. She requested we each take a brief nap and accomplish whatever cosmetic enhancements were required to make ourselves socially presentable. Grateful, I watched as she excused herself through the parlor door and locked it from the outside. She was a remarkable woman and even though she had been a child in the diary and a matron in my room, there was something about her that felt as though we were the same inside.

I listened at the door as she walked down the hall and then heard her footfall on the steps rising to the third floor. I wrote the number for the turret room on the tablet next to the phone, gathered my things and headed to the bath. It was odd to know her so well although so little time had passed. In one day we had traversed the key points of her life and some of mine. I held some in reserve.

After all, it would have been unfair to have heaved such a heavy load on her slight shoulders. I thought of the way she had taught me to prance with delight in front of a mirror that could hold a lifetime at a glance. And though she was no longer the image from the pages I had read, she had that same sensual air about her that hinted there was still so much passion left. I now understood why Haydon had sacrificed everything to be at her side.

When I emerged from the bath, the phone was buzzing and the light on the cradle blinked red with enthusiasm. My initial intention was to ignore it, but then I remembered the Police Chief and decided the prudent thing would be to answer and feign illness if the conversation became lengthy.

Connie's voice boomed into the receiver. Charlene had heard from a reporter friend about the showdown at the Danburg the evening before and was concerned. Not able to locate me, she got a hold of the landscaper who told her where she could find me. We talked for what seemed forever, she asking questions and I trying to supply the answers. She apologized for taking me to the bridge that day and placing me in danger, but there was nothing to apologize for. Had she not, I would have never known the truth about the Danburg diary... the world would never have known. I thanked her and told her it was because of her I was on my way to spend an evening with the maiden in the diary. She wished me God speed and I closed to prepare myself for the meeting of my life.

* * *

I mounted the stairs one by one as the clock in the lobby two floors below bellowed the first of eight gongs. I was neat, I was clean, I was punctual and I was terrified! Having heard what I felt was the bulk of what had happened, I felt certain she would eventually drag the rest of it out of me with those kind eyes, and I did not want to ruin the magic of the day.

The room was at the end of the hall and the runner stretched out before me in swirls of emerald and paisley. By the time I reached the end of the hall, the eighth bell echoed up through the winding staircase and bounced off the mahogany doors on either side of me. The door on the left stood at an angle and up two steps from the hall floor. I knocked and it opened before I had chance to strike for a third time. I was about to call out her name when the door swung fully open and Joe excused both the cart and himself, leaving the door ajar for my entry.

Timidly I entered to the underscore of an instrumental piece of sweet violins. Joe bid me a pleasant night, closing the door behind me and I found myself alone within her inner sanctum. The ceilings climbed twenty feet into the air and the furniture was bulky and dark. The walls were washed with a deep shade of sage, accented by the thick bands of rich chocolate brown moldings and stained glass jewel-toned transoms. Heavy upholstered furniture of renaissance flavor graced each corner, along with accent pieces that flashed with gilt and deep bronze. The room spoke of aged grace; period paintings and prints of the masters hung in every conceivable space. It was a space that advertised a full and cultured life.

The main room was approximately twenty feet by twenty feet, with an alcove that jutted out another eight feet to the turret, which boasted 360 degrees of stained glass and a panoramic view of the square. It was gloriously decorated with tall, thin book shelves that lined the wall segments between each window, festooned with well-used leather bound sets of the classics. In the center was a burgundy oval rug fringed at the edges with hand-tied gold tassels. An ornate mahogany desk with marble top and cabriole legs crushed the monogrammed rug below and was topped by a beautiful tiffany lamp that glowed amber and magenta. Neat stacks of papers and small reference books dotted the upper desk corners and a leather satchel sat squarely in its center. It was perfect.

I re-entered the main sitting room and searched for my host, but she had not made an entrance. To my right I noticed a sliver of light coming from a door that stood slightly ajar. I assumed it to be her bedroom and that she was still attending to personal matters, so I wandered the gallery to wait.

Just above the tiled and tiger oak fireplace hung a magnificent portrait of a young woman with flowing, burnished copper hair. She simmered in the painted sunlight, seductively folded onto a fainting couch in front of and just beneath a marble balustrade facing an ocean view.

The rain had ended late that afternoon and the clouds had finally parted ways. The sun, though happy to have engaged in the day at all, began to exhaust and continued to lower itself slowly behind the buildings on the opposite side of the square. Shadows stretched and yawned into the side streets, preparing to go to sleep for another night.

I watched a shadow drift back and forth from the other room, un-offended at the delay as a mantle clock chimed the quarter hour. She called out and excused herself for one more minute. I acknowledged my agreement and returned to the painting, captivated by the portrait's subject whose features were smoothed and serene in slumber.

There was casual grace calculated in her pose. The artist had poised one arm under the curve of a swollen breast and then draped it seductively down the length of her elongated thigh. The other he folded neatly beneath her head as she dozed. Her dress was delicate and sheer. Painted a vibrant shade of burnt sienna, it clung unapologetically to the silhouette of her voluptuous frame. Barefoot, she beckoned, and I sensed cool breezes that traveled inland from the ocean that lazed beyond the banister in a sedate shade of blue. A portrait lamp hung just above, and the lighting effect, combined with the orange rays of the setting sun set the room afire. There was something so familiar about the face…

"A remarkable likeness," she whispered through my hair into my right ear. Her exhale tickled at the curve in my shoulder. I felt her hand and reached to touch with mine.

"Please forgive the delay. I am unaccustomed to entertaining and wanted to do things properly."

I nodded in acceptance of her apology, though none was truly necessary.

"It's a beautiful reproduction," she whispered again. Still mesmerized by the colors and the content, I failed to respond so she continued to educate me.

"It's called *Flaming June*, and it's by Lord Frederic Leighton. It was Haydon's favorite. He said it reminded him of me."

I turned and suddenly saw the uncanny resemblance to the woman child in the portrait. She faced me and for a short second I saw the woman from the portrait lean into the curve of a settee and mimic the pose. Her evening attire, though not identical to the portrait's, flowed with the same ethereal enchantment and shade. She was aglow with memory. I had no doubt he had said that and a great deal more, looking at the image she projected even now. When engaged she was still a striking beauty. Leaning forward into the space between us, she continued.

"For years we had been kind and considerate of one another, but something changed the beginning of my seventeenth summer. I hungered for his eyes upon me. I was full breasted by then and my hips had rounded out. My hair had grown a considerable length, and no longer a child; I wore it down the better part of the time. Frankly, my presentation did little to tame his or my rather unruly natures."

"I bet you were quite the picture," I said, and meant it. She was plain in some ways and yet, when she smiled, she broke all patterns of appraisal. It was her seductive voice, though, that was her greatest gift, and she applied it generously when animated. "Yes... pretty as a painting," and she smiled with devilish delight. There was a story in that kind of smile and so I took the bait and swallowed the line.

"So... what was the spark that began such a fire?"

"Oh, don't be fooled. The fire had always been there in some fashion. I think I just finally had the right equipment to flame it!" and she winked again. "As odd as the distance in our ages looked to the outside world, it never mattered to us. He lit my soul on fire with his love of literature and art and in some twisted fashion I supplied the exotic measure of the forbidden which he craved with his addictive personality. It really took to flame the night he called me by my middle name in the throes of climax…June."

I was dumbstruck by her candor. I stood and took in the entire painting with new appreciation for its subject. The fullness of the hip and the curve of breast with its darkened punctuation under the drape of burnt orange screamed for intimacy and violation of innocence.

Haydon was no idiot. He had education, class and could turn a girl's head with nothing more than the charm he oozed in print. Although one could ascribe his romantic gesture to a simple ploy… the fact was, she truly resembled the painting.

"He said the nickname 'Maggie' no longer fit my form nor my passions. He had showed me that portrait from one of his many art books long before. I had even tried to mimic once with unsatisfactory results. But that night… that night there was magic in the air. It was the night we made love for the first time."

Awed, I stood motionless. She brought a glass of wine to my side and we appreciated the art silently. She toyed with the dangling tendrils of my hair as I studied the languid curves of the oiled goddess and she gave me the history of the painting.

"…Some scholars have suggested that this painting is Leighton's homage to a grand tradition in art history that goes back to Giorgione and Titian…"

Lost in the mastery of the piece, I took a sip of wine and she brushed my cheek with a velvet kiss. The act was sensual and I realized why Haydon had been so drawn to her. Celine could not have affected such a state in either a man or a woman, and yet this woman, at a substantial age, still emitted such powerful sexual presence that I was aroused by her touch.

"She's breathtaking…" I whispered.

"I thought I was," she quipped. "At least …that's what I was striving for."

I moved cautiously to the settee. There were other paintings in the room with just as much artistic command, but none nearly as inspiring. I removed my shoes and walked the polished length of the floor to gaze upon the twinkle lights in the trees that were erupting into the dim of evening tide outside and sipped again at the glass within my hand. She was a glorious specimen of life, causing both sensual and emotional circuitry overload all at the same time. It was little wonder the man had been smitten beyond recourse.

I moved away from the turret windows, uncertain as to my role within her evening. The furniture pieces were exceptional examples of the Renaissance period, but she obviously meant them for living, as she told me to pull my legs up and get comfortable upon the settee with her. I followed her invitation and without further introduction, she began to divulge with eager honesty the details of the night she and Haydon's had become lovers.

The walls began to flicker with the reflection of the twinkle lights that hugged the branches of the trees just outside her sage and chocolate cocoon. The effects were enchanting. I could not have designed a more convincing set for the remainder of her story to unfold if I had had a lifetime to orchestrate it. The music's sensual strings, her scent and the wine intoxicated me as I took in the better part of the first glass like air.

She took a sip of her wine and toyed with the rimy stem of the glass as she held my hand and submerged us into 1946. "The day had been long. I had been in Danburg a whole week and he had not made even the slightest nod in my direction. Convinced he had somehow come to find Celine's company more appealing than my own over the seasons in between visits, I took to my room early to pout and ponder how I had misjudged my prowess."

I tried to release my hand from hers, but she held fast and pulled us both deeper into her intrigue.

"The air was still and swollen with humidity. June that summer had arrived with a vengeance. Even in the waning hours of the evening, the earth was hot and there was little way to cool one's fever. Restless and damp with disappointed desire, I went to the window to see how Haydon was spending his usual banishment from the main house, when I heard Celine's voice from the other side of the courtyard and despaired.

Below in the breezeway I saw the lighted tip of a cigarette and surmised he had taken to the night air to escape the unrelenting stillness of the ironing shed. Whatever their conversation was, it was abbreviated and I watched as the glow of his cigarette increased with every puff. More agitated than enraptured with what she'd said, he turned to crush the dying butt in the sand. Sensing opportunity, I threw my hair pin to the ground and let my hair fall to my bare shoulders. Following the projected pattern of its flight he searched the upper floors with his eyes. I stood unadorned in the open casement for his review. I read the hunger in his eyes and bid him goodnight... hoping.

Minutes went by and when there was no footstep upon the lattice that climbed the rear porch to the center upstairs hall, I surmised I had not inspired but merely amused. Disenchanted, I fled my bed and retired to the attic to find something suitable to be my consort through the long sleepless night. Resigned I had humiliated myself; I made my way to the moonlit shelf beside the small window in the eave of the gable.

The room was stuffy, so I opened the window to invite the evening air to waft through and cool my skin. I had risked discovery by borrowing one of my aunt's diaphanous evening slips to tempt Haydon. Angered at my failure to allure and with the tepid air mocking my exaggerated heat, I pulled at the inner lining and accidentally tore the seam. Frustrated in my pitiful attempts to exude a more womanly demeanor, I threw it to the floor and began to sift through journals to distract my injured ego."

Her eyes remained closed and the air about her pulsed with the electricity of her reverie. I was uncertain as to whether interjection was necessary, so I kept silent vigil.

"I never heard him mount the stairs... I only noted his arrival as my eyes adjusted to the dim and I saw the shadow of his arms as he eased the shirt from his chest and shoulders. I had fallen asleep tearfully in the fainting couch. I was aware of the lustfully perfumed sweat that had pooled in the cratered notch at the base of my back as my chest began to heave the closer he came. I should have been frightened. There was such a look of unapologetic longing in his eyes and yet...he did not seize to take, or reach to ask for my favors. He simply stood there silently in the moonlight flooded in his own desires. When I reached for him, he pulled me upward to crush any objection from my mouth with his full lips.

The pressure of his groping hands sent a spiraling chill of primal ache that wound its way all the way to where I pulsed with anticipation below. I shuddered in the slight breeze...both his lips and movements teased and I arched in acceptance as he lowered himself into my rapture..."

She closed her eyes and I felt the pheromones in the room dance with delight as she signed with the signature... "I was devoured by his touch... mind, body and soul and had no shame in my equal response of consumption. Death by inches my darling... it was such a delightful way to die."

I could hardly breathe, let alone respond. Theirs had not been a mere dalliance. It had been a burning perpetual flame of passion that flared and flourished. It raged out of control from that night forward as defiantly as the fire of revenge that was set in response.

She sipped heavily from the remaining wine in her glass and excused herself to the turret room and retrieved the satchel from the center of her desk. Unprepared to embark upon conversation I avoided her gaze. I had felt the same climax of emotional and physical energy in the afterglow of his words and the green monster of jealousy raged for but a second.

She walked from behind her desk and engaged my eyes as she came to the face of the settee, handed me the satchel and returned to the fireplace where she reached to touch the fiery hem of the image of her past and dipped her head in silent lament.

Watching as the shoulders before me rippled in grief, I came to appreciate her pain. How horrid to have held him, felt the weight of both his passion and his form imprinted upon her soul not once, but forever, and then yearned for its patterned crush the remainder of her exile.

I opened the satchel and found inside a stained envelope that had been worn velvet to the touch with time and perusal. The parchment boasted the letterhead of the hotel and its date screamed the anguish of the young maiden who waited for a response that was never to materialize.

July 27ᵗʰ, 1946

Dearest Haydon,

Without you by my side, I remain unrealized, divided, unresolved. – these are needles that no matter how diligently I try to thread, the relief of a closing knot escapes me in your extended silence. Given your delayed arrival, I question not your fidelity but your safety after the final events of Danburg. I know you secured your escape from the horrors of her rage that night. I believe she meant to burn us both at the stake of her revenge. Thank God for the recent memory of our trysts— I used your lattice to secure my safety. In the chaos, it would have proven ill advised to try and find you in the dark. So I fought freedom from Celine's grip and begged the safe shelter of the church. Compassionate Lucy housed me while they battled the flames and till I could find the comfort of my father's arms days after.

I have told him everything, and though he disapproves of our irresponsible execution, he is compassionate toward our situation and begs you to come home to work out issues of peripheral concern. As I have pledged my passion, so also have I pledged myself to you. Again and again with each touch of your phantom fingertips and the distant echo of your kiss, I honor our vows in a marital bed of one. Where are you my darling that I can neither feel your touch nor taste your lips?

The woman upon the canvass where you have now made me believe I belong weeps for the artist's hands that made her whole... you, my love. I am your Flaming June. How is it you cannot follow the torch of my affections and find your way back to me?

Come to the Fitzgerald. Your father is distraught with worry and we wait with the knowledge of another horrible event which has heightened everyone's concerns for you. Where you there? Was it really you they saw? Is that what you were trying to tell me before we were confronted? I have lost the diary, love... If I had your words perhaps I could discover your course, but your words exist nowhere I have been inspired to look. Find me, Haydon, and we will lay all to rest...

In the words of Virgil, "'Quisque suos patimur Manes' – we each one suffer our own ghosts."

Let us no longer hide behind our own ghosts. Let us dance in the sunlight... Come home to me.

I love you without measure,
Your Flaming June

***

The evening passed from one profession of love their love to another, each more poignant than the previous, and all leaving me with a sadness that could not have possibly paralleled her own. And yet, she was gracious enough to allow the fact that mine felt as fresh and naïve as hers must have over half a century before.

I asked her to tell me everything from the day she could remember entering the Danburg manor to the night of the fire. The later the evening, the more I began to understand the dichotomy of our clandestine meeting. We each carried with us separate pieces of the puzzle. She, the intimate inside story of trials and tribulations and I, the outside shell of rumor and gossip. It only stood to reason that somewhere between the two lay the truth of what happened that day.

Small talk was nonexistent. Huge chunks of their relationship lay gutted out on the table in diary entries, shared passages of *Green Mansions*, and oral history, and we dissected what parts could be reduced further to glean further clues. So much of their history was not even their history. Celine and time had fogged the map of war so brilliantly that it was hard to decipher truth from local legend. The research materials surrounding the Moores Ford Bridge lynchings were similarly redundant. Though there seemed to be a multitude of renditions, there seemed to be a minimal amount of information. Thus far the best source had been the book by Laura Wexler, but I was hoping for the gaps to be filled by Richard Rusk's chronicles and the 500 page FBI report.

I tried to recall the less salient facts that could help me puzzle together what might have happened from the time he left her at the Danburg, until the next evening when Celine sold him down the river. A timeline would be my best bet.

A bottle of wine and a thousand fading twinkle lights later, I left her curled up in her coral gown tucked underneath a beautifully patterned throw across the room from her alter ego. I would have kissed her on the cheek but chose to leave her with the last whispers of a sonata speaking into the dawn. She was exhausted both emotionally and physically and she was not alone. I had forgotten my shoes at the foot of the settee, but there was no reason to go back. I knew we were not finished. Still unaccounted for were the 24 hours of the 25th of July, 1946 but there was no way to face them without full reserve.

As I walked down the hall and towards the flight of steps to the second floor, I recalled a passage from Green Mansions: "...I envied them not their wings; at the moment earth did not seem fixed and solid beneath me, nor I bound by gravity to it. The faint, floating clouds, the blue, infinite heaven itself, seemed not more ethereal and free than I, or the ground I walked on..." I turned to look back at the door at the end of the hall that read 307 and understood what it was Mr. Hudson had meant.

The light on the phone blinked as I set the keys on the table near the door. I picked up the phone and dialed Joe for my message. "A Miss Connie McCann called. The anniversary is the day after... well no, looking at the clock...tomorrow," he said, "...is the annual re-enactment and memorial service for The Moores Ford Bridge incident. She asks, would you care to attend? If so, please call her for details. I can bring you a paper and your coffee and then perhaps after reading the article about it you can get in touch with her later this morning? Miss Caroline? Oh... of course. It's very early. Shall I ring you later?" He wished me a good morning and I placed the DO NOT DISTURB sign on the doorknob and wished him a good night!

Chapter Thirty-nine

I slept fitfully for a few hours, breakfasted with Maggie, excused myself and then returned to Danburg to tie up loose ends. The day in between was a godsend as it gave me the chance to respond to more questions posed by agents, as well as conduct a little more detective work on my own. Aside from the connection to Moores Ford, I had another Danburg mystery yet to solve. I returned the call to the jeweler as soon as I hit town most anxious to learn what he had found. What he'd discovered inside the final weight was nothing shy of remarkable and grateful, I made him my first stop. By the time I made it back to Washington I was exhausted. Several phones calls and a half a dozen emails later, I met with Joe who still held the final pieces to the puzzle. Hungry, but desperate to complete my work I begged off from dinner with Maggie promising to meet her later that evening.

I could not present my scenario as infallible. In fact, some of my composition was little more than intuition and conjecture based on hearsay and lore, but I felt certain that there were undeniable corroborations between the authors of the diary and actual records that could not be denied. Factual time lines of events and outcomes that once paralleled with confessions and entries could have held no other plausible explanation than what I was proposing. I met Maggie in the turret room just as the twinkle lights began to light the trees and with trembling hands offered her my unofficial account of what I believed happen to her young husband.

Written in third narrative form allowed me to distance myself from its events and provide information in the best way I knew how. Nervous I paced the floor and watched the sun slip over the edge of my reason as she read what I believed happened in the shadows it must have cast that black day back in 1946.

Supposition:

They had been wed in secret only 24 hours before the hideous event… spent the night at the Fitzgerald in the honeymoon suite and she had been returned before daybreak to eliminate discovery until the arrival of her parents days after. The events of their epic tragedy played out to the best of my constructions as follows…

In his knowledge of her feeble ability to weather his searing gaze, he baited from below night after night until she consented to marry. At seventeen, she had achieved the age of emancipation from her family, but not the blessing. Leery of the long arm of his step family, Haydon secured the services of an agent of the court in Monroe to do the nuptials. The distance of some ninety odd miles allowed them the privacy of their venture, but presented complicated logistics as well. Both by her verbal admission and confirmation of entry, the elopement occurred the day before the incident and in full anticipation of Haydon's company on a private picnic the next afternoon of the 25th. But Haydon did not arrive until the night of the 29th… the night of the fire.

At four in the morning on the 25th, Haydon put his child bride in the front seat of his biological father's sedan and returned her to the edge of the Danburg property and then drove back to the hotel to discuss the issue of fulltime employment.

Cautiously the new bride re-entered the house through the open jib windows across the front of the porch and made her way to her room, just as Celine crossed from the outhouse back into the open hall of the lower alcove. Thinking Maggie had just returned from a sordid rendezvous with the dark haired devil she thought lay sleeping off his booze in the shed, Celine censored her anger and devised a plan to have the maiden forever removed from the house.

Upon Haydon's return at approximately 7:00 a.m., his father instructed him to move their things into the second floor room nearest the elevator. It was the smallest room in the hotel, but with access to kitchen and surrounding grounds it wasn't such a bad deal. After setting up house in the 12'x15' space, Haydon hustled to the kitchen and helped with the first rounds of coffee and donuts to the patrons as he had promised. He worked all day with the hired help and finished his chores round about 3: 00 p.m. and collected a day's earnings to get to the courthouse before it closed to retrieve another copy of the marriage certificate to present to Maggie's parents on the 27th when they were scheduled to fetch her back to Atlanta.

It was now late in the afternoon on the 25th of July, 1946. Knowing Maggie would be desperate for his company and unprepared to venture away from the main house after supper hour, Haydon did his best to secure a ride back to the Danburg. While waiting for the clerk, he struck up a conversation with a suited gentleman to his right which seemed impatient for some word as to the release of a particular jail mate. Pleasantries aside; Haydon explained he was desperate to return to home to see his new bride. Counting on empathy for his newly acquired status, Haydon tried to press present company into his employ.

Few traveled that way, but the young husband was certain he might be able to buy his passage and reach the Danburg before Maggie was confined to quarters for the remainder of the evening. Not wanting to exploit his father's good graces any further, he continued to solicit his way back to Danburg and Maggie's side.

Having been turned down by several men with apparent means outside the courthouse, he decided his best bet was to find someone less fortunate whose head might be turned by a few extra dollars. There was a small gathering of white folks all milling about the courthouse steps curious as to the rumored release of the colored man named Roger Malcolm that had sent a white farmer by the name of Barney Hester to the hospital. The bail was $600.00 and had been posted by a gentleman by the name of Loy Harrison who was on his way to the jail to meet the other colored members of the group that would eventually be killed that day.

Haydon, tunnel visioned by his date with desire was unimpressed with the local racial dilemma at hand and continued to concentrate on his travel plans. When volunteers seemed to be scarce, he found a young man in an army uniform (possible FBI interest; Jack Malcom, a twenty six year old Hestertown man who returned home from the army the day before the shooting) with a beat up pickup truck who seemed more interested in Haydon's green than the growing crowd.

As news of the release reached the courthouse stairs, there was a stream of cars that flowed out of town in disgust at the jailbird's freedom. Fortunately for Haydon, there were several cars heading east. It was in one of those vehicles that Haydon bought his transportation. During the brief sojourn out of the city limits and into the rural countryside, the driver began to voice his rather colorful opinion at the turn of events in Monroe. and Haydon began to relax. The more agitated the driver got, the quicker he drove and for Haydon, that was a very good thing! At the rate of his anger, the driver would have Haydon in Lexington before seven thirty and hopefully in a bed by nine... Maggie's! Not knowing if it was the chore of transportation or the news at the foot of the jailhouse that continued to irritate, Haydon did his best to entertain his host. The young driver seemed reticent to talk so Haydon settled into the seat and did his best to carry the conversation.

Looking out the window at the vacant cotton fields, Haydon filled the void of silence occasionally with obvious commentary. When the driver's mood lightened, Haydon took this as a sign of approval. Enthusiastically he showed the driver his polished wedding band and spoke of his lovely bride and their plans to relocate from Danburg to Washington as soon as he could return to her side. It was a confidence he would soon live to regret.

Shortly before 5:17 p.m. on the afternoon on the 25th of July, 1946 the car driven by Loy Harrison that carried the four African Americans, turned onto a seldom used dirt road and rolled to a stop. Three of the four cars ahead of Haydon continued straight and so not anticipating the scenery to break in pattern, Haydon was surprised when the driver of the truck turned abruptly onto the same dirt road and headed towards a rickety old wooden bridge. Hoping this was some sort of shortcut to the Atlanta Highway, Haydon kept his concerned vigil silent. The ruts in the road made the ride bumpy but Haydon remained tolerant, although it made more sense to continue due east than northwest only to turn due east again several miles later. The uniformed driver focused on the rise of dust far ahead in the distance. Sensing that perhaps the drivers ahead had run up behind a farm equipment or into a dead end, Haydon bit back the urge to question and decided to try and entertain with friendly banter.

Five hundred feet from the bridge the truck rolled to a stop and the debris flew high in front of the hood and blocked the view. The driver muttered something under his breath and waited for the dirt cloud to settle before he opened the door and stood on the running board to get a better view. Hearing a man call out for help, the driver leapt to attention pulling a rifle from beneath the front seat and warned his passenger to stay quiet and sit tight.

Published accounts reference upwards of twenty plus men and at least one vehicle that blocked the other end of the bridge. The car in front of them had stalled and refused to let the truck pass. The driver raised his rifle and ran forward into the dust. Suddenly Haydon heard yelling come from the wooded area up ahead. Five or six men (possible FBI interests Weldon Hester, Melvin Hester, Clarence Hester, Hughlon Peters and Alvin Adcock) including his chauffer (the uniformed Army soldier and possible FBI interest, Jack Malcom) surrounded the Harrison car.

Harrison was carrying the recently released black sharecropper (Roger Malcom) and those that surrounded the vehicle began demanding with weapons that the nigger be removed. When objections arose from the other passengers, a frenzy of activity and obscenities erupted.

At first, just the second black man (George Dorsey) was dragged from the car. But when the women went to cursing (Dorothy Malcom and Mae Murray Dorsey) and hollering calling out one of the bystander's names, they too were evicted from the vehicle. The driver (Loy Harrison) claimed he was threatened with the same. Those in the area quietly at bay infected by osmosis and soon become involved and party to the following events...

The last vehicle furthest from the bridge still contained the frustrated and impatient newly wed, Haydon Fitzgerald. It was now approximately 5:48 p.m. and the unexpected interruption and congestion on the tiny road made no sense to Haydon. Curious at the delay, Haydon made an attempt to remain patiently inside the idling vehicle, as the uniformed driver had cautioned. Minutes later at approximately 5:52 p.m., Haydon panicked and then sparked since he had paid handsomely to be carried as far as Rayle and the hour of suppertime was fastly approaching.

Fearing he would miss his rendezvous, he wandered towards the bridge to see what the delay was. Hearing the yelling of obscenities and screams, he carefully covered the distance. At approximately 5:57 p.m. the first volley of shots rang out and echoed off the pines. Haydon scrambled to the lee of the shoal for safety. In horror he covered the last sixty feet or so to the edge of the bridge. Bullets flew overhead and he leaned into the path that traversed the south west side of the bridge parallel to the waters edge. Before he made it through the first twenty feet of scrub, the second volley of buckshot ricocheted through the trees. Garbled screams of both women bounced off the hollow underbelly of the bridge. Startled by the volume of rifle fire, he dove amongst the briars as chiseled bark fell from stray bullets that shredded the towering pines.

Caught by kudzu and wisteria vine he twisted his ankle, tripped and watched with disbelief at the escalation of the events as he tried to untangle himself without notice. The third round of buckshot danced among the woods and Haydon screamed into the madness as bodies thirty feet in front of him folded into hideous positions within the ropes that bound them. Heads turned immediately to calculate the origin of the foreign rejoinder as Haydon continued to vomit into his sleeve. Seeing nothing, a few of the men appraised the sound nothing more than the echoed aftershock from the crumpled pile of victims. Haydon held his breath and all was silent for a few seconds while Moores

Ford Bridge lay suspended above the Apalachee River, riddled with arrogance and shotgun shells.

Satisfied with their work, the murderous group stabbed at the victims with their rifle butts, one kicking at the pregnant woman who lay slaughtered in a muddy pool of her own blood. With men running the length of the shoreline for thirteen feet to secure the scene, shallow pools at the waters edge started to churn with the red earth, staining the rocks as the water did its best to filter.

The last body slumped further into the straining ropes, releasing as much air as blood from its deflated lungs. Satisfied they had completed their mission without compromise; the first of the murderers piloted their way up the hillside and broke into shocking insensitivities. As if they had done nothing more than putting old plow mules out of their misery, they patted one another on the back, collected themselves and began to clear the bridge with stern resolve.

Blood continued to drool from the upper chest cavities of the two males and a single stream of crimson flowed from the abdomen of the pregnant female towards the waterline. Unable to collect his breathing, Haydon cringed in a fetal position and vomited into the underbrush as a last volley of bullets burrowed into flesh and bark alike. The sound of blood dripping nearby echoed and amplified in Haydon's ears as the last three men mounted the bridge. With a sudden shift in the tenor of the conversation above him, he tried to focus and contemplated his options for escape. Their voices continued to jumble and bounce off the pines. Haydon wiped at his mouth and wondered how long the mob would brave possible discovery.

As several men crossed to and from Harrison's car, the wooden slats of the bridge creaked under their collective weight. Haydon didn't understand the delay. He couldn't go back up the hill now and pretend as though he had not seen anything, nor could he pretend not to have been affected. His complacency would have been taken as advocacy and then what kind of a human being would that make him? He estimated they had come at least eight to ten miles out of town and that he was still a good 80 miles from home. He looked at his watch.

It was now just before 6:10 p.m. and there would be no way to get to Danburg before nightfall without re-engaging with the young soldier (possible FBI interest Jack Malcom) who had been his currier thus far. He hadn't heard an engine fire up, so the odds were good the soldier had been as frightened as he and fled the scene. If he could just get back to the road further down, he could steal the truck and make his own escape.

Climbing higher into the brush he assessed the dirt path he was on was nothing but an old tractor road and there was no telling exactly how far down from the bridge the next crossing might be. He knew only one direct way back to the main thoroughfare and that was right through the carnage he had just witnessed. Bargaining on the crowd dissipating to make a hasty retreat, Haydon sat tight figuring to wait them out. Voices muffled and laughter pitched as he did his best to keep his sanity in check and his eyes averted from the vacant stares of the corpses that now began attracting flies from every corner of the wood. Finally one by one, engines fired up. Sensing possible freedom, he waited for the last set of tires to cross the bridge.

Ants began to invade the area and nauseated by his own smell he removed his soiled jacket and picked at the smaller clots that had clung to the inside of the cuffs at the bottom of his slacks. A final car door opened and then slammed shut, but no ignition followed.

Less than fourteen minutes after the event had begun, he heard what he thought was the voice of his paid courier (possible FBI interest Jack Malcom). At first none of the words registered. Several pairs of feet scuffled at the far end of the bridge followed by a single pair of boots as they clomped to the railing and paced with deliberate measure. The young man in the uniform (possible FBI interest Jack Malcom) approached Harrison's car that sat idling in the center of the wooden bridge. Another few seconds passed as Haydon moved further into the brush and the masculine voices muffled. The car engine shut off and Harrison opened the door, but did not emerge.

Soldier boy hugged the rail canvassing the riverbank and then suddenly sent out a yell to the others that his young hitchhiker had fled the car. Haydon froze as the young uniformed man then rushed the other side of the bridge and paced that rail. Another voice soon entered the fray and announced the young hitchhiker was most likely still somewhere close in the woods. Haydon tried not to make a noise as three more men rushed the rails.

For a moment he thought his white shirt had given him away and then realized they hadn't seen him yet or surely he would have been addressed. Slowly he dug into the mud and smeared the reddened clay across the front of his shirt and down the sleeves to camouflage. As the men paced the bridge peering into the pines, Haydon carefully upended the vines that kept him captive and made for the heavy briars that edged the denser woods. A branch snapped as he lost his footing.

Antennas alert, the noise sent one man into motion. Suddenly the woods were charged with electricity and another car door slammed not more than 100 feet from where Haydon sheltered. Grumblings irritated the silence and then seconds later, a new man breached the side of the wooden rails and called out..."

"Haydon? Haydon Edison Fitzgerald? You out there.... boy?" Haydon shuddered in his own waste and waited to appraise the intention shocked that the stranger had called his full name.

"You listen and listen good, son... you can come out now. No one's gonna hurt you. We just took care of a little business, that's all. No harm to you... Haydon? Ya hear me boy?"

Paralyzed with fright, Haydon tried to discern the man's intention. The voice called out again. Haydon refused to reply still dumfounded. They had used his name as if they had known one another all his life. His lack of response was deafening.

Under orders, two men from the other end of the bridge began to canvass the path that fed down from the Oconee county side. Another man sent two more down the Walton county side and into the woods. The simultaneous rustling of leaves bounced off the walls of the banks and broadcast from beneath the warped boards of the bridge with wayward destinations. A fourth man carrying a rifle entered the fray and sidled up along side the carnie-barker in the dark suit. Maniacal laughter ensued and the huge man with the black rimmed hat (possible FBI interest Lester

Little) came to the edge of the bridge, smiled and spoke with even timbre as if he could see Haydon's face squinting in the sunlight.

"I got your Marriage Certificate son." He bent over the rail and baited into the bloody stream below. "I gotcha boy... I gotcha by the short hairs. You best come on out now, for I have to send these here boys in after ya." And he waved the document in the air above his head hoping that its owner might still be in the area to see.

"Says right here where you at, son. Who your daddy and your mamma is..." There was a brief pause and then he smiled into the wind.

"Well, well... well. Look-ey here, boys!" And he waved the document, pointing to a line laughing into the group of men at his side. Receiving no response from the woods, he slammed his fist onto the rail and then addressed the air between them.

"Lord, son... you done robbed the cradle! Says right here...Magnolia June, age 17! Bet she's a pretty thing... ripe as a peach for certain. You a little old to be playing dolls, with this one, son. What you gonna do with such a young girl, Haydon?" and he let the words filter through the evergreens.

"I know what I'd do if she was mine..." the man with the black rimmed hat bit at the air and then groaned for affect. "Sure would hate something awful to happen to such a fine piece of southern ass if somebody was dumb enough to go runnin his mouth off bout what he'd seen here today...." And like the flies that hovered above the bodies below, his warning buzzed in the air above Haydon's head.

"You understand me boy? I don't know where to find you just this minute... but I do know where to find her. I have eyes everywhere and there ain't nothin or no one in this here entire state I can't get to if I have a need to. This weren't none of your concern, son. This nigger had it comin to him... his friends just got in the way and things got a little messy. But it's done now...just let it go. You walk on outta there right now quiet like and we'll call this a warning and not a threat, ya hear? I find out you've gone to the authorities, you won't ever see that lovely little bride of yours all in one piece again. You understand me.... boy?"

He wiped the smile from his lips as he swiped the sweat from his brow and placed his hat back on his head, motioning with his other hand to the two men next to him to fire a round into the woods.

Buckshot rang from every tree within fifty feet of Haydon. They'd promised him safety if he'd come on out, but he'd seen what kind of safety southern justice provided those who could call their names. Both his head and his ankle hurt like hell. If he came out now, they'd be hard pressed not to see his fear. The men began to work the river banks. While they beat at the underbrush with their rifle butts, he pulled himself higher into the woods above the rutted path till the voices began to fade with the sun.

Somewhere after 9:00 p.m. dehydrated and disoriented, he flagged down an old sedan that was headed into Lexington. Sick at heart, he lay in the back seat and kept his mouth shut till they dumped him out in front of the courthouse and took off down another road. He walked for an extra mile and collapsed inside the door of an abandoned roadside store called Morton's. Three more days passed as he did his best to stick to the back roads and cover of night to travel. It was now five days after the lynchings. The bodies had been lowered into their graves and all of Georgia was mystified with the national attention they were receiving. It appeared as though Talmage had won the vote and promised the South could get back to normal implying the incident at Moores Ford had been unfortunate, but not insurmountable.

Seven miles out of town Haydon borrowed a ride and a shovel from a colored man who had worked his stepdaddy's fields. Terrified by the events of Monroe though, the colored parted ways with him a mile from the Danburg drive. The time was now just after 8:00 pm so Haydon waited for the lights to go out on the lower level before he entered the house.

The clock chimed 11:45 p.m. as he made his way through the jibs in the front parlor and down the hall to the desk for paper and pencil to record his thoughts. Hearing footsteps in the upstairs hall he quickly relocated to his sanctuary out back. Lured by the sudden appearance of light flickering in the ironing shed, Celine threw on her house robe and made her way to the lower porch and out to the shed. After a brief encounter with Celine, he pretended to settle in for the night as she returned angry to her room.

When enough minutes had passed, he made his way back inside and up the worn steps to the second story hall and the room on the end where he found Maggie asleep in her bed. Hunched in the corner, he tried to keep his breathing steady. Frightened for them both he recorded what he'd seen first and then tried to warn her second why he could not stay... mindful of Celine's fury building just across the hall.

Foreign hounds sent up a yelp that carried across the emptied cotton fields and down into the hollow. Haydon panicked, and then realized the first place they would look for Maggie was in Atlanta. The certificate had listed her permanent address, not her summer one. It was not her, the hounds were after ...they had come for him and the distance was closing fast. He could only bring her harm now by staying! Convinced he could lead them away and come back to safely get her the following day, he decided to leave with a kiss, his undying devotion and a clue in her diary as to where to look for his description of the men and the massacre of Moores Ford Bridge.

His death was recorded as a drowning. Local authorities never investigated allegations of foul play made by the father. Those fearful of KKK's retribution filed Celine's account of their argument and his alcoholic tendencies, writing the whole thing off to unfortunate circumstances and accidental death. The FBI never received information they needed in Monroe and thus were never able to make the connection to Haydon's death in Danburg ninety miles away. The marriage certificate was filed in Walton County and not Wilkes and the diary was lost to all parties till the state's acquisition of the property and its subsequent restoration sixty one years after the event. The FBI still has not closed the case and remaining suspects are either dead or still at large.

Chapter Forty

Aside from the more current calamity of the Danburg, I was amazed that no one else had ever figured out the calamity of its past. It had never been Maggie or Haydon's whose background that was compromised. It had always been Celine's and the direct descendants of her great, great grandmother Hannah.

I laughed to think that with all my skills, it had really been my over-ramped neurosis that had done most of the work for me. My instant messenger had wanted me to find a Mr. Jenkins. A Mr. Welborn V. Jenkins to be exact. He was a young black man who had written a famous poem about the lynchings at Moores Ford Bridge and the messenger's intention had been to educate me and to solicit my signature for a petition to have the poem and author recognized for his contribution to the Moores Ford cause. It had nothing to do with the Danburg at all.

However, convinced that it had to have been something so much more covert, I did find something else! It was the last name Jenkins that lead me to the series of articles on the ramifications of the one drop rule, which affected whether or not you were considered black in the eyes of the law or community, which in turn affected your legal rights and your ability to vote, marry and/or own land! Lots of land: land like the Danburg plantation. As the oldest, most direct descendant to the family fortune, Celine had a lot at stake.

It was lucky that my landscaper shared my sense of morbid curiosity. After he excavated the suspected cremation pit, it proved to have been nothing more in its current history than a burn pit, surrendering mostly bone fragments of animals, bits of crockery and miscellaneous refuse. Digging deeper, however, convinced of a more clandestine find, my landscaper found the missing weight and chain to the grandfather clock! What the jeweler and I found inside the last weight was more precious than all the Danburg silver and gold put together! Inside the hollowed out cylinder that would usually be occupied by lead, the core revealed the original Danburg Diary from 1864. I imagined the author hid it with the other treasures in hopes that someday the curse of the Danburg would be broken and that the family heirloom would valued for its real wealth...the truth.

The descendants of the union between Celine's great, great grandmother and a slave by the name of Able Jenkins had produced a bloodline that while it passed the one drop rule, was half African American at its core... thus terminating the Danburgs' right to legal ownership of the Danburg manor back as far as the late 1800's. This must have been the reason for so many law volumes about the study of land grants hidden in the attic. Previously, it had made little sense to me, but apparently it had made sense to Haydon.

Had Celine not been found out as such an integral part of Haydon's discovery at the Danburg by those defending their actions at Moores Ford Bridge, I felt certain no one would have taken such an interest in my exaggerated theories. But it wasn't until after the discovery of the weight's interior and the feeding frenzy of facts that followed, that it all began to fit. Upon my request they cloistered Cattalieu and Celine separately for further questioning. During this round of interviews the fact there had been another diary was finally confirmed and this is what my jeweler had been trying to tell me he'd found hidden inside the final weight. That was the reason for his phone call while Celine was squaring off with me in the kitchen with a knife. It was also the reason why I left Washington and Maggie the day after.

This original diary from the Danburg dated back to 1857, well before the declared secession of Georgia and Jeremiah

Calhoun Danburg's decision to join the Confederate Army. It canvassed the years before and after he was gone. Among the recorded ledgers of crops and other financial familial business it registered births and deaths. In the years that followed Jeremiah's departure, it became more personal. Its author, lonely and frightened, comforted herself penning the hardships the family faced in his absence.

The bulk of recordings dealt mostly with news of the war efforts, until word of his death arrived early in the spring of 1864. Large gaps filled the spaces between dates until the recording of another birth in late August of 1865. In the first entry since the great fire, the author began to confess of her fatigue and weariness, the loneliness of widowhood and the strain of being both master and mistress of the house. Several pages had been ripped out and then abruptly the confession appeared, containing clues to the true origins of the first fire.

Celine had not known of the diary's location until the night she had confronted Haydon in the ironing shed. Convinced the affair between he and Maggie had gone too far, she finally told Haydon about her manufactured pregnancy. Haydon tried to be gentle in his rejection, but when Celine pressed his compliance with the bomb she had already gone to his stepfather with the contrived confession, he dropped a bomb of his own. All the years spent in the attic had produced not only a love of literature, but evidence of supreme controversy that threatened the very foundations of the family. He never turned it over to her. He had merely added it to his arsenal of insurance should his stepfather ever cross the proverbial line again with his mother or himself.

Haydon threatened Celine with the journal's publication. This was why she had been so particular in trying to salvage the damaged contents of the house alone the day after the fire—she had been searching for the original diary. She had mistaken Maggie's diary for the coveted diary of 1864 that night in July, but after breaching its pages, discovered it was an imposter and her rage increased!

Since Celine was already being interrogated for her involvement in the hate crimes committed that summer of 1946, she finally gave up the remaining ghosts of Danburg so to speak. She told the FBI and GBI everything she knew about Haydon's murder and about the terrible events that led up to it.

As to the original diary, she could add nothing further beyond the fact that Haydon had sworn to its existence and as she had stated before, he had never lied about anything else.

* * *

It was absurd to think that after all the man-hours this case had devoured over the course of 61 years, that one little girl's diary had been the key to breaking everything wide open. Even more absurd that one email had triggered the discovery of the real root of Celine's abhorrence... the original Danburg Diary!

The matron, swollen with child in the very print Celine had shoved in my face had kept a diary of her own, confessing the loss of the Danburg and its wealth was God's punishment for her sins. Unlike the version Celine had been told, not all the slaves had abandoned the Danburg in the anticipation of Sherman's armies.

One never left her side...a light skinned slave called in the diary only by the name of Abel Jenkins.

* * *

Widowed for over eleven months, but over two months pregnant, I can no longer defend my thickening waist. Nor can I afford to absorb the public shame of having shared my bed with a slave, as now I am solely dependent of the good graces of my family and neighbors to survive. With the hysteria created by Sherman's armies traveling towards Augusta, I shall use the cover of their atrocities to hide my own. I will stage a catastrophe believable enough, but survivable enough to squelch any rumors of my impropriety...

The diary continued to explain that when it appeared Sherman's troupes were changing directions and heading south, the matron of the Danburg put the final touches of her plan into action.

First she sent the household servants with her five young children in wagons with directions to visit and thank neighboring family. Each wagon was loaded with several baskets of the Danburg's harvest spoils and several more filled with articles of clothing and personal trinkets from her husband's wardrobe. The communication they carried was her undying gratitude for their compassionate support in her new status as widow, followed by a heartfelt wish that their hero, her husband, and his generous belongings not to go to waste. That she was exhausted and needed respite from the younger ones for a day or two to garner strength and complete preparations for the winter ahead. This got the children out of the manor and safely away from the plantation.

When the wagons had cleared the distant border of the plantation, she moved into the second stage of her plan. With the help of slave Jenkins, she removed the lead from the weights of the grandfather clock at the foot of the stairs. While she ran through the house collecting other family heirlooms, Jenkins melted down the family silver in the blacksmith shed. When the silver was ready, they poured the liquid back inside the weight casings of the clock. When it cooled, they rehung the weights inside the cabinet of the clock.

Family jewels were sewn into the hems of her skirts, while below in the front parlors, Jenkins broke a few of the lesser valued furnishings and then tumbled the residual pieces into the four corners of the rooms. Under cover of nightfall they fled to the yards, killing several of the barnyard animals, flinging their bloodied carcasses about and staining Jenkins' shirt with their blood and dirt and ash. The remaining valued livestock was driven deep in the woods and corralled inside pre-constructed paddocks until they could secretly retrieve them later.

Their tasks ran late into the night and at last in the pre-dawn morning, errands accomplished, she sent Jenkins running to the neighboring plantations with claims that soldiers had broken into the Danburg home. Claims that when he tried to stop them, they had beaten him and left him for dead, then stolen livestock, killing or dragging what they could carry into the woods. Claims, that his mistress was hiding in the swamps, in dire straights and needing help. With Jenkins on his way, she rested in the front parlor, watching the horizon for first signs of her neighbors' arrival. Calculating the time it would take for him to return with help, she slept throughout the morning. When she awoke, she dowsed herself with coal dust from the fireplace, water from the well, and waited. When she saw what she thought was the first onslaught of wagons coming to her rescue upon the horizon, she set the ironing shed on fire.

But the slave's heart had apparently changed from the first hint of freedom and along with it the winds that fanned the flames about the Danburg. Perhaps, no sooner had he cleared the acreage, than he headed in the opposite direction back into the woods and the waiting arms of other slaves who had camped the night through waiting on his arrival. They tied the remaining livestock to the backs of the wagons and hitched their courage in the direction of the northern star and were gone.

Soon flames jumped from the tiny wooden structure to the fields... then from the fields to the out buildings. The main structure soon became caught in the eruption and before her eyes the Danburg and all its glory were ablaze. There was no help coming, because Jenkins had not delivered either the message or the children.

She was incapable of stopping the fire on her own. Panicked and pregnant, she gathered what she could, but by the time the neighboring families saw the blaze on the horizon and came to her aid, the first Danburg lay in smoldering ruins.

The widow was found collapsed, inconsolable, hugging the only things she had managed to save: a table, two chairs and the grandfather clock rolled inside a floor rug from the front parlor, and, known only to herself, what few precious gems had been sewn in the lining of her petticoat. In the following days she discovered the true depth of her tragedy. None of her children had arrived at neighboring plantations because they had all been left in the surrounding swamps to die in order to keep the plan of the escaping slaves silent.

Everything she had tried to save, in the end had been destroyed by her guilt and shame. In her melancholy, relatives assumed the unwanted pregnancy to be the result of the brutal demands of an itinerant Union soldier. When the child was born, its features were foreign. But as the child grew, rumors did too. Folks commented that the child resembled the fair skinned slave more than a faceless stranger. When they considered that no other plantation suffered that night at the hands of the Yankees, they closed their eyes to the obvious.

***

Had I never Googled Jenkins, the truth about both diaries might have been written off as silly feminine wiles. Ironically in the end, it was just like the beginning. The question now was, had Maggie ever known the whole horrible truth about how Haydon had died and why? According to Celine, it was quite possible Haydon never understood how much the information about their compromise might cost them as a family until that day at Moores Ford Bridge when he saw the cost of color.

***

Celine's stated in her final interview she had pieced together conversations between her Aunt and Uncle's many volatile marital spats. Haydon's grandparents had sent their seventeen-year-old girl, Haydon's mother, to stay with friends in the country when it was discovered she had been compromised by one of the garage help. Those who knew had been bought off to keep the scandal quiet and those that didn't were told she'd run off with a cotton farmer from rural Georgia who'd run up upon bad luck. Everyone soon forgot about Haydon's questionable beginnings. Everyone that was, but Celine. The more seductive Haydon became, the more she saw the secret as a way to further blackmail her "cousin" into love.

She told everyone she was fearful for his wayward soul and as a good steward of the faith, she would continue to provide guardrail and conscience for him. It wasn't until the night Maggie dropped her hair comb that Celine realized her plot for romance had failed. No one else had known of the young man's compromise. In fact Haydon himself may not have known the truth about his birth until the night he broke in on a domestic squabble between his mother and stepfather. After he learned that any shame he might be branded with paled in comparison to the hidden Danburg shame, he kept the secret of the ancestral documents in his emotional bank account as currency to buy Celine's tolerance for his secret marriage to Maggie.

The rest of the events we pieced together from clues in the diary and both public and private records. The only logical explanation for the missing grave of the fourth Moores Ford Bridge victim must have been Haydon! It was the only theory that made sense. Haydon must have robbed a grave and reburied the body with whatever names and descriptions he could remember of the men at the bridge. He must have returned to Monroe after his night at the Danburg and robbed one of the graves for protection, believing government agents would do what ever necessary to protect him and Maggie until he could testify.

Sadly, it was also an insurance policy that never got cashed in. Several days after the shootings Haydon turned up, face down in the swamps less than two miles from the Danburg. Rumors that he had been seen in the truck of the uniformed soldier heading towards Moores Ford Bridge, but not from Moores Ford Bridge, died the same unquestioned death as he.

Chapter Forty-one

Thank God for Joe! Insistent that I not oversleep, he placed a call to my room at 11:00 a.m. and another at 11:10 and then another at 11:20. The Moores Ford Bridge commemoration was going to start in Monroe at 2:00 p.m. at the First African Baptist Church just off Hwy. 11 across from Church's Chicken. I had exactly ten minutes to shower, dress and meet Miss Maggie, who had been down in the lobby studying the article. I had not even the time to think better of what we were about to do, but it wouldn't have mattered. With what she knew now from both Cattalieu's and Celine's interviews, she was hell-bent on attending.

I pressed Joe to supply me with a large cup of coffee, but he assured me his employer had already put together a sampling of goodies and beverages to keep us satiated and free from side trips throughout the remainder of our day. Grateful that she had fallen asleep hours before me, I left the remaining schematics of the day to her and focused on showering and brushing my teeth.

When I arrived on the first floor, Joe motioned towards the door where my companion sat waiting with newspaper and notebook. On the ride in, we said not a word about the night before. It was as though the magic of the twinkle lights and the thesis the evening after had been the only things needed to catapult us from the past into the present. As the miles stole away the morning, the tension surrounding our adventure built.

We arrived in Monroe just before two and followed the instructions to the church. I parked the car and noted the demographics. The church began to fill. I could count on two hands the number of white people. We stood out. Four minutes before the first speaker, a woman of color in the pew behind us thrust her hand forward and said, "I'm just dying to know what brings the likes of you two here."

I scanned the room, looked at Maggie and realized what a sight we must have been. Self conscious, I smiled weakly, uncertain how to explain. When I didn't answer the woman right away, Maggie squinted an apology with her eyes. Reading her thoughts I turned to the woman behind us.

"Compassion, I think would be the best word for it." I smiled.

For over two hours we listened to orations about the Moores Ford Bridge lynchings. There were representatives from the black press, the NAACP, the ADL, all doing their best to canvass the issues at hand. Each spoke to the horrors and the injustices of historical and current events. When the speeches had finished we left the confines of the little country church and made our way back to the parking lot to retrace the events that had given birth to the moniker, The Last Mass Lynching in America. It was evident law enforcement agencies in the area had done their best to minimize opportunities for chaos. There were squads and uniformed presence in every visible direction.

There we were; two white women... one younger, one older ... both there for the same man. So much of my own heart-ache had been entangled with hers; I'd forgotten how truly peripheral this was in my real life. Haydon was gone. Maggie would eventually leave, and then I would be alone again. I had but one life, same as they and it was the one I would have to return to after the Danburg was finished.

There was an uneasy feeling of bridled fury amongst the crowd as we departed to our individual cars. Maggie and I exited the church and those that accompanied us through the doors distanced themselves immediately from our sides once we left the threshold of the church. Alone and very much the minority we walked quickly to our car. There was electricity in the air that made me nervous. The exit out of the parking lot was staggered.

The roads were clogged with participants and onlookers alike. As we waited in line, I was surprised as the late afternoon sun in Monroe cast rays of tolerance. Faces of people behind windshields showed more grace than grimace as we passed in review, never shying from the spectacle.

I shook my head in amazement at the symmetry. Motionless vehicles embroidered the moving as we traversed the main street through town. Every twenty feet or so another vehicle swung into or away from a curb. I commented at the delicate dance that was taking place before us. In a stream of conscious thinking, I heard myself say without guardrail...

"Look at them... car after car, pulling to the side of the road just as if this were a funeral procession." I sighed heavily and then from the seat next to me, the tiny voice spoke softly into the bloated silence.

"It is, my darling... it is."

She held my hand and we drove the rest of the way in silence. She was so much better than I at life. Alone for so much of the time the last few months, I had become tunnel-visioned and self absorbed. For her it **was** a funeral. A funeral for her and for every other person who had lost someone or something that day they could never get back. It didn't matter what it was, be it a son, a daughter, a lover...their dignity or their innocence. Everyone in Monroe...in Georgia... the United States had lost. Hell, everyone in the world had lost something that day. Things that no man, white or black ever had a right to steal from anyone. What right had I to place more value upon my lost innocence than those others who had suffered far greater than I?

The first stop out of town was a fiasco. The site of the Hester home was now the site of a new three story estate home under construction. The only thing blacker than the crowds mood, was a new Hummer that sat in the gravel drive. As the vans and busses slowed into the shoulder of the road and the hordes began to unload, a bewildered family of four held their dog in horror as an endless parade of people began to multiply at the edge of their driveway. A few un-pleasantries passed between the property owners and the leaders of the tour and we were quickly shuffled back into our cars. Each unorganized site after became a blur.

An hour later, we stood at the lower banks of the Apalachee River in the pandemonium of a carnival atmosphere. Actors were pulled from a car, thrown to the asphalt of the road and tied while camera crews and photographers jockeyed for position amongst the clearing. The effect was surreal. Crowds rushed the shoulders of the roads just as the clouds began to drool. The event ruptured and the integrity of the moment was lost on all, but for the two women before me who represented the core of the human civility. With ketchup bottles and memorexed rounds of gunfire the actors pursued their version of the truth, while I continued mentally to pursue mine.

Maggie had been standing in front of me for the better part of the sequence until they forcibly delivered the four African Americans down into the clearing. As they filed the victims into an execution line, she started to drift away from me towards the crime scene tape. I urged her to remain, to merely close her eyes and listen, but she never heard me over the caterwauling of the crowd. I broke through another line of folks who had formed to my right and reached again to hold her back, but realized at the last second that I had no right to secure her for my own comfort and so lowered my arms. It wasn't trying to save her as much as I wanted to save myself. I knew why she was going. She wanted to see what he had seen, but that was where we had both gone wrong. She could never see what he had seen, just as I would ever be able to feel what he had felt.

The sun hid behind angry clouds and the rain began to patter at our feet with great fervor. With the blaring third memorexed round of gunfire and theatrical screams of well meaning citizens, I watched as an actor pretended to carve the infant from the woman's womb with a condiment as garnish and I heard a black man in front of me say, "Ain't it so. Don't tell me the white man ain't the devil... don't tell me it ain't so..."

Instinctually I stepped forward several paces and grabbed Maggie's hand to drag her back beside me. That one single act of fight or flight told me the minute had been lost on us all. We could sit side by side in a church... we could work next to one another till our hands bled in the fields... we could break bread and break each others hearts, but we could never come to build a bridge that could replace the one damaged that day at Moores Ford without more than lip service. It was going to take a continued conscious effort on everyone's part, each second of the day to make the moment of understanding and acceptance a reality and to see each other as something other than threat.

The rain began to fall as steadily from the sky as from my eyes. Maggie stood cataleptic in the rain as I heard the final hush of the crowd at the fallen four and the plastic doll that lay swathed in store bought blood. Suddenly the drops echoed hollow above our heads without ever touching our skin.

Directly to my right was a woman of color, sophisticated and smiling. She was dressed to the nines in a beautiful green embroidered skirt and jacket of the same shimmering emerald and her eyelet lace shirt with Peter Pan collar stood starched beneath her well coiffured silver hair. Her glasses and jewelry were simple but elegant, her shoes worn but stylish. I looked at her eyes. Deep chocolate brown with centers of black, they held my gaze. Without hesitation she raised her hand to me, not in anger but in shelter. Just as the clouds exhaled with a vengeance, she adjusted her blue and white umbrella and took a step closer to cover our heads. Without hesitation Maggie turned, patted the woman's hand fixed upon the handle and whispered her heartfelt thanks. Together we stood, side by side in our own private digestion of what lay prostrate in the clearing before us. Maggie crushed my hand, asked if I had seen enough and when I acknowledged I had, she turned to the woman still sheltering us, smiled and we walked away.

Twenty years Maggie's junior, I was impressed as she moved swiftly along the embankment, up the ravine and around the cars that lined the road for a 1/8 of a mile. As the rain became a silver meshed backdrop to her silhouette, I watched her as she navigated the road as purposefully as she had navigated her life. If something was in the way, she would move it, if it was too big she would maneuver around or wait until someone else maneuvered it for her, but she never stopped. Not once. Not to catch her breath or defend her hair from the falling downpour. She was a driven soul and I learned why it was Haydon had been so drawn to her. She was a beacon, whether seventeen or the woman with the graying temples who finally turned and stood silent in the rain waiting for me to catch up.

Looking at her I marveled. Haydon had given her as gift to me and in return, I was going to be able to give him back to her through his final words. I wiped at my own damaged coiffeur and picked up the pace. She dabbed at the rain that flecked her cheeks, but never budged to get out of the rain and under shelter.

I finally saw her from Haydon's eyes.

Maggie was her own person. She never apologized for having outlived the one person she adored. She never dishonored his affections for the sake of conformity and she never regretted. Not the good, nor the bad things that happened in her life. Maggie lived! It was the most powerful epiphany.

I watched her face. It should have reflected something else, but there was joy. She wasn't looking back at the events of Moores Ford Bridge behind me, she was looking at me. She smiled, blew me a kiss, mouthing the words "Thank you for this day," and then she was off again. She never broke her cadence. I turned one more time to imprint the moment forever.

The woman with the blue and white umbrella too had never looked back. Her gaze remained focused on the clearing and what lay beyond the other side of the bridge, the setting sun and the closing ceremonies. Without any fanfare or farewell, I picked up my pace and moved forward under a new steam of my own. I too needed to learn how to just live, each day, everyday. No matter what happened to me, I had an obligation to myself and to those that survived me to keep plowing through.

It was in *that* moment I knew there was hope. It was the simple act of kindness acknowledged by the simple act of gratitude between these two women and the beauty of their effortlessness in doing so that became more binding than any document or declaration of civility that any government could have ever procured for either race that day.

As we walked the final steps back to the car side by side in silence we could hear the soulful voice of a gospel singer whose lamentation begged the Lord's forgiveness for transgressions of every kind. I do not know if Maggie had need of forgiveness for herself, but I knew I had need of dispensing some of my own. The rain kept time with the clicking of the hazard signal as I reversed our direction and drove slowly past the sixty or so cars and buses that continued to add and mar the shoulders of Moores Ford Bridge Road. When we reached the crossroads, there were squad cars with lawmen on every corner waiting to direct the crowd which was still more than a mile and sixty one years behind us.

Uncertain as to which road to take to get Maggie back home, I rolled down our window. The officer came to it with ease and asked if we were lost, but before I could even answer Maggie replied with absolute calm, "Not anymore...my dear man. Not anymore."

I turned my head in amazement. She thanked the officer, smiled and instructed me to turn left and head home the long way. I learned that with this Flaming June, there was no such thing as taking short cuts!

Chapter Forty-two

An hour into our ride back to the Fitzgerald, she finally spoke.

"I know where to find him... I know where Haydon would have gone." And that was it. She never said another word as we drove the remainder of the time in absolute silence. Just outside of Rayle she told me to slow down and so I lowered my speed to 35 and continued to keep in the right hand lane. I reached for my hazard signal and she cautioned against it.

"Let's not attract any attention to ourselves. It's no longer an emergency. I've waited 61 years... another few minutes won't harm me."

I never turned to look at her face. Never took my hand away from the steering wheel or the other from where she left her own tucked inside. And together, we never wiped away the tears that had always clouded our vision, but guided our hearts towards another horizon.

The Mustang cruised at a slower and more comfortable pace and the earlier rain had cooled the air enough to bring pleasure to our cheeks. The day had been emotionally exhausting and a battered sun began to dip just beyond the horizon in agreement. Had it been any other day, it would have been less appreciated and taken for granted, but today was beside itself with significance. I wondered if sixty one years ago some one else had made this same drive, passed these same rocks and knolls, emotionally exhausted, trying to reach the Fitzgerald.

The countryside rolled past us with the splendor of a burning sky that painted the fields and face of the Flaming June in the seat next to mine. I had no idea where she meant us to go or what she meant us to do when we got there. This was her day and it was my honor to do nothing more than follow her lead.

Just outside the limits of Rayle, the landscape on the left side of the road suddenly became empty of trees and opened into a clearing of fallow hayfields and burnished sky. Maggie seemed to enjoy the scenery and for a while the minutes slipped by without any hint of what where we were about to end up. Heading due east, the glare of the sun had given way to evening hues and I moved my sunglasses to the top of my head to keep my wayward hair out of my eyes. I seldom got to enjoy the top down on the car in the company of others and I was grateful that Maggie seemed as content as I with an uncompromised view of the countryside. The white lines stretched as the land began to flatten out. Freshly cut schematics of green and gold ripped past my peripheral view until the pattern shattered and I saw it standing alone in the center of the field.

She never announced it. She never had to. I had passed this way a hundred times in my coming and goings with the Danburg and never once made the connection. The diary sat in her lap and though she never broke its back, I could read the entry in her eyes when she turned to look at me. The entry was one of the first. "...hiding something in plain view is the best way to keep a secret...secret."

I had been so foolish not to have grasped what he had been trying to tell us both from the very start and yet, in truth, how could I have possibly known this was where the man was trying to lead me? I slowed the car by ten miles an hour and watched as the sweeping motions of the clouds clung to the horizon and kissed its rim.

I took a deep breath and let the sweet evening air fill my lungs, but still I felt as though I could not breathe. The reference had never been about the diary being hidden in plain view—it had always been about the physical truth, and he had been right. Seldom do we ever see anything before us in its proper light. Even our sorrows or the sorrows of others become colored by our personal perceptions and needs. My approach to the world had been with eyes veiled. I returned my focus to the structure in the distance. He had been so right. Everything we had needed to know about that day had been right in front of us the entire time. He had tried to explain in his final entries, but I had only read what I wanted to see and not what he had written.

I tried to release her hand in what I now viewed as my diminished worth, but my fingers caught the intensity of her squeeze. She needed me and it was time I stepped out of myself and made certain I was there for her. I hit my blinker and without any further instruction other than our collective sigh, I pulled into the tractor path that breached the first eighty feet of the vacant field. The car idled at the edge of a rusty gate and we sat in awe taking in the solemnity of the moment. To the left the sky continued to brush the horizon with color and we were cemented into the painting by the omnipotence of orange that ruptured violently at the edges then into elongated streaks of purple and pink. You could feel the sinking weight of closure descend from above as the sun began to die.

I turned off the engine and the sounds of rural life infiltrated the air that sat still and heavy upon our shoulders. Maggie breathed unevenly. An orchestra of crickets crescendoed into the evening air and a single bird stopped in flight to review us. Maggie lifted herself out of the seat, swung the door open and hesitated. She had said we, but there was singleness in her purpose, so I waited. She closed the door and stood still while I kept vigil over her silhouette in the sunset from behind the wheel. The ragtop of the Mustang had been down since Moores Ford Bridge and though the night air was beginning to chill, the goose bumps on my arms were for another reason. You could feel something here that cried for validation and exposure. I left the top down and waited for her to move.

"We were supposed to picnic here that day." she said, and closed her eyes.

"There was a small pond just the other side of that thicket..." Her smile began to breach the corners of her mouth and I knew she was gone. "When we first fell in love, we used to come here. He would read to me and I would fall asleep in his lap and when the sun began to dip but not our desires, we used to slip outside our clothes and into each other. If I had only known..." she said with even calm, and gathered herself into her arms. "I packed a lunch for us that day. A blanket, his favorite books and I... I waited for the longest time, but he never..."

Her voice cracked and with it my heart. Her thinned hair whipped softly about her cheeks and neck. The sky spewed forth one more burst of brilliant orange and for a second she and the Flaming June were as one again. Her skirt billowed and swished within the breeze, her silk blouse rippling under its gentle touch. Had I not known better I would have sworn that Haydon had come as wind to caress and welcome her home.

She didn't speak another word. As she edged forward, the crickets bowed and hushed themselves. Cooing doves that sat atop the telephone wires watched and trilled. She took tiny steps and then braced herself upon the hood of my car, afraid to advance further.

I asked if she was all right. She moved her mouth but no sound emitted that I could hear. Whatever she could have said no longer held any importance for either of us. It was he she had wanted to hold onto. Not memory or regret.

The silo raised its bulk to the darkening sky at the end of another day. I noted the moon at the edge of the horizon as it began to make its climb. Maggie pulled her skirt away from her ankles and took one step closer to fate. It was his spirit she craved. The wind rounded the stone structure and raced along the wispy spires of greenery that danced and bowed slightly at the touch of her hem. With the same calculated measure as I had seen her traverse the lawn of the Danburg, I watched as she inched her way to the base of the decapitated silo. She stood and bent her head in reverence. He had been there, his footfall perhaps touching the same earth as hers. Her hand extended outwards to touch the cold and mossy stones that had both sheltered and imprisoned him. The sun had set and though there was light there was also dark approaching, and I did not wish to be apart from her side when she finally made her tattered peace.

I unfolded myself from the driver's seat. The shovels and bag Joe had been instructed to place in my trunk at the beginning of the day were now to be used for another purpose. It was clear we would not be weeding and decorating Haydon's grave at the churchyard in Danburg. He no longer had need of the flowers we could offer.

Moving quickly, I found the breach in the wall that had been the only point of entry or exit other than the sky for over a century of the silo's existence. The scent of sweet jasmine clung to the foundation as I lowered the satchel to the ground. The see-saw of emotion kept me off balance but nothing could have prepared me for the look upon her face when she turned to meet mine. It was a palette of tears and smiles. She ran her fingers across the brittle wall before her and whispered his name.

"Haydon...we used to come here. I used to come here after it was all over. I would sit right here. Right outside this tower and read aloud from our book, hoping to make sense of it all. I never knew he made it this far... never knew I had been sharing the last place his soul could have been with mine... all these years. I only knew it was here we were supposed to have met."

She turned and faced me for a moment, her cheeks damp with anguish.

"I waited, you know. I may have even been here the day he..." and her voice cracked again. As she had been rushed from the Danburg the likelihood of that was slim, but I had neither the right nor the desire to advise her otherwise.

"I can search the silo by myself... if you wish to remain here." I said and waited for her response.

She ran her fingers across the mortared section of pitted stones again and shook her head. "Together..." she whispered. "Together... this time." And she turned to me, "He wanted you to find me first, so that I would not be alone when I finally found him."

I lit the Coleman and we made our way under a full moon and mantle of cobwebbed ivy into the inner sanctum of the silo. It smelled no more offensive than the inside of a barn, and thinking of Haydon's description, I was grateful for the passage of time.

Once adjusted to the light, we centered ourselves equally opposite to the circumference of the walls. I instructed us both to put on the leather gloves and painter's masks. We held our breath as the two of us dove deep into the chatteled flooring. Syncopated puffs of dehydrated debris spiraled upward into the air. Again and again we duplicated the chore until finally the hollow sound of metal bounced within the vertical stones. Shocked at the resounding affirmation, we each froze. Her hands let go of the shovel handle and it fell to the earth. Shocked, she stood with gaping eyes that flashed wildly from the earth to me and back again.

Monitoring her panic, I demanded that she rest and dug deeper three more times, building upon the small mound beside me. On the fourth plunge I finally made discernable contact with what appeared to be the surface of a rusted tool box. I laid my shovel to the side and reached down through the uneven silt. Her eyes danced with watery anticipation as they met mine and I removed the box from its earthen grave and placed it at her feet. Slowly I moved it to the center of the silo. She followed with her eyes as it captured a fractured path of moonlight. Once convinced of the box's reality, she tenderly brushed away the soil that clogged the hasp. I looked once more at her face, asked for permission to unseal it, and with gentle courage she nodded.

Gingerly I lifted the wavered edge of metal away from the rusted lower lip of hardware. I blew at its soiled edge to clear the remaining dirt and keep from admitting any further compromise to the contents contained within.

Inside the box was a smaller one and an envelope addressed to Maggie.

She lifted out the parcel that bore her name and then opened the tiny container, while I lowered the larger box. With arthritic fingers she brought forth from its velvet womb a perfectly polished band of gold. The engraving on the inside was still as crisp as the day it was cut and she traced it with tenderness. She took a deep breath and continued to caress it with a grace and dignity I have yet to see reproduced by any other human being since.

Moved, I watched as she placed it on a finger beside her own and then kissed its oversized rim and whispered his name. She looked into my eyes, then broke into racking sobs of despair. Helpless I watched, frozen inside the echo of her desolation and my own inability to console her. The moon shifted overhead, the light came full, and she unfolded the parchment and read.

Dearest Maggie,

I knew you'd come. I never doubted for a moment that you would find me and save me....mostly from myself. I have left my ring here for you, certain that you will place it upon my finger when I can renew my vow of fidelity and love. I cannot tell you of the things I have done this night and yet you must trust that I have done them all for the right reasons and for us. You once told me you could not live with a truth that must be kept silent. For you I would cut out my own tongue and remain mute forever, but for those whose voices have too long remained silent, I know that you would ask me to speak. There is another box, buried deeper. Stop with this one and seek out trusted help to raise the other. Take this message to your father. He will know what to do and who can be trusted with such information as lies within. Keep this ring as a symbol of my affection and abiding love and let these words remind you that I will return to reclaim it and you both....

She broke at that point and was inconsolable. The tattered page fell to the soft earth between our feet. I bent to pick it up and read the remainder of the script and manuscript for her. It was a page torn from the book Green Mansions...

"You are you and I am I – why is it?' – the question asked when our souls were near together, like two raindrops side by side, drawing irresistibly nearer, even nearer: for now they had touched and were not two, but one inseparable drop, crystallized beyond change, not to be disintegrated by time, nor shattered by death's blow, nor resolved by any alchemy."

Then in his own pen, he signed off.

Stay safe, my darling, and make a wish upon the moon tonight, just as I... that once more and forever we are as one. All my love...
Your adoring Abel,
Haydon

I handed the paper back to her.

"I always thought I had lost that page..." she sighed and the tears welled over the dam of her lower lash. "It was always my favorite passage..." and her lips quivered and then gave way to the crushing weight of discovery. His fingers had been upon the same words. She rubbed at the velvet of the parchment. He must have taken it the night he made the last entry in the diary. Overwrought, her grip failed her again and the discolored paper floated softly to the floor of the silo as she slowly collapsed into the earth and whimpered his name.

"Haydon...Haydon. Oh my darling.... I'm here. I'm here now... come back to me. I cannot bear the separation any longer..."

It broke my heart to see her so and I could do little more than hold her as she swayed with infinite sorrow. In the hollow of my silence her weeping pierced the night. Clouds humbly parted company, leaving her devastation to search the whole of heaven for a sympathetic ear. As I watched, the years melted away and I saw the supple frame of an errant child in supplication and could not understand how a god, any god could have begrudged such a dear child such heartfelt desires.

I do not know how long we knelt there clinging to each other in the bottom of that great tower. I only know that the moon was high when we each let go a final howl of anguish and mustered our courage to raise our shovels one last time, pressing them into the forgiving earth in search of an even more distant truth...the location of the fourth grave and the inked description of those that had been with Haydon that day at Moores Ford Bridge.

* * *

Maggie and I made the phone call to the GBI together with Joe, who had finally confessed himself my mysterious emailer. He had grown up in the area and heard rumors about a young white sympathizer who'd made the fatal mistake of trying to hitch a ride out of Monroe that day, but never made the connection. Haydon's murder took place days later and more than ninety miles away, so no one ever put the two together. Celine had woven a tale so pathetic, folks were ashamed they had known him at all and he was forgotten with almost as much haste as he was buried.

Joe admitted he had never thought much about the rumors surrounding Moores Ford until his friend Bennie the cop told him about a young woman preservationist who had been asking questions down at the café about the Danburg Plantation and its famous fire. Later that week, the librarian talked about the same woman having asked if there had been a multiple murder scene recorded in the local archives the year of 1946 that sounded similar to that of the mass murders at Moores Ford Bridge. When he put what history he knew about the hotel's family, Maggie's brief, but tragic marriage and the date of the Moores Ford massacre... he felt there was more to the story than just coincidence.

Once the first call had been made to the GBI, a second was made to FBI agents who were still investigating the case. After that it was all we could do to stay calm and wait for the next barrage of questioning.

Hours later men stuffed inside pin striped suits and good intentions flooded the hotel. The third floor was cordoned off and the inside of the turret room became our only view to the outside world for two more days. In our interviews we told them the location of the silo, what we had discovered and how we had located it. We told them we suspected the larger box left behind in the bottom of the silo, was the final resting place of the fourth body from the mass lynching that day at Moores Ford Bridge.

When they asked me how I had found the location I told them I hadn't. Instead, I stated that I had followed the clues left in the diary and they had led me to Maggie. Maggie had found Haydon and in doing so; found the last victim of Moores Ford Bridge. When they asked Maggie how she had found the site, she twisted the oversized band of gold on her finger and said she had simply followed her heart. Together we were both right.

We told them everything we thought was important for them to know. We told them about the silo, the grandfather clock and the bitter history between Celine and Haydon. We told them about Catty's cooperation and Celine's confession. We told them about Maggie's diary and the Jenkins essays and what little we knew about the Klan and their alleged involvement. We showed them the tool box and the letter and then described what our shovels had hit beneath the dirt floor of the silo.

What we didn't tell them about that night was finding Haydon's wedding ring, or about the horrendous heartache suffered when I read the yellowed page he'd stolen from the book *Green Mansions*. Those we decided Maggie should kept for her. When they were finished, we were left alone again with what had happened to her, to him, the victims of Moores Ford Bridge and to an entire nation.

Chapter Forty-three

For those who wished still to exact revenge, most of the folks named on Haydon's list would provide little satisfaction. Most had either died or weren't far from it. For those few guilty remaining, the law would afford them the luxury of the counsel and protection they had denied others sixty-one years before. But for Maggie, it had been enough to know that Haydon had loved her beyond measure and that together they had loved each other for better or for worse, until death forced them to part.

For me, it was enough to know the possibility of that kind of love existed at all.

I cannot tell you how it is that God places in our paths those that we need and those that need us at exactly the moment of greatest necessity. I could not tell you even now with certainty that what transpired both sixty-one years earlier in his lifetime and what transpired now seventy-two hours earlier in ours did anything to change the overall understanding of humanity. We humans are feeble and fickle creatures. We wake up each day and forget to feel the warmth of the earth that supports our feet. We see the sky above our heads and forget to marvel at its cobalt beauty. We forget to look with love upon the faces that grace the daily portraits in our lives and we hardly remember that in the blink of an eye they can be removed to another canvas we cannot begin to paint.

In truth, I know only this: That within this weary world there is but one reward worthy of all our trials. One gift that bestows itself without obligation, without instruction and without selfish gain... One gift that renews itself and those that hold it gently in their hearts who have learned its truth...love.

This was the final entry in the Danburg Diary, dated August 26, 2007. The diary Maggie started. The one Haydon shared and the one I ended.

The moon hung low in the sky and though the Coleman was burning dim, there was one final chore to perform. Exhausted and covered with dirt, I wiped the tears from my eyes. We had faced our ghosts with equal bravery, shouldered our heartaches with grace and dignity. She had lived her life without apology and when it had ended shortly after our discovery that night, she had left me with a roadmap to finish my own—to live each day, no matter what happened. Good or bad.

No one outside those silo walls would ever be able to take the truth from us again. We might not have changed the world that night, but we had done exactly what we had set out to do.

I placed Maggie's diary inside the small plastic box along with her obituary, Haydon's letters, what was left of the tattered book of *Green Mansions*, their wedding bands, a rendering of *Flaming June*, and a promise that I would never forget. I secured the lid, drove into the new dawning of another day and hours later laid them all to rest in another dilapidated silo just this side of my own heartache.

When I finally returned to the Danburg hours before the grand opening, I walked to the rear of the upstairs alcove, unhasped the lock on case thirteen and placed the final archived piece into place upon its velvet bed.

"...That is my philosophy still; prayers, austerities, good works – they avail nothing, and there is no intercession, and outside of the soul there is no forgiveness in heaven or earth for sin. Nevertheless there is a way, which every soul can find out for itself – even the most rebellious, the most darkened with crime and tormented by remorse. In that way I have walked; and, self-forgiven and self-absolved, I know that if she

were to return once more and appear to me – even here where her ashes are – I know that her divine eyes would no longer refuse to look into mine, since the sorrow which seemed eternal and would have slain me to see would not now be in them...”

The card beneath it simply read: “Excerpt from the novel *Green Mansions*, by W. H. Hudson, once owned by two of the Danburg’s most cherished residents. This passage and several other Civil Rights related documents were rumored to have been discovered tucked inside a diary that was found inside the charred belly of a grandfather clock that once stood on the first floor of the Danburg home. An additional Civil War related document was also discovered coiled inside one of the original weights that hung within the same great clock.

The entire contents of case thirteen have been donated to the state by Magnolia June Fitzgerald. Born November 21, 1929. Died August 26, 2007. ‘Maggie’ as she preferred to be called, was the child bride of Haydon Edison Fitzgerald, the secondary victim of the mass lynching at Moores Ford Bridge July 25th, 1946. These documents were discovered just prior to the opening of this museum and the solving of the mystery at Moores Ford Bridge. The remaining pages and location of the second Danburg Diary, purportedly written by Miss Fitzgerald as a young child who visited seasonally, is currently unknown.”

August 29, 2007

The End

Dedicated to the memory of those loved and lost at the Moores Ford Bridge July 25, 1946. Many thanks to my children for their eternal patience when I am writing. To my husband, Don who never loses faith in me. And finally to my colleague and friend Sandi Huszagh, for her inspired contributions to the character Maggie and the diligent support of M.D. for her insistence that this story be written.

Notes:

Reference materials which assisted the writing of this book include:

Fire in the Cane Brake by Laura Wexler

Athens Banner Herald June 15, 2007

Richard Rusk chronicles 1997 Oconee Enterprise

Moores Ford Bridge Committee Organization

Flaming June by Lord Frederic Leighton, National Art Gallery

Green Mansions by W. H. Hudson

Who Loves You Jimmie Orrio by Cheryldee Huddleston

Special thanks to:

The Moores Ford Bridge Memorial Committee

Contributing author Dr. S. Huszagh

Rich Rusk

The Fitzpatrick Hotel

The town of Washington, Georgia

The Callaway Plantation

Monroe, Georgia

S. J. Hardman/ View From the Victims

www.ingramcontent.com/pod-product-compliance
Lightning Source LLC
Chambersburg PA
CBHW060533180626
46817CB00002B/548